A LONG TIME DEAD

A D.I. DUNCAN MCADAM MYSTERY

THE MISTY ISLE
BOOK 1

J M DALGLIESH

First published by Hamilton Press in 2023

Copyright © J M Dalgliesh, 2023

ISBN (Trade Paperback) 978-1-80080-291-9
ISBN (Hardback) 978-1-80080-888-1
ISBN (Large Print) 978-1-80080-494-4

Look out for the link at the end of this book or visit my website at **www.jmdalgliesh.com** to sign up to my no-spam VIP Club and receive a FREE novella from my Hidden Norfolk series plus news and previews of forthcoming works.

Never miss a new release.

No spam, ever, guaranteed. You can unsubscribe at any time.

SCOTTISH NAMES
PEOPLE AND PLACES

Characters;
>   Ruaridh - (Ruer-iy)
>   Èibhlin - (Eve-leen)
>   Mhari - (Vh-ari)
>   MacEachran - (Mack-Eck-ran)
>   Catriona - (Cat-treena)

Places;
>   Portree - (Por-tree)
>   Benbecula - (Ben-beck-u-lar)
>   Kensaleyre - (Ken-sal-ayre)
>   Carinish - (Car-in-ish)
>   Trotternish - (Trott-er-nish)
>   Waternish - (Water-nish)
>   Dunvegan - (Dun-veh-gan)
>   Raasay - (Raa-see)
>   Isay - (I-say)
>   Uist - (Yoo-uhst)
>   Edinbane - (Eee-din-bane)
>   Airdrie - (Air-dree)

SCOTTISH PHRASES AND SLANG

Slang;

    Scunner - (whiner / nuisance)

    Wee - (Small)

    Deid - (Dead)

    Cannae - (Cannot / can't)

    Dinnae - (Did not / Didn't)

    Disnae - (Does not)

    Nae - (No)

    Mind - (Remember / recall)

    Tae - (To)

    Blether - (Chat / conversation)

    Braw - (Good)

    Bùrach - (Mess)

    Laldy - (Lots of energy / vigour)

    Weans - (Children)

    Bairns - (Children)

A LONG TIME DEAD

PROLOGUE

WERE IT NOT FOR THE cool breeze drifting in off Loch Dunvegan, she could have been dancing on a beach in the Mediterranean, the crushed white coral beneath her feet giving off an iridescent sheen in the moonlight. The water was clearer here than anywhere else on the island, of that she was almost certain, and if they were in southern Europe then this coastline would be lined with villas, hotels and restaurants. As it is, here on the Waternish peninsula of north-west Skye, the water was cold almost all year round and even following the hottest of summers, the October swim was still only for the keenest bathers.

The sun had dipped below the horizon now, but they'd have another hour or so of light. This summer had been kind to the islanders, at least with regard to the weather. Although the influx of tourists each year had stayed on an upward curve since the bridge connecting them to the mainland at Kyle opened four years previously – ending a four-hundred-year-old ferry operation – the growth promised to the community by the new infrastructure had so far failed to deliver. People still came to the Misty Isle much as they had done before, only now they could get onto the island more quickly. Things were changing on the island, to her mind very much for the better, but she knew not everyone agreed.

The song ended and the music stopped, the murmur of general chat and laughter carrying to her on the breeze. In the twilight, she could see Dougal fiddling with the shuffle, either puzzled as to why the music had stopped or he was trying to select something else to play. If he couldn't figure it out, then they were stuffed for the dance tunes. Dougal always had to have the latest bit of kit and he wasn't happy unless everyone knew he had the latest bit of kit either.

Sitting down on the grass bank, *Ghrobain* rose up behind her, a solitary hill standing watch over Coral Beach. She turned to hear excited shouting and cheering from the handful who'd made the short climb to the top for the view of what was a stunning sunset over Duirinish in the west. She'd seen it before, so hadn't felt the need to go this time.

Roddy sauntered up to her on unsteady feet, sinking to the grass beside her and offering her a bottle of beer. She made to decline but he forced it into her hand.

"Slàinte," he said, chinking his bottle against hers.

She smiled but the bottle didn't reach her lips, instead she sat there, cradling it in her hand.

"You all right, lassie?" Roddy said adopting that tone of voice that he only ever used when mimicking their old S5 science teacher, Mr McClintock. The question came accompanied by a single raised eyebrow and Roddy's best attempt at being cross-eyed just like the great man himself. The reason for his sporting a glass eye was a hotly debated topic throughout high school; one that never realised an unequivocal conclusion. It was quite possible that the truth was known, but that it was far more mundane than the causes they could each come up with and was, therefore, discarded. The

favourite suggestion was always that he'd had a sideline making explosive devices and got careless. The fact the man was in his late fifties and couldn't tuck his shirt in correctly only led teenage pupils to think this was entirely plausible.

"I'm all right," she said quietly.

"Really? Because that doesn't sound like the Isla we've all come to know and love."

"Why are you staying here, Roddy?"

He looked at her, feigning hurt.

"Well, I had come to see if you were okay but, if you're going to be like that, I can always leave you to it."

She smiled, leaning into his shoulder with hers and gently barging him affectionately. "Not what I meant, and you know it."

He returned her smile before turning his focus towards the others gathered around the fire a short distance away. "Why aren't I leaving the island?"

She nodded. "It feels like everyone wants to leave the island."

"That's because most of us do!" he said, taking a swig of his beer.

"Everyone says so, but they don't all mean it," she said with a sigh, lifting her bottle and drinking from it. "Argh… Roddy, what is this?" She held the bottle up towards the light trying to read the label. "It's… it's…"

"Delightful? Tasty?"

"Awful!"

"Aye, that too," he said, grinning. Undeterred, he lifted his bottle once again. Wiping his mouth with the back of his hand, he licked his lips. "It's the aftertaste that really gets you, isn't it? It's like dog slobber."

"It'll be repeating on me all night," she said. "Seriously, where did you get it?"

"Remember that craft beer home-brew kit my mum got my dad last Christmas?"

She nodded.

"This is it. Well," he said, cocking his head, "the first batch that he's got around to doing anyway."

"It's disgusting, Roddy. Truly, truly awful."

"Why do you think he let me have it?" Roddy said, winking at her. He leaned a little closer to her, tilting his bottle towards the crowd who were up and dancing again now the music had restarted. "I see you're making friends," he said, subtly pointing at one boy in particular, "but does he deserve that?"

"Ian?"

Roddy nodded. "He screwed up and he knows it. I think you broke his heart."

"Well, if he was interested then he wouldn't have kissed Ashlee earlier, would he?"

"Ah… she only pounced on him to annoy you."

"Well, it worked," she said, lifting her bottle once more.

"Poor lad," Roddy said, chuckling. "He preloaded this afternoon so as to summon up the courage to make a play for you. Little did he know the machinations of female jealousy and etiquette would force his ex to try and drive a wedge between you."

She snorted with derision. "If he's still hung up on her then I'm better off out of it."

"Poor lad," Roddy said. "Although, he's a proper wee scunner now. I think the afternoon courage session has caught up with him."

"He didn't need to," she said. "I was in the bag already."

"Were you indeed?" Roddy said, open mouthed and arching his eyebrows in shock. "How forward of you… but let not the fine steward of island virtue, Reverend Matheson, hear such things pass your lips."

"Och… sod off with you," she retorted, elbowing him in the ribs. Roddy winced, complaining bitterly. The mention of her father brought on a wave of melancholy and she toyed with the bottle in her hands. "That's not what I meant."

"I know!"

"Good, so long as we're clear."

"But…" Roddy said, mock grimacing, an expression he did well.

"But what?"

"Did you have to get off with pretty much every guy here tonight?"

"Are you channelling my father or something?"

He shook his head. "Even Alex noticed."

"Good. Tosser."

"Me or him?"

"Alex, of course," she said, smiling.

"You'd think he'd be happy with… what's her face?" Roddy asked, searching the group for Alex's new girlfriend. The faces were now lit by the dancing flickers of orange and yellow as the fire properly took hold.

"Catriona," she said flatly.

"Aye… that's her. Only moved to the island this past spring and she's already sinking her claws in to the weak minded."

"You don't need to hate on her just for my sake, Roddy."

"I dinnae." He looked at her, splaying his hands wide apologetically. "I don't trust anyone from… where's she from again?"

"Airdrie."

"Aye. Says it all, doesn't it?"

She laughed, leaning over and putting her head on his shoulder. "You're very kind to me."

"I know. You dinnae deserve it, but I try my best."

Conversation died and for a few minutes they listened to the water gently lapping on the beach mixed with the laughter coming from the others, all celebrating their end of summer blowout before everyone parted and went their separate ways. Some of them were leaving for university, others starting apprenticeships and the unlucky few, Isla being one among them, with no idea what lay ahead of them at all.

"So, why are you staying, Roddy? I mean, you could go anywhere."

She sat up and he adjusted his seating position, suddenly taking on an air of maturity that didn't sit well with him.

"Where would I go to?"

"Wherever you like. I thought you'd take up that offer of a place at Glasgow."

"Nah! Who wants to go to live in Glasgow? Full of people... it's dirty... and I'd never see the sun again," he said, saluting the orange glow on the horizon.

"Seriously, why did you knock it back?"

Roddy picked at the glue on the surface of the bottle where the original label had once been before the glass was repurposed by his father.

"My dad needs me. The business... it's too much for him to do on his own."

"He's forcing you to stay?" she said, incredulous.

"No, quite the opposite. Besides," he sighed, "life in the big city really isn't for me. Can you imagine me not going out on the water every day?"

"Your webbed feet would dry out and drop off," she said.

"Exactly." Roddy leaned back on his elbows. "What about you?"

She shrugged.

"That's not an answer, Isla. What are you going to do?"

"I don't know. I really don't."

"Follow in the big man's footsteps?" Roddy asked without a hint of sarcasm.

"Into the church? Me?"

Roddy laughed. "No, I meant your brother. Follow him to university… bright lights, drink, drugs and rock and roll… or dance tunes, clubhouse… or whatever they call it these days?"

She smiled. Roddy always had a way of seeing the best in things. It was why she loved him.

"I don't know," she repeated quietly.

"Well, there's one thing I know," Roddy said, sitting upright and taking a deep breath.

"Yeah, what's that?"

"You're a long time deid, lassie."

She winced. Roddy noticed; his expression turned serious. "Now that's definitely not the Isla I know. Are you okay?"

She waved away his concerns, taking a deep breath. "I'm all right, honestly."

"Honestly, you're not," he said, coming up onto his knees, concerned. "You've not looked great all day."

"Roddy, will you just leave it!" Immediately she felt bad for rebuffing his concern, reaching out and grasping his forearm. She squeezed him gently. "Please, just leave it."

Clearly against his wishes, he nodded solemnly, pursing his lips. Sitting back down, he allowed a moment of silence before staring out across the loch.

"Do you fancy a swim out to Lampay?" he asked, pointing to the island.

"Are you mental?" she asked, shaking her head.

"Just a thought," he replied, sniffing and sipping at his

bottle. She leaned into him again and he put a comforting arm around her, drawing her to him.

"What would I do without you, Roddy?" He didn't reply. The two of them sat there in silence, watching the other party-goers tearing up the night. "What would I do?" she whispered to herself.

"We could sit here and talk about the good times," Roddy said, "or we could sing a sad song and lament the passing of our youth as we stumble into adulthood, bemoaning how good things used to be before they were ruined by the youth of today."

She laughed, getting to her feet. Reaching down, she took Roddy's free hand and hauled him up too.

"I think we should go and join the others, sing, dance and have some fun!"

"Really?" Roddy said, looking glum. "I was kinda thinking it'd be good to have a right old moan."

CHAPTER ONE

KELLY THUNDERED away at her keyboard, Lord only knows what she had to write about. She knew he was watching her. There was a knack she had of tilting her head in such a way as to catch sight of someone in her peripheral vision but without making it apparent she was looking.

He checked his watch, then the clock on the wall to make sure they married up. They did.

"He'll be with you as soon as he is," she said without looking up. Her talent was uncanny.

"I didn't say anything," he replied.

Her fingers ceased moving on the keyboard and she glanced up at him. "You were about to ask."

He couldn't argue. She was right. Taking a deep breath, he considered nipping downstairs to the canteen and grabbing a cup of coffee and maybe a sandwich.

"And don't think about leaving, Detective Inspector. It will only make matters worse."

DI Duncan McAdam raised both hands in a gesture of innocent denial and Kelly almost allowed herself the luxury of a brief smile passing her lips before the fixed, matronly expression returned. He got up from his seat, stretching his legs and casually wandering around the office, glancing at the pictures on the wall as if it was the first time of viewing them. He felt Kelly's eyes on him.

Turning, she averted her eyes but a second too slow. He crossed the short distance between them and perched himself on the end of her desk. She looked up at him before her eyes drifted to where his backside was positioned. Duncan didn't move. He leaned in conspiratorially, glancing at the corridor as a uniform walked by.

"So, is he in a good mood this morning?"

She frowned at him.

"Bad mood then?"

"He's in a... professional mood."

That didn't help. The old man, as they liked to call him, was always professional, at least when it came to his manner. One piece of advice that Duncan was given when starting out was to always get to know your governor. It was a word of wisdom he'd failed to heed in the first part of his career and, in the latter part, he tried, but despite often learning what they wanted he had still catastrophically failed to turn that knowledge to his advantage. At least, thus far.

"Any idea why he wants to see me?"

She fixed him with a dismissive look, shaking her head.

"Come on, you must have some idea," he protested. "Nothing comes out of this office without you wiping his bum..."

The door opened and the man himself appeared. Duncan hopped off the desk, nodding at the detective chief superintendent.

"Good morning, sir."

"Is it?"

Duncan smiled. "I thought so, sir. I got a space in the car

park this morning. First day back. I feel like I should buy a lottery ticket."

DCS Mullen eyed him. Duncan couldn't tell if he was irritated by him or just plain despised him. He doubted it would make much of a difference.

"Come through, DI McAdam."

He turned and went back into his office without looking back. Duncan smacked his lips, glancing at Kelly and raising his eyebrows. He'd been addressed almost full title. It was almost like his father was speaking to him after catching him rifling through the bicky tin when he was eight.

"I think I'm in trouble," he whispered, drawing himself upright and moving off. Kelly smiled. "Any last-minute advice?"

"Maybe fewer jokes?"

"Then I am in trouble," he said, hastening into the office.

"Close the door, Duncan."

He did as requested. Coming before the desk, his superior gestured for him to take a seat opposite him. The ageing head of CID fixed Duncan with a stern look, leaning forward he rested his elbows on his desk and pitched a tent with his hands before him.

"How are you feeling?"

Duncan was momentarily thrown by the question. Mullen wasn't a touchy-feely sort of boss. He was old school. One of the few remaining, wheeled out by a new generation of senior officers who spent as much time on management performance courses as they did policing.

"I'm… well, thank you, sir."

"Any nerves about being back?"

Duncan arched his eyebrows, smacking his lips as he contemplated the right answer, whatever that should be. "No… I've done this before." He said the last bit with a brief smile, immediately regretting doing so as Mullen rolled his tongue against the inside of his cheek, the tell-tale sign of irritation. What Duncan would give to play a game of poker against this man would be substantial. He might not be able to please him, but he could read him when the need arose. It was just that this was usually far too late for him to be proactive.

Mullen opened a folder in front of him on his desk, glancing down as he scanned the document on the top. Duncan was certain he'd already read the contents, likely memorised them too, knowing Mullen. He tried to angle his own view to see what he was looking at and was almost busted as the senior office met his eye. Duncan smiled innocently.

"I understand that you have chosen not to appeal. Is that still your decision?"

Duncan nodded. "It is, sir."

Mullen returned his gaze to the folder in front of him, Duncan straining his neck to see what he guessed were the notes from his disciplinary panel.

Mullen took a breath. "The panel's decision was to issue you with a verbal warning. This will remain on your file for a period of six months."

"I'm aware, sir, but thank you for the reminder."

Mullen fixed him with a stern look.

"Your conduct... is not what I expect from an officer under my command, DI McAdam."

Duncan felt awkward, unsure of what he should say. He'd accepted the outcome of the investigation and was pleased it was over. The formal process was over, at any rate. The fall out, however... was still raining down.

"I understand, sir. I will learn from it."

Mullen's eyes narrowed. He was, no doubt, considering the sincerity of the pledge. Drawing a deep breath, Mullen closed the folder and double tapped the cover with two fingers.

"So be it, the matter is closed."

Duncan examined his superior's expression and came to a very different conclusion, not that he voiced it. Instead, he smiled warmly.

"Right, onto other matters," Mullen said. Any thoughts that Duncan had of leaving the office any time soon were dashed upon the rocks of those words. "Northern Command have requested your presence, Duncan."

He was surprised. "Me? Whatever for?"

"Heaven only knows, DI McAdam, but we all have our masters, don't we?"

"I've been off for two months, how do they—"

"You've been on suspension for two months, Duncan... it was hardly supposed to be a holiday."

"I kept my eye in, sir. I can assure you."

"Indeed, I'm sure you did," Mullen said, scepticism dripping from his tone. "I accepted on your behalf. After all, your caseload was reassigned while you were... off... and so we have no need of you."

Duncan felt that last comment like a knife to the heart. Mullen noticed, smiling apologetically.

"No *immediate* need of you," Mullen said, although Duncan was absolutely certain he'd chosen the original words purposefully. "I'm sure you understand. Besides, it's a good opportunity to get yourself back into the swing of things away from the goldfish bowl of Glasgow."

It was the first time he'd ever heard the greater Glasgow metropolitan area, housing forty percent of the country's entire population, being described as a goldfish bowl, but Mullen was known for hyperbole.

"So..." Duncan wondered aloud, "where exactly am I

going?"

"Home, DI McAdam." Mullen laid his palms flat on the desk before him, smiling. "You're going home for a spell."

If it was possible for his heart to sink even further, Duncan's did. Mullen studied his expression.

"I thought you'd be pleased, heading home to familiar places... and faces. I doubt all that much has changed since you left."

That was entirely the problem and one of the driving motivators for his leaving in the first place. The prospect of heading back to the island didn't cheer him. There were many questions he could have asked at that point. Many more he perhaps should have asked. Instead, only one word emerged in a pitiful tone.

"Why?"

Mullen sat back in his seat, his mood lightening as he analysed Duncan's discomfort.

"Because you were asked for. I should imagine it's down to you being from Skye. You know better than most what island folk are like."

"Sir?" Duncan was unsure if he should know the answer or take offence.

"People are entwined in those communities, Duncan. Everyone knows everyone else... and they don't take to outsiders."

That was something of a myth in Duncan's experience. In any community he'd ever worked in, people trusted what was familiar and not all that wasn't. It didn't make a difference if it was a remote island community of crofters or The Carlton here in Glasgow. People knew what they knew and often distrusted the unfamiliar.

"Maybe they'll open up to one of their own," Mullen finished. Duncan realised he'd stopped listening part way through the statement. "It shouldn't be for more than a week or two at the outset, perhaps three at the most."

"Sorry, sir. What case is this?"

"You recall the disappearance of a teenager one summer, twenty or so years ago?"

Duncan didn't have to think hard to recall it. The case shocked the entire island when a girl vanished into thin air never to be heard from again. A huge air and sea search and rescue operation got under way and that was replaced subsequently by a police investigation into her disappearance. Nothing was ever found of her at the time, or since as far as Duncan knew. He'd been just a boy in short trousers, in primary but preparing for high school at the time and could remember his parents speaking about it in hushed tones when they thought he and his sister weren't listening. The case was mired in rumour and gossip to this day.

"Isla Matheson," Duncan said quietly, the name he hadn't thought of for years, although it was on the tip of his tongue.

"Yes, that's the one," Mullen said, nodding firmly. "Well, they've found her." Duncan looked at him expectantly, knowing he didn't have to ask the question. "Her body was found three days ago. A DNA match was found in the database and the next of kin have been informed."

"Was she murdered?"

"That's what the team is there to determine, Duncan," Mullen said, sitting upright and pointing towards the door. "DCI Jameson will be expecting you there later today."

"Today?" Duncan said aloud, a multitude of thoughts flashing through his mind. "I mean... I have to speak to my other half."

Mullen raised one eyebrow in query.

"I can't just up and leave without a word..."

Mullen glanced at his watch. "You can be there in less than

four hours, so that leaves you plenty of time to get yourself sorted."

A flash of irritation passed over him and Duncan winced. Being away might not be the worst of all possible scenarios, but to be heading back to Skye was like leaping from the fireplace onto the stove. Either way, Mullen didn't care. In fact, he seemed to delight in his reaction.

"Yes, sir. I'll... make my way up there this afternoon."

"Good man." He gestured to the door. "That will be all DI McAdam." Duncan, momentarily lost in reverie, looked up and nodded, hastily getting up. Mullen turned to the screen on his desk and made as if he was moving onto his next assignment but in reality, he was only brushing Duncan away.

As he reached the door, Mullen called after him. "No hurry for you to return, Duncan. A change is as good as a holiday, right?"

Duncan, hand firmly gripping the door handle so tightly he could see the whites of his knuckles, looked back and smiled as convincingly as he could. "Aye, sir. I'm looking forward to it."

"Good man," Mullen repeated, looking away. Duncan left the office and gently closed the door behind him, finding Kelly looking his way, smiling. She rose from her seat and picked up a sheaf of paper held together with a large paper clip. He approached and she offered the papers to him.

"Your travel itinerary, accommodation, contacts and all the details you need for your trip."

He gave the top sheet a cursory inspection, spotting his hotel reservation and smiling said, "Well, at least it's a decent hotel."

Kelly lowered her voice. "I was supposed to put you in a B&B but I won't tell anyone if you don't." She winked and he smiled.

"Thank you, Kelly. I've always liked you."

The phone buzzed on her desk and she turned to pick up the receiver.

"Yes, I'll tell him, sir." She put the phone down again and looked sheepishly at Duncan. "He says not to hang about for a blether."

Touching the edge of the papers to his temple, he silently mouthed the words *thank you* to her and left the office. Once out in the corridor he contemplated his return home. It wasn't going back to the island that necessarily bothered him – although he could do without it to be sure – because he'd made the trip back several times over the years, but leaving now wasn't the greatest timing for him.

The corridor was empty and Duncan checked his watch. If he called now, he'd catch Natalie before she left for work. Taking out his mobile, he leaned against the wall and took a deep breath as he dialled her number.

"Hey, it's me," he said. "How's it going?"

"What's going on?"

He was taken aback. "What do you mean?"

"That tone, you only use it when you're about to drop something bad on me."

"I don't…" he said, but inwardly he knew that was likely true. "But I do have to talk to you about— "

"I knew it. You've been back in for one morning and you're being suspended again, right?"

"No…"

"So, what is it?"

There was something about Glaswegians that Duncan had always admired and hated in almost equal measure, dependant largely on whether he was on the receiving end or not, and that was their almost brutal honesty. Natalie had it in spades.

"I have to go away."

"Away?" she asked, annoyed or just curious, he really couldn't tell. "Away where?"

"Skye... for a case."

"And it has to be you?" The question was definitely asked accusingly. "Because Big Dunc McAdam is the only polisman in Scotland who can investigate a crime in the arse-end of nowhere?"

"It's not quite like that," he said, trying to keep his tone calm and neutral, "and it's not like I have a choice— "

"There's always a choice, Dunc. Always."

"Well, you can take it up with my DCS if you like?"

"When are you going?"

"Today. As soon as I can get a bag packed."

"And what about ma fether's birthday party this weekend?"

"Ah..." he grimaced. He'd forgotten about that, not that there was anything he could do about it. "Yeah, I'm not going to make it."

"Is that right?"

He knew that tone, and he readied himself for facing both barrels.

"I know the timing isn't great— "

"No, Duncan. The timing is perfect."

"It is?" he asked, lowering his voice and nodding to a colleague passing him in the corridor.

"Aye, it is and I'll even help you pack."

This was it, the denouement he'd anticipated.

"You will?" he asked, bracing himself.

"Aye, don't worry about packing, I'll put yer bags out in the street fer yer."

"Natalie, come on. I told you, it's not like I have a choice in any of this—"

"Well, maybe if you'd kept yer trousers on in the first place you wouldn't have pissed everyone off," she said, "me included, and they wouldn't be sending you off to inspect the sheep, would they?"

He had to admit it, she had a point. "Nat—"

"No, I think you've said enough, Duncan. I'll have your stuff ready to pick up before I go tae work. Enjoy yourself on Skye and don't hurry back, yer wee prick!"

The call ended and Duncan pursed his lips, wincing as he lowered the phone and stared at the screen.

"Well, that went quite well," he said quietly to himself, slipping the mobile into his pocket, "all things considered."

"You all right, Dunc?" It was the familiar voice of his DCI, Lyndsay Scott, approaching him in the corridor. He looked at her and smiled, nodding. "When are you off to Skye?"

"As soon as I've retrieved my clothes from the gutter, I expect." She looked at him quizzically and he waved the comment aside. "I'll get my stuff together and leave after lunch."

"Not what you were expecting from your first day back, I suspect?"

He frowned. "Tell me, does everyone in the station know I'm heading up there?"

She grinned. "Only those of us in the loop. It'll be good for you, Duncan. A chance to regroup, sort yourself out."

"Now you sound like the old man," he said, nodding towards their superior's office.

"Keep me posted," she said, before continuing on along the corridor.

"Will do." Pressing into his eyes with his fingertips, he then dragged both hands down his face while looking skyward. "Back home," he said, slapping both cheeks with his hands. "Jesus wept."

CHAPTER TWO

DUNCAN FOUND a parking space opposite the bus station in Somerled Square, something that was akin to winning the lottery in peak tourist season and, even at this time of the year, was fortunate during the day. The blue sky and pleasant sunshine belied the cutting wind that tore into him as soon as he got out of the confines of his car.

Looking around, the old place hadn't changed much. The trees lining the open-air seating near the war memorial had grown significantly. Some of the buildings had changed hands, restaurants or bars undergoing rebranding but from the outside they hadn't changed at all. The Lodge of St. Hilda was still present, bearing a sign out front proudly displaying the masonry heritage although the sunlight had aged the paper from cream to a tanned, almost smoke-stained greyish brown.

The image of his father haranguing the members as they left their meetings came to mind. He often wondered if his father's mockery was misplaced jealousy at never being considered worthy of an invitation or if he really did have truck with what he called a secret society; one so secret they advertised their meetings on a public street.

The Megabus rumbled up Wentworth Street, navigating the narrow road with a line of cars parked in the short-term bays to the left, slowly making the turn into the bus station and drawing up along the raised platform. People emerged from parked cars, nearby shops and cafes dragging wheeled cases or with bags slung over their shoulders. The turnaround would be swift, the bus hitting the road again within minutes.

Looking past the bus towards the police station, Duncan checked his watch. He'd made good time up from Glasgow. The clement weather made the drive through Glencoe a wonder to behold, although doing the same drive even a month ago would have seen him running the gauntlet of foreign drivers, tour buses and bikers meandering through at low speeds. Although Highland tourism was almost an all-year-round business these days, they were currently in the lull as the year end approached. He wasn't expected for another hour at the station, so he decided to have a look around.

Crossing the car park, he skipped across the road and walked past the Sheriff's Court. In front of him was an old building which was now a travellers' hostel, painted bright yellow with deep blue accents mimicking the famous-coloured terrace lining Quay Street overlooking Portree's old harbour. Turning left he stopped at the end of the building looking down over the coach park and across to the water of the bay where a handful of small boats lay at anchor.

Traffic thundered past him as he continued to his left, heading for Bank Street. This was the route traffic took to bypass the town centre and head up the east coast of the island towards Staffin. Rounding a tight corner onto Bosville Terrace, the vista opened up and he could see across Portree Bay, over the harbour and the Sound of Raasay to the island itself in the distance. If the island wasn't visible it meant one of two things; either it was lashing it down or it was about to lash it down.

"I'd know that walk anywhere!"

Duncan, hearing the raised voice, turned to see a man standing at the entrance to the mini Co-op, two carrier bags, one in each hand, watching him. The man hurried across the road in between passing traffic navigating the tight turn up the hill onto Bosville Terrace where Duncan stood. It took a moment for Duncan to realise he knew him but, although he looked familiar, the name didn't come immediately to mind, not until he closed the gap, beaming a smile through a mass of an unkempt ginger beard.

"Archie Mackinnon," Duncan said, breaking into a smile of his own. "How are you, mate?" He offered his hand. Archie looked at the offer of a handshake, sneering as he dropped the green plastic bags and threw his arms around Duncan, embracing him in a bear hug and hauling him off his feet. At five foot ten and weighing in excess of fourteen stone on a good day, Duncan was surprised to feel air beneath his feet but, then again, Archie had always been freakishly strong.

"Wee Dunc!" Archie said, grinning and dropping him. Duncan, glad to feel the reassuring touch of firm ground beneath his feet, took a step back. "What are you doing back here?"

Duncan took his friend's measure. He looked very similar to the young man he was the last time they'd been together when they were teenagers readying themselves to set out in the world. The boyish grin and mischievous gleam in his eyes were still there, even if the face beneath the mass of curly hair, sticking out from beneath his beanie and hanging from his cheeks, was now lined with the unappeasable creep of ageing. Duncan looked around, shrugging.

"I'm here for a bit of work, you know?"

"Oh aye. What are you up to these days?"

Duncan looked Archie up and down. He was sporting stained jeans and an all-weather coat that had seen better days. He was wearing wellies, so it was fair to assume he still spent a lot of time outdoors. No doubt he was working his father's croft, or one of his own, but what else he did to make ends meet, as many crofters often had to do, he did wonder.

"I... work in the public sector," Duncan said, never keen to volunteer that he was in the police. People looked at you differently when they learned that and, more often than not, were immediately put on their guard.

"The council? I thought you went off to university to study... what was it again?"

"IT."

"Aye, that's right... computers and that. Much call for your expertise in Portree is there?" Archie sounded sceptical. To be fair there wasn't a great deal of modern industry on the island, so it was a good shout.

Duncan shook his head. "Those days are well behind me."

"Not surprised," Archie said, shaking his head, a gesture that irritated Duncan for a reason he couldn't immediately understand. "I never did see you as one of those bookish sorts thumping away on keyboards."

"No, that's true," Duncan said, looking past him and searching for a route out of the conversation. At high school they'd been friends, but what he'd have in common with the big guy now after all these years escaped him.

"So... Highland Council, eh?" Archie said, scratching his beard. Duncan slowly nodded but didn't offer any more information. "Well, I hope you're going to be able to do something about all these people coming on to the island."

Duncan shot him a quizzical look. "People? What sort of people?"

Archie shook his head. "Not people as such, they're all right... well, some of them. No, I mean the numbers. The damn tourist board have been overselling the island again. Been doing it for years! The roads... shops and all that just can't cope with it. It's mental here much of the year these days."

Duncan wrinkled his nose. "Sorry, Archie, but that's not my... field of expertise."

"Ah, fair enough, Dunc." He looked disappointed. Duncan figured he'd managed to steer clear of a rant. "How long are you about for?"

Duncan shrugged. "A few days... a week or so, maybe."

"Grand. We'll have to grab a pint later." Duncan was noncommittal. Even if he had time, which he doubted, he didn't really fancy a trip down memory lane. Archie, his exuberance returning, had other ideas. "Hey, you know what? Macnabs has a Ceilidh on tonight. Why don't you swing by, and we can have a couple of pints and a catch-up?"

"Oh... well, I've only just got into town— "

"Nonsense, man! I haven't seen you in what... fifteen years? Come on!"

Duncan smiled. "All right, I'll see what I can do."

"Good man!" Archie said, clapping him on the arm with such force it knocked Duncan off balance.

"No promises," Duncan said, raising a pointed finger. "I've still got to check in with... work and all, so I'll make it if I can."

"Great! Where are you staying? I'll—"

There was no way he was allowing this information out there, so Duncan raised a hand and cut Archie off. "I'll see you in there... eight-ish. What do you think?"

"Great," Archie said, beaming and nodding. "Ah… Duncan, it's so good to see you."

Duncan smiled back at him. "Yeah, it's nice to see you too, Archie." He slipped past him on the narrow pavement, offering him an encouraging thumbs-up gesture as he did so. "We'll catch up later, yeah?"

"Cheers, Dunc."

Duncan crossed the road and hurried onto Wentworth Street, the most direct route back to Somerled Square and the relative safety of the police station.

Entering the station, he approached the front desk and pressed the buzzer. A civilian clerk opened an opaque sliding glass screen a few moments later. He looked Duncan up and down.

"Can I help you?"

Duncan showed his warrant card. "DI McAdam, up from Glasgow. I'm to report to DCI Jameson."

"Do you know the way?" he asked. Duncan shook his head. He'd never been inside this station, not as a policeman through the public door at any rate. "Take a seat and I'll have someone come and get you." He pointed to the seats behind Duncan lined up side by side against the wall opposite. Duncan thanked him and crossed the reception. The glass screen slid closed with a thump.

He didn't have to wait long before the security door into the station opened and a man stepped out, looking around reception. He was tall, at least six-two but lean, and walked with a straight back which was a dead giveaway that he had at one time served in the military. His hair was cut close, receding and he sported a thick moustache that would have been all the rage in the late seventies when he was probably barely out of his teens. His expression was impassive and emotionless as he eyed Duncan, offering him an almost imperceptible nod in greeting.

"DI McAdam?" he asked, his tone flat and a little gruff.

"The very same," Duncan said, standing up and accepting the man's offered hand.

"DS Alistair MacEachran. Welcome to Portree." The handshake was firm and he held Duncan's eye. Duncan felt as if he was already being assessed. "Long drive?"

"Ah, it's an easy run up from Glasgow."

"Aye. You ever been up to Skye before?"

"Not for a while," Duncan said as he was led through the door and deeper into the bowels of the station proper. "But I know my way around."

He felt MacEachran's eyes on him as they climbed the stairs to the first floor.

"I thought I recognised the island accent."

Duncan laughed. "Yeah, it never leaves you. How about you? You're not from Skye. West End of Glasgow?"

"No," he said. "Dumbarton."

"Ah, the ancient mighty Kingdom of Strathclyde," Duncan said, glancing sideways. The detective sergeant was looking at him, probably trying to decide if he was taking the mickey out of him. "I picked up a few things since I lived down that way."

"Ah, did yer... aye?"

Duncan figured the DS wasn't one to joke with and the rest of the short journey up to CID was made in silence. As they were approaching the operations room, DS MacEachran slowed the pace, coming to a standstill a few metres from the door.

"Just so you know, there's a briefing under way," he said, lowering his voice and glancing down the corridor to ensure they were alone, "and the boss figured you'd have been here earlier."

Duncan nodded. He was certain he'd got the scheduled times right. He wasn't late, not as far as he was concerned. It was true that it took him a while to pack his things into the car. Natalie hadn't been hyperbolic when she said she'd put his bag in the street for him. She had, along with everything else of his that he'd left at her flat in the two years they'd been seeing one another. All of which was now in his car parked outside.

"Thanks for the heads-up."

"You're welcome. Jameson's a wee shite…" he looked around, lowering his voice conspiratorially, "between you and me."

He didn't wait for a reply and pushed open the door into the Operation Room, Duncan following on. A sharply dressed man in a tailored suit with fastidiously-styled hair was at the front addressing what was a fairly crowded room. Duncan couldn't figure out which of the assembled officers were locals and who had been drafted in from elsewhere. Presumably most of them, seeing as Portree didn't have a massive contingent of CID officers. Although the island's capital, the town wasn't massive and the population of Skye couldn't be more than fifteen thousand, although bearing in mind what Archie had been bemoaning earlier, perhaps the population massively increased with the tourists.

"So, it's been officially confirmed," the man at the front of the room said, looking around the room. Duncan presumed he was DCI Jameson. "The body found out at Waternish has now been positively identified as that of Isla Matheson, a young woman who was reported missing in 1999. DNA samples compared with those provided by family members leave us in no doubt." A murmur of what Duncan thought a mixture of shock and anger reverberated around the room. The DCI was forced to raise his voice to ensure they quietened down. "I know this is shocking for all of you, in particular those locals with ties to the community and perhaps even with the Matheson family, but I ask you to park your emotions at the door. We are still to determine what ended the young woman's life and I need everyone focussed on that objective."

The DCI looked around the assembled officers, his gaze settling momentarily on Duncan, standing at the back of the room alongside DS MacEachran, before moving on to those around him.

"As I said, the cause of death is still under investigation," Jameson went on, "and so let's not lose sight of what we are trying to achieve here."

"Which is?" MacEachran muttered under his breath.

"And that is to find out what happened to her," Jameson said.

MacEachran raised an eyebrow, glancing sideways at Duncan. "You can see why he gets paid the big bucks, right?"

Duncan had to suppress a smile.

Jameson continued. "I want everyone to stick with their designated assignments for the time being. Local CID, I want you revisiting the witness statements, Isla's friends and family and anyone else who was spoken to at the time of her disappearance. See if anything has changed with their memories over time. I know it's mundane, but even the slightest snippet of information missed or overlooked back then could turn out to be very important and you're the best placed to really drive down deep into the local mindset." He looked around the room again making eye contact with a few before addressing the group as a whole once more. "Everyone else, we're still tracking the movements of known sex offenders, violent criminals and reviewing intelligence from the time, tying it into the present day. Stay focussed. Stay alert… and I assure you, we will catch this guy."

"You see… a wee shite," MacEachran said, leaning into Duncan. "We get the donkey work while his drone army of high-flying super soldiers get to play hunt Hannibal the cannibal."

Duncan shot him a questioning look. MacEachran's expression changed and he smiled sheepishly.

"Figuratively speaking, obviously."

"So, I'm up from Glasgow but I'm from the island. Does that make me a super soldier or something else?"

"That's to be determined, laddie."

Duncan hadn't been called *laddie* for years. Things weren't quite as formal in the police on Skye. Either that or it was just MacEachran who held little respect for the rank. He wondered which scenario was accurate, but guessed it was probably the latter.

"Detective Inspector McAdam?" Jameson said, striding purposefully towards him as the briefing broke up and the general hubbub within the incident room increased as people made their way back to their desks.

"Yes, sir," Duncan said, shaking hands with the DCI. "I'm sorry if I am a bit late. There must have been crossed wires somewhere along the line.

"My office, Detective Inspector," Jameson said, offering a curt nod to MacEachran who returned it with one of his own. As the two senior officers turned away Duncan could have sworn he heard two heels click together and stamp on the floor as if MacEachran was standing to attention. Glancing back, Duncan half expected the man to be offering an extended salute, but he wasn't. MacEachran was already off across the room hailing a colleague, his voice rising well above all others.

CHAPTER THREE

DCI JAMESON WALKED into his office, a small room set off the incident room, and went around to the other side of his desk.

"Close the door, would you please, Duncan," he said as he took his seat. Duncan shut the door and immediately the noise level lessened but telephones ringing and chitter chatter was still audible in the background. There were no other seats available in the confined space, so Duncan was forced to stand. "A good drive up?"

"Very good, sir, thank you."

Jameson fixed him with a look that Duncan found hard to decipher.

"It's a wonder you were so late for the briefing." Duncan made to respond but Jameson switched tone and pace, waving away the comment. "No matter. You're here now. I have you in mind to be my liaison between my team and..." he looked up, frowning as he tried to find the right word "... the locals."

Duncan was perplexed. "Aren't we all on the same team, sir?"

Jameson stared at him, disapprovingly. "Of course, we are,

Duncan. Only we have levels… think of them as proactive versus reactive or the A Team and the B Team, if you prefer?"

Duncan smiled. "Right you are, sir."

"And you're captaining the B Team, Duncan." Jameson sat back, assessing Duncan as he entwined his fingers and cracked his knuckles. "I need someone to be my eyes and ears among the locals." He sat forward and pointed at him. "And that's you, Duncan."

"Wouldn't their own DI be a better fit for that, sir?"

Jameson shook his head. "No go, I'm afraid Duncan. DI Johnston is signed off long term. He'll not be back any time soon, and certainly not before we have this case put to bed."

"You're confident, sir?"

"Always. A positive mindset is invaluable in this line of work. Wouldn't you agree?"

Duncan nodded, although internally he seldom met a police officer with any significant time served, who hadn't been ground down by wading through human garbage for years.

"Eyes and ears," Duncan said aloud.

"Exactly. Now, you recall the case? Isla Matheson went missing when you were on the island, right? It was a big story back then, in and around the millennium?"

"Aye, it was," Duncan said, remembering. "Just before the millennium, '99 I think. I was only just about to start high school, mind."

"What do you remember about it?"

He shrugged. "Not all that much. Playground gossip had her abducted by aliens, I think." Jameson didn't laugh. Duncan thought better of making light of it again. He cleared his throat. "From memory, as a child I remember my folks were scared for me and for all the children on the island. It was different back then. We were used to tourists, new faces visiting in the summer months but life hadn't changed much for centuries around these parts. Here on Skye, you're pretty much shielded from stuff going on in Glasgow or Edinburgh. And let's face it, anyone in the central belt thinks they're the be-all-and-end-all of this country. The rest of us, particularly the highlanders, just live in the back end of nowhere, sheep-shagging our way through the day..." Jameson's eyes narrowed and Duncan realised he'd inadvertently just described the man sitting opposite him "...sir."

"You were saying about the locals?"

"Aye, right. People were scared. It's not unknown for someone to clear off from time to time, but a teenage girl... that was unusual. And I hope it stays being unusual, sir. Most people, as I recall, myself included, figured she'd just run off with her boyfriend and would come back in a couple of days. As the time passed though, I remember my mum insisting on taking us to school and collecting us too, me and my sister. Other parents started doing the same. Islands can be strange places—"

Jameson snorted. "You're right there."

"I mean, everyone knows everyone else. We all know who the weirdos are... who to avoid. Who likes a drink," which was most people, he said to himself, "and who likes a scrap." He shrugged. "You just avoid them. People got scared. I think the boyfriend was interviewed by the police at the time. Rumours and gossip were swirling around as well."

"He was interviewed, yes," Jameson said, glancing down at an open file on his desk. "Alex Macrae. Although he stated that he and Isla had recently split up and he was in another relationship." Jameson shrugged, absently turning the top document over before looking back at Duncan. "He said he was happy about that, and he had no idea where she was.

Seemingly, she was making quite an exhibition of herself the night she disappeared."

"An exhibition?" Duncan asked, not liking Jameson's tone or choice of adjective.

"Yes, flirting with the young men within her group. You'll remember she was last seen attending a beach party?"

"Yes, sir. It was out on Coral Beach, out Dunvegan way."

"That's right… some kind of *rites of passage* among the local teenagers. Is that something you got up to in your day?"

Duncan thought back to his latter teenage years, momentarily recalling the mayhem and chaos he and his friends often wrought on the islanders. He shuddered internally. "Similar, I expect sir. Don't we all?"

"Can't say I was ever a drink and drugs man," Jameson said haughtily. Duncan believed him. He looked as straight as a broom handle… and less interesting.

"Were drugs involved, sir? I don't remember anything being said at the time."

"True enough, I'm making an assumption. Good spot, Duncan."

"It's common for kids to have a bit of a blowout at the end of the summer, sir. Things are different here on the island. If you want to continue education then you have to leave for the mainland and, similarly, if you're looking to get into industry or the modern workplace, then you have to leave. There's nothing for you here. Everything in Scotland is geared towards Glasgow or Edinburgh and everywhere in between." He shrugged. "A party like that is the closure of a chapter in your life you're never likely to revisit."

Jameson nodded along thoughtfully. "Well, someone happened across the… young lady… and she came a cropper."

"Is that the main focus of the investigation, sir?"

"All lines are open at this time, Duncan. And that's why I want you to oversee the locals as they reinterview those who knew and spent time with her. Nothing was thrown up when she disappeared twenty-odd years ago, but now, with the passage of time, maybe someone saw something that they didn't think was significant."

"And you really needed me to come all the way up here for that?"

Jameson didn't appreciate the comment, glaring at him. "You have something better to do with your time than investigate the mysterious death of a teenager, Detective Inspector?"

"No sir."

"Good, because there is a dead girl in the morgue and I want to find out who put her in the ground."

"That's been confirmed, has it, sir? That she was killed twenty years ago?"

"That she died, yes," Jameson said. "But, as you'd have heard during the briefing, had you been on time and listening, the cause of death is still to be confirmed."

"But someone buried her," Duncan said, his brow furrowing in concentration. "What is the condition of the body?"

"Well preserved, according to the pathologist who came up from Glasgow at the weekend. The peat content in the ground preserved her remains rather well. DS MacEachran can provide you with a copy of the report."

Duncan considered the information. If Isla died that night, then he figured there were only two possible scenarios; either she happened across a dangerous individual by chance in the dark or, what he thought was more probable, that someone attending the beach party hadn't told the police the truth about the events of that night. Thinking back to what his group often got up to; it was likely that would apply to more than one of the party goers.

Duncan realised he'd been lost in thought. DCI Jameson was looking at him quizzically.

"Sorry, sir. What did you say?"

"I asked if you needed anything further," he said. "And it was a rhetorical question."

"I see," Duncan said, smiling. "I'll crack on then, sir."

He turned to leave but Jameson asked him to wait.

"Sir?"

Jameson took a deep breath, then pursed his lips before exhaling. "I wasn't going to say this, Duncan, but you seem like the sort of fella who appreciates people shooting from the hip."

Duncan had no idea why that term would apply to him, but he waited expectantly.

"Let me be frank with you, Duncan. You were not my first choice for this case. I requested Tommy Gibson."

Duncan knew Tommy. He was a decent detective, a bit fake… plastic coppers they were known as in the trade; degree graduates, fast tracking their way to the top. It was also the exact opposite of what he'd been told back in Glasgow.

"But he wasn't available… apparently." Jameson sighed, clearly disappointed. "And so here you are." The last was said with intonation, the fact Duncan came in Tommy's place was evidently quite a big disappointment.

He smiled. "And here I am, sir."

Jameson nodded ruefully. "You're one of them, Duncan. An islander. That can be both a bonus and a hindrance to me." He fixed Duncan with a pointed stare, gently wagging his forefinger towards him. "Keep the locals in line… and out of my team's way, and I'm sure we'll have this wrapped up in no time. Then… you can go back to Glasgow." His gaze lingered on Duncan, who remained tight-lipped. "Understood, DI McAdam?"

"Crystal clear, sir."

"Good man. Crack on."

Jameson was already focussing on something else as Duncan opened the door to be hit by a wall of noise coming from the incident room. DS MacEachran saw him leaving Jameson's office and got off the edge of the desk he'd been perched on chatting to a young woman in a business suit, crossing the room to meet him.

"So, you're with me?" MacEachran said with a knowing smile.

"Relegated to the B Team," Duncan said.

"What? Does that make the rest of this lot," he said, glancing around the room, "the A Team?"

"Seemingly so, yes."

"That's bollocks. I'm second battalion. I've never been on the back-up team ever... what does he think I am, One Para?"

The military reference was lost on Duncan, but it did confirm his earlier thoughts that MacEachran had served in the forces at some point. Duncan looked around the room. The activity levels were high and all he really wanted to do was find a quiet corner and run through the established details of the case.

"Is there somewhere we can go..." Duncan said, "...that isn't here?"

"Could do with grabbing a sandwich myself," MacEachran said. He glanced at a clock on the wall. "I know just the place too."

The mention of food made Duncan hungry and he realised he hadn't eaten since breakfast; such was the whirlwind of a day he'd had. Getting out of bed this morning, he was facing up to his first day back in the office in months and now, less than eight hours later, he was back on Skye with a car outside stuffed full of his belongings, investigating a two-decade old mystery with a bunch of people who likely would prefer it if he wasn't there.

"Something to eat sounds good," Duncan said. "Is there a Pret or a Subway around here these days?"

MacEachran snorted with derision. "Are you absolutely sure you're from the island?" Duncan shrugged apologetically. "Pret..?" he asked, laughing.

"Guess not then," Duncan said, slipping his arm through his coat sleeve. "Lead on, my Guru Keck."

MacEachran laughed. "Alistair will be just fine."

Five minutes later they were in a pick-up truck driving out of the town past the largest, and indeed the only, supermarket of note in the island's capital heading west towards the ferry terminal at Uig which served the islands of the Outer Hebrides. Not that they were going that far. Alistair turned off the main road onto an industrial estate on Portree's outer limits. The estate wasn't large in comparison with those found serving Glasgow, but it was definitely larger than Duncan remembered being present years ago when he lived on Skye.

The island had grown in the intervening years since his departure, and not only in tourism. They drove past two timber and builders' merchant yards and he saw several units occupied by consultancy firms as well as others that he struggled to determine the nature of their business. They were all however, looking busy.

"Things sure are changing here on the mountain," Duncan whispered, referencing an old American television show he recalled watching during the school holidays long before streaming and catch-up TV was ever a thing. It was set around the turn of the twentieth century and even when Duncan watched it, it was already repeats.

"What's that?"

Duncan glanced across at his driver, shaking his head. "Doesn't matter."

They pulled into a lay-by on the main thoroughfare between four commercial units. One of them was a prefabricated house manufacturer, highlighting the rise in demand for-quick-to assemble modular homes that could stand up to the harsh Atlantic weather fronts that rattled across the island daily. With few resources open to the local community of their own to build modern, insulated and efficient-to-run homes, these designs were proving popular. Duncan had seen them popping up across the island every time he'd returned home, not that that was often.

"We're here," Alistair said.

"We're where?" Duncan asked, looking around at a few cars parked in front of the units. Alistair checked his watch and, as if on cue, a small red van rounded the corner and pulled into the lay-by in front of them. The driver sounded three blasts on the horn before getting out and coming to the side where she opened a panel, revealing the contents of her van.

"Better get a shifty on," Alistair said, cracking open his door and clambering out. Duncan saw people almost streaming out of the nearby buildings and all of them were making a beeline to the little red van. He followed suit, hurrying to catch up with the DS. The sandwich van was well stocked with a mixture of rolls, pastries, chocolate bars and various other snacks and drinks. A queue formed rapidly behind them and Duncan felt his mouth watering when he caught a whiff of the hot food on offer. He delighted in choosing a chicken bridie; a pastry stuffed with diced chicken breast and vegetables.

"Best restaurant in town," Alistair said, taking a bite of his roll just as Duncan reached for his wallet, cursing. "What is it?"

"I left my wallet in the car."

"Typical weegie," Alistair said, laughing whilst taking out his wallet to pay the bill. Duncan was grateful and they walked back to the pick-up. Reaching the car, Alistair tutted, stopping Duncan in his tracks. "You'll no' be eating that in my pick-up."

Duncan glanced down at the pastry bits sticking to the front of his coat and the jumper beneath. "Fair enough." He put his can of drink and unopened packet of crisps on the bonnet, and before taking another bite of the bridie, he caught Alistair's attention. "So, what do you make of this case?"

Alistair tilted his head to one side, arching his eyebrows. "I reckon Jameson's got it all wrong."

"In what way?" Duncan asked, taking a bite.

Alistair was thoughtful. "I don't care what he's said in that briefing, they're scouring Scotland for a serial killer or a sex offender and hoping they find one on or around the island at the time of her disappearance… and I'm no' buying it."

"No? Why not?"

He scoffed. "How's your maths?"

Duncan shrugged.

"About as good as mine," Alistair said, smiling, "but let's run the numbers. Isla goes to a party with all her pals, right. They're drinking, having a great time and at some point in the evening, unseen by any of the other attendees, she wanders away from the group. No one sees her go and no one comes looking for her." He leaned on the pick-up and with both hands mimicking an explosion, he said, "Poof! The girl vanishes without trace!" He shook his head. "Isla Matheson had to stumble across a murderer who just happened to be passing at the exact same time... and that'd make her the unluckiest lass in the whole world..."

"Or at least, on the island," Duncan said.

"Aye, that's right. Now, my maths is awful which is one of the many, many reasons I shovel shite on this beautiful island for a living rather than running a blue-chip business somewhere else, but I'll tell you this... someone there that night must know who killed her and, to my mind at least, they've been sitting on that knowledge for twenty years. It must be eating them up inside."

Duncan, with a mouthful of food, raised a hand full of bridie in his direction, covering his mouth as he spoke with his free hand. "That's the second time you've mentioned her being killed. Do you know something the rest of us don't because Jameson said the cause of death is yet to be determined?"

"Aye, well who put her in the ground?"

Duncan tilted his head. "You got me there."

"No one's going to tell me she died of natural causes and then buried herself. Some of us on the island aren't as thick as mince, you know?" He smiled and winked. "And I'm not even from the island, but I've been here long enough for my superiority to lose a bit of its sheen."

"I was thinking much the same thing, about someone burying her," Duncan said. "Did you work the original case, back when Isla was reported missing?"

"Nah, well before my time. I was still jumping out of planes on Her Majesty's pound back then."

"Right." Duncan finished his bridie, licking the end of his fingers and wishing he'd bought a second. The van was closed up now, the driver accelerating away to her next stop somewhere in the town no doubt. He looked back at Alistair.

"Did you get to see the body?"

"Aye, when they first found her and after they brought her in. The poor girl. What a place to be laid to rest... a more beautiful place in the world you will not find, but to be put down out there... with your kin not knowing your whereabouts." He shook his head. "Nah, that's no' right, no' right at all."

"Is she still on the island? The body, I mean?"

"Aye."

"Can we get in to see her?"

"I guess we could do that."

"Let's do it then."

"You want to go now... right after eating?" Alistair asked, screwing up his nose as if he'd smelt something awful.

"Weren't you in the army?"

"2 Para, aye. No finer fighting men in the British forces."

"You must have seen much worse then?"

"Aye, but I didn't stop to eat over the dead bodies, did I? That'd be plain weird."

"I have an island constitution," Duncan said, tapping his chest with a balled fist, "not like you metropolitan softies." He sighed. "Maybe we should have hired a former Royal Marine."

The trace of a smile crossed Alistair's face and he pointed to the pick-up, silently gesturing for him to get in. "Royal Marines... my arse," he mumbled through a smile.

It was good timing as the first pitter-patter of rain cast down from a fresh weather front struck the windscreen as Duncan shut his door. Such was the way of things here on the island, he figured there was a decent chance the rain would be replaced by sunshine before they reached their destination.

There was an equal chance it would be far worse too.

CHAPTER FOUR

A SHORT DRIVE LATER, DS MacEachran pulled his pick-up into the car park of a nondescript single-storey building. There were only half a dozen parking spaces and Duncan observed the building. It was of modern construction, a simple rectangular timber-framed building wrapped in white-painted harling with three evenly spaced square windows along the side and one brown, wood effect, plastic door.

"The morgue," Alistair said, pointing to the one other car in the car park. "And that is our pathologist." The occupant of the other vehicle got out when Alistair switched the engine off, crossing the parking lot to greet them.

"Hello, Alistair," the pathologist said in a distinctive island accent, shaking hands with Alistair before looking at Duncan. He was a slight man but portly, with straw-like red hair rapidly shifting to grey and disappearing away from his forehead. The hair sprouting from either side of his head above the ears was an untamed wilderness with a mind of its own.

"DI McAdam," Alistair said, introducing him. "He's joining us from civilisation for a week or two."

Duncan took the man's offered hand. "Duncan," he said, warmly. "I'm up from Glasgow for a wee while."

"Craig Dunbar," the man replied, smiling. "Pleased to meet you."

"Dr Craig Dunbar," Alistair said but the correction was dismissed. Alistair angled his head. "Don't do yourself down, Craig, all those letters after your name were earned, after all. Wouldn't want him thinking you're just the janny around here."

"And those letters mean next to nothing unless I'm at a conference or testifying in court!" Dunbar said, smiling and turning his collar up against the wind. "Come on, let's get inside. I wish this weather would make up its mind today."

The doctor unlocked the entrance and led them inside. The building was cold, unsurprising for a morgue one might think, but this was only the entrance lobby. The two detectives followed the shorter man along a corridor where he unlocked another internal door, opened it and ushered them through. He flicked several light switches and fluorescent tubes stuttered into life overhead.

"Now, remind me," Dr Dunbar said, looking between them. "What are we here for?"

Alistair nodded towards Duncan. "The big man wants to see Isla Matheson's body."

Dunbar looked at Duncan and simply nodded. He didn't ask why, just turned and led them through another door. This was the cold store where they kept the bodies refrigerated. There were only six steel doors, each securely closed with large over-sized handles.

"Now… let me see," Dr Dunbar said pointing at the closed doors in turn. "One… two… and number four," he said, opening the fourth and grinning triumphantly. "Here we are." He grasped a handle and pulled the tray out. The runners were well oiled and the bagged body slid out effortlessly. The pathologist crossed the room, returning seconds later with a box of forensic gloves and some disposable masks. He plucked a pair of gloves from the box and passed it to Duncan before turning to the body, donning the gloves and then gently unzipped the black bag. "I'm sorry to disturb you, my dear," he said. "We won't keep you long."

Duncan, gloves on purely as a precaution as he had no intention of touching the body, stepped forward. He was immediately shocked by what he saw. He almost did a double take to check if this was Isla Matheson. The teenager had been missing for over two decades and yet she looked like she'd only passed away recently. Dr Dunbar noticed his reaction and smiled knowingly.

"I know. Beautiful young girl, isn't she?"

Duncan wasn't sure if beautiful was an appropriate adjective, but he was right. Isla Matheson had an almost angelic bone structure to her features, high cheekbones and a slim nose that most would consider classically attractive. Were it not for the discolouration of her skin and hair, she could easily be judged as sleeping.

"That's... remarkable," Duncan whispered. "She's so..."

"Well preserved," Dunbar said. "I know. It's the soil. Where she was found is akin to a raised bog." Duncan looked at him quizzically. "It's a natural basin which due to the lay of the land is saturated... then waterlogged... and the lack of drainage slows plant decay and over time sphagnum moss accumulates to form a dome of sorts which is in turn fed by further rainwater. You may have noticed that we have a fair bit of that around these parts."

"And that process preserves the body... like this?" Duncan asked.

"Well, not only that. The land has very few minerals and

even less oxygen…" he drew breath "… and if you throw in the cool mean temperatures this far north you find the land itself acts as a natural refrigerator. A body in this environment decomposes extremely slowly." He frowned. "Although, it's not a perfect system. Soon after burial, the acid begins the tanning process to the body's skin, hair and nails."

"Which is why she's this reddish-brown colour?"

"Quite right, Duncan. And as the sphagnum moss dies, which it does each season before renewing, it releases a carbohydrate polymer called sphagnan. This binds the nitrogen, halting the growth of bacteria and de facto further mummifying the corpse." He arched his eyebrows in wonder. "It really is quite a special reaction within nature's mix of chemical reactions. The effect is not unlike what we find with all of these ancient sacrificial victims archaeologists have been hauling out of the peatlands across Europe in the last couple of hundred years." He looked at the body glumly. "Had we discovered the poor lass in a thousand years or so, this process would have extracted the calcium from her bones and she'd have been flattened," he made a gesture, pressing his hands together, "squashing all the shape out of her. Very sad indeed. Not that I think this lovely girl was sacrificed to appease any gods, past or present."

"We still don't have a cause of death for her," Duncan said. "Is that correct?"

Dunbar shook his head, his brow furrowing. "No, we don't I'm afraid. Which is something of a puzzle, I have to say. I found no sign of external trauma to the body." He waved his hands around him in the air. "With these sacrificial lambs of the past we've found they've been garrotted, strangled and or stabbed… throats cut… hanged or even bludgeoned to death." He tilted his head, examining Isla's face as if it was for the first time. "On occasion, a combination of those, but none of this happened to you, did it, my dear?"

"Was there any sign of sexual assault?" Duncan asked.

"No," he shook his head, "none that I could see. Before you ask, there's no trace evidence left by any would-be perpetrator either. Twenty years lying, effectively, in a peat bog does not lend itself to forensic criminal analysis. Much of what I can do is merely supposition… and I am a little baffled with this one, I must say."

"But you are able to date the time of death with a good level of accuracy?"

"Well, I can't tell you what she would have been missing on television the night she died, Duncan… but yes, with a fair degree of certainty, I can say she died around the time of her disappearance."

Alistair came to stand by Duncan's shoulder. He could easily see over him. "Which lends itself to the reason no one saw her after that night, if she was already dead. There were no sightings on public transport, not hits on her cash card at the bank… so it stands to reason she died at the time she went missing."

"She was in good health?" Duncan asked neither man in particular. Alistair was familiar with the case and Dunbar had carried out the autopsy.

"Nothing wrong with her as far as I know," Alistair said. "The family described her as the picture of good health."

Duncan looked at the pathologist.

"I've still some work to do there," he said. "Having not found any obvious cause of death I've had to dig further. I've sent blood samples away to Glasgow for further analysis because there's no reason a fit and healthy young woman should drop dead unaided, unless of course, there's some disease or illness we –

and her family and GP – were unaware of. I did read through her medical records and there is no known ailment to speak of." He shook his head, frowning. "Hence why I am baffled." He looked between them and smiled. "Don't worry, I'll spend some time with the wee girl and no doubt I'll figure it out."

Duncan took one last lingering look over the body, lips pursed in solemn thought. He had wanted to come and see her for himself. It was something he always tried to do if at all possible. You could stare at photographs for hours and, shocking as they were, you would never feel the same about the victim as you would having stood over the body in person. Many detectives preferred not to expose themselves to it, and he couldn't blame them. One had to keep a degree of separation from a victim, thereby insulating yourself from the emotional pain and trauma but, for Duncan, it was that very pain that would spur him on. This girl needed a champion and, like it or not, he was hers.

"Thank you for seeing us at such short notice, Dr Dunbar," Duncan said, nodding and stepping away from the body, peeling off his gloves. "I think we're done here."

"Right you are," the doctor said, carefully zipping up the bag and returning Isla to her refrigerated locker. "Back to sleep, my dear."

Duncan hurried back to the pick-up with Alistair at his side, the wind howling around them and driving sheet rain in their faces. Neither man spoke until they got back into the sanctuary of the cabin.

"She looks just like she did the day she vanished," Duncan said quietly. "I can see the pictures taped up on the lampposts and in the newspaper in my mind, clear as day."

"Aye… boils my…" Alistair didn't finish the comment but the meaning was clear, "… that someone on this island did that to the girl and they're still wandering around as we stand about discussing it."

"You really think someone local did this, don't you?"

Alistair laughed but it was without genuine humour. "Like I said before, she'd be unlucky to meet some crazy all the way out Dunvegan way, especially at that time of the night."

"Statistically possible," Duncan countered.

"Aye, and statistics can tell you how many boils you have on yer arse by the time you're forty, but it doesn't make it so, does it?"

Duncan arched his eyebrows. "Colourful analogy. I didn't know they studied that sort of thing."

"I have plenty more where that one came from," Alistair said, sighing. "Not that what I think really matters. Jameson has his team casting a historical dragnet over the island, metaphorically speaking, and they're determined to catch someone in it. He doesn't think it was someone local."

"Why do you think he's done that?"

"Because he's left the local investigation to the likes of us," Alistair said with a rueful smile. "If he thought for a second that the killer was still walking among us, do you honestly think he'd leave it to the country bumpkins to handle?" He shook his head. "No way! We'd be assigning parking tickets, teaching self-defence to eight-year-olds in the primary schools or something else. Anything to keep us side-lined."

Duncan considered that point as Alistair started the engine, reversing quickly out of his space and pulling up to the junction with the main road.

"Reasons why it wouldn't be a local?" Duncan asked, playing devil's advocate.

Alistair held the car in place on the clutch, thinking. "Only one victim," he said at last before pulling out onto the main road. "If it was an opportunistic killer who took his chance when he had it, why would he stop there? Let's assume it was a first-timer, seeing as we haven't had a serial killer on the island – if you don't count the absentee landlords of the clearances – once a killer makes that step up and takes their first kill, the itch only starts again shortly after. No one sick in the head enough to do that is satiated by the one kill."

"No, they are compelled to do it again," Duncan said. "And again… and again, usually with a decreasing timespan between their victims."

"And we'd expect to have more than one victim after twenty years," Alistair said. "So… let's look at it from Jameson's viewpoint. If the killer was transient, a tourist, seasonal worker… someone passing through, then it would stand to reason that they moved on."

"One victim," Duncan said. "Sound logic."

Alistair glanced sideways at him, his eyes narrowing. "But you don't buy that either, do you? I can tell by the look on your face."

Duncan cocked his head. "Small community… even smaller back then. The island was opening up, but if someone took off around the time of Isla's disappearance, people would have noticed and likely commented on it."

"That's what Jameson is looking for," Alistair said. "Someone who was around beforehand and left shortly after."

"If they had form," Duncan said, "then they'd want to get off the island pretty quickly after Isla went missing. Preferably before too many questions were asked. And certainly before a body was found."

"Which it never was," Alistair said, "until now."

"Yeah, until now," Duncan repeated. He felt the vehicle slowing.

"What the heck is this?" Alistair said, allowing the car to slow further. Duncan followed his eyeline, off to the left. A man was walking along the pavement, pushing a pushchair. The pushchair, however, was glowing orange and dripping molten plastic globes to the ground as he walked, tiny flames eating their way up the synthetic material stretched around the metal frame. Alistair pulled the pick-up alongside, lowering the passenger window as they came to a stop alongside.

"What the feck are you doing?" he called out. The man stopped, teetering to both left and right as he turned to look at them, clutching a can of beer in one hand, the pushchair's handle in the other, pretty much the only thing keeping him upright. He was dressed in grubby jeans and a khaki-coloured parka overcoat, the hood down revealing a shock of lank, mousey hair. His thin face was pale and lined with several patches of dry skin, cracked, red and angry, his expression vacant.

"Eh?" the man asked, leaning down and peering into the truck from his vantage point on the pavement.

"What... are... you... doing?" Alistair repeated.

Unsteady on his feet, he glanced at the pushchair, open mouthed, then pointed at it with his beer.

"A wee fire."

"You're having a wee fire?" Alistair asked.

"I thought I would, aye."

"Oh, did yer, aye?" Alistair said, glancing at Duncan and shaking his head in disbelief. He released his seatbelt and cracked his door open. Duncan did the same and got out, thankful the rain had eased to a light drizzle, although it still came across them in sheets.

The man watched them get out, shuffling back a couple of paces. Duncan braced himself, unsure of what this dubious character might do seeing as he was clearly on some form of narcotic but didn't appear threatening, although often it was hard to tell. Alistair reached into the back of the pick-up, coming around to the pavement with a small fire extinguisher in his hands.

"Are you the polis?" the man asked Duncan, sniffing hard.

"You know I'm the polis, Charlie," Alistair said, joining them. He looked at Duncan. "DI McAdam, meet Charlie Lumsden, resident addict and Portree's greatest waste of oxygen." The insult didn't register, and Charlie merely rocked back and forth, looking likely to keel over at any moment. "Well, Charlie, I do hope neither of your weans were sitting in that pushchair when you lit it?"

Charlie grinned, revealing several blackened or missing teeth. Alistair pulled the restraining catch from the extinguisher's trigger guard and blasted the pushchair, immediately exhausting the oxygen feeding the fire and smothering the flames. Charlie laughed, eyes widening. Alistair turned the extinguisher on him and let off another blast of CO2 straight in his face. Stumbling backwards, coughing and spluttering, Charlie inadvertently upended his can, the beer trickling out unfettered to the ground.

"Get y'self off home, Charlie," Alistair said firmly, jabbing a pointed finger at him. "And don't go setting fire to anything else on the way."

"Aye, right," Charlie mumbled, gripping the pushchair's handle and stumbling away, using it as a stabiliser.

"Why can't you be like every other stoner and stay home rolling around on the floor laughing and eating pickled onion Monster Munch?" Alistair shouted after him. Charlie didn't hear or if he did, he didn't respond. Looking at Duncan, Alistair smiled. "One of Portree's finest."

"You see a lot of him?"

"Uniform do… although they hate picking him up because he usually wets himself in the cells."

Duncan grimaced. "Nice."

"Back to the station?"

Duncan checked the time. "No, I think I should check in to my hotel."

"Shall I drop you off?"

"The car is parked in Somerled Square, so there will do just fine, cheers."

They got back into the pick-up for the short drive back into town. Alistair pulled up at the side of the road and Duncan made to get out, but Alistair stopped him.

"So, who did you annoy to get lumbered with the locals?" he asked him.

Duncan smiled, cocking his head. "Who says I annoyed anyone? I figured it would be a good opportunity to come home for a bit, see the old stomping ground."

Alistair's face split into a broad grin. "Oh, did yer, aye?"

That was the third time Duncan had heard him use that particular phrase, a well-known sarcastic phrase used by someone who knows full well that someone is talking absolute rubbish. Duncan smiled. "I'll see you in the morning."

Alistair nodded. "Bright and early. Jameson likes a morning briefing, seven o'clock."

"Seven?"

Alistair winced. "Aye. Everyday... like clockwork. I assume his wifey doesn't like him much, sends him on his way."

"Tell me," Duncan asked, as he got out, looking back, "who did you annoy to get lumbered with me?"

He chuckled. "Ah... that'd be telling, laddie."

Duncan closed the door, waving him off as Alistair drove away. He crossed the road and went to his car. It was one of only four left parked in the square at this time of the evening. Seeing it packed to bursting with pretty much everything he owned brought a wave of melancholy over him. He didn't have time to empty the car before leaving, not that he had much free space in his little apartment in the West End anyway.

He stood for a moment, scratching his head.

"There he is!"

Duncan turned to see Archie bounding across the seating area next to the war memorial with a woman in tow. As they came closer, Duncan felt a stab of something in his chest, feeling it tighten as he realised who Archie was with.

"I told you he was back," Archie said, coming to stand before him and glancing at his companion, beaming another of his wide smiles. "She didnae believe me, but I told her it was you."

"It is you, Duncan," she said, smiling. He didn't know what to say, no words came to mind, not even hello, which would have been a safe and rather obvious choice. She spread her hands wide, surprised. "Are you not going to say hello?"

Duncan coughed, feeling his face flush. "Y-Yes of course. Hello, how are you doing, Becky?"

"I'm well, Dunc," she said, smiling. "I'm… doing all right. You?"

"Aye… all right."

Archie looked between them, shaking his head. "You'd think the two of you had only just met. What are yous like?"

Duncan cocked his head, smiling away his embarrassment. Becky looked great. She looked older than she did when he'd last seen her, but she would do because it'd been fifteen years, maybe more since they'd last been together. Becky's blonde hair still hung to her shoulders, although it was tied back and away from her forehead. Her blue eyes, although lined at the edges, still sparkled with that gleam that drew him towards her much as they'd done back when they were kids walking to school together, catching the bus home and for countless hours wiling away their free time.

Becky Mcinnes looked great. Duncan suddenly felt self-conscious.

"We're going for a couple of drinks," Archie said. "Aren't we, Duncan." He put his arm around Becky's shoulder, drawing her to him. Duncan felt a pang of jealousy, immediately silently chastising himself for doing so.

"Ah… well, I really need to…"

"Nonsense! We're going," Archie said.

Duncan relented. "All right… aye, we are."

"You'll come too, won't you, Bex?" Archie asked.

She made to protest. "I've only just finished work and I really need to be getting away home, Archie— "

"No way!" Archie said. "When was the last time the three of us were all together? Come on, one drink? It'll no' kill you, will it?"

Becky also relented, smiling bashfully. "One drink, and that's it!"

"One drink," Archie repeated, "Maybe two," he added, with a wink. Throwing his other arm around Duncan and pulling the three of them together, he grinned. "Back again!"

Duncan looked past Archie, meeting Becky's eye. They shared a brief, but silent, exchange before Archie dragged them away to his pub of choice.

CHAPTER FIVE

THE PUB WAS ALREADY JUMPING. One of the most popular ceilidh bands was playing that night and the event had been advertised for months in advance. It was like half the island had turned out to make the most of it. The three of them squeezed their way through the press, making their way to the bar. The patrons were two to three deep already but everyone seemed in good spirits, looking forward to their night out.

Duncan felt his apathy for the day's events lifting. There were worse places to be than on a night out surrounded by his own people and he felt warmer this evening regarding his homecoming. That said, he didn't fancy a late one. A session on the beer wouldn't be a good look when rolling into the station, half cut, for 7am the next day.

Becky eyed free seating off in the far corner. The tables were laid out around the room leaving a huge space in the centre for the Scottish dancing that was already getting under way. Children were taught traditional dancing at school from a very early age, and it was remembered fondly by most as they passed into adulthood. A wedding, birthday or any other celebration wasn't quite the same without a good ceilidh. The table Becky chose was only half occupied and the others seating at one end offered it to them as they approached.

"My round first then," Archie said, raising his voice to be heard over the music.

"One drink!" Becky reminded him as he set off for the bar, waving a hand in the air to indicate he understood. Duncan looked at Becky as they slid onto the bench seating.

"He'll no' be taking one drink for an answer," he said, smiling ruefully.

"Aye, he bloody will if I have anything to say about it, but you're right, Archie hasn't changed much over the years."

"Still takes things too far?"

She nodded. "Aye. That inbuilt sense of when you've reached the acceptable limit... just never kicked in with Archie. I reckon that's why Fiona left him."

"Fiona. Fiona Mutch?" Duncan asked and she nodded. "Did they get married then?"

"Aye, years ago."

"I'd never have seen the two of them as compatible."

"Well, you'd be right. She ditched him two summers ago... shacked up with some guy down Broadford way. Runs a post office these days, I think."

"Ah... that's a shame. Any kids?"

"No, but I don't know why seeing as Fiona always wanted them. It's not the kind of question you should ask people though, you know?"

"Why not?"

Becky shrugged. "I guess you never really know the circumstances."

"People do though... ask," Duncan said. Becky nodded glumly. "Can I ask you?" He regretted the question immediately and tried to take it back. She dismissed his concern.

"Kids?"

He nodded.

"Two," she said, glancing away and scanning the room. "Boy and a girl."

"I see you're married too," Duncan said, casting an eye down at her ring finger. The words felt like they were sticking in his throat which was odd after all these years. Becky looked at him with an expression he found hard to read, sadness perhaps. Or maybe he was just projecting.

"Yes, to Davey." She looked away which pleased Duncan because he would have failed to mask his shock.

"Davey Mcinnes?"

She nodded.

"Ah… right… Davey," he said again. Duncan would never have pictured the two of them together either and their compatibility also seemed unlikely without one or both of them massively compromising on their personality. Perhaps he was a terrible judge of such things, seeing as his own relationship record was an often-lamented succession of failures. Maybe things had changed. He caught sight of her expression and he felt embarrassed for reacting so negatively. "Sorry… I didn't mean any offence. It's just… I don't know," he said, flushing. "Are you… happy?"

She snorted a laugh, catching herself and putting a hand over her mouth.

"It's a fair question," he said, stiffening before smiling at her reaction.

"Well, in the most part. I mean, it's life… and… you know Davey."

Duncan grinned. "Aye. I guess he hasn't changed much either then?"

"No, he's not the type of guy who embraces change, let's be honest."

"So, what do you do now?" Duncan asked. "You said you'd just finished work."

She didn't seem keen to talk about it, but he persisted and she sighed. "It's only part time. I work in a shop, here in the town, selling pottery, knik-knaks and stuff to tourists." She shrugged. "It's all handmade... by people here on the island and some from a couple of folk on North Uist. It's not exciting, but it adds to what we bring in from Davey's work and the old croft."

"Davey working his old man's place, is he?"

She nodded. "Davey's dad passed away some time ago, and he was always going to take it on. He also works over at the ferry terminal."

"Uig?"

"Aye," she said. "What about you? What are you doing back here?"

He really didn't want to talk about his work, so he was deliberately vague. "I'm back for a few weeks... probably. Maybe less."

"You still stay in Glasgow?"

He nodded. "For my sins."

"Have you been to see your mum?"

He shook his head. "No, not yet. I only got in this afternoon."

"Well, make sure you do," she said, admonishing him with a stern look. "It'll make her day."

"Have you seen her then?" Duncan asked, surprised.

"Davey's mum is in the same place, and I have to pop in to see her three or four times a week, check in on her."

Duncan didn't reply, hoping the conversation would move on. He felt her eyes on him though.

"How is she looking?"

"Well," Becky said, "I think. How about Roslyn? Does she know you're here?"

"Hah!" he said, grinning. "You must be joking, right?"

Becky shook her head. "Honestly, the pair of you are a nightmare. Always have been."

"How is she?"

Becky laughed. "She's your sister, Duncan!"

"Aye, well… you know how it is."

"I know how the two of you are with each other," she said, shaking her head. "Besides, she doesn't really speak to me."

"Ros and you never did see eye to eye."

"I wasn't good enough for her wee brother, that's what it was."

Duncan smiled ruefully. "Amazing that she could be so protective over someone she…" He shook his head. "Ah, well… I guess it doesn't matter now."

Further conversation on the subject ceased, much to Duncan's relief, as Archie appeared bearing a tray with a pitcher of beer and three, already full, pint glasses, almost slamming it down on the table before wiping the sheen of sweat from his brow.

"Damn, that took ages. I thought I'd better stock up, save the trip back like."

Duncan rolled his eyes, but Becky laughed. She jabbed a pointed finger at Archie. "I'm still only staying for one. I've got the family supper to make and if you think I'm leaving that to Davey, you've got another think coming."

Archie cocked his head and smiled, setting a glass down in front of each of them.

"Slàinte!" he said, raising his glass. Duncan and Becky matched his action and they knocked their glasses together. Becky put her pint down and slid out from her seat.

"I'm off to the ladies'," she said, disappearing into the throng.

Duncan watched her go until he lost sight of her, a cascade of old feelings and memories returning in a jumble which left him feeling... confused.

"You've missed her, haven't you?"

Duncan turned to Archie, finding him staring at him with a hint of a smile. Duncan shook his head. "Get away with you, man."

Archie's smile widened. "You have. I know it."

Duncan sighed, sitting up and looking around. "Being back here... the town... it's like I never left."

"You can leave the island, Duncan, but it'll always be a part of you," Archie said, raising his glass and tipping it in his direction. "As will everyone you know on it."

Duncan exhaled heavily. "Ain't that the truth. Excuse me," he said, getting up and heading for the gents. He passed Becky in the crowd, who'd stopped to speak with a couple of friends, and as they eased by one another, their bodies pressed together and he felt an almost electric sensation pass through him. She winked at him as they touched. Duncan tried not to read anything into it. Shaking his head, he pressed on through the crowd trying to remember where the toilets were.

Getting back to the table proved to be quite a challenge. The bar was filled to capacity by then and the music, along with the dancers and those keeping to the periphery, was loud and raucous. Archie was standing next to their table but of Becky there was no sign. Her glass was half full, and the level in the pitcher was much lower too. Duncan looked around for her but couldn't see her anywhere.

"Becky had to go, Dunc," Archie said, passing him his drink. He accepted it, trying to appear nonchalant but, surprisingly to himself, he felt deflated that he'd not had more time to catch up with her. It was probably for the best anyway. Sooner or later, they'd find themselves going over old ground and the shine of their reunion would likely dissipate rapidly to leave nothing but a sour taste, much as it had when they'd briefly moved to Glasgow together back in the day. He pushed her from his thoughts, turning to watch the Gay Gordons getting under way. Becky would have dragged him onto the dance floor for that one, he had no doubt. Or maybe that was the Becky of their youth; a person from another life entirely, as was he.

From his right a big man sauntered up to him, slamming a meaty hand against his shoulder causing Duncan to spill some of his drink. He glared at the newcomer and it took him a moment to recognise the face.

"Wee Dunc McAdam," the man shouted above the music and cheering, leaning into him. The smell of beer and stale tobacco smoke on his breath was intense. "You come crawling back to the island have you?"

Duncan attempted to put space between them, taking one step to his left. Murdo Grant, a pupil from the year above him at school, followed suit and Duncan found himself sand-wiched between the two larger men. Murdo had aged pretty much as one might have expected him to. He was overweight, which was nothing new, red-faced, a complexion borne of too much drink, too often, the capillaries of his nose almost burst-ing, and he must have started early because he was already wobbling on unsteady legs.

"Hey, Murdo," Duncan said, trying to be amiable. "Long time no see. How are you?" he asked, not particularly caring for an answer.

"I see you with Becky just now," Murdo said, grinning mischievously. "You gonna hit that again?"

Duncan bit his lip, almost imperceptibly shaking his head.

"I'm fine, Murdo. How are you these days, you keeping well?" This time he added a smile to the question. The guy was a complete arse back when they were at school and, by the looks of things, he still was, only now he was bigger, carrying another five or six stone in weight.

"She always was a bit of a slapper, that Becky," Murdo said, slurring his words as he spoke. Duncan couldn't tell if he was trying to be antagonistic or if being offensive just came naturally to him. "I'll bet half the island's been through her before she settled on poor Davey."

Duncan felt a flash of irritation. He was being goaded and he knew it, not that it didn't stand a chance of working, mind you.

"Well, that'll see you on the other half, wouldn't it, Murdo?" Duncan said calmly. Archie glanced at the two of them, suitably concerned enough to place his pint glass back down on the table behind him.

"Come on fellas, play nice," Archie said with as much authority as he could muster.

"Came back from Glasgow a broken woman," Murdo said, looking past Duncan at Archie. "Didn't she, Arch? Wee Dunc here was finished with her. Ruined her for other men—"

Duncan snapped, shoving Murdo away from him. The big man, off balance and slightly worse for drink, stumbled backwards into the crowd only to be pushed straight back at Duncan as if he was on a bungee cord. Murdo returned the favour, shoving Duncan forcefully, his momentum and larger size seeing Duncan clatter into Archie who disturbed the table behind sending pints sloshing over their owners. Cries of outrage went up around them.

Undeterred, Duncan came forward just as Murdo took a swing at him. The wild punch flew over Duncan's head as he bobbed to his left before throwing a punch of his own.

The blow landed square on Murdo's nose and the big man staggered backwards, pitching over and sprawled onto the dance floor, taking out three people who failed to see him coming.

Duncan let out a howl of pain, his hand feeling like he'd just thumped a brick wall. It was years since he'd been in any kind of a brawl. He clutched the wrist of his right hand, staring open mouthed at his hand. Murdo, clambering to his feet, let out a guttural roar of anger, blood streaming from his nose and he lurched forward only for Archie to stick out a wonderfully timed foot and trip the big man up. Murdo hit the ground face first with a grunt.

Archie stepped over him and grabbed Duncan by the arm, hauling him away.

"Come on, let's get out of here before he gets up," Archie shouted, dragging Duncan towards the exit, "or someone calls the police."

"Don't worry, I'm already here," Duncan said, trying not to fall over such was the pace Archie was manhandling him towards the exit. The two of them hustled outside, almost breaking into a run once they were in the street, not easing up until they were around the next corner and onto the relative safety of Bayfield Road and out of sight of the pub.

Both men were breathing heavily, Duncan doubled over, resting his hands on his knees while Archie leaned against the wall of the florist's shop. Archie started chuckling. Duncan shot him a dark look, feeling the shakes coming on with the amount of adrenalin coursing through him as the fight or flight reflex subsided.

"What are you laughing at?" he asked.

"You, of course! You can take the man off the island," Archie said, shaking his head, "but you cannae take the McAdam out of Duncan."

Duncan glared at him but then, he too, saw the funny side, relented, and started laughing.

"Right, where to now?" Archie said, righting himself and looking up the street.

"Home, that's where to," Duncan said. Archie looked crest-fallen but nodded.

"Aye, I guess so." He took a step to his left, stumbled on the kerb and fell to the floor, exhaling hard as he struck the tarmac without managing to raise his hands to break his fall. Duncan winced. That would have hurt. "I'm all right," Archie muttered as Duncan made to help him up. "Just get me to my car and I'll be right."

"No way are you driving," Duncan said.

"I bloody am," Archie replied, eyeing him suspiciously, looking slightly off balance as he ham-fistedly dusted his coat down. Duncan had a hold of him and realised there was a fair chance he'd topple over if he let go.

"Did you make a start before you met Becky and me in the square?"

Archie shot him an innocent look. "May have had one or two. Just an appetiter, you know?"

"Appetiser," Duncan corrected.

"Apple something," Archie said, grinning at his own joke.

Duncan sighed. "Give me your keys."

"No way! How will I get home?"

"I'll drive you, now give me the keys."

Archie conceded defeat and rummaged through his pock-ets, finding the key ring at the third time of asking. He thrust them reluctantly into Duncan's hand and the two of them set off for where Archie had left his car.

"Hey, what did you mean back there?" Archie asked as they walked.

"When?" Duncan asked, feeling the strain of supporting the larger man as they walked.

"Back in the pub, when I said they might call the police."

"Oh… I said I was a policeman."

Archie stopped, turning to face him with a look of surprise. "You? In the polis?"

Duncan was unsure of what this reaction meant. He nodded. "Aye."

"Bloody hell," Archie said, shaking his head. "I never saw you doing that."

He leaned back onto Duncan and they moved off.

"No, neither did I, Archie. Neither did I."

Archie lived in Kensaleyre, a small crofting community situated on the A87, the main road up the west side of the Trotternish peninsula towards Uig and the ferry terminal serving the islands of the Outer Hebrides. The small house was in darkness as Duncan pulled off the highway and bounced along the uneven access track in Archie's beaten-up old Land Rover Defender. Archie had long since fallen asleep, only stirring as they passed over the cattle grid which kept the sheep from venturing out onto the main road. The cattle grids helped, but it was still common to find sheep sitting in the middle of the road almost anywhere on the island. They were a special surprise, often to be found on an early morning commute cresting a blind hill or a bend in the road.

With difficulty, Duncan manhandled Archie out of the defender and towards the house, propping him up on a bench seat alongside the back door as he fumbled in the dark with the keys. A dog barked excitedly inside. By the sounds of it, it was a small terrier type, and Duncan hoped it took kindly to strangers. Once the door was open, he was greeted by a friendly dog, running around his feet and jumping up at him. Putting Archie's right arm around his shoulder, he levered his old friend up and hauled him to his feet. Archie acquiesced, grunting under the strain of movement, but managing to mutter an incoherent protest. Trying several light switches as they progressed through the house, Duncan was annoyed to find no power to the house. *One thing at a time,* he thought, wondering where he'd locate the fuse board.

Duncan only managed to get Archie into the sitting room before his strength failed him and he had to admit defeat, lying the man down on the sofa and watching him roll sideways, his head coming to rest on the arm, one leg overhanging the edge leaving his foot on the floor.

The dog, still at Duncan's feet, wagged his stumpy tail, looking between his owner and the newcomer expectantly. Duncan angled his head and smiled wryly.

"Well, wee fella," he said, shaking his head, "that's where your man will be staying the night." Finding a blanket on a nearby chair, he cast it over Archie who was already snoring. The dog barked at him. Duncan looked down. "I guess you need feeding, do you?"

The dog barked again, tail and ears raised in understanding it might be about to eat. Duncan made his way back into the kitchen in search of dog food. The kitchen was a mess. He wouldn't even dare to describe it as a bachelor pad; it was too untidy for that. The sink was full of plates, a saucepan and associated utensils, scum floating on the surface of long-cold water suggesting they'd been there for days. Every inch of the counter tops had something on them and there was a strange smell lingering in the air, a mix of damp and mould. Finding a sack of dry dog food leaning against the wall beside the back door, he took a guess that a cup full was more than enough for this size of dog and emptied it into a bowl he found in the corner of the room. The dog didn't stand on ceremony, hurrying over to set about it.

"You're welcome," Duncan said. He looked to his left, spotting a photograph in a frame hanging on the wall above a small dining table. Moving closer, he saw it was a shot of a much younger Archie, his arm draped around a smiling woman. Judging from the trees in the background, it looked like it was taken somewhere far from here, perhaps in the Mediterranean. Duncan recognised Fiona from their school days. The two of them looked happy, Archie happier than Duncan ever remembered him. "Shame it didn't work out for the two of you."

He heard movement to his right, half expecting to find Archie stumbling out of the dark, but another face appeared at the back door, peering in at him.

"Hello, Archie?"

Duncan stepped out of the gloom in the corner of the kitchen to greet him. "No, sorry. Archie is…" he looked through the door into the sitting room, "indisposed. Can I help?"

The man eyed Duncan warily, but then he seemed to relax, probably guessing that he was likely a friend of Archie's and therefore had cause to be present in his house.

"I just wanted to let him know that a man was here earlier, from The Hydro."

The Hydro referred to the Scottish Hydro Electric Company, once the state provider of electricity to the Highlands and Islands, but long since privatised along with all the power generation assets in the UK. Despite this, and a change of name, most people still referred to the energy company as *The Hydro*.

"Aye, anything important?"

The man shifted his feet nervously, handing Duncan an envelope. He opened it and glanced inside. There was a folded letter along with a small plastic key. Duncan knew what that meant; Archie had been cut off, his electricity now needed to be purchased from a shop and the credit loaded onto the meter via that little key in order for him to put the lights on.

Duncan sighed. "I'll pass it on to him... when he... you know?"

The neighbour nodded appreciatively, glancing towards the living room where Archie's resonant snoring carried to them. He seemed in a hurry to leave. Duncan put the envelope down on the table, feeling for his friend's predicament. Hurrying to the door, he called after the retreating form of the neighbour.

"Excuse me! Any chance of a lift back into town?"

CHAPTER SIX

DS MacEachran called for silence in the little room just off the main incident room where the local officers had gathered to be introduced to their new temporary detective inspector, Duncan. It took a moment for the conversations to die down and everyone in the room looked at Duncan expectantly.

Duncan's head was thumping. It wasn't the level of alcohol consumed the previous night, seeing as he'd barely got to drink much before he came across Murdo Grant and they had their little catch-up. It was as if they'd managed to roll back the years to when they were sixteen, bold, brash and up for anything. Duncan felt bad for the scrap he'd allowed himself to be baited into. He should know better. *He did know better*.

Moreover, whatever Murdo had done to his face – lined it with a concrete cast judging by the havoc striking it had done to Duncan's right hand – the back of his hand had swollen overnight, the pain keeping him awake. Duncan wondered if he'd managed to break a bone or something. Luckily, the night porter at the hotel had been able to sort him out with a champagne bucket of ice and he'd kept his hand submerged for as long as he could, pleased to see a reduction in size as a result. It still hurt like hell though.

"Right, introductions," Alistair said, pointing out the individuals sitting around the room. "You've got two of our resident detective constables in Angus Ross and John Mclean, there," he pointed at the two of them. "Don't let Angus fool you, he is as old as he looks, fresh out of school, and John's name is John but everyone calls him Russell." Alistair tilted his head towards Duncan, smiling. "And we have a book running on how long it takes you to figure out why he's called Russell, so don't even ask because we'll no' tell you. Take it seriously though because there's money riding on it."

Duncan frowned, observing the portly middle-aged detective constable smiling up at him. Everyone else was grinning and nodding along. "Okay, is this normal procedure?"

"Aye," Alistair said. "It's something of a tradition. If it takes you more than a week, then you're not considered a very good detective. No pressure though."

Duncan arched his eyebrows and the assembled officers excitedly offered him a little cheer of encouragement, two of them adding a drum roll on the tables for emphasis. Russell himself was still smiling, opening a bag of crisps and evidently enjoying his moment. "I'll try not to disappoint. Put me down for a tenner. I'm good for it."

"Will do," Alistair said. "Good to know you're backing yourself." He smiled and the others did too. "Caitlyn Stewart is our other full-time DC, but she's on annual leave at present. She's the token female in Portree's CID and…" he looked around the room, "…also happens to be the finest detective on the island." Faces turned to Angus and Russell, jeering them. Both men smiled, Angus shaking his head. Alistair turned to Duncan. "However, if you tell her I said that, I will deny it."

"Understood."

"Lastly, the three men to your right are, collectively, the MacDonalds; Ronnie, Fraser and Robbie. They could form their own boy band," Alistair said with a sideways smile, "if they could go without eating for a very long time seeing as they cannae sing, dance and don't have a modicum of talent in any way, shape or form between them."

The three protested loudly before mutually agreeing that Alistair was indeed accurate, if not complimentary.

"Are you all related?" Duncan asked.

The three glanced at one another, looking the others up and down before turning their attention back to Duncan, and replying in unison. "No," they said, shaking their heads.

"At least your line manager won't have difficulty typing out the annual appraisals... cut and paste must make things quicker," Duncan said.

"Not to be confused with Malky, who looks after the custody suite," one of them said. "He's another MacDonald. No relation."

Duncan looked at the man who'd spoken. "Which one are you?"

"Fraser."

"Right, I'll try and remember, but give me a bit of leeway until I get used to you all."

"How long are you with us for, sir?" Angus asked. He sounded as young as he looked. Duncan found himself wondering if he'd ever looked that young, either in CID or uniform.

"Until we find out what happened to Isla, or until I'm told otherwise," Duncan said. "Your regular DI is off long-term sick, I understand."

Alistair nodded. "Aye, not sure what's wrong with him but he's been admitted to hospital in Inverness for tests and the like. No idea when he'll be back."

"Well, for now, you have me," Duncan said. He looked at the MacDonalds. "Do I take it that the three of you have been drafted from uniform for the duration of this case?" They nodded. Duncan scratched the back of his head, wincing as the movement sent shots of stabbing pain through his sore hand. "Okay, I want you to bring me up to speed on everything you've done up until this point. We've been tasked with revisiting Isla's friends and family statements, witness statements…"

"All the donkey work that none of us will be pleased with," Alistair said, causing them all to groan, "but we will do it with a smile, won't we, lads? After all, we get paid whatever they have us doing, right?"

A general murmur of acknowledgement passed through the room.

"Okay," Duncan said, gesturing for quiet, "where was Isla's body found?"

"Buried on some rough grazing land," Alistair said, "out near Trumpan on the Waternish peninsula overlooking Ardmore Bay."

"Who found her?" Duncan asked.

"Linesmen, working on restringing the overhead lines that run out to the Trumpan township," Russell said. "The last round of storms brought the power lines down and they've been upgrading the line this past week. The community have been on diesel generators in the meantime. About time too. Those lines have been up for nigh on seventy years. It's amazing those towers haven't come down before."

"She was fully buried though, right, not partially?" Duncan asked Alistair.

"Aye, but the volume of water we've had these past few months has saturated the hillside… and those patches of rough grazing are the banks where in days past the crofters would have dug the peats, you know?" Alistair said, citing the traditional process the islanders would go through in the summer of digging the turf, stacking it and allowing it to dry throughout the year to then use as fuel over the winter. These days, the process was done by fewer and fewer people, and where it was still practised it was often mechanical, but the method hadn't changed much over the centuries, getting something of a resurgence at times of high alternative fuel prices. "The weight of the water pulled the hillside apart, forming a foot-wide trench, and the linesmen came across her as they crossed the hill."

Duncan considered it. That location was isolated. Rugged, beautiful even, but remote. Although everyone living there would likely know anyone who frequented the area, it would be easy to come and go unseen, particularly at night or during inclement weather when the locals would be hunkering down to see out the passage of the storm. Isla Matheson could have lain out there for centuries without anyone finding her, her fate only revealed by pure chance.

"I want to go out there," he said. "See where she was for myself."

Alistair didn't question it, and simply nodded. "I'll take you out as soon as we're through here, if you like?"

"I would."

"We'd better not take any of the MacDonalds with us or the locals will be after us with pitchforks," Alistair said with a sideways smile. The others laughed at the reference to the raid launched from Uist by the Clan MacDonald where they burned the Trumpan church along with the local churchgoers inside it, known historically as the *Battle of the Spoiling Dyke*. The retribution by the MacLeods had been swift, killing all the attackers before they managed to leave the island.

"Is anyone still digging that bank?" Duncan asked.

Alistair shook his head. "Not as far as I know." He looked at Angus. "Check that, would you?"

Angus nodded and made a note.

"I know you've probably already done this, but I want you to gather all the witness statements, divide them up between you and start talking to people. See if their memories still marry up with what they said twenty years ago. Don't feed them reminders, I want authentic reactions, even if they try and press you to tell them what they'd originally said. This is the whole point of redoing the statements. They might recall something previously omitted or give up something they had intended to keep quiet. We'll regroup and run through everything we have this afternoon. Until we know more, everyone within Isla's circle or anyone with the slightest potential motive is a suspect."

"Ah... she was a popular lass. That's going to be a long list," Fraser said, frowning. "Everyone liked her, you know?"

"Did you know her?"

"Sort of like, aye. I was at school with her big brother, Donnie. Good bloke was Donnie."

"I knew of him," Duncan said. "He had something of a reputation as a tearaway when I was at school."

Fraser laughed, as did Ronnie who nodded along. "Infamous, wasn't he?" Fraser said. "A rock star persona among the kids! Things have changed a bit now, mind."

"He was a few years older than Isla, wasn't he? He left for university on the mainland," Duncan said.

"That's right," Fraser said. "Came back to support his folks after his sister went missing." His expression turned glum, and he sighed. "Her disappearance tore that poor family apart. Not knowing what happened to her... to Isla, just broke her mum's heart."

Ronnie agreed. "The mother couldn't hack it. She took her own life, what…" he looked at Fraser "… three years after?"

"More like four," Fraser said. "But it was no' just that, was it? The father being paralysed in that accident must have added even more stress to it."

"Accident?" Duncan asked. He remembered the case from his childhood but he didn't recall anything about an accident.

"Oh aye," Ronnie said. "Isla's father… what was his name, Fraser?"

"Ruaridh."

"Aye, that's it, Ruaridh. The week of Isla's disappearance… his car came off the road in a storm. He was there for a good few hours before anyone found him. It looked like he wasn't going to make it for a while." Ronnie shook his head. "That must have tested his faith like nothing before."

Now they mentioned it, it did sound familiar. Duncan knew of Reverend Matheson prior to Isla's disappearance. Never one to attend church himself, leaving that to his mum and Roslyn, he only knew of the man through the way others spoke of him. They'd met once, he recalled, with Duncan still a child and decidedly preoccupied that day, and Ruaridh had struck him as quite a pious, almost austere man who was difficult to read.

"The community missed him in the pulpit, I reckon," Fraser said. He took a deep breath. "He couldn't do that anymore."

"He left the church?" Duncan asked.

"No, no, no," Fraser said, "but he's wheelchair bound as a result of the crash… and much of Skye isn't geared up for that level of access, you know? The Episcopal Church kept him on, mind, so he's still a minister."

"Well, we'll need to speak to the family again in any event.

Has anyone been assigned as a liaison to the family yet, to keep them up to speed with developments?"

They all exchanged looks. Alistair frowned. "No, but we have been keeping them advised of proceedings."

"That's something we'll need to sort out." Duncan's decision was twofold. Not only did he want to ensure the family were not kept in the dark, hearing news through gossip or the media as had happened in the past, but also Duncan meant what he said, everyone in Isla's circle was a suspect until he decided otherwise. This included the family, and he didn't really care what Jameson thought about it.

DUNCAN BRACED himself against the wind barrelling towards them over the outer islands, driving across The Minch and buffeting them as they stood on the steep incline above the hamlet of Trumpan. They were standing on one of the most remote parts of the island. Whereas other parts of Skye had their own particular draw for travellers, there was little to entice tourists to this spot beyond the view of The Minch and a ruined church. The view south over Ardmore Bay towards the Isle of Isay and the Duirinish Peninsula beyond that was stunning on a clear day, and even on a dreich one such as this. Looking west, the sweeping vista over The Minch towards North Uist was also a view to behold. Not that the outer islands were visible today. A cloud bank was rolling across the water and Duncan could smell rain on the breeze.

Turning his attention to the scene, blue and white police tape fluttering in the breeze as it strained against the metal poles it was wrapped around, marking off the spot where Isla's body was found. The ground underfoot was marshy, a nearby burn carried water noisily off the hillside. There would be many more doing similar along this length of hillside, but sometimes it wasn't enough. The ground near to where they were had opened up, parting as if the hand of God had unzipped a parcel of land some thirty feet in length allowing Mother Nature's contents to spill out, offering up her secrets.

Alistair stood off to Duncan's left, his hands thrust into the pockets of his overcoat, his back to the wind.

"It's a beautiful spot," he said, "but it's no place to leave a wee girl to rest."

Duncan nodded but didn't say anything. Looking to the south, past Isay, in the direction of Claigan, the nearest community to where Isla was last seen alive, partying with her pals on Coral Beach. The proximity to where they were now was not lost on him. It was not a quick drive from there to here, and far from easy, but if this was Isla's final resting place he had to wonder how long she'd remained alive once she left that party. Could it be a coincidence that she disappeared on the Waternish peninsula only to be buried there much later? In all likelihood, the killer – if indeed there was a killer – would have abducted, murdered and disposed of her body in quick succession, otherwise the kidnapper would have to live nearby… or had somewhere to take her to, either a holiday residence or be travelling in a camper van or similar.

To be fair, at the time of year Isla went missing, late summer, there would have been plenty of those people on the island, so perhaps DCI Jameson had a point. The pathologist's inability to determine the cause of death threw Duncan though. The lack of injuries to the body, either offensive or defensive, was an anomaly and such anomalies seldom helped to solve crimes. They only worked to confuse matters further.

"Do you have the photos?"

Alistair stepped forward, unzipping his coat and producing the photographs he'd brought with them. Passing the folder to Duncan, he struggled with the wind, it was gusting so strong now that it threatened to tear the images from his hands and send them whirling across the island.

Duncan oriented the crime scene photos before him, matching the image to his view. Isla looked very serene to him, much as she had done in the cold storage, as if she were sleeping. Her body had been wrapped in a patterned material, once blue and white, woven in a checked pattern. The peaty water had soaked into the blanket, turning the white fabric a muddy, reddish-brown colour in the same way it had stained her skin and hair.

Swapping image after image, Duncan looked at every angle, picturing the body exactly where it was found in the ground. He could see Alistair shifting his weight between his feet, arms clamped tightly to his frame. Irritated perhaps? Cold, certainly. Feeling drizzle on his face, Duncan took a breath as he stared at a full-body shot, head to toe, of Isla in her makeshift grave. Angling his head, he frowned, looking between the picture and the earth at his feet.

"What is it?" Alistair asked.

"Did anyone disturb the body prior to these pictures being taken?"

"Only to reveal her face," Alistair said. "Beyond that... I don't think so. Why?"

Duncan wasn't sure and so he said nothing. Isla lay on her side in the ground, facing down the slope, her face and upper body uncovered, arms folded across her chest.

"She was found clothed?"

"Aye, fully clothed," Alistair said, raising his voice to be heard above the wind. "And there was no indication of sexual assault, tears or bruising to the body... and so I don't see sexual assault as the motive." Duncan glanced at him and Alistair shrugged. "Jameson has it in his head she was the victim of some wandering predator… but the evidence doesn't suggest that. At least, not to me. I've seen death, Duncan… too much in my time and something's no' right about this one."

"Maybe he was disturbed… seen nearby and was forced to change plans?"

Alistair was pensive, nodding, but it was clear he didn't agree.

"Do you have a theory then?" Duncan asked. Alistair met his eye with a wary look. "Come on, don't be shy. It doesn't suit you."

The DS smiled. "I think whatever happened to that wee girl came as a result of some aspect of her life *on this island*, and I reckon someone's been sitting on that knowledge for these past twenty years… and, if I'm right, it'll have been eating them alive."

"You have any evidence to back that up?"

He turned the corners of his mouth down, exaggerating the expression. "No, I cannae say that I do."

"A good old-fashioned hunch?"

"I prefer experience," he said, shrugging, "but whatever works for you."

Duncan nodded. The rain was increasing, falling steadily in sheets sweeping across The Minch and driving at them. Isay was no longer visible to the south.

"Come on. Let's get out of the rain."

"About time," Alistair said.

CHAPTER SEVEN

BACK AT THE station in Portree, the local CID officers and their seconded counterparts from uniform were waiting for them when Duncan arrived with Alistair. Duncan wasted little time in getting the briefing under way.

"Okay, I want to know who was spoken to in the original investigation into Isla Matheson's disappearance, and then where those people are now," Duncan said. "Then we can set about revisiting them and going over what they did or didn't say at the time. Who wants to go first?"

A hand raised straightaway. It was Angus Ross. Duncan gestured for him to begin.

"I've read up on Isla's ex-boyfriend, Alex Macrae. He was at the beach party that night. He and Isla split up a few days before the party and apparently she didn't take it too well."

"Anyone else involved in the breakup?"

Angus shook his head. "Apparently not or, at least, that's what Alex said at the time, but he was there at the party that night with another girl so," he shrugged, "who knows."

"How did the new girlfriend go down with Isla?" Duncan asked, picturing the prospect of a confrontation.

"No one said there was any grief between them – Alex and Isla – or the girl for that matter, Catriona, her name was. A number of people said Isla was particularly flirtatious amongst the other boys that night."

"Trying to make her ex jealous?" Duncan wondered aloud.

"Or just seeking attention," Angus said, shrugging.

"Okay. Where is Alex now, do we know?"

"Aye, he's living here in Portree. Works at *Driftwood House*."

Duncan looked at him quizzically.

"It's a care home, on the outskirts of town," Alistair said.

"Right," Duncan said. "Any criminal record?"

Angus shook his head. "No, nothing to write home about. He got himself into a bit of bother in his teens and early twenties, but no more than any other young lad around these parts."

Duncan found Angus curious. He was barely in his twenties himself, and looked much younger, but he had a measured maturity about him.

"Thanks, Angus." He looked around the room. "Who's next?"

Fraser MacDonald cleared his throat, an action that saw everyone else defer to him.

"I looked up every islander's favourite salesman, Dougal Mackenzie."

There was a groan from most of them and Duncan had to smile. He'd never heard one name elicit such a response at their mention before, *forced overtime* would be the only comparison that sprung to mind. His curiosity piqued.

"Who's Dougal Mackenzie?" he asked.

Fraser sucked in a large breath, exhaling loudly. "Dougal owns an estate agency here on the island. He specialises in selling land and property at high-end figures. It's made him unpopular with a lot of people."

Duncan shrugged. "Aren't all estate agents considered to be less popular than scum? Generally speaking, I mean."

"Not like Dougal," Fraser said. "He takes it to a *whole* new level."

Alistair nodded. "Dougal pitches to investors usually, bringing buyers in from off the island... and we all know how local people feel about absentee landlords, don't we lads?"

"Arseholes," Ronnie muttered. "Do nothing for the island aside from leech it dry."

Robbie MacDonald agreed. "Driving the house prices up, forcing locals off the island. Just like back in the old days."

"So," Duncan said, "he attracts buyers from off the island. How does that sit with the Crofting Commission? Nothing's changed there, right? They still insist on owner-occupied crofts, yes?"

"Oh aye," Alistair said. "And they've had many a run-in with Dougal's buyers. I hear some of those aren't too keen on Dougal's sales practices either." Duncan frowned, seeking explanation. "These corporate types often use their own conveyancers, solicitors and that. If they're not up to speed with the crofting regulations, which let's face it, are an absolute nightmare at the best of times, then they can fall foul of them too without realising. Dougal's way of doing things often pitches crofter against landowner one-way or another. He seems to get off on the antagonism."

"A popular guy then?" Duncan asked.

"Disnae help that Dougal is minted either," Fraser added, sniffing hard. "Puts a lot of people's backs up, you know?"

"Only cos his father came onto the island with his pockets bulging twenty-five years ago."

"And he was at the party?" Duncan asked. "Dougal?"

Fraser nodded. "Aye. By all accounts it was his idea to go out there that night. I couldn't find any reference to him and Isla fraternising though. If she was getting around the guys, then it's possible he got, or sought, her attention as well."

"Was Dougal popular back then, before he got into the property game?"

Fraser shrugged. "No idea, but I'm sure I can find out."

Duncan looked around and saw Russell doing similar, eyeing up his colleagues, his hand dipping lazily into a packet of crisps.

"You go next, Russell," Duncan said. The detective constable put his snack aside, wiping the grease from his fingers on his trousers and smacking his lips to clear the crumbs.

"Right, I had Nicol Nicolson," Russell said, tilting his head to one side. "Son of parents with a lack of imagination when it came to baby names, but whatever…" he shrugged. "Nicol was at the party too, and a couple of the lasses there said he had a thing for Isla, but it wasn't reciprocated. He's interesting because he does have a record, not at the time back then, but he does now."

"What for?"

"Sexual harassment," Russell said, drawing intakes of breath around the room. He glanced at his colleagues. "I know, right? Straight to the top of the pile. He was arrested and cautioned for sexually assaulting a woman at a gig on the mainland a few years ago, but it didnae get to court. He accepted a caution. And reading through the statements taken during the search for Isla Matheson, Nicol was nick-named by some of his pals *Nicol the Octopus* because he tended to get a bit handsy with the girls once he had a few drinks in him."

"Where is he now?" Duncan asked.

"Works on the ferries serving the Western Isles… they run out of Uig."

"I'm aware of the Western Isles, thank you, Russell. Definitely give him a tug at some point," Duncan said. "Next?"

"Roddy Mcintyre," Ronnie MacDonald said aloud, "Isla's best pal. The two of them were inseparable, apparently. My reading of what was taken down in his statement was that he was devastated by Isla's disappearance. A few people held the view that she may have taken her own life that night, throwing herself in the sea like, you know? But Roddy was adamant she'd no' do anything like that. Absolutely adamant, he was."

"If they were close, he should be the one she'd confide in first then, right, if she had a problem?" Duncan asked and Ronnie nodded.

"I'd reckon so, aye."

"So, where did he think she'd gone?"

Ronnie shrugged. "Never offered up a theory of his own. Or, at least, it was never written down if he did."

"Still around?"

"Aye, he works the family business."

"Which is?"

"Sightseeing… tours of the islands and that. Him and his dad operate a small boat that ferries people around the inner islands."

"I'll pay him a visit too," Duncan said. "Any other notable people we need to speak to?"

Alistair nodded. "There was a small group of girls in that peer group. They were pretty tight, although Isla wasn't part of the *in-crowd* by all accounts. From what I can gather she was seen as something of a liability because of who her father was on the island, and some of the girls kept their distance as a result."

"The fact he was a minister?"

"Aye. He was pretty old school about what his daughter should and shouldn't be allowed to do. I guess they didn't want the grief."

"That must be one reason why her brother, Donnie, went so far off the rails," Duncan said. Donnie Matheson was a local legend, to many of the teenage islanders anyway. He'd been the local lad who'd made it in a rock band, formed during high school, leaving for Glasgow to hit the big time. It never really happened for him or the band, but they had managed to get an appearance on some television documentary about up-and-coming bands in the Glasgow music scene. Duncan couldn't remember the name of the band Donnie played lead guitar for, but it was still the stuff of legend to Skye's teenagers dreaming of fame and fortune.

"Donnie's back now though," Fraser said.

"Didn't one of you say he came back when Isla went missing?" Duncan asked, picturing the long-haired rock star sporting dark sunglasses, wearing cowboy boots with insane heels and make-up. His own father had been quoted in the paper, citing Donnie's appearance as *ridiculous* when they printed a picture of him. The Mathesons were a story in and of themselves even before Isla went missing; the rock star son of the pious local clergyman. The tabloid papers, if Skye had had a tabloid paper, would have found it irresistible.

"Aye, but he came back for good a couple of years later," Fraser added.

Duncan hadn't realised the first return had only been temporary. The details of the case had faded from his memory and likely others too, as Isla's disappearance became a foot-note in the island's folklore, painful to those who knew and loved her but merely a topic of occasional conversation over a beer for those who didn't.

"Were you part of the original investigation, Fraser?"

"No," he said, shaking his head. "But I keep my ear to the ground, you know?"

"Because you're lying around doing nothing most of the time anyway," Ronnie replied and the others laughed.

"There's one more," Robbie MacDonald said. "Ian Fraser. He was someone who Isla was knocking around with that night, early on. Everyone thought he and her were going to become an item, and they were all watching to see how her ex, Alex, would take it, the two of them being together. Although he'd seemingly moved on, he still had half an eye on what Isla was up to."

"And?" Duncan asked.

"Ian's ex-girlfriend wasn't keen on the match either and – oh, she was there too, forgot to say – she waded in to scupper it by pouncing on a slightly drunken Ian in front of Isla. He kissed her back... and it didn't go down well at all."

"With?"

"Isla. That's probably what triggered her doing the rounds that night, trying to make everyone jealous."

"So, Ian got back with his ex... what was her name?"

Robbie checked his notes. "Um... Ashlee. And no, she was just stopping Isla from getting it on with her ex. She didnae want him for herself though."

"Ouch," Duncan said. "That's cold."

"But another one whose skin Isla got under," Alistair said.

"It all sounds like pretty standard teenage stuff," Duncan said. Seeing several blank faces looking at him, he shrugged. "Well, maybe you guys have never screwed your friends over..." he smiled awkwardly "...which is a good thing. Right, let's get out there and start talking to these people, and see if anyone has changed their recollections of events over time, especially now we have a dead body. Who knows, that might shake someone up a bit?"

Duncan looked at Alistair. "Can you take me out to Driftwood House? I'd like to speak to the ex-boyfriend."

"As good a place to start as any," Alistair agreed.

CHAPTER EIGHT

DRIFTWOOD HOUSE LAY on the east side of the town, on the main road into Portree. It was a modern, purpose-built building set across two floors. Duncan could hear the television playing daytime game shows to some of the residents in what he guessed was the day room while he and Alistair stood in the reception waiting for Alex Macrae to appear.

Looking along the corridor he saw several nurses moving between rooms, presumably checking on residents, passing out medicine or generally caring for their needs and doing their rounds. They didn't have to wait long before the matron reappeared at the top of the stairs leading a man down to them.

"Alex, this is Detective Inspector McAdam and Detective Sergeant… I'm sorry, what was your name?"

"MacEachran," Alistair said, waving her apology away. "Easy name to forget."

The matron's eyes narrowed as she searched Alistair for any sign he was being sarcastic, but he remained expressionless. It was a skill that Duncan guessed he utilised frequently.

That way, he couldn't get himself into trouble. At least, not easily.

Alex Macrae looked them both up and down. He seemed nervous to Duncan, unless it was just his way.

"Hello," Alex said, eyes flitting between them.

Duncan smiled. "Is there somewhere we can talk in private?"

"Yes, sure," Alex said, looking around. "I don't think there will be anyone in the games room."

He gestured for them to come with him and they crossed the lobby to their right and made their way to the other side of the building, to a glass-roofed extension overlooking a mature garden to the side. The games room, as Alex referred to it, was little more than a large room with tables and chairs laid out. Duncan could see a stack of jigsaw puzzles, board games and it looked like two tables were set up to play bridge on with green felt table liners and cards ready to be dealt.

Alex caught Alistair looking around. "Something wrong?"

"Wrong? No, not at all," Alistair said, arching his eyebrows. "Just when you said *games* I figured…"

"You were expecting table tennis and a squash court?"

"No," Alistair said, rolling his tongue across the inside of his cheek. "I just thought there'd be more to do."

"Most of our residents are here because they cannae look after themselves, let alone attempt pole dancing or the lambada," Alex said. "We provide end-of-life care for the disabled and the infirm."

"All right, Mother Teresa," Alistair said. "I didnae suggest charades weren't a thing."

Alex smiled, his nerves dissipating, and he turned to Duncan. "What can I do for you gentlemen?"

"You've heard about the human remains that were found out near Trumpan, I presume?"

"Aye, of course I have." He laughed nervously. "The whole island is talking about it. It's the most interesting thing to happen on the island since Bonnie Prince Charlie came ashore."

"A statement hasn't been confirmed to the public yet, but the remains belong to Isla Matheson," Duncan said, watching Macrae closely for a reaction. The colour drained from Alex Macrae's face, his lips parting as he stared hard at Duncan, his right eye twitched involuntarily. Duncan didn't speak and all three men stood in silence. Alex eventually looked away, reaching for the edge of a nearby table, using it to steady himself.

"Isla… are you… I mean, it's really her?"

Duncan nodded. "Yes, DNA tests have confirmed it."

"My God," Alex said, putting the one hand not grasping the table to his face as he turned and sat on the edge. The hand was shaking. "I always thought…" he looked at Duncan, his eyes moistening, "… hoped, maybe, that she'd just done a runner and one day she'd walk back into our lives with that cheeky smile of hers… like it had been some massive joke, you know?" He shook his head. "I didn't think she'd… that'd happened to her."

"That what had happened to her?" Alistair asked. Alex looked at him, shrugging.

"What do I mean?" Alex asked. "That she was dead, that's all. I didnae believe it."

"Any idea who might have killed her?" Alistair asked. Duncan was irritated by that. They had no confirmation she'd been killed yet, but he could see Alistair was seeking to rattle Alex, and it was working.

"Hey… now look, here," Alex said, glancing between them, his pale cheeks flushing red with rising emotion. "I didn't have anything to do with that!"

"With what?"

"With… with… someone killing her!" Alex said, his voice raised. A passing colleague stopped as she passed the doorway, casting a glance in at them before hurrying off when they saw her. "Yeah, cheers," Alex said, watching the nurse leave, "now everyone'll think I'm a sex pest or something."

"Are you?" Alistair asked.

Alex shot him a steely look, annoyed.

"No one is implicating you, Alex," Duncan said which drew a snort of derision from him.

"Then why are you here? It's not because I was her boyfriend because I told you lot *at the time* that Isla and me had split up."

"And how did that breakup go for you?" Duncan asked.

"Fine," Alex said. Duncan arched his eyebrows in query and Alex shook his head. "All right, it was a breakup. They're never pleasant are they? But… it was time to move on. I had… and she was moving on that night too."

"Who with?"

Alex looked away, sighing before pinching his eyes with thumb and forefinger.

"She was having fun that night. A lot of people were into her. I mean, who wouldn't be. Isla was great."

"So, she dumped you?" Alistair asked, suppressing a smile. Duncan wondered if he was still agitating or if he was genuinely amused.

Alex glared at him. "What are you, five years old?"

Alistair shrugged. "A wee bit older."

"It was mutual, but I initiated it," Alex said.

"Did Isla think it was mutual?"

"What is this?" Alex asked, glaring at Duncan now. "Do you think she was so angry at being dumped that she killed herself to get back at me? Because that's ridiculous."

"Aye, that would be ridiculous," Alistair said. "Even more so that she buried herself afterwards, too. Talented lass."

Alex stared at him, shaking his head.

"We're only asking what the nature of your relationship was the night of that beach party," Duncan said. "That's all."

Alex shrugged. "I didnae even speak to her that night… at all. And anyone who says otherwise is lying."

"You're anticipating someone saying otherwise?" Alistair asked.

"People say all kinds of stuff, don't they? Especially when the police come calling. So, let me be clear," he said pointedly. "Isla and me were fine. It was over. It had been over for a while, but neither of us were wanting to say it, that's all. I don't know what happened to her that night, but what I can say is I had nothing to do with it."

"That's very clear, Mr Macrae," Duncan said.

A man poked his head around the door, peering in at them and catching Alex's attention.

"Joan needs you," he said, looking between the three men. "Sorry to interrupt but she'll not let anyone else lift her out of her bed, you know?"

Alex nodded. "Okay, I'll be there in a minute."

Satisfied, the man left and Alex looked apologetically at Duncan. He held his hands up in a placatory gesture. "I'm really sorry if I sounded a wee bit off there, Detective Inspector, but… Isla's disappearance and all of that has been hanging over me for years now."

"Hanging over you, how?"

"She never came back," he said, "and this is a small island with small-minded people inhabiting it." He directed the last comment at Alistair, who didn't react but the intent was clear. "People pointing fingers… whispering. The rumour and gossip just never goes away." He shook his head. "Look, if I can do anything to help you find whoever did this, I will. I mean it. But I'm done. I need to move on, you know?"

Duncan held the eye contact for a few seconds trying to gauge his sincerity, which struck him as genuine, but he'd been wrong before.

"Can I go?" Alex asked. Duncan nodded. Alex Macrae thanked him, shot a dark look at Alistair as he passed and left the room.

"Making new friends, Alistair."

"Everywhere I go!" he said, grinning.

"Duncan!"

He turned upon hearing his name to see a sandy-haired woman standing in the doorway, a look of surprise on her face.

"Ros," he said, equally surprised. She walked into the room, a trace of a smile on her face. Duncan looked at Alistair. "My sister, Roslyn."

"I knew it was you!" she said, bounding up to them with a warm smile, glancing briefly at Alistair, but not acknowledging him directly. The smile faded following the initial greeting as she stood before Duncan, her eyes narrowing. "Why didn't you phone and tell me you were coming?"

"I… I…" he shook his head, "…didn't really know myself until yesterday, otherwise I would have."

"Mum will be so pleased to see you," Roslyn said. She looked at Alistair again, clearly wondering who he was. Alistair, for his part, just smiled at her, glancing between them. "Duncan," she said, shaking her head and taking his hands in hers, "I can't believe you're here."

He laughed nervously. "Neither can I, to be honest Ros."

The matron entered the room behind them, catching Alistair's eye.

"Did you two get everything you needed?" she asked.

"Oh aye, thanks very much," Alistair said. The matron smiled and left.

Roslyn looked at Duncan with disdain, releasing his hands with a firm push downwards.

"And here was me thinking you'd come to see your old mum… and you're working, aren't you?"

Duncan winced. "I am… on a case," he said, contritely, "but that doesn't mean— "

"Oh right, I see," Roslyn said, folding her arms across her chest defiantly. "Did you even ask after Mum?"

Duncan decided not to lie. "Is she here? I thought she was in that place on the far side of town."

"Aye, she was. Moved her last year."

"You did?"

"And I tried speaking to you about it, but you're nae free to take my calls, are you? You sent me a text in the end."

"I…"

"Don't remember," she said, accusingly. "Do you?"

He shook his head. "No, sorry."

"Never mind, Dunc." She let out an exasperated sigh and turned, stalking towards the door. "Maybe see you again in another ten years or so, yeah?" she said over her shoulder.

She left before Duncan had a chance to reply. Looking skyward, he exhaled, mouthing a silent curse. Perturbed to find Alistair looking at him, grinning, Duncan rolled his eyes. "What?"

"That had to smart a bit," Alistair said, nodding towards the door Roslyn had passed through. "What she said, a heck of a slap in the face."

"No need to enjoy it so much."

"The most fun I've had today."

"I planned to call…"

"Oh, did yer, aye?"

"I did," Duncan replied. "I swear."

"Aye, but it's no' me you need to convince though, is it? Your sister always that fierce, is she?"

Duncan briefly arched his eyebrows and tilted his head to say yes. Alistair's grin broadened.

"A formidable lass."

"That she is," Duncan said quietly.

CHAPTER NINE

DUNCAN MADE his way along the first-floor corridor, checking the room numbers as he went. The door to one room was open and he glanced in as he passed. Several members of staff were attempting to get a woman into or out of bed, he couldn't tell which. She was resisting, both physically and vocally.

"Get off me, yer bugger!" she yelled at one of them. Hesitating, Duncan stopped just past the door, keeping an eye on proceedings. He was relieved to see the staff keeping calm, speaking softly but firmly and managing to get the woman out of her bed. People who worked in environments like this needed to have a particular mindset, empathy and compassion, otherwise he was certain each day would be an arduous trial... both for staff and residents.

Continuing on, he came to his mum's room. The matron seemed surprised when he identified himself. Evidently, she didn't realise her resident had a son, which only increased his feeling of guilt. Easing the door open, he peered inside.

Roslyn was sitting in a chair by the window, his mother sitting opposite her, both looking out over the garden. He was startled by his mum's appearance. She'd always been a slight woman, barely over five foot four tall, but wiry and with a strength in her body mirrored by the firmness of her character. Now though, she looked ever so frail. Her hair was incredibly thin, revealing liver spots on her scalp and face, her skin was pale and clinging to her bones.

When had he last visited? It couldn't have been so long ago, could it? His memory let him down, sadness threatening to overwhelm him. Roslyn glanced up and, seeing him in the doorway, reached across and placed a hand gently on their mother's forearm.

"Mum, Duncan's come to visit," she said, smiling warmly. She slowly turned away from the view over the garden towards her daughter and Roslyn pointed to Duncan. His mother looked across the room at him and Duncan forced himself to smile, stepping forward.

"Hello, Mum," he said, wishing to be as upbeat as he could. "How are you?"

He walked around the bed and came alongside her, dropping to his haunches in front of her chair and reaching out to take her right hand in his. She looked at him suspiciously, he thought. She didn't return his smile, nor did she speak. Her eyes were trained on him though, and she appeared to be taking his measure.

"Mum," Roslyn said, "it's Duncan."

Their mum sighed and she frowned, slowly withdrawing her hand from his. Duncan watched it go, trying to keep smiling whereas inside he felt the instant stab of rejection. Maybe he deserved it.

"Hi, Mum," he said again.

"And what time do you call this?" she asked him accusingly.

He frowned, glancing at Roslyn and then the clock mounted on the wall opposite her bed.

"It's a quarter after five, Mum," he said.

"I'm well aware of what time it is, Duncan!" she scolded him. "You should have been back to pick the weans up from the school bus at four."

Unsure of what to say, he looked at Roslyn for help, but she stared at him impassively. He cleared his throat, buying himself a moment to think. Her dementia had been steadily getting worse this past decade, he knew that, but he found her current state to be a stark wake-up call. Reaching out again, he gently placed his hand on top of hers.

"I'm sorry, Mum," he said. "I'll try not to be late again."

She eyed him warily and he smiled. Her expression appeared to shift momentarily and she offered him the hint of a smile. His own widened and he squeezed her hand.

"Hi, Mum. I've popped in to say hello. I'm back on the island."

"What have you been off the island for?" she asked.

He cocked his head. "A bit of work, Mum, you know?"

"Just make sure you're back to pick wee Duncan up from the bus stop, won't you?" she said, fearful. "You know how anxious he gets if he's left on his own."

A memory leapt to mind. The feeling he had when he arrived back in the township and neither of his parents were there to meet him. Roslyn would stay on at the end of the school day from time to time to study and he'd take the school bus home on his own. Back then, when he was in primary, the schools used to bus the children in from the outlying crofting communities. Once they reached high-school age, many of the children would board at the school in Portree, heading home only at weekends. That used to be what everyone did until investment came through from central government, improving roads and public transport. At that point, the number of pupils boarding halved and Duncan figured it would be far fewer now.

His father would often be busy working, so busy he'd forget to pick up wee Duncan. His father was also named Duncan, *Big Dunc* and *Wee Dunc*, as they came to be known. Wee Duncan would often find himself standing at the bus stop waiting to be collected. On occasion, one of the passing neighbours would pick him up and drop him off at home. Often there would be no one there, his mother would also be out tending to the animals or working whatever job she could find just to bring in a few extra pounds to make ends meet.

His mother must have mistaken him now for her husband, his father. She smiled at him, years dropping away from her face. He loved to see her smile. When it was genuine, she seemed to radiate beauty. Some of the family photographs they had, ones taken on the odd occasions when they'd dressed in their Sunday best, their mum looked fabulous. Her regal stature, high cheekbones and Hollywood starlet eyes made her one of the most beautiful women on the island, on any island, as Duncan recalled thinking when he was a child.

Sadly, those days were few and far between in his memory. Most of the time he pictured her with a sour expression, preoccupied, a negative demeanour that permeated throughout the household infecting everything within reach with the same malaise.

She reached up with her hand, cupping his cheek with her palm and gazing at him affectionately. Duncan felt emotional, his eyes brimming, and he blinked back tears.

"Don't cry, Duncan," she said. "Everything will be all right, dear. You will collect him, won't you?"

He nodded, leaning into her hand. "I'll not forget, Mum. I promise." She smiled at him, taking her hand away and turning her gaze back out of the window towards the garden.

"I'll be there to pick him up, don't worry," he whispered. Glancing up at his sister, he saw her touch the corner of her eye as well. It all felt too much and he stood up, stepping out of the room. His mum didn't notice.

Roslyn followed him into the corridor. It was deserted. He leaned against the wall, quickly wiping his eyes fearful someone would pass by and see him. His sister touched his arm in a gesture of support. He glanced at her before looking away, past her and along the corridor at nothing in particular.

"How long?"

Roslyn shook her head. "She's like that a lot of the time now. Sometimes she can be more lucid, but you never know when it will come... or go."

Duncan took a deep breath. "Strewth. You might have bloody warned me."

Roslyn's scornful reply was a snort of laughter. "Well, it's not like I haven't tried, is it, Duncan? I mean, you're not exactly available, are you?"

He couldn't deny it, so resolved not to even try. He went to speak but choked on the words.

"She... she thought I was Dad."

Roslyn nodded, smiling supportively. "She talks about him a lot. They say the strongest memories are the last to go. It's kind of sweet once you get used to it. And you do look like him."

"Does she... only talk about the good times?"

Roslyn pursed her lips, in Duncan's mind she chose not to answer. He didn't press it.

"Ros, I'm sorry I didn't let you know I was coming. It wasn't planned, you know? They only told me first thing yesterday... and it's been a bit mental since I got here."

She accepted his apology. The anger she'd vented at him earlier seemed to have waned in its ferocity.

"So how are things with you?" she asked.

Where would he start with a question like that? He'd deliberately kept his work life separate from that of his family, keeping them at arm's length to avoid questions and the potential for judgement or meddling. He shrugged. "Been better."

"Are you still seeing that lass…? What was her name, Linda?"

"Linda?" he asked, chuckling momentarily and then shaking his head. "I've not been with her for a while."

"Still playing the field, Duncan?"

He laughed, but it was a bittersweet sound. "Ah… you know how it is."

"I do, when it comes to my little brother, aye."

He sought to switch the conversation. "How about you? How are things with you and Ronnie?"

"Aye, all right," she said, referring to her husband. Having been together throughout high school, Ronnie Macdougall and Roslyn married soon after they'd graduated, moving onto Ronnie's parents' croft. His parents had been quite old when they had their one and only child and when his father took ill, when Ronnie was all but fifteen, it became inevitable that he'd take the reins as soon as he was able. "And Mel is doing well too, seeing as you're asking."

Duncan smiled awkwardly. He would have got to his niece sooner or later.

"How old is she now, ten?"

Roslyn shook her head, laughing at him. "She's nearer fourteen, Duncan. Honestly, what are you like?"

He flushed with embarrassment. "Sorry. I lose track."

"So, if you're not knocking about with that Linda anymore, are you seeing someone else?"

He sighed. "Another time, Ros, please."

She laughed again. "As bad as that, is it? All right. How about tonight? You could come over to ours for your supper."

Duncan checked his watch. "I don't know, I might have to work—"

"Oh, come on Duncan. You can manage to come to the house for something to eat, can't you? It's nae too much to ask. I won't even force you to reveal details of your sordid love life. In fact, I'd rather not know."

He shook his head. "No, of course it's not too much to ask." He scratched his forehead. In the absence of a good excuse, he opted to not go for a bad one. "All right, I'd like that. Thanks."

Roslyn smiled, genuinely pleased and maybe a little shocked. "Great. I know Ronnie will be pleased to see you."

"Really?"

They'd never really been close, Ronnie and Duncan. Duncan's desire to get off the island and head to Glasgow was never something Ronnie could understand. He'd never considered leaving Skye, let alone a future away from crofting. It was what his family were, not something to choose to walk away from. He'd challenged Duncan about it the week he'd left for university. It was a conversation that quickly escalated into a slanging match. The two men had barely spoken since.

"Oh, it's all water under the bridge now," Roslyn said, dismissing his concerns. "You were children back then."

Duncan didn't share his sister's optimism, but if she thought he should come round for supper then so be it.

"What time?"

"Half seven for eight?"

He nodded, checking his watch again. "Listen, I really need to go. I'm still on the clock, so to speak." He glanced past her and into the room. Their mum was still staring out of the window. "Can you say goodbye to Mum for me? I'll pop back and see her tomorrow or something."

She nodded, crossing her arms at the waist. "Okay."

"Do you want me to bring anything tonight?"

"No," she said, turning away and making for the room to go back to their mum. "But showing up would be a definite plus."

He smiled. "I'll be there. I promise."

She smiled back at him, walking into the room with a spring in her step. Duncan took a breath, considering saying goodbye to his mum, but the thought of facing up to her vacant expression once more, her seeing him as a total stranger or, worse still, as his father, saddened him. Would she ever remember her son again? It was a strange thought, and one that'd come to mind every now and then after her initial diagnosis, but this was the first time it had been front and centre and it dawned on him that he wasn't prepared. Not prepared at all.

Heading back downstairs, he walked out into the night. It wasn't raining now, but the wind was strong and he drew his coat about him as he crossed the car park to where Alistair was waiting for him in his pick-up.

"Has she forgiven you?" he asked as Duncan got in beside him.

"Aye… sort of… it's complicated."

"Families always are lad. They always are." Alistair started the engine. "I had a call from Russell. He says Isla's family and friends are gathering tonight out at Coral Beach for a vigil."

"Christ!" Duncan said. "I thought we were keeping this under wraps for as long as possible. The media circus will go ape when they get wind of it."

Alistair shrugged. "The family want to get the community

involved, remembering Isla and all that. You cannae blame them."

Duncan bit his tongue. He didn't know Alistair well enough to openly speak his mind, and certainly not when it would be littered with expletives. Alistair read his mind.

"Besides, you're an islander."

"Meaning?"

"Meaning you know as well as anyone you cannae keep a secret on this island for long."

Duncan scoffed. "Unless it's a dead girl buried in the peats, aye."

Alistair looked glum. "Station?"

Duncan bobbed his head and they set off.

CHAPTER TEN

THE NEAREST CAR park to Coral Beach was in the crofting community of Claigan, situated five kilometres north of Dunvegan. There were already more than a dozen cars parked there when Duncan and Alistair arrived. The rain had long since passed revealing an almost cloudless sky offering them a quite stunning backdrop as they looked out to the west over Loch Dunvegan towards the Duirinish Peninsula. Duncan spotted two bright lights in the twilight sky, planets, visible to the naked eye before the stars which were sure to follow.

Checking his phone, Duncan cursed the lack of signal, holding it aloft in the hope of catching a few bars.

"Problem?" Alistair asked. "The storm last week knocked out a transmitter this way. The forensic guys were having a nightmare while working up at Trumpan, but I figured it'd be back up by now."

"No problem," Duncan said, hastily typing out a text message to Roslyn apologising for not being able to make it to supper. He offered to call round in the next couple of days instead. He'd prefer to speak to her, believing she would assume he was making an excuse if he didn't. He tapped send before putting his phone away and zipping up his coat, thrusting his hands into his pockets and the two of them set off along the path towards the beach.

The path crossed the fertile pastures of the township's crofting land before reaching the coastline. From here, they walked along the shoreline towards the rising beach rock, Ghrobain, at the tip of the headland overlooking the beach. This initial stretch of beach, the length of which one had to pass before reaching their destination, the ground calcified algae, known as maerl, looked like crushed coral that afforded the beach its name, was packed with stinking seaweed brought in on the tide and deposited for several hundred yards.

A naive tourist could be forgiven for thinking the guide-books had duped them. That is, until they rounded that last turn and their eyes fell upon the pristine white of the maerl beneath their feet. At low tide, it was possible to walk out to Lampay, the small island nestled off the coast between the two great land masses.

In the distance, Duncan could see the assembled group standing together, heads bowed, the tide gently lapping at the shoreline. Intent on not disturbing the vigil, they approached cautiously. A priest stood at the head of the group reciting a passage from the bible. Although not religious in any way, Duncan had attended Sunday School as a child, at his father's insistence, and found himself pondering which passage the words came from.

"… this is what the Sovereign Lord says: Again and again you remind me of your sin and your guilt. You don't even try to hide it! In everything you do, your sins are obvious for all to see. So now the time of your punishment has come…"

Their arrival was noted by several people, curious glances coming their way but the priest continued and Duncan and

Alistair remained detached from the group, observing. Alistair leaned into him.

"Donnie has changed, hasn't he?"

Duncan frowned, scanning the group for Donnie Matheson but was unable to recognise him. He looked quizzically at Alistair.

"Standing at the front," Alistair said, "preaching."

Duncan looked again and was taken aback. Donnie Matheson was leading the vigil, dog collar and all. "He's…"

"A minister, aye."

Duncan exhaled slowly. "I'd never have seen that one coming."

Alistair allowed himself a hint of a smile, unseen in the failing light. Duncan contemplated the transformation of the lad he'd once known – not known personally as such, but certainly by reputation – and it was a stark one. The recital ended with a prayer and both he and Alistair closed their eyes and bowed their head in respect with the silence that followed.

Donnie Matheson said amen, the rest of the group repeating it, as did Alistair, but Duncan remained silent. The group then disbanded with people turning to one another, some hugging while others formed their own conversations, likely discussing the service and remembering Isla in their own way. Donnie detached from the group, closing his bible and walking over to greet them. He offered Alistair his hand.

"Alistair, thank you for coming," he said warmly, although he was clearly pained to be there. Duncan took his measure. Donnie's face was drawn, deep lines etched in his skin particularly around the eyes which looked weary.

Donnie Matheson had been something of a legend to the teenage Duncan McAdam and his peers, although they'd only seen him once or twice when he came back to the island for a visit. He'd had shoulder-length hair at that time, highlighted with blond streaks much like the soft rock stars of the day, very Bon Jovi-esque.

Now, Donnie Matheson had morphed into a pretty decent replica of his father, another man who Duncan could picture in his mind's eye, tall, serious and balding. Donnie's hair was scant atop his head, a few wispy strands fluttering on the breeze and the sides were shot with grey. It was a far cry from the lion's mane he used to sport. He was sure if Alistair hadn't said so, he'd never have put this man as the same one from his youth.

"Do you remember wee Duncan?" Alistair said, introducing him. Donnie looked at Duncan, his brow furrowing as he tried to recall him, but eventually shook his head.

"I'm sorry, I can't place you," he said. Duncan smiled reassuringly, dismissing any perceived offence with a flick of his hand.

"DI Duncan McAdam," he said, shaking hands with Donnie.

"Ah… a relative of Roslyn's, by any chance?"

"Aye, that's right. I'm her brother."

"I'm so sorry… I didn't realise Roslyn had a brother on the island, let alone him being a policeman."

"I stay in Glasgow these days," he said, mildly surprised that his existence had gone unnoticed for so many years.

Donnie nodded, understanding. "What brings you home?"

Duncan cocked his head. "I'm here to help with Isla's case."

"I see. Well, it's good to have one of our own on the case," he said, glancing around. No one else was within earshot. Most people were saying their own particular prayers for Isla, laying flowers or setting down candles at a makeshift shrine they'd constructed at the edge of the beach where it met the pastureland, safe from the incoming tide. "I must admit, we've found the police investigation thus far to be... somewhat lacking." He glanced at Alistair apologetically. "I don't mean with you, Alistair," he said, "but these detectives who are from the mainland... they don't really understand the island like we do."

Alistair nodded. "I know their ways can seem a bit odd to us, but we are all looking for the same outcome."

Donnie smiled politely. "I hope so, Alistair. I really do, but it seems as if the family – the island – is nothing but an afterthought."

"I can assure you," Duncan said, "that not all of us are coming at it from that perspective."

Donnie studied him, gauging his sincerity perhaps, and seemingly satisfied he smiled. "Thank you, Duncan. I appreciate that."

"Tell me," Duncan said, looking past him to where the others stood, gathered around the shrine for another moment of silence, "why did you choose to hold the vigil here and not across the way, at Trumpan?"

Donnie pursed his lips, thinking on it. "I... we... thought that here would be more fitting. Isla's last night was spent here among her close friends, enjoying everything good that the island has to offer... nature, her people..." he took on a faraway stare "...no, this is a fitting place. Trumpan is a place of pain to Isla... to all of us. It is where she was laid to rest, but not somewhere for us to remember her." He shook his head. "Far better to be in a place of positive memories, wouldn't you say?"

Duncan couldn't argue with the logic. He looked at the priest. "I hope you don't mind me saying so, Donnie, but you've changed a fair bit over the years."

Donnie grinned, revealing a line of perfect teeth, top and

bottom. That wasn't common, at least not among Duncan and his pals.

"Sometimes, when I look in the mirror of a morning, I can hardly believe it myself," Donnie said. "But, in the end, I found my calling."

"Quite a change though, eh?"

Donnie nodded. "Yes, I suppose so. Looking back, I was running away from everything... and yet, once you take the time to stop and to think about it, and I mean really sit down and analyse yourself, you realise you're not getting away from anything at all. You are your own person and it is inescapable. You'll always have your demons with you, wherever you go or whatever you do, successes and failures, because it is all a part of you. It is all a part of the plan."

"The Lord's plan?" Duncan queried.

"Exactly. Once you recognise that fact, there's no going back."

"Even so, the church?" Duncan said, trying to mask his scepticism.

Donnie laughed. "I know, I know. But do remember my father. He is a formidable man, and everything he used to say to me... all those teachings I poured scorn upon year after year, were actually spot on." He smiled ruefully. "I came to see that once I returned."

"Gave up the music career," Duncan said.

Donnie sighed. "Yes, all of that seems like a different life now. I lived the dream – the perceived dream anyway – which became a nightmare, I might add. I was a different person then... living a life of debauchery and sin."

"Sounds all right to me," Alistair said.

Duncan ignored his DS. "And now? How do you live now?"

"I live a simpler, more holistic life. One that is far more spiritually balanced and fulfilling."

"Saying no to the drugs?"

"As I said, Duncan," Donnie replied, arching his eyebrows, "that was a different path I was on back then. No temptation has overtaken you that is not common to man. God is faithful—"

"And will not allow you to be tempted beyond your ability," Duncan said, drawing an appraising glance from Alistair.

"Quite right," Donnie said. "I could say that I see a believer before me, had you not refrained from joining in our prayer to my sister just now."

"Ah…" Duncan said. "You saw that? Good eyes."

"It pays to study my flock, Duncan," Donnie said, accompanied with a slight smile. "These days, I try to steer others away from the path I walked." He spread his hands wide. "After all, who better to act as a guide than someone who has walked that particular path of temptation?"

"There is that," Duncan said. "The path of temptation can be quite a fun place, mind?"

"I would be pompous…and a liar, if I argued otherwise, Duncan. I'm not quite the pillar of austerity that my father hung his dog collar on, but for every five souls who walk that road, at least one of them will destroy themselves and possibly, also those around them whom they love. Personally speaking, I was on a path of self-destruction. I had a choice to make on the road, take the fork to the right and find a future worth living or go left… a path that would have led to my death. I'm quite certain of that." Donnie's brow furrowed momentarily before his expression lightened. "You know, my father and I used to butt heads almost daily… and now, I realise that we are not all that different to one another, after all. Maybe that was why we used to clash so much?"

Duncan scanned the group standing in the background. "Would it be out of order for us to have a chat with a few of these people? I promise we'll be discreet."

Donnie shrugged. "No, I don't mind, not at all. Many of them were Isla's friends. Some were here that night, I believe," he said, turning his focus to the people standing a little way away from them. "I dare say they will help if they can."

Duncan excused himself and made his way towards the group. He introduced himself to people as he mingled, sharing words with a few. One woman in particular caught his eye, sidling up to him with a slight smile.

"No wonder you slipped away pretty sharpish last night," she said, lowering her voice so as not to be overheard. Duncan was surprised.

"Sorry, do I know you or have you mistaken me for someone else?"

She shook her head. "That was you last night, wasn't it... you popped one on Murdo before legging it with your pal, Archie?"

Duncan flushed red. "You were there?"

"I work there," she said. "I tell you, Murdo was spitting feathers afterwards. I dread to think what would have happened if you'd stuck around."

"Aye..." Duncan cleared his throat, embarrassed.

"Nae bother," she said, dismissing his obvious concern with a shrug. "You can unclench now. He likely deserved it, knowing Murdo. He's always getting into something with someone or other. Gets himself barred several times a year." Duncan was pleased to hear that their altercation was par for the course. The incident was far less likely to cause much fuss in that case. "You're investigating what happened to Isla then?"

He nodded. "You knew her?"

She shrugged. "Sort of. In passing like, you know?"

"You are?"

"Catriona Sinclair. I was a Murray back then mind."

"Ah… right. You were seeing Isla's ex-boyfriend, Alex."

She nodded. "They'd split before we got together, though. I didn't really know her. I'd only moved up with my folks from Glasgow a wee while beforehand."

"How was she with you? Around the breakup and you being with her ex?"

Catriona shrugged. "Never said anything to me about it. I get the impression Alex fancied himself as something of a player back then." She chuckled. "I thought he was so cool. What a loser."

"Him or you?"

"Both," she said, raising one eyebrow. "Besides, rumour was that Isla was knocking around with someone else anyway, behind Alex's back."

Duncan thought on it. "Do you mean the lad she was with the night of the summer party, Ian Fraser, wasn't it?"

She shook her head. "He was in and around her, sure. One of the magnificent seven… but no, I didnae mean him. It was some guy over on Uist. Alex mentioned it at one point."

"Uist?" Duncan asked and she nodded. He was unaware of any mention regarding a man she was seeing on the islands. "North or South Uist?"

Catriona shrugged. "No clue. I mean, it was gossip, so who knows? Maybe it was rubbish. You know what islands are like for Chinese whispers. And the lasses around these parts back then were a catty bunch, you know? Girls talk… and it may have been nonsense."

"Right enough," Duncan said. "What did you mean before when you said the magnificent seven?"

Her expression changed, embarrassed. "Oh, I didnae mean

anything by it. It was just a joke from back then... before we knew anything had happened to Isla."

Duncan didn't want to let it lie and waited for an answer. Reluctantly, Catriona obliged.

"That night, at the party, Isla was jumping between the guys, flirting and kissing pretty much anyone who crossed her path. At the last count, we had seven..."

"Hence, the magnificent seven," Duncan said.

"Aye... sorry. I know it's bad taste to bring it up."

"That's okay. So, if you weren't exactly friends with Isla, why are you here tonight? If you don't mind me asking?"

"No, of course I don't mind." Her expression clouded and she seemed pensive. "Back then, I was young, stupid. We all were, let's face it. We thought the world was ours to do with as we pleased." She shrugged. "I'm older now, wiser. The world is a dangerous place, especially for women. Knowing what we know now... maybe if we'd been more inclined to look out for one another, then Isla would still be here." Her expression took on a faraway gaze. "And on the other hand, if some things went differently that night, it could be me they're lighting candles for tonight." She sighed. "Who knows?"

Duncan nodded solemnly. "Alex Macrae told us he was with you all night during the party and beyond."

Catriona smiled awkwardly. "To the best of my recollection, yes."

"That sounds particularly vague. You were more specific at the time."

She shrugged. "It was a party... a few drinks, quite a few if I'm honest... and, you know, I was a party girl up from Glasgow."

"Meaning?"

She hesitated but he pressed her for an answer. "I brought

the sweets that night, you know?" she said reluctantly. "Not that I was dealing."

Duncan took a deep breath. "What did you bring? I'm not interested in what you were up to twenty odd years ago, but…"

"A few wraps of speed… nothing heavy."

"Speed? Who took it?"

Catriona shrugged. "Like I said, I wasn't dealing or anything… but whoever was up for it could… you know, dip in?"

"Good stuff, was it?"

She laughed, nodding. "Always."

"So… it'd be fair to say you – and possibly a few others that night – may have struggled with accuracy regarding the passage of time?"

She grimaced. "Fair, aye. Had I known back then that something had happened to her, I'd have said something. I really would."

"Can you back Alex's account that he gave in his statement?"

She nodded slowly and then changed her mind, shaking her head. "No, not at all."

"Right."

"Disnae mean he's lying though, does it?"

Duncan shook his head. "No, that's true. Even so, I'll have someone come by and take a fresh statement from you regarding that, okay?" She seemed reticent but agreed. "And make sure you tell the truth this time."

"I will. I promise."

"Did any of these girls you're talking about ever say who Isla might have been seeing on Uist?"

She shrugged. "No one specific as far as I know. Mind though, she'd been over that way a few days before. I remember someone mentioning it after she disappeared. We wondered if she'd gone over there on the ferry, shacked up with someone for a bit and that she'd be back soon enough, but was staying away cos of the fuss and all. And she did have a wee bit of a reputation for… putting it around a bit." She dismissed her own suggestion. "I'm not trying to speak ill of the dead, as I say, I didn't really know her all that well, but it's just what people were saying."

Duncan thanked her before stepping away. Alistair was talking to others in the group, breaking off from them to join him.

"Alistair, do you remember reading anything about some guy Isla might have been involved with over on Uist?"

Alistair thought hard. "No, not that I recall. Involved with, how?"

"A relationship of some kind. Someone just said it… and that Isla had been over there a short time before she disappeared."

"Aye, that last bit rings a bell. She was supposed to be visiting her aunt or something. She lives on North Uist, so maybe that's what they were on about? The aunt was spoken to and she said Isla never made it across though."

"So… where was she, if she wasn't with the aunt?"

Alistair shrugged. "I don't know if they ever established for sure that Isla went over to the islands, and certainly not whether anyone ever followed it up."

Duncan nodded. "Let's follow it up now." He looked around. "Did you turn up anything of interest?"

"A few names notable by their absence tonight," Alistair said. "Surprised a few."

"Oh yeah. Like whom?"

"Isla's best pal, Roddy Mcintyre is a no-show; a lot of raised eyebrows about that. Alex came though," Alistair said, pointing out Alex Macrae. Almost as if he'd heard mention of his name, he glanced over at them, immediately looking away again. Duncan hadn't noticed he was there.

"Nervous soul, isn't he?" Duncan said.

"Aye. So is someone else," Alistair said. Duncan enquired with a look. "Nicol Nicolson. Made his excuses and left before I got to have a word with him."

"Coincidence?"

"Nah, don't believe in them."

Duncan smiled. "Wise man."

CHAPTER ELEVEN

DUNCAN ENTERED THE INCIDENT ROOM, spying DCI Jameson deep in conversation with several members of his team. He saw Duncan approach but didn't make anything but the briefest of eye contact and Duncan was fairly sure he carried on his conversation longer than necessary just to delay speaking with him. Either that or his paranoia was getting the better of him.

"Duncan," Jameson said, a curt greeting accompanied by a sharp nod.

"Good morning, sir," Duncan said. "Could I have a moment?"

Jameson checked his watch, frowning. He looked up at him. "Make it quick if you can, Duncan. I have a media briefing in fifteen minutes and I need to get myself prepared."

"Of course, sir. You wouldn't want to get on the TV without looking your best."

Jameson eyed him warily, likely trying to discern if he was taking the piss out of him. Duncan remained straight faced, leaving the DCI unsure.

"This vigil stunt the locals pulled last night has really

sparked interest in the case, interest I could well do without, Duncan." He stared hard at him, almost as if it was somehow Duncan's fault Donnie Matheson had set the vigil up. Jameson shook his head. "People around here are a law unto themselves. Now, the press are questioning me personally!"

"To be expected, sir."

Jameson was taken aback. "Why?"

Duncan shrugged. "It was a big story, sir. Stands to reason now we have a body, it will be up and running again. It was always going to happen."

"Hmm… I suppose you're right." He looked at him. "Well, what is it, Duncan?"

"I was talking to some of those who attended the vigil last night—"

"You were there?"

Duncan nodded. Jameson's eyes narrowed, but he didn't comment further.

"One of Isla's peers confessed to being under the influence that night, meaning she couldn't be clear on the night's timeline. Specifically, regarding the movements of Isla's ex-boyfriend, Alex Macrae." Jameson nodded thoughtfully. "She also referred to Isla potentially having a boyfriend in the outer islands. Have you or your team followed that up?"

Jameson thought about it and then shook his head. "Reviewing the files, Isla apparently made some trip to Uist to supposedly visit an aunt, but she was back on Skye for the party, so I don't really see the relevance."

"DS MacEachran said the aunt denied the visit took place."

Jameson shrugged. "Well, there you go. What of it?"

"I'm wondering why she went to the islands if not to visit the aunt?"

"Irrelevant to her disappearance," Jameson said, frowning.

"Until we know what she was doing there, I'd beg to differ."

Jameson straightened his back, raising himself several inches higher, making him a little taller than Duncan. "Duncan, if you want to spend your time traipsing across the Outer Hebrides, then be my guest. It will keep you out from under my feet. Excuse me, please."

Duncan made way, allowing his DCI to walk past him. Another officer fell into step alongside him, passing a file across and Jameson began studying it as he walked. Duncan shrugged and made his way across the room to where the local CID team were working. Alistair was waiting for him.

"How did you get on?" he asked.

"Pretty well," Duncan said. "We have the green light to explore the islands."

"Holidaying on the taxpayers' shilling?"

Duncan shook his head. "Did you find anything in the files about this guy on Uist?"

"Not specifically, no. However, that spring, the one prior to Isla going missing, she got a couple of weeks' work experience alongside a vet on North Uist. Isla had some plans to explore being a veterinary nurse after she left school."

"When was that exactly?"

"The first couple of weeks of April during the Easter school break. Mid-lambing season, so the vets are always busy."

Duncan considered it. "She'd have spent a fair bit of time among the locals, wouldn't she?"

"Aye," Alistair agreed. If she was likely to be seeing someone, it was the perfect chance to meet. Should I give the vet a phone?"

"No, no," Duncan said. "Give me his details and I'll have a word." He checked the clock. "What time does the next

Calmac sail?" he asked, referencing the ferry company, Caledonian MacBrayne, who served the islands with their fleet of distinctive black and white ships.

"You want to go out there today?"

Duncan nodded. "It's too easy to be dismissive over the phone."

Alistair frowned. "First sailing to Lochmaddy leaves at half past nine." He tilted his head. "You'll be pushing it to make it to Uig for the check in."

Duncan did a quick bit of mental arithmetic. "With a car, half hour before—"

"Forty-five minutes," Russell said, looking up from his desk. "And if you dinnae make it the next sailing will be half six this evening."

Duncan frowned. "Can you call ahead, get me booked on and tell them it's a police matter."

Alistair laughed. "That'll probably make them leave early out of spite."

Duncan gathered his coat. "Someone book me somewhere to stay tonight as well. I'll come back on the first sailing tomorrow morning." Alistair nodded. "And can you email me everything you have about Isla's stay on the island that spring? I'll read it on the boat."

CHAPTER TWELVE

THE RUMBLE of the mighty diesel engines sounded as the *Innse Gall* lined up her approach around the South Basin of Lochmaddy, heading for the ferry terminal. Duncan, standing on the passenger viewing deck at the stern, beneath the red funnel with its familiar Lion Rampant badge emblazoned on the side, stared off the starboard side towards Flodday, a large uninhabited island, one of many, situated off the east coast of North Uist.

He wasn't alone on the deck. An elderly man, wrapped up in a thick coat and sporting a flat cap, sat in the first row of seats, his collie dog lying on the green painted deck at his feet. The wind was fierce, normal for this part of the world, but the hour-and-forty-minute sailing had been across calm waters which was unusual. The crews manning these vessels were a tough bunch. The Minch could be incredibly hostile to shipping when the Atlantic storms swept across the islands, which they did frequently, and these ferries were all that linked these remote communities to Skye and the mainland. There were flights to the islands, but these were largely made by light aircraft. The bulk of travel between the islands was done via the Calmac fleet.

Duncan spent much of the journey reading through the old files Alistair had sent him. He'd downloaded them in his car while he was waiting to embark. The vet who'd given Isla the work experience was a man by the name of James Turnbull. He lived in Carinish, a small community in the south-west of the island.

All of the communities were small in this part of the Western Isles. The population across the fifteen inhabited islands making up the Outer Hebrides had been steadily growing over the last two decades with current numbers running into the mid-twenty thousands, however the bulk of those lived on Lewis and Harris. On the smaller islands, the largest recorded inhabitants were those on South Uist, where the population fell well short of two thousand. From memory, Duncan recalled the smallest known recorded figure was on Flodaigh, where the occupancy was counted in single digits. He wondered if that was still the case or had those people moved on?

The tannoy sounded, issuing instructions for passengers to return to their vehicles and make ready to disembark. Duncan made his way down the staircase to the vehicle deck and returned to his car. Pleased to have managed an early meal in the restaurant, he didn't know when he'd next get the chance to eat. The times he'd been out on the islands, he'd found them not well stocked with hotels or restaurants and the convenience stores consisted of small independent units or Co-ops, and these were few and far between. But that was life in the Western Isles.

The car shook momentarily as the engines were put into reverse, guiding the ferry into the harbour and docking seamlessly at the terminal. He didn't have long to wait before the bow doors lifted and the crew began gesturing for the line of cars to move forward. Once clear of the terminal, he followed the main road north through the town before turning left and cutting across the island in the direction of Benbecula and South Uist. He would reach his destination, Carinish, and the home of James Turnbull, before crossing the North Ford Causeway to reach Benbecula where Isla's aunt lived.

The islands were low lying, close to sea level, and the route took him through a mix of terrain unlike any other he knew of in the British Isles; blanket bog, wet and dry machair – the arable and grazing land formed close to the coast by the deposition of sand and shell fragments by the wind – as well as both fresh and saltwater marshes. Duncan knew the coastline of these islands were like no other, coastal dunes, white sandy beaches and clear water stretching for miles where you'd be unlikely to register another soul. If you caught it right it was the most beautiful weather on earth, although within the space of half an hour you could find yourself leaning into horizontal rain or being lifted off your feet by the Atlantic winds.

The single-storey white-painted croft house belonging to James Turnbull was located a little way off the main road and in view of the ruined Trinity Temple and its smaller twin chapel, the Church of Clan MacVicar.

Seeing them brought back a memory from childhood, a school trip he went on with Becky by his side. The entire class had been present, but he'd only ever had eyes for her. They were still in primary and couldn't have been more than ten years old. The trip was exciting, an incredible adventure for children, many of whom had never left Skye at that point let alone ventured onto a ferry to cross the water. This site had been of significant importance to the religious community in the thirteenth and fourteenth centuries but fell into disrepair after the reformation. Now, only the gable ends and part of the south wall remained of the smaller chapel whereas the larger of the two had fared better, although it too bore no resemblance to what it must have once been to the community who lived here in its heyday.

"Can I help you with something?"

Duncan snapped back to the present, turning to see a woman standing at the entrance to a barn to the left of the main house. She had dark hair, shot through with grey, and it was tied at the nape of her neck. She sported a thick hoodie with a padded gilet over jeans and wellington boots. Setting down a bag she'd been carrying from the barn, she eyed him suspiciously as he approached.

Presenting her with his warrant card, he smiled. "DI McAdam. I'm over from Portree."

"What can I do for you?" she asked, curious.

"I was hoping to speak to James Turnbull. Is he around?"

"He is," she said, looking back at the house. Duncan followed her eye. The croft house was built with two agricultural barns springing from either side. The one they were standing in front of was likely original whereas the other was modern and purpose built. Presumably, this was where the veterinary clinic was housed for any medical procedures that were needed. "James is inside, doing a bit of paperwork. I'm his wife, Andrea. What do the police want with James?"

"You might be able to help actually. How long have you lived here?"

She shrugged. "It feels like forever. James and I moved out here…" her expression was thoughtful as she worked it out in her head, "…thirty-odd years ago, to make a different type of life away from the treadmill."

Duncan could think of easier places to build a life. It was

hard out here and it was rare to find outsiders who could hack it, but fair play to them.

"Do you remember a teenager who came out here for some work experience, Isla Matheson?"

Andrea's face dropped and she nodded slowly. "How could I forget her. I remember her going missing a few months afterwards... nice girl as I recall. Why do you ask?"

They were interrupted by her husband James, who came to meet them pulling on a wax jacket as he crossed the gravel-lined drive towards them.

"Hello," he said, smiling at Duncan. "I've just had a call from Rab MacPhee's, over in Samala. He needs me to—"

"James, this is DI..."

"McAdam," Duncan said, offering his hand. James took it, perplexed.

"He's here to speak to you about Isla. You remember Isla—"

"Yes, yes of course," James said, looking between them. His gaze lingered on Duncan, and he ran his tongue along his lower lip before checking his watch. "Is it... important? It's just I said I'd see Rab—"

"It's about a dead girl, Mr Turnbull," Duncan said, "so yes, I would say so."

James looked at him, open mouthed, glancing sideways at his wife, who gasped, before nodding. "Dead? Isla is... dead, you say?"

Duncan nodded. "Yes. I'm afraid so."

"Well... of course it is much more important... of course." He looked around but appeared reticent to invite Duncan inside. "What... what can I do for you?"

"Isla worked here for a time; the spring prior to when she went missing. Is that correct?"

James nodded. "Yes, she was here for a week or so, ten days at the most."

Andrea agreed. "We've had a few students come to work for us over the years, haven't we, James?"

"Yes. Not all that many, three or four perhaps. Often, they are already here on the island and looking for a bit of work in the summer, school holidays… that sort of thing."

"And Isla?" Duncan asked. "What was she doing here?"

James blew out his cheeks, shaking his head. "A bit of everything and nothing. Whatever we needed at the time."

"What was she like?"

"Nice girl," James said, glancing at his wife. "Wouldn't you say, dear?"

"I think so. I never really got to know her all that well," Andrea said. "You remember, my mother was getting out of hospital, and I had to travel to help her for a bit when she came home?"

James looked thoughtful, his brow furrowing. "Ah… yes, I remember."

"So, you weren't here, Mrs Turnbull?" Duncan asked. She shook her head. Duncan looked around. "Do you have any other staff around here to help you?"

Andrea shook her head. "There are several vets who service the island. We all tend to muck in when needed. That's how it works out here. There's no one to count on but each other."

James Turnbull was lost in thought. Realising she was talking to him, he looked at her, his expression lightening. The moment hadn't gone unnoticed by Duncan.

"Sorry…" James whispered. "What was it you said there?"

"The community here," she said, shaking her head and smiling apologetically at Duncan, "all pulls together when needed. You can't be an island on an island."

"That's right," James said, nodding and drawing a deep breath.

Andrea reached out and touched his arm. "Are you all right, love?"

To Duncan, James did seem to have turned a little pale. He shook his head slightly. "I don't feel particularly well," he said. He turned to Duncan. "I must admit to feeling a bit off today."

Duncan nodded. "Well, I hope it isn't catching."

James smiled awkwardly. "I think I need to have a sit down."

Andrea put a hand of concern on her husband's back, gently rubbing it. "Maybe you should come inside and have a lie down. The MacPhees can wait for a bit."

James nodded. Looking at Duncan, he was apologetic. "Sorry, Detective Inspector. Is there anything else I can help you with?"

"Oh, just one more thing," Duncan said. "Isla travelled to North Uist a few days before she disappeared. I was wondering what she came to see you for?"

James and his wife exchanged glances, James shaking his head.

"I... I don't recall her coming to see us at that time," he said. Andrea's expression was stern. She looked at Duncan, concerned.

"What about you, Mrs Turnbull? Can you think of a reason why she would come here? It would have been late August."

Andrea shook her head, "No, I'm sorry. I don't remember her coming here either. Why would she?"

Duncan smiled. "That's why I'm here, to ask that very question."

Andrea focussed on her husband, and he also shook his

head. He didn't seem to be feeling any better, in fact, he looked quite the opposite.

"Are you okay, Mr Turnbull?" Duncan asked.

"I'll be all right, I'm sure," he said, putting a hand on his stomach.

"One more question, if that's okay? Where was Isla staying when she was over here working with you?"

James glanced at Andrea, frowning. "She stayed with a relative who has a place on Benbecula, but if we were working late… and had an early start in the morning…"

"Then she would have the option to stay in the bothy," Andrea finished for him. She met her husband's eye and he nodded. She pointed towards the new barn extension. "Before we built the clinic there, we used to have an old barn that we let tourists use from time to time. That was before half the island converted crofts to holiday lets anyway. It wasn't much, little more than you'd get with a bothy, hence why we called it that, not that it was ever a real bothy of course."

"I see," Duncan said. "And Isla stayed here with you?" James nodded. "How often?"

James seemed uncertain, looking at his wife who shrugged. How could she know. She was on the mainland. "A night or two, I guess… but I really don't remember."

"Strange," Duncan said, capturing both their attention. "I think if a young girl had stayed with me for a short time before she vanished in mysterious circumstances, I'd likely remember how long she was with me."

James snorted with derision. "It was lambing season… one of the busiest times of the year, if not the busiest time of the year. Give me a break."

Duncan clicked his tongue on the roof of his mouth, nodding, but he didn't say anything. James held his gaze. Was it fear, anger or irritation in his expression, Duncan couldn't tell?

"When Isla went missing, were you both here on the island?"

Andrea thought about it. "Late August? I was spending a lot of time between here and my mother's. I'd need to check."

"Where does your mother stay?" Duncan asked.

"Fife, or at least, she did. She passed away."

Duncan exhaled. "I'm sorry to hear that."

"Oh, don't be, it was some time ago now."

"That's quite a trip, Uist to Fife… not one you'd want to make regularly."

She shook her head, smiling ruefully. "No, I wouldn't recommend making it at all!"

"Could you have a think about it for me, try and recall your movements at the time?" Duncan asked. "I know it's a long time ago, but it'd be a great help."

Andrea seemed a little puzzled, but she nodded. "I will, of course. If you think it'd help."

"How about you, Mr Turnbull. Do you remember much about that time, late August?"

He looked thoughtful. "I think there was a conference around that time… given by the BVA. I believe it was held in Glasgow that year."

"The BVA?"

"The British Veterinary Association."

"How long were you away for, do you remember?" Duncan asked.

Concentrating hard, James took a moment, exhaling deeply. "Three, maybe four days. I would have stayed for the duration of the event. It's a good opportunity to catch up with friends and former colleagues. I recall there was a lot of concern about the spread of Avian Flu that particular year."

"Right, thank you."

"Is there anything else, Detective Inspector McAdam?" James asked pointedly.

Duncan glanced between them. "No, I think that covers it for now."

Andrea put her arm around her husband's waist, supporting him. "Come on, love. Let's get you inside. You're not as young as you used to be, darting off here and there at the drop of the hat."

James made to gently ease her away from him but she was having none of it.

"Thanks for your time," Duncan said, handing Andrea a contact card for future reference and then he watched them go. Andrea looked back and smiled, James did not. Duncan assessed James Turnbull. He must be in his late fifties now, which would have put him late thirties around the time of Isla's death. Isla was an attractive girl who, by all accounts, enjoyed the attention of the opposite sex. Could she have drawn the eye of a married man while Andrea was away nursing her mother?

It was certainly possible.

CHAPTER THIRTEEN

IONA SUTHERLAND, Isla's aunt, lived in the Benbecula community of Torlum, only a twenty-minute drive from the Turnbulls' home on North Uist. Much of the east side of the Isle of Benbecula was uninhabitable whereas the western side had fertile grazing land and a stunning coastline. Here, Duncan was booked into his hotel, so it made sense to visit Iona last.

Her home was a small, white-painted croft house, the nearest neighbour was situated at least a hundred yards away. Like many of the houses in these parts, the garden was surrounded by a wire fence to keep the grazing animals from getting too close. Duncan could see a herd of cattle huddled close to one another amid the sand dunes off to the west.

Iona's home looked shabby compared with many of the others he passed on his way here. The exterior paintwork to the fascia was peeling and several of the roof slates had slipped or were missing. This was a harsh climate and even the most fastidious of owner-occupiers might struggle to tame the wilds of Mother Nature. The metal five-bar gate offering access to the drive was wide open and he pulled his car up at the front of the property. A plume of smoke drifted out of the chimney before quickly dispersing on the wind.

Drawing his coat about him, Duncan knocked on the front door. He waited patiently and soon enough he saw a hunched figure approach from inside. The door wasn't locked which didn't surprise him. Very few people felt the need to do so in such a tight-knit community.

"Mrs Sutherland?" he asked, looking at the woman. He figured she must be well into her eighties. She was perhaps five foot five, tall for a woman on the islands in his experience but hunched as she was, she appeared shorter. Dressed in a thick woollen jumper and skirt with thermal leggings under-neath, she craned her neck to look up at him.

"It's been a long time since anyone has called me that, dear," she said, her face splitting into a toothy grin. "Iona will do just fine, young man."

Duncan smiled, producing his warrant card and holding it out for her to see. "I'm DI Duncan McAdam," he said. "And it's been a while that I've been called young, too."

"I'll never be able to read that, not without my glasses," she said, squinting at his identification.

"I'm over from Portree," he said, "investigating what happened to your niece, Isla."

Iona's smile faded, her expression clouding. "Of course. You'd best come in," she said, stepping back and releasing her grip on the door. He reached out and caught it with the flat of his hand before the wind slammed it shut. Following her inside, he closed the door and immediately the wind noise dropped to a dull background roar. "This way," she said, shuf-fling away with the use of a walking stick."

She went into a sitting room, Duncan followed. An open fire crackled in the hearth on the far wall, Iona crossing to it and struggling to lower herself down to add a log from the basket alongside the hearth. Duncan hurried over and knelt beside her.

"I'll do that," he said. Gratefully, Iona patted his forearm, rose, and shuffled a few steps to her right to a chair and sat down. "Do you live here alone?" Duncan asked as he added the wood, ensuring it was settled on the embers and would catch quickly.

"Just me these days," she said. "My Ian left me years back. Heart attack, they said." She shook her head. "Far too young, but they say the Lord takes the best early." She chuckled. "I'm not sure what that says about me."

Duncan was impressed. The folk of Skye and the Western Isles were undoubtedly hardy, they needed to be but, even so, to live alone out here took someone with strong fortitude. Satisfied with his efforts around the fire, he stood up, looking to sit down.

"Are you any good with electrics?" Iona asked him, her heavily-lined face staring hard at him.

He shrugged. "It depends…"

"Oh, my storage heater isn't coming on. The one in my bedroom."

That was beyond any knowledge Duncan would have, he was certain, but he was willing to take a look. He glanced past her and out into the hall, pointing in that direction.

"Second door on the left," she said, smiling.

Duncan inclined his head and headed out of the room. Iona stayed where she was. She was clearly a trusting soul. The first door on the left was the bathroom and the second was a bedroom at the front of the house. It wasn't very large; these houses being built for form and functionality rather than space or luxury. The storage heater was on the wall beneath the window. Casting a quick glance over it, he found no loose cables or any exterior sign as to why it wasn't working. It was hard wired into a fused socket on the wall.

Stepping out into the hall, he called, "Where's your fuse board, Iona?"

"In the pantry, at the top."

He went into the kitchen and found a small cupboard next to the back door. Inside the shelves were well stocked. She certainly believed in being prepared which wasn't a bad thing bearing in mind where she lived. The old fuse board was above the top shelf and Duncan had to use his mobile as a torch to see. He was surprised to find a traditional board with the old plug-in fuses. He cursed. These things could be lethal. At least they were labelled and he found the one for the heaters and pulled it. The fuse wire was broken.

"Do you have any spare fuse wire… and some tools?" he shouted.

"In the cupboard to the left of the sink," Iona shouted back. Duncan turned, located the cupboard and found a small tool bag at the back inside an old shoe box. Alongside the bag he found spare fuse wire, a couple of candles, a box of matches and some assorted batteries. It didn't take him long to cut a new length of fuse wire, tie it in and then replace it in the board.

Heading back into the bedroom, he found the red light in the wall switch lit and he exhaled. Returning to the sitting room, he found Iona was now in the kitchen making them both a cup of tea. She smiled at him as he walked in.

"That's you sorted," he said. "But you really should have someone update that fuse board for you. If you get a shock off that it'll be the death of you, quite literally."

She waved away his concern. "We all go when it's our time."

"No need to speed things up though."

She smiled at him. "You're starting to sound like my nephew. Always on at me to leave the island and move over to Skye." She pointed towards the corner of the kitchen. "The biscuits are in the tin over there, next to the eggs," she said. Duncan gathered the tin and brought it over to where she'd put a side plate onto a tray and set about filling a teapot with freshly boiled water. She arranged some of the biscuits on the plate and asked Duncan to get the milk from the fridge while she put out a sugar bowl. "As if I belong anywhere but this island. I'm far too old to go upping sticks and moving some-place new." Iona put two upturned cups onto saucers on the tray, smiling at her own handiwork. "There. All done."

"You needn't have gone to any trouble," Duncan said.

"Don't be daft. It's not like I get all that many visitors over this way these days."

"Did Isla visit you a lot?"

She stopped, her expression taking on a faraway look. She nodded. "When they were little, Ruaridh and Èibhlin used to bring the wee ones over quite a bit. Not so much as they got older, to be fair. Donnie was always less keen." She cocked her head. "It wasn't the done thing to enjoy visiting your old aunt once you reach a certain age."

"And Isla?"

Iona smiled. "She still liked to come across, always. She described it as her safe space." She frowned. "I always thought that referred to this house, but maybe she meant the island. I don't know."

"Safe space? Was she troubled then, your niece?"

Iona sighed, looking glum. "I never thought so, not really," she said, looking at Duncan. "Always such a sweet girl, a bright soul... someone people liked to be around."

"Have you spoken to your brother?"

She hesitated, pursing her lips and bracing herself against the countertop. She nodded.

"I spoke with both Ruaridh and Donnie," she said quietly. "I'd almost given up hope of ever knowing what became of her… of Isla." Her eyes flickered to Duncan and away again. "I did wonder whether she'd…" The words caught and she swallowed hard, glancing at Duncan. "I thought maybe she'd taken her own life."

"You thought that likely?"

She shook her head. "Not likely as such, no." She shrugged. "But… I couldn't fathom a reason as to why she would up and vanish like that? Not that I know why she might contemplate suicide either… but in the absence of any other reason… Do you understand?"

"I do, and I appreciate this is difficult for the family," Duncan said, "but I need to find out what did happen to her."

Iona met his eye, blinking back tears. "Whatever I can do to help," she said. She made to pick up the tray but Duncan gestured he'd take care of it and having picked up the tray he followed her back into the sitting room. They sat down either side of the fireplace, Iona pouring them both a cup of tea before offering him a biscuit from the plate. He didn't want one but accepted out of politeness.

"Isla caught the ferry over to Lochmaddy a few days before she disappeared," Duncan said, sipping at his tea. "Several people at the time thought she would be visiting you."

"Oh… she visited me a lot, that's true," Iona said before shaking her head, "but she didn't that week."

"You're sure?"

She nodded. "I'd remember. Someone called to ask me if she'd been here… who was it now?" she asked herself, cupping her chin with thumb and forefinger, frowning deeply.

She shook her head. "No, I can't remember. It must have been a policeman."

"Asking if Isla stayed here?"

She nodded. "And asking if she was here at the time… when she'd been reported missing by Ruaridh. They wondered if she'd come to visit and not told anyone." She scoffed. "As if Ruaridh hadn't already been on to me."

"Have you any idea who else she may have been here visiting on the island?"

Iona thought hard. "No, not really. I mean, we all know each other, and she certainly knew people around and about to say hello to. She was here working for a time earlier in the year. Did you know that?"

"With the Turnbulls," Duncan said. Iona nodded. "Did she ever mention her time with them, with James and Andrea?"

"Oooh… you know what, she loved working with animals. I think that was her calling and what she would have wound up doing had she…"

Duncan saw the pain in her expression. He'd come across these cases from time to time. Far too often during his time in Glasgow, but it would be less common on the islands. Families often built narratives around the motives and reasons for their missing relative's failure to reappear; needing a break from society, a fresh start or even amnesia caused by an accident. While there was still no body, there was always hope, however faint. The discovery of a body changed all of that. It was final. There was no hope of their return now and the reality had to be faced.

The wound was reopened, it was bleeding freshly once again. And it was painful.

"Isla stayed with you while she was on the island for her work experience?"

"Yes, she did. Sometimes she stayed at the Turnbulls'

house, if she was working late, but she'd always let me know."

"And she got on well with them?"

"With James, yes. I'm not so sure Andrea liked her very much."

Duncan found that odd. Andrea spoke highly of Isla earlier in the day, albeit admitting she didn't know Isla well, but he said nothing of it now.

"Andrea was always ordering her around, speaking down to her," Iona went on. She laughed dryly. "The children of today… they expect to have the same respect as those a generation older. I told her, *Isla, you have to work your way up, my girl. You can't expect to walk into things and immediately be calling the shots.*"

"So, she didn't get on with Andrea?"

Iona was dismissive. "I wouldn't say that. Just that they didn't match as well as she did with James. He took a shine to her." She winked at him. "Like a lot of the boys, I suspect."

"James Turnbull wasn't a boy though, was he? He was a grown man, and a married one at that."

"Oh, I'm not saying he was attracted to her… well, maybe a little." Iona's eyes sparkled with the memory of her niece. "Isla had that… magic about her. I would expect every full-blooded male would be drawn to her." She appeared thoughtful. "From what I read in the papers, probably a lot of girls too."

Duncan smiled. Iona pointed to a row of picture frames on the mantelpiece above the fire.

"That's her, fourth from the right."

Duncan stood up and picked up the photograph, one among many shots of individuals or groups at parties or walking the many miles of golden sands available on the Western Isles. This particular photo was faded now by the passage of time and exposure to light. Isla Matheson, paddling through the surf. She looked in her early teens. A pretty girl, right enough. Not classically beautiful perhaps, but the shot captured a wonderfully innocent smile.

"That was taken just over the way," Iona said, pointing behind Duncan as if they could see through the wall towards the nearby coast.

"How old?" Duncan asked, tilting the photo towards her.

"Thirteen or fourteen, I should think," Iona said, smiling wistfully. "Lovely wee thing. I'd have done anything for my niece, I really would."

Duncan put the photograph back in the row among the others before returning to his seat. Iona looked preoccupied, wringing her hands.

"To think... where the poor wee thing ended up," she said quietly. "Just awful."

"Yes, it is," Duncan said. The words sounded hollow and inadequate, but what else could he say?

"After all this time..." she said, looking at him, "... you'll still find the man responsible?"

"That is my job," he said, not wishing to over promise.

"But are you good at it?" she asked. He felt her eyes upon him conveying both her hope and expectation. Instinctively he wanted to make a light-hearted comment, self-deprecating, but it wouldn't be appropriate. Instead, he nodded.

"I don't want to offer false hope, Iona." He met her gaze. "But I'm good enough."

Iona smiled weakly, putting her hands together in prayer. "In which case I will pray that will be enough, young man."

CHAPTER FOURTEEN

DUNCAN STOOD BESIDE HIS CAR; hands deep in his pockets as he braced against the wind buffeting him from behind. The drive back to Lochmaddy was uneventful but sitting in the car had somehow aggravated his back and stretching his legs with a brief walk about while waiting seemed to help. His stomach growled and he regretted not having gathered a snack or something to bring with him from the hotel he stayed in last night, besides the complimentary shortbread biscuits he'd snaffled from his room prior to checking out.

The first sailing to Uig would depart at 7:15 and he watched the crew making ready. The ramp was already down, and Duncan looked around at the waiting vehicles, two delivery trucks and a couple of locals making trips to Skye. His phone rang and he glanced at the screen. It was Alistair.

"Good morning, Alistair," he said, pressing the phone to his ear to try and minimise the wind noise passing over the microphone.

"Good morning, boss," Alistair said cheerfully which set Duncan's antenna waggling. He was pretty sure he had the measure of his DS, and he wasn't the sort to be so upbeat. "Are you on your way back?"

"Waiting to embark now," Duncan said, glancing towards the ferry. "Why?"

"Just thought you might take the opportunity to speak with Nicol while you're there?"

"Nicol Nicolson?"

"Aye, I stopped by his place yesterday and his mum told me his shift pattern has him on the Uig to Lochmaddy run, so he'll be on your sailing."

Duncan cast an eye over the crew readying the boat to set sail, in their high viz jackets and woollen beanies, wondering if any of them were Nicol.

"I'll see if I can find him." Duncan saw one of the crew stride down the ramp, waving towards the waiting vehicles. Engines fired up behind him and Duncan opened his car door. "We're just about to load up, Alistair. Is there anything else?"

"Yeah, the pathologist has emailed me. Those extra tests he commissioned... well, the results are back from the lab in Glasgow."

Duncan waited, one hand on the roof of the car watching the first truck move off. The ferry crew wanted the trucks on first which stood to reason. The heaviest vehicles would sit in the centre of the vehicle deck with the smaller cars parking to either side, evenly distributing the weight. He always found that unnerving, logical, but unnerving, as if the crew expected the ferry to capsize on its way across The Minch.

"And? What did they find?"

"Strong suspicion of sepsis."

"Blood poisoning," Duncan said, surprised.

"Aye, but that's not all the good doctor has to say. During the autopsy, he found a... let me get this right," Alistair said, breathing into the mouthpiece as he adjusted his position,

probably to read from his screen or a file in front of him, "…
here it is, a minor tear in the uterine wall. Yep, that's how he
described it."

"Which means?" Duncan asked, his eyes narrowing,
contemplating the significance.

"Initially, he put it down to decomposition over time as
well as the shifting position of the body along with the movement of the peat bank, you know?"

"And now?"

Alistair hesitated. "Well… he thinks Isla may well have
been pregnant."

"Say that again," Duncan asked, unsure he heard correctly
over the noise of the wind and the vehicle engines
around him.

"Pregnant… with child… well, not pregnant as such. More
like, had been pregnant recently, before she died. When the
test results came back, he took another look at the pathology
and has concluded she died from septicaemia, the result of an
infection likely originating in her uterus, hence looking again
at the uterine tear."

"No one said she seemed ill the night she disappeared,"
Duncan said, thinking aloud.

"Aye, and although sepsis is a killer, it does take time to
knock you down. Which means…"

"She didn't die the night she went missing," Duncan said.
"She must have been somewhere else for a time beforehand."

"Several days at least. Maybe more."

"Is the doctor's conclusion she miscarried or—"

"He doesn't believe so, no. His best guess, and he stressed
it is a guess, is that the pregnancy was aborted which would
explain the damage to her uterus."

"Right."

The crewman signalled for Duncan to get his car aboard

the ferry. The driver of the car behind him in the queue to embark gestured for him to get a move on and Duncan waved for him to go past, which he duly did.

"I really need to get aboard or they'll sail without me," Duncan said. "Have you checked to see if Isla—"

"She wasn't booked in for any procedure here on Skye in the weeks leading up to her going missing," Alistair said, "if that's what you were about to ask?"

"I was," Duncan said, getting into his car and turning the key in the ignition. Condensation had formed on the windscreen and he leaned forward, giving the moisture a cursory wipe with his sleeve so he could at least see where he was going, enough to get aboard anyway.

"Doesn't mean she couldn't have gone to a clinic somewhere on the mainland for it, mind."

"Yeah... but without anyone knowing? Is that likely?"

"Who said no one knew about it?" Alistair countered. "Just because they didn't tell us."

"Fair point," Duncan said, switching the call onto speaker and driving slowly towards the ramp. "Maybe that's why she went missing, leaving the island for that? What about aftercare?" Duncan asked. "They check these things. You're not discharged without support."

"I wouldn't know," Alistair said in jocular fashion. "Never had the need personally, but I'll happily bow to your knowledge on the subject."

Duncan felt defensive and he snapped back, "Yeah, well anyone who's lived a bit knows this kinda stuff."

"All right, all right," Alistair said, his tone changing to conciliatory. "I just meant—"

"No, no," Duncan said, following the directions of the crew as to where they wanted him to park, "it's me, don't worry. I didn't sleep well last night, that's all... and I'm hungry."

"Shame. I had them book you into the best hotel on the island."

"Yeah, it's not the hotel. I'm sure it's me… a lot of upheaval these past few days, you know?"

"Aye, right enough. You've got nearly a couple of hours to kill on the boat. Hit the Mariners Café first, the Stornoway Black Pudding is fantastic, and then you can always see if you can have that word with Nicolson."

"Sounds like a plan." Duncan switched his engine off. The other passengers were already making their way to the upper deck, so he guessed he'd be at the back of the queue for food. "Okay, I'll be back in Portree around ten o'clock. We'll regroup and go from there."

"Don't be tempted to throw Nicol overboard when you speak to him," Alistair said, finding his joviality returning. "He's a horrid wee bam, so I'm told."

"Thanks for the tip."

Duncan hung up and got out of the car. He could smell the seaweed and taste the salt on the air as he made his way to the stairs. Something about being surrounded by the immense steels, welded together to form this ship, along with the sea mist lingering around him and the pooled water in places on the deck made it feel colder somehow.

A crewman finished securing the ramp in place and was heading towards him as Duncan caught his attention.

"Do you know if Nicol is about this morning?"

The man looked at him as he passed, nodding. "Aye, he's about. You wanting him for something?"

"Aye, when he has a moment."

"I'll let him know."

"Cheers. I'll be in the cafe."

The crewman nodded and disappeared through a door off limits to passengers and Duncan climbed the steep stairs to the upper deck following the signs to the cafeteria, the smell of bacon ensuring his stomach reminded him of its presence.

Duncan was mopping up the last of his beans with a bread roll when a man entered the cafeteria stopping near the till, his eyes searching the assembled passengers. He was easily six foot tall, with thinning wispy hair swept up in a quiff that wouldn't pass muster at an Elvis impersonation contest. Dressed in an orange coverall with high viz patches to the cuffs and across the shoulder, his face was drawn with dark circles beneath the eyes. He wiped his nose with the back of his hand, his gaze settling on Duncan.

"Are you looking for me, pal?" he asked, coming to stand at the table.

"Aye. Duncan McAdam," he said, introducing himself as he wiped his fingers with a paper napkin before screwing it into a ball and tossing it onto the plate in front of him. Nicol Nicolson cast an eye over him.

"Do we know each other?"

Duncan shook his head, producing his warrant card from his back pocket and gesturing for Nicol to pull out a seat opposite. Nicol seemed puzzled but took the offered seat anyway.

"DI Duncan McAdam," he said, presenting his identification to Nicol who shifted uncomfortably now he knew he was in the presence of a policeman.

"The polis?"

Duncan nodded, sipping from his coffee cup to aid swallowing the last mouthful of roll. "I'm investigating the death of Isla Matheson."

"Oh right, Isla… aye," Nicol said quietly, nodding. He was a slightly-built man, wiry, and apparently of a nervous disposition. Although Duncan often had that effect on people when he first met them in an official capacity. It was an almost routine response that any police officer would recognise. He was used to it.

"You remember that night on Coral Beach, the night when Isla was last seen alive?"

"Aye, of course."

"What do you remember?"

Nicol frowned, his eyes flickering around them. "It was a good bash, like, you know? The last big party before the end of the summer."

"Isla was popular, I heard."

He nodded. "She was having a big night, it's true."

"A lot of attention from the men."

Nicol smiled awkwardly. "Aye, you could say that."

"A lot of attention from you?"

His intonation made it sound accusatory and Nicol's smile faded to an expression of concern.

"Ah… hey, we were all having a good time that night… you cannae single me oot like."

"No, I won't, Nicol," Duncan said, sitting forward and resting his elbows on the table. The boat lurched to the left, the contents of his coffee cup sloshing and spilling over the rim. Duncan steadied it with his right hand. "But, of all the people present at that particular party, only you have an arrest for sexual harassment."

Nicol flushed red which Duncan had expected. He seemed to shrink into himself, checking they were out of earshot of other passengers and crew.

"That was all a misunderstanding… it wasn't like—"

"A misunderstanding?" Duncan frowned. "You were arrested at a gig in Glasgow—"

"Aye… but we were all dancing…"

"Drinking… having fun…"

"That's right, drinking and having fun. It's not like I was out on the prowl or anything. It just got a bit... misconstrued."

"That night on Coral Beach, you were all drinking, dancing and having fun too, weren't you?" Duncan asked. Nicol nodded. "And Isla was having a better time than most. Maybe things got a little... misconstrued then too? You thought you'd join in and—"

"Now look!" Nicol said, his voice rising as he jabbed a finger angrily towards Duncan, drawing everyone's eyes towards him. He cleared his throat, realising people were slyly watching him from the corner of their eyes and lowered his hand, looking pensive. A few eyes stayed focussed on him, no doubt watching his outburst keenly. It was the most entertaining spectacle passengers would see on such a crossing.

Nicol leaned forward on the table, his hands clamped together forming a ball and he raised it to cover his mouth. His gaze lifted to meet Duncan's but they didn't convey anger; it was fear that Duncan now saw in his expression. "I didn't... I wouldn't hurt Isla. She was lovely... and I knew back then that a girl like her would never look at a guy like me. Not ever. I'm not daft, you know?"

"Some men don't worry about that sort of thing, Nicol. Some won't take no for an answer."

Nicol shook his head, deep creases forming on his brow.

"Some men don't even ask," Duncan added, "and they just help themselves."

"No' me," he said, forcibly shaking his head. "That's no' me, not anymore."

"Not anymore?" Duncan asked, arching an eyebrow.

"I'm not..." he looked around, lowering his voice. "You make me sound like... a... a... I'm no' a rapist!"

"Then what are you?"

Nicol met his eye, thrusting out his lower jaw. Closing his

eyes momentarily, his eyelids fluttered in an involuntary movement as he stammered a reply. "I-I-I'm friendly… o-overly… friendly," he said at last. "I dinnae mean anything by it, and I only drink to be sociable… and it sort of comes out of me sometimes. I swear, I dinnae mean anything by it, I really don't."

Duncan was curious. Nicol's twitch and stammer only appeared when he felt under pressure. It was not quite the cold, calculating response of a man who had been getting away with murder for two decades or more. Although admittedly, caught off guard, who knows how one might react if they were guilty. After all, he'd never met this man before.

"And were you *overly friendly* with Isla that particular night, on Coral Beach?"

Nicol cast his eyes downwards at the table in front of him, his hands cupped in his lap now. He nodded.

"Did she let you know she wasn't interested?"

Nicol's head snapped up. "It was just a wee kiss… nothing heavy."

"And how did she react?"

He shrugged. "Seemed fine with it. She smiled… and just walked off. Didnae seem bothered by it at all. I reckon she took it as a compliment, you know?"

"That must have stung though, her walking off like that; discarding you like you're not worthy of her."

Nicol looked at him quizzically. "What's that you're saying?"

"To be rejected by Isla… in front of your peers? Painful. The humiliation could make someone angry, especially someone who can't control their urges."

"Oh… it was nothing," he said, glumly, lowering his gaze. "Isla was in a funny mood that night… toying with people, winding them up. I was one of many. I canna take it personally."

"Who was she winding up?"

He shrugged. "Anyone she could, as I see it. Guys, girls… the ex-boyfriend. It was like she was craving the attention. People with low self-esteem need attention, don't they? That's what they say."

"You're saying Isla was… what… depressed?"

"Oh, I wouldn't know about that like, but that's what people do when they feel bad about themselves, isn't it? Either they hide or they come out as larger than life, masking it all behind a quick smile and a bit of flirting. Isla was the latter."

"What did she have to be down about?" Duncan asked. Nicol made to dismiss the question without answering, implying he wouldn't know, but Duncan persisted. "Hazard a guess for me."

"She wasn't happy with her lot I suppose," Nicol said. "A lot of us knew that, so it's no' my imagination. She wasn't exactly the shy type, Isla. Unsurprising I guess, bearing in mind who her father is."

"Ruaridh?"

"Aye. The most pious figure on the island. You know he was a Stornoway man, right?"

Duncan shook his head.

"Well, no greater killjoy there is on this here island."

"She could have followed her brother's example," Duncan said, "and left for the mainland. As I understand it, she had no plans to though."

Nicol scoffed. "Donnie was something else though, eh?" He smiled. "A real character, special. What I'd have given to be in his shoes for a few years."

"He's back now though."

"Aye, he is," Nicol said, the smile fading. "The pendulum

swung aways off but then it comes back, doesn't it? The apple disnae fall too far from the tree like."

Duncan smiled. "I suppose not." Thinking of his own father, he hoped that wasn't always the case.

The PA crackled into life, announcing a garbled message that Duncan couldn't understand, but Nicol, familiar with hearing it daily, cocked his head. He frowned, appearing thoughtful, but didn't say anything.

"When was the last time you saw Isla Matheson, Nicol?"

He looked at Duncan, his mouth must have been dry because he struggled to swallow. "On the beach," he said, nodding, "when I was with everyone else. I've no idea what time it was… I'd been drinking."

Duncan held his gaze, gauging Nicol's reaction. The PA burst into life again and Nicol listened to the message.

"I'm needed," he said, turning to Duncan and spreading his hands wide. "I really need to go. Are we through here?" he asked, hopeful.

Duncan nodded. "What is it you do on the boat?"

"I'm a mechanical tech… keep the engines running and that."

"That sounds important."

He shrugged, standing up. "It is if we break down. I spent three days adrift a few years back… and trust me, you dinnae want to be on the boat when that happens, eh."

"Good job though, is it?"

"Aye, the pay is good… and the hours, regular."

"I may need to speak with you again, Nicol."

Nicol's eyes stared at him, still fearful. He replied with a curt nod and departed. Duncan exhaled and stifled a yawn, watching the man walk away.

CHAPTER FIFTEEN

DUNCAN'S TIMINGS WERE ACCURATE. The ferry put into Uig just before nine o'clock in the morning and he found himself returning to Portree a little earlier than expected having had a clean run back across the island. He'd found Nicol Nicolson to be an underwhelming man: nervous, awkward and a couple of degrees removed from reality. Nicol was self-aware, at least to the point that he knew a girl like Isla wouldn't be interested in him, but not aware enough to stop him from trying it on. The man's history of overstepping the mark, or being *overly friendly* as he saw it, was troublesome. He genuinely didn't seem to think he had done anything wrong in that scenario. It was this element of delusion that kept him in Duncan's thoughts.

Was Isla as blasé about his approach as he said or was he glossing over his inappropriate behaviour? What else could Nicol justify in his own mind that any reasonable person would recognise as at best, odd, and at worst downright dangerous?

Planning to park his car in front of the police station, Duncan turned onto Bridge Road leading him into Portree

centre. The first turning into Somerled Square was momentarily blocked by a tour guide's minibus and another coach
negotiating the junction and Duncan had to wait while they
passed each other at the pinch point outside the Sheriff's
court. Looking down the road, people were milling about as
they made an early start on the shops. Two outdoor clothing
stores to the right looked busy and Duncan saw someone
unlocking the door into another small business opposite them
on the other side of the road.

Reading the sign above the door, he realised that must be
Dougal Mackenzie's property shop. The road clear, Duncan
acknowledged the grateful thanks of the coach driver who
looked relieved at successfully navigating the turn before
moving off and heading out of Portree. Parking his car,
Duncan made the short walk around the corner to see if he
could speak to Dougal.

Pushing open the door, Duncan stooped to enter. This was
one of the older buildings in Portree, narrow with a low
ceiling and only one small window facing out onto the street.
It was a classic example of how traditional buildings were
now adapting to modern life, but a far cry from what one
might expect from any major town or city. Built for function,
the town's harbour was once the hub of a large fishing
economy and used as a way point for ships heading to the
Americas in previous centuries. Now though, things had very
much changed.

"Good morning!" a man said with an accompanying
broad grin. He was in his forties, slightly overweight but
wearing a smartly-tailored Oxford-style shirt and shiny
chrome cuff links, a bright burnt orange tie completed the
look. He had his landline phone in his hand but he replaced it
upon the desk as Duncan entered. Standing, he came from
behind his desk, his eyes narrowing as if trying to decide if

they'd met previously or if Duncan was a potential new client.

"Duncan McAdam," he said, shaking hands.

"McAdam... ah, you must be Roslyn's brother. Am I right?"

Duncan nodded.

"I thought I recognised you."

Duncan couldn't see how; he bore little resemblance to his sister in his mind.

"Dougal Mackenzie," he said, grinning.

"You know my sister?"

"Very well," Dougal said, and then he tilted his head, mock grimacing. "Sort of. I've lost count of the number of times I've spoken to her about your father's old croft out in Balmaqueen." He sighed. "It's a shame to see such a beautiful old place like that falling into rack and ruin, don't you think? I know it's painful for Roslyn too."

Duncan pursed his lips. He hadn't been home for years and, if he was honest, he wasn't inclined to take a trip down memory lane either. Dougal was building up a head of steam though and he wasn't finished with what Duncan guessed was his pitch for an instruction.

"You know, the old byre you have there as well... you could make good use of that these days; convert it to holiday accommodation or just obtain the planning and sell it as is. You know, I was telling Roslyn that if we split the croft into two parts, one building and another of the land and the byre, we'd likely get more offers and generate a larger profit than selling it as a whole. You could even add a contemporary extension to the house first, orient it towards the water. What do you think?"

"I think it's a working croft," Duncan said, shaking his

head. "The Crofting Commission would need to be involved, along with local crofter assent and—"

"Details," Dougal said, waving away Duncan's argument. "The land can be tenanted, no problem. Besides, that can all be sorted out later, let the solicitors do their thing. It's all they're good for, after all." He held up a hand. "That spot, overlooking the water, is absolutely *to die for*. People will be falling over themselves to bid on it."

"Aye, probably," Duncan said, understanding that although Dougal was probably right it would not be the easy transaction that he made it out to be. That community fiercely defended the traditional way of life on the island. They welcomed newcomers, in his mind, but they valued their heritage and rightly so. He could already see how Dougal had got certain people's backs up with this type of approach. "I thought there was a downturn in the housing market coming anyway?"

"Ah… only in the areas where you've seen under supply and high demand. What goes up the most, the fastest, usually takes the biggest hit on the way back down. It's simple economics." He offered a dismissive wave of his hand with an exaggerated exhale. "And you know what they say about economists?"

Duncan turned the corners of his mouth down and shook his head.

"That they successfully predicted six of the last three recessions." Dougal grinned at his joke. Duncan smiled politely. Dougal cleared his throat. "Comedy isn't my thing, so I should stick to what I'm good at, which is selling property. I'm a bit surprised."

"About what?"

"That Roslyn sent you to see me. She hadn't mentioned

your involvement. I thought you were living on the mainland. Glasgow, isn't it?"

The man certainly retained information well.

"I do," Duncan said. "You know your stuff."

Dougal grinned. "Property is a details business, Duncan. "What brings you home?"

"I'm just back for a wee while, but I'm not actually here to talk about my parents' place. I need to speak to you on another matter."

"Oh…" Dougal was surprised. "What about?"

Duncan took out his warrant card and presented it to Dougal who baulked.

"I'm investigating the death of Isla Matheson," Duncan said.

"Oh… Isla… right. I didn't know you were in the police."

Duncan cocked his head. "I think Ros is a little embarrassed about it. Some people can be a bit funny about the police, and as for having a family member in the law…"

"Not me," Dougal said. "Very supportive of the police. I donated to the Federation fundraiser last year, same as I do every year."

"That's… very generous," Duncan said, smiling politely. "About Isla, I understand you gave a statement around the time of her disappearance…"

"I did, yes. Although, I wasn't much use, I don't think."

"It was your party, wasn't it?"

"Oh no… it was all of us… a group thing. I did bring the music and got things jumping, as we used to say back in the day. I don't think that counts as making it *my* party though."

"I understand you were romantically involved with Isla that night."

Dougal's lips parted and he looked vacantly at him.

"I… wouldn't say that."

Duncan nodded. "Then what would you say?"

He frowned, rolling his lips as he thought. "We had a wee kiss... but... I wasn't the only one. She was on the wind-up that night, quite a tease."

"So I understand," Duncan said. "How did it make you feel, Isla's behaviour that night?"

He shrugged. "Didn't feel anything to be quite honest with you."

"Really? A confident young woman taking an interest in you, only to discard you and move on to someone else. It can't have been nice."

Dougal frowned. "What is this? I heard you're looking at a guy off island who may have been responsible." Duncan was surprised to hear the rumour but, knowing Jameson was exploring that notion, he couldn't rule it out as being true. Not that he let on.

"It's an ongoing investigation," Duncan said. "Details of which I won't discuss, however we are speaking to everyone present that night to see if their recollections have changed at all with the passage of time."

"Oh, right." Dougal visibly relaxed. "Yes, of course. I... erm..." He shrugged. "I don't think I have anything else to say. It was all much like any other night when we all got together. A lot of drinks... laughs... it didn't rain for once," he said, smiling. "It was a fun night. There was no indication of anything untoward going on that I noticed. What happened to Isla... is shocking to this day."

Duncan nodded.

"I'm really sorry," Dougal said. "I wish I could help more. It's a nasty old business. Poor Isla."

"Looking back, was there anyone who seemed to you to be annoyed with her?"

"Annoyed enough to kill her?"

"I didn't say that."

Dougal exhaled, his eyes flickering away from Duncan and around his small office. "I guess she got under the skin of a couple of the lasses who were there. The flirting didn't go down well with some." He tilted his head, wincing. "Who can blame them for getting annoyed. The boys who were there… well, let's say it was slim pickings for the girls, so Isla being as she was wound some of them up."

"And the guys? Did anyone take exception to being picked up and dumped in quick succession?"

"Ah… well, no one likes to be dumped when they think they're in with a hot girl, do they?"

"No." Duncan shook his head. "No, they don't. Any names spring to mind? Besides yours."

Dougal wagged a finger at Duncan and then thought about it, pursing his lips. Bobbing his head, as if answering an unspoken internal question, he looked at Duncan. "I reckon Roddy was a little bit tense about it all."

"Roddy Mcintyre?"

"Yes. He was tight with Isla. We always reckoned he had it bad for her, but it was always unrequited love where she was concerned. It must have burned him that she wouldn't come near him. The lad was definitely in the friend zone, you know? He left it way too long to make his move, destined to forever see her stroll out with other guys."

"Okay," Duncan said, making a note of it. "Thanks for that. So, you were one of the magnificent seven then?"

Dougal looked at him, puzzled.

"One of the seven Isla kissed that night?"

"Oh aye, right." He smiled sheepishly. "Was it seven? I don't remember, but these things get exaggerated, don't they? I remember it being the Famous Four… or Five." He offered a dismissive flick of his hand. "It was a few kisses randomly thrown around the group, that's all. I wouldn't pay too much attention to gossip," he said, still smiling. "Those lasses I was telling you about. Isla really got up their noses... and they didn't let us guys forget about how enthralled we were with Isla that night either. They had the hump with us *for weeks* afterwards as a result."

"What brought that on do you think?"

"Jealousy... a horrible trait," Dougal said. He sighed. "And very unattractive too. Thankfully, it didn't last. My Kirsty forgave me anyway." Duncan looked at him enquiringly. "Kirsty... Blake, as she was back then. She was there that night. We got married... eventually, some years later obviously." He smiled wistfully. "She made me work for it though."

Duncan smiled. "Okay, thanks for your time, Dougal."

"No problem at all. Now, if you want to talk to me about your parents' place, then I'm available whenever you need me." He grinned, the quick ersatz smile of a salesman flashing across his face. "Seriously though, you'll want to make a move soon because who knows how long the seller's market will be around. Things change quickly."

"Not on this island, they don't," Duncan said, flatly. Dougal cocked his head, raising one eyebrow and nodding approvingly at the comment. "But I'll certainly bear it in mind."

"Aye, do that. Have a chat with Roslyn and then give me a call." He scooped up a business card from the top of a small pile on his desk, handing it to him. Duncan glanced at it before slipping it into his pocket.

"Thanks again," he said, making his way to the door.

Roslyn hadn't mentioned she'd been considering selling the old place, although he shouldn't be surprised. Roslyn's husband was working their family croft alongside his own, and Ronnie wasn't getting any younger. And as Duncan knew from the way his dad struggled to get by, crofting alone didn't pay the bills. That was always the way though. The landowners ensuring they maintained a tethered labour force to the island by parcelling up the croft land in such a way as to guarantee it wasn't large enough to provide for an entire family; a deliberate policy to maintain serfdom via the back door.

Back outside, it was drizzling. It wasn't heavy, annoying more than anything else and it aligned with Duncan's mood. The mention of his family croft clouded his mind, memories flooding unbidden and confusing his thoughts. Trying to push the images away, he sought to focus on the conversations he'd had with Dougal and Nicol Nicolson before on the ferry ride. Both men recalled that night on Coral Beach differently. Dougal was dismissive of Isla's behaviour, seeing what was said afterwards as jealous gossip aimed at Isla, a teenage girl having fun, whereas Nicol gave the impression of Isla as calculating in her actions. It wasn't impossible for them both to be remembering accurately. Opinions often differed; it was about perspective.

Perhaps they were both right, or neither.

Rounding the corner into Somerled Square, Duncan looked at the police station. He didn't want to go inside. DCI Jameson had made it clear to him that his presence wasn't deemed necessary and the task he'd been set could easily be overseen by a competent detective sergeant. Alistair MacEachran was such a DS.

Taking out his mobile, he called him.

"Alistair, I've got an errand I need to run."

"Oh, do yer, aye?"

Duncan laughed, detecting the sarcasm in his tone and picturing his facial expression. "You can hold the fort and I'll be in at some point later on."

Not waiting for a reply, he put his phone away. Walking to his car with the station in the background, he felt like he was pulling a sickie but he didn't care.

He had one quick stop to make first, but then he'd be out of town for a few hours.

CHAPTER SIXTEEN

THE TRACK WAS PITTED and uneven in places, the car pitching into the potholes and making protestations via shrieks and groans as he progressed towards the old house. Although, some work had been done in recent years because the access road had been resurfaced and was far better than he remembered.

The rain was still falling steadily and, when he drew the car into a gravelled turning area before the house, he couldn't make out the distant Western Isles usually visible across The Minch. On a clear day they loomed out at him on the horizon, the last tracts of land before the vast expanse of the Atlantic Ocean. Many an evening as a child he'd sit by the water's edge at the foot of the croft watching passing ships, often late into the evening. On occasion he'd see a Royal Navy flotilla making its way around the British Isles and he'd become quite adept at making out the different type of vessels.

His grandfather had served in the Navy, fifteen years, signing up as soon as he could, leaving school early having gained his parents' permission. Having travelled the world, he'd come back to Skye and would regale his grandchildren, Duncan and Roslyn, with his adventures in the Middle East, notably Bahrain, visits to South America and anywhere in between. The children, Duncan especially, had been captivated by the stories, but that's all they were, according to their dad anyway, stories. *Nothing as real as a lie that's told with a grain of truth* their dad had repeatedly told them, dismissive of his father's tales.

Duncan's dad had a troubled relationship with their grandfather; a situation that seemed to follow in the family with the next generation too. Was his grandfather a man who liked to spin a yarn or was the negativity directed at the stories the result of Big Duncan's own perceived inadequacy at having never left the island to explore the world? Duncan didn't know. And now he never would.

Getting out of the car, he drew his coat around him. A ewe made her presence known, calling from above him on the gentle slope up from the side of the house. Duncan walked towards the property, casting a cursory glance over it. It was stone built, once white-washed, but the salt carrying on the sea air alongside the harsh climate had stripped much of the colour away now. Wild grass grew in clumps at the foot of the exterior walls and the stonework looked damp with moss growing on both the internal and external walls. Much of the glazing was missing from the windows, the wooden frames having rotted away to such an extent they could no longer hold the panes in place.

The roof, once traditionally thatched but subsequently replaced with cheaper, easy to maintain corrugated metal sheets, painted red, had now collapsed in on the house. The rafters and roof joists, exposed to the elements had deteriorated to such a degree Duncan was reluctant to go inside. The corrugated sheets still fixed in place rattled and shrieked, encouraged by the stiff sea breeze whipping between the exposed walls. The place was in a sorry state. It wasn't the house pictured in his mind's eye anymore.

"What are you doing up here?"

He turned, seeing Roslyn standing beside the barn located at the gated entrance to the croft. A quad bike was parked behind her, the engine idling. He hadn't heard her arrive which he found unnerving. Despite the prevailing wind masking her approach, he was still surprised he hadn't heard her but so lost was he in the memories of his past he must have zoned out.

"Hi, Ros," he said, slowly walking to meet her halfway. She waited for him, hands on hips, watching him closely. She must have been tending to the sheep, dressed in her wet-weather gear and wellies, ready to face whatever Mother Nature threw at her.

"Are you out here looking for me?" she asked.

He shook his head, then looked back at the house. "No, I just figured I should come out and have a look at the old place."

Roslyn arched her eyebrows; she didn't believe him. It was fair enough, as he hadn't said it with much conviction.

"I've just come from town," he said, turning back to her. "I was chatting with Dougal. You remember Dougal Mackenzie?"

Her expression clouded and she crossed her arms in front of her, nodding slowly. "Aye, I know Dougal. What's he got to say to you?"

Duncan smiled, feeling like he was walking into something he possibly didn't understand. "He said he's been talking to you about selling the house."

She smiled then, but it wasn't warm. "Oh, did he, aye?"

"You haven't?"

"Oh… he has, right enough. It's non-stop with Dougal. He's been getting onto me and Ronnie for the past eighteen months or so… promises the earth does Dougal."

"You don't think he can deliver?"

"I don't care either way, Duncan. The man's a shark."

Duncan cocked his head. "If you're selling then that's what you want, isn't it, the biggest shark in the tank?"

"And who says I'm interested in selling the place?" she asked, looking past him at the dilapidated house.

Duncan shrugged, casting an eye over the croft as well. "Maybe we should consider it? Not the land – I know you and Ronnie are working it – but the house. We could apply to decroft the house… sell it on as is," he glanced at the ruined shell of their childhood home, "or do it up and sell it on."

Roslyn sneered. "To some city type who'll rent it out to the tourists flitting about the island?"

"Yes… if they want to buy it. Who cares what they do with it?"

She snorted with derision. "What's this *we* anyway, Duncan?"

"Well, we both own the croft… don't we?"

She laughed. It was a dry sound, which was the only thing dry where they were standing, the rain was lessening now although the breeze was stiffening.

"Isn't that just typical of you, Duncan."

"What?"

"You swan in here for the first time in years… make some sweeping statements with your grand ideas and then you'll no doubt sod off back to the mainland. Stop me if I'm getting ahead of myself."

Duncan grimaced. "I didn't think it would upset you—"

"Did you *actually* think at all, though, Duncan? I mean, really consider it or are you just lashing out the same as you always have? The petulant little brat that you've always been?"

Duncan's jaw clenched and he tilted his head. "That's a bit harsh, Ros."

"Is it? You think so, do you?" she asked, nodding sarcastically. "Nothing changes, does it, Duncan? You drop in when it suits you, kick the litter tray over and then clear off leaving everyone else to clean up your mess. Always running away."

He was puzzled. "What the hell is that supposed to mean?"

"It means the rest of us have to stay here... and *take responsibility* for the consequences of our actions. Whereas others," she said, pointing at him accusingly, "do exactly the opposite."

"What are you on about? Are you still not over the fact I moved to Glasgow or something?"

"Among other things, aye!"

"Sweet Jesus, Ros, that was nigh on fifteen years ago! Get over it, yeah."

"Leaving me to deal with the fall-out as usual—"

"I had to go!" Duncan said, feeling his anger rising. "You know I had to go when I did—"

"Do I? Why... why then, Duncan? Tell me now because you never bothered before."

He turned away from her, mindful of not wanting to say something he'd regret. Roslyn was having none of it though and she chased after him, the colour rising in her cheeks. She grabbed his forearm, pulling him and forcing him to turn and face her.

"Why, Duncan?"

He yanked his arm away from her. "I had a place at university."

"You didn't leave to get an education, Duncan. You never gave a damn about school, so that's just an excuse. You couldn't wait to leave school and you applied to university through clearing... it was all last minute—"

"Yes, because I *had* to go!" he snapped.

"Why?" she shouted at him as he made to leave again, pursuing him as he walked away. Duncan spun on his heel, squaring up to her.

"Because otherwise I'd have bloody killed him... and you know it!"

His aggression saw the colour drain from her face and she hesitated, taking a step backwards. Duncan saw the fear in her eyes and immediately backed down, holding his hands up in apology and lowering his eyes. When he raised his head, he saw tears in Roslyn's eyes. Her expression reminded him of her face the day he'd packed his bag, leaving with only an hour's notice. She'd followed him outside, begging him not to go but he'd made his decision and he'd ignored her pleas.

"I had to go," he repeated quietly.

Roslyn held his gaze, wiping her eyes clear of the forming tears. She nodded. "I know you did."

Silence. It was awkward. After a moment, Roslyn broke it with a question.

"Have you ever wondered what it might be like if things had been different?"

He looked at her quizzically. "Different? How different?"

She shrugged. "You know... at home. You might never have left the island."

"Oh... I'd have to have left the island sooner or later. I mean, could you see me moving sheep around from field to field?"

"What's wrong with that? It's honest graft."

He placated her with a raised hand. "I know. I don't mean anything by it, but… for me?"

She smiled. "I guess not."

"Do you then?" he asked.

"Do I what?"

"Wonder how different things might have been for you. I mean, you married Ronnie to get away from home. It could have been anyone—"

She snorted. "You utter bastard, Duncan."

The words came out completely wrong. That wasn't what he'd meant to say and he felt guilty. "I-I didn't mean it like—"

"Duncan!"

He turned to see his brother-in-law, Ronnie Macdougall, striding towards them, grinning. Their collie ran past him and hurtled up to Duncan and Roslyn, running rings around them, sniffing at Duncan's ankles before deciding he was of little interest and leaping up at Roslyn who made a brief fuss of him before sending him on his way. The dog wandered away to find something else more entertaining.

"Hello, Ronnie. How are you?" Duncan asked, shaking hands with him, hoping he hadn't witnessed his outburst.

"Braw, Dunc, braw." Ronnie leaned away from Duncan, still gripped in a handshake, casting a searching eye across Duncan's expression. "Much better than you by the looks of you. What have you been up to? You look dreadful, man." Glancing sideways at his wife, Roslyn sought to avoid scrutiny by looking away, keen for him not to pay too close attention to her, perhaps to not see her emotion. Not that it mattered. Ronnie read her expression and instantly figured he'd walked in on something. "Catching up, I see."

Duncan smiled awkwardly. "Digging up the past."

Ronnie winced. "Ah well… for everything else that it is, the past is a forgotten country. Best leave it that way, eh?"

Duncan smiled politely. If only it was that simple. Ronnie was a decent man. He was a few years older than Roslyn, pushing fifty now he guessed. He was carrying a bit of extra weight from the last time he'd seen him but that had been years ago. Ronnie's hair was now more grey than red, his beard thinner and he was fuller in the face.

"So, what are you doing up here at the croft, Duncan?" Ronnie asked.

"Duncan wants to sell it," Roslyn said flatly before he had a chance to answer.

"Is that so?" Ronnie said, looking at him with a stern expression. "Cashing in on the scenic view, are you?"

Duncan looked out over The Minch. The weather front had passed swiftly and with it the rain, which was lessening as they stood there, allowing the sunshine to stream through the break in the clouds, reflecting off the water. The Western Isles were visible through a haze of sea mist signalling another bank of cloud was on its way to them.

Duncan shrugged. "It's not that. I just thought if you were thinking of selling up, then it might be a good idea."

Ronnie glanced at his wife. "Are we thinking of selling up?"

"No, it's that sod Dougal stirring it again. He knows damn well we're not up for selling."

"Aye…" Ronnie said, looking at Duncan. "Dougal has been sniffing around for ages. He'll no' take no for an answer."

"I got the wrong end of the stick," Duncan said. He turned pointedly to Roslyn. "I'm sorry. I really didn't mean to upset you… about anything."

"It's fine," she said, turning away from him without

meeting his eye. It clearly wasn't fine at all. "I've got to crack on," she said, walking away. "Give me a call and let me know when you're wanting to come over to ours for your supper."

Duncan took a deep breath, releasing it slowly. Ronnie fixed him with a judgemental gaze.

"I see you still have your special knack for dealing with women, Duncan."

"It's a gift. What can I say?" he said, shrugging with an embarrassed smile.

Ronnie grinned, revealing stained teeth. He swung an arm around Duncan's shoulder and drew him in for a bear hug. Duncan didn't appreciate it but said nothing. When Ronnie released him, Duncan was relieved, so tight was the man's grip.

"What's the craic now then, Duncan?"

"Ah... I figured I'd stop by and have a drink with the old man."

Ronnie stared at him, his eyes narrowing. "Oh, did you? That's... interesting."

Duncan shrugged. "It's what he would want."

"I dare say you're right." Ronnie smiled. "Come by the house soon, Duncan." He looked across at Roslyn, who was keeping half an eye on them but making out she wasn't. "Don't let it fester, man."

Duncan nodded. "I will." Ronnie arched his eyebrows, indicating scepticism. "I promise."

"Aye, promises, promises," Ronnie said. Duncan smiled and shook his hand again, making for his car. Slowing as he came past the house, Duncan stopped and looked into the ruins of his childhood home. The state of it seemed in keeping with his memories. *How could he carry so much pain from a place that existed within such a beautiful setting?*

The engine of the quad bike picked up and, looking back,

he saw Roslyn riding away without a backward glance. Ronnie was gathering the sheep together and funnelling them into the adjoining field with the aid of his dog. Duncan toyed with the car keys in his hand, feeling the first spots of rain on the incoming breeze.

"Come on then, Dad. Let's go for that drink," he said to himself.

CHAPTER SEVENTEEN

DUNCAN ARRIVED at the end of the track, drawing his car to a stop in the hardcore parking area beside the church yard. This was almost the most northerly tip of Skye, at the site of the old ruin of St Moluag's Church, little more than one stone gable end wall remained, two feet thick, standing like a giant monolith to the dead ancestry of the Isle of Skye. The rest of the church had long since fallen into ruin, the stones carted away for use elsewhere or assembled to form the boundary walls of the graveyard. Within the church grounds were several small enclosures marking off the graves of local dignitaries or wealthier families who could afford to have their resting places separated from those of the common folk. Not that the Old Churchyard of Kilmaluag was home to many with fewer than twenty headstones dotted around.

Reaching across the passenger seat, Duncan opened the glove box and took out the small brown bag he'd put in there earlier before heading out to his family croft and got out of the car. The wind was gusting now, his coat trailing behind him as he made his way towards the walled cemetery, accessed through a metal five-bar gate akin to those used at the entrance to every croft and field to keep the sheep in or out depending on your needs. The hinges of the gate were well maintained and it opened effortlessly.

Duncan closed it behind him, walking across the grass, impressed at how well maintained the ground was. It was rare on this part of the island for as far as the eye could see the ground was largely machair, boggy with sporadic vegetation growth. Someone was paying attention to the churchyard here. Coming to stand before a single, finely crafted and yet simple headstone, he stared at it for a few moments in silent thought. The wind gently buffeted him and the sound of his coat flapping was all he could hear besides the wind itself. Despite Kilmuir, where the old church and cemetery were located, being in the lee of the surrounding hills, they were still susceptible to the prevailing westerly winds coming over the island off the Atlantic.

Behind him, beyond the crest of the hill, Duncan knew there was the famous bothy at Rubha Hunish. It was a timber structure housed on top of the cliffs offering unparalleled views out to sea and across to the Western Isles. Tourists hiked up there regularly and it was a wonder to behold, for the hardy.

Taking the bag out of his coat pocket, Duncan took out the small bottle of scotch, unscrewing the cap. He took a stiff draught of his own, hissing after swallowing as the liquid fire spread throughout his chest. Upending the bottle, he poured the remaining contents onto the grass before the headstone, watching the liquid gurgle and splash its way out until the final trickle dripped from the neck to the ground at his feet.

Duncan sneered, his lip curling. "Here's to you, Dad," he whispered, feeling a shadow cloud over his thoughts. Screwing the cap back on, he put the now empty bottle back into the paper bag and slipped it into the side pocket of his coat. Rubbing at his jaw and cheek with his left hand, he shook his head, turning to leave.

Becoming aware of someone else present on the other side of the wall, Duncan slowed as he approached the gate. It was an elderly man, well wrapped up against the weather in thick coat and trousers, woollen hat and gloved hands, cupped together in his lap. In one hand he loosely held onto a clear tube which draped across his lap and around to his left where it connected to an oxygen canister mounted on the side of his motorised wheelchair. He watched Duncan as he reached the gate, unhooking it and pulling it open.

"We usually prefer flowers when one pays their respects," he said with no hint of aggression or sarcasm. It was merely him stating a fact.

Duncan closed the gate, turning to face him. "Flowers won't last long out here," he said, shuddering from the cold.

The man angled his head. "Whatever works for you, Duncan."

Duncan narrowed his gaze.

"You are wee Duncan McAdam, are you not?"

Duncan felt disadvantaged. He was certain they'd never met and he eyed the man suspiciously, nodding. "Aye, that's me. I'm sorry, but do we know one another?"

The man smiled, revealing tar-stained teeth and deeply receding gums giving his upper canines an almost vampiric look to them. "No, not so as to speak about but I know the names of every individual entombed in this cemetery." He glanced around the surrounding landscape. "In all the cemeteries locally. It was my job after all; the spiritual wellbeing of lost souls in this life and, some would argue, preparing them for the next."

Duncan guessed he was a minister, but Reverend Geddes

had presided over his father's funeral. The man appeared to read Duncan's mind.

"Old John Geddes retired some years ago. He lives in Inverness now."

Duncan nodded. "I see… and you took over from him?"

The man smiled, an action that morphed into a tickly cough and then into wracking, lung-bursting hacking, making Duncan concerned for his wellbeing.

"You shouldn't be out here in this weather."

Although the rain had eased, falling in odd showers now, it was still brutally cold in the wind and for someone chair-bound it wouldn't take long for the elements to seep into you. The man waved away his concern.

"It's far too late for me, young man. When He decides it is time for me to join Him, then I shall go gladly. I live there, next door," he said, pointing to a house barely thirty yards away. He extended his hand towards Duncan and he took it. "I saw you arrive. I must admit to being curious. We don't get many visitors to the cemetery… and certainly not ones I don't recognise… man or car."

"Duncan McAdam," Duncan said, officially making his acquaintance.

"I thought as much," he said, holding Duncan's gaze. "Ruaridh Matheson. Isla Matheson's father."

Duncan was taken aback, but realised he should have guessed, so preoccupied was he with the moment he had planned with his father, the penny had failed to drop. He looked at the house where Ruaridh was living.

"How did you end up all the way out here?"

Ruaridh laughed, before it morphed into more coughing and he raised a gloved hand to his mouth. Duncan wanted to assist, moving closer but was waved away.

"When I had the car accident," Ruaridh said, indicating his

legs, "and I couldn't work anymore, the ministry were able to sort me out with this place." He pointed to the house. "It's owned by the Island Crofting Trust... protecting properties of significant interest, old crofts and the like from becoming business investments. It is a nominal rent, for which I am grateful, and these places help keep people on the island. Giving your life to your God is not wealth generating, I can assure you."

Duncan smiled. "Even so... it's some way out for someone..." he didn't want to offend him and he didn't finish the comment.

"Yes, it is," Ruaridh said, looking across the cemetery, pointing to a grave marker newer than the others and protected by a knee-high railing around it. "My beloved Èibhlin was laid to rest here and it is important for me to be near her. In time, Isla will join her too... as will I."

Duncan nodded solemnly. "And you manage out here by yourself? It can't be easy."

"Don't let the scenery fool you, Mr McAdam. The community is strong here and we all look out for one another."

"I don't doubt it, it was ever thus."

"And my son is not far away, should I need him."

"Yes, I've seen Donnie," Duncan said, and then he cocked his head. "And I remember him in times of old."

Ruaridh's expression leeched disapproval. "Yes, well thankfully those days are behind him now. He came back once he found his calling. He called me late last night to say they'd brought an island man back to investigate Isla's death."

Duncan knew that wasn't quite how it had come about but didn't see the need to explain.

"Is that what brought Donnie back to Skye then... to be a clergyman?"

Ruaridh chuckled. "No, I doubt that very much. He came back to support the family... despite our somewhat fractious relationship, Donnie knew his mother needed him. May she rest in peace. I did too if the truth be known."

"She took her own life, didn't she, your wife?" Duncan asked. There was no way of dancing around what happened. It was common knowledge.

Ruaridh's expression shifted and he stared into the distance at nothing in particular, seemingly lost in thought. After a moment. he nodded. "Yes, she did. The stress of losing one's child, Mr McAdam... is something no parent should have to go through. Without knowing..." he frowned, pensive. "Without closure... it is difficult to find peace with oneself."

"I can only imagine."

"Do you have children?" Ruaridh asked, turning his steel grey eyes upon Duncan. He shook his head. "Then forgive me, but you will find it difficult to understand the sheer scale of the pain that loss imparts. Not that I believe you are not empathetic, but it is such a wicked wrench to lose a child."

Duncan didn't wish to speak, and so he waited patiently.

"Couple that with what happened to me," he said, patting his right leg with his hand."

"What did happen if you don't mind my asking? I understand you were involved in a car crash."

"No, I don't mind at all," he said, drawing breath. "After Isla went missing... we knew the police were out looking for her, as were our friends and my congregation, everyone pulling together to find our daughter. But, despite everyone's best efforts, it wasn't enough and I couldn't sit by the telephone waiting for it to ring with news. I've never been one to wait for things to happen around me. You see, I'm someone who has to be out there, making a difference... usually to other people's lives rather than my own." He sighed. "But it is what it is."

"You were out looking for Isla?"

He nodded, glumly. "Every night I would find myself driving around the island, looking everywhere where I thought she might be. Old haunts that we visited as a family... places her friends told me she liked to frequent... places a parent isn't supposed to know about," he said, tapping the end of his nose with the tip of his forefinger. Duncan smiled. "After all, having been through all of this with her brother, Donnie, I had some idea of places she was likely to go to."

"And you had an accident?"

He sighed, shaking his head. "I was dog tired... and I'd been out scouring the island for what felt like days. I mean, it had been day after day after day. It was relentless, particularly those first few days after she went missing." He leaned forward in his chair, grimacing with discomfort. Duncan frowned, offering help but Ruaridh dismissed him. "There's nothing that can be done aside from getting out of this blasted thing," he said, tapping the arms of the chair. "And then I have to sit in another chair... or go to bed. It's not much of a life, Mr McAdam, but it is the one planned for me."

"Did you fall asleep at the wheel?" Duncan asked, returning to the accident.

Ruaridh blew air through his clenched teeth. "Possibly. I don't recall. I remember coming round inside the car. It was on its side at that point and I was still restrained by my seatbelt. I couldn't move. I was there for what seemed like hours... and it was hours," he said, laughing dryly. "I came off the road very late at night and I wasn't found until dawn the following morning. By that time," he looked down at his legs... "they struggled to make good, so to speak." He smiled at Duncan, looking heavenward. "I was lucky. Someone was looking out for me that night. It wasn't my time."

Duncan nodded. "Where was it that you came off the road?"

"Just west of Edinbane." He shook his head. "For the life of me I can't think how I managed it there... the road is good but, maybe as you say, I fell asleep." He fixed Duncan with a stare. "And now you're here to find out what happened to my daughter all those years ago?"

"Not only me," Duncan said. "There is a dedicated team that's been drafted in to review the case."

"No one knows this island like we know it, though. Isn't that right, Mr McAdam?"

Duncan smiled again. "Perhaps. I'm confident we will though, get to the bottom of it, I mean. I'm sorry that our efforts will not bring comfort to your late wife."

"Thank you, Mr McAdam. It was a tragedy... what happened to my beloved Èibhlin. I do so hope that the Lord will offer her dispensation for the choice she made to end her suffering."

"Is your God a forgiving god or a vengeful one?" Duncan asked.

Ruaridh eyed him warily. "Now that is a question for a theologian. The Old Testament God was a wrathful god... and I would hope that the God I've devoted my life to would not be so rigid in His views."

"Is that a more recent standpoint you've adopted there?" Duncan asked, knowing the man's reputation for piety.

Ruaridh smiled. "I have... softened in recent times, I must say. Is that a result of ageing... experiencing my own suffering or seeing that of my wife and son? Perhaps." He lifted his chin, gently scratching at his neck. He hadn't shaved for a couple of days based on the stubble he was sporting. All of this, his words, the way he presented himself... it all seemed a far cry from the Reverend Ruaridh Matheson people close to Isla spoke of from the time she disappeared and their view of him now.

Ruaridh began coughing again, putting one hand across his mouth, the other moving to fix his nasal cannula in place from where it had been resting in his lap. He breathed deeply and the coughing subsided. Duncan winced at his discomfort. Swallowing hard, Ruaridh struggled to breathe normally, his expression pained.

"The cold air," he said, tapping his chest with two fingers. "It seems like the cancer doesn't care for it. I'm supposed to keep this blasted tube in my nose... but it is so very irritating."

"Lungs?" Duncan asked and the man nodded.

"Who'd have thought that filter less cigarettes could do such damage when they once told us they were healthy?"

Duncan smiled at the sarcasm. "That night, when your daughter was out at Coral Beach, you were supposed to be collecting her from the party?"

Ruaridh nodded. "That's right. She was supposed to call me to come and get her but... she never called."

"Were you worried?"

He snorted. "No, I can't say I was. Isla was with her friends and despite my reputation to the contrary I did understand that teenagers like to have fun. I thought she was likely staying with one of her friends and would return home in the morning."

"Was she prone to that sort of thing, changing plans without telling you?"

His forehead creased and he seemed pensive. "No more so than any other child of her age, I would say. But it was normal enough for us not to be overly concerned, not until her friends came calling for her the following afternoon. They were expecting her to be at home, you see?" His expression turned grave. "Then, we became worried and started to phone around asking after her."

"Some people found it odd," Duncan said. Ruaridh looked

at him quizzically. "For a man, a religious man… as you said, with a reputation for being—"

"A pious Stornoway priest?"

Duncan smiled. "Something like that, yes. Some found it odd that you reacted so slowly, whereas others thought you would never have allowed Isla to stay out like that."

Ruaridh tilted his head, thrusting out his lower jaw. "We live in a world of opinions… many are forceful and people make a judgement without ever considering they might be wrong about something… or someone. These are the people who are incredulous that others hold views distinct from their own. To be fair, I was always quite the barnstorming performer from the pulpit, that's true." He sighed. "I was so concerned about my family's moral wellbeing, along with that of my flock and the wider community, that I neglected to protect that which is so precious to me."

"You couldn't have known."

He exhaled through his nostrils, shaking his head. "Very kind of you to say so, but a parent's first duty of care is to their spouse and their children. And in that, I failed. There's no two ways about it."

Duncan contemplated the impact of asking his next question, but it would save him from making a subsequent trip, and there would never be a good time to ask.

"Forgive me for asking this, Reverend Matheson," Duncan said. He immediately felt the heat of Ruaridh's eyes upon him. "The autopsy report revealed some information that the police were unaware of at the time of your daughter's disappearance."

"Which is?"

Duncan paused, choosing his words carefully. "It would appear that Isla had been pregnant around the time she went missing."

Ruaridh stared at him; his lips parted but he didn't speak for a moment. His complexion was already pale, but he seemed to look greyer as the seconds passed.

"Are you… sure?" he asked, reaching for his oxygen bottle and increasing the flow to his cannula. He fixed Duncan with a stern look. "I mean really sure?"

"We are, yes. I'm so sorry."

"I… I don't know what to say about that…" Ruaridh looked lost. He seemed unsteady and had he been standing, Duncan figured he'd have passed out and toppled over. He still might. Duncan placed a gentle hand on his shoulder, and Ruaridh looked at him, glass eyed.

"Are you with me, Reverend Matheson?"

For a moment it seemed as if the words hadn't penetrated that vale of confusion, but then the light returned to Ruaridh's eyes and he blinked away the tears, slowly nodding.

"Isla… was with child?"

"Around that time, but not when she… passed away," Duncan said, feeling for the man.

"I-I see."

Ruaridh put a gloved hand to his face, just as he began coughing again. The fit continued for over a minute, enough time for Duncan to conclude he needed to get the old man inside.

"Come on, let's get you somewhere warm," Duncan said. Ruaridh agreed and once he was over his coughing fit, he steered his chair back along the track to his house. Duncan walked beside him, keen to ensure he returned home unscathed. A purpose-built pathway led from the road to a ramp up to the front door, negating any accessibility issues.

Whether DCI Jameson would be happy with Duncan for revealing the pregnancy, he was unsure, but it was too late now.

CHAPTER EIGHTEEN

DUNCAN TOOK the road down the east coast of the Trotternish peninsula heading back to Portree. The route wasn't as quick as cutting west and then picking up the A87 at Uig, but it would take him past The Quiraing and Kilt Rock. Both were places he would drift away to in his mind when in need of a mental escape.

The weather was closing in around him as he viewed the Old Man of Storr in the distance. The mist was swirling around the stoic rocks, standing with the centuries-old monumental grandeur that drew tens of thousands of people to walk around them each year. It made for an impressive sight. Even at this time in the afternoon the car park was full of hikers and families making the trek up to capture the views across the Isles of Rona and Raasay with the mountains of the mainland in the west or to look south over the Storr Lochs towards Portree and the Cuillin Hills.

He was tempted to return and make the same walk he'd done many times before, should the opportunity arise before he left to return to Glasgow. Thoughts of leaving the island and Glasgow brought images of Natalie to mind. He felt guilty then. He had barely given her a thought since he'd arrived on Skye. She hadn't called him, not that he expected her to. Finding his belongings in the street outside her flat had given their relationship the air of finality in his head. Natalie was many things, headstrong and stubborn were two of the more prominent character traits she exhibited, but she was also kind and loving. She deserved better than what he'd offered her during their relationship, particularly these past six months.

Rounding a slight bend and cresting a blind incline, Duncan was forced to slam on the brakes to avoid a handful of sheep who'd decided the road was a great place for a rest. Only two of the animals moved as he swerved the car to his left to avoid making contact. The others stayed put, rooted in fear or purely nonchalant at the sudden approach of the vehicle, he didn't know. Cursing himself for not paying attention, he slowed the car down.

On the approach into Staffin, he came upon a small 4x4 stopped on the highway, hazard lights flashing. Pulling alongside he saw Becky in the driving seat, peering at her mobile phone screen. He drew his car in to the side of the road behind it and got out. Recognising him, Becky did the same and they stepped onto the grass verge away from the road.

"Problem?" he asked, realising the question was obvious.

"It just died on me," Becky said, attempting to move the hair away from her face but the wind merely caught it and blew it back again. "The damn thing has been playing up for a while."

"I'll take a look if you like?"

"Thanks, but I think you'll struggle. Davey has been saying the head gasket is on its way out, and we've been coaxing it along for the last month or so until he could get around to dealing with it."

Duncan looked at the car, frowning. If that was the case, then there really was nothing he could do about it. Not that he knew his way around an engine beyond the basics anyway. It was a genuine offer, but one deep down he'd be unlikely to turn his hand to. However, he resolved to try. Getting into the driver's seat he turned the key in the ignition, the engine attempting to turn over and making the strangest noises he'd ever heard emanating from a machine. It would be better if he didn't do that again.

Becky opened the passenger door and looked across at him. "Told you."

He nodded. "Yeah... it's... um..."

"Knackered."

"Pretty much. Have you got breakdown cover?"

She laughed, closing the door. Duncan exhaled. "I guess not." Looking into the rear of the car, he saw several carrier bags from the Co-op. Getting out, he rejoined Becky. "Have you called Davey?"

"Aye. He's out on the croft and has at least another hour's work to do out there before he can call it a day." Becky looked stressed. Breaking down when you were out and about wasn't the best, but it was more than that, Duncan thought. She didn't look as if she'd slept particularly well. It was all in stark contrast to how she'd seemed when he'd briefly spent time with her the other day.

Duncan frowned, looking around. "I can give you a lift home, if you like. The car will be fine here for a bit." He shrugged. "It's not like anyone is going to steal it."

"If they did, they'd be doing me a favour. Could you give me a lift home?" she asked, hopeful his offer was genuine. She smiled and the years fell away from her face.

He nodded. "Sure, it's no bother."

"That'd be great Duncan, thanks." Becky glanced at her

watch. "I need to get the shopping back and the kids will be home from school soon."

"No problem," Duncan said, opening the door to the back seat and picking up the first two bags of shopping. Moving out of the way, Becky picked up two more and they made to transfer the groceries into Duncan's car. He popped the boot with his fob, the motor whining as the boot lid came up. He'd forgotten the boot was full and Becky scanned all his worldly possessions packed into the relatively small space.

"Duncan... why have you got a toaster in the boot of your car... and is that an espresso machine too?"

"Erm... it's a long story," he said, embarrassed. "We can put your stuff on the back seats."

The rear seats of his car also had some of his belongings on them, but at least these were in a holdall and a gym bag. Duncan put them down in the footwell of the passenger seats to make room. Having finished the transfer, Becky locked her car and got into the passenger seat of Duncan's car, shivering after being caught out in the wind but very grateful to be heading home.

Becky and Davey Mcinnes lived in a white house in Maligar, a couple of miles outside Staffin, off the main road and up into the hills at the end of a long road which petered out into boggy moorland. It was a five-minute drive in summer and sometimes impassable in the winter.

"What were you doing in Staffin?" Duncan asked, looking at the shopping in the rear-view mirror. To reach Staffin, she'd have passed the turning to take her up across the high road to Maligar.

"Just had an errand to run," she said. "Nothing interesting." She spun in her seat to face him, a mischievous smile crossing her face. "What's this about you and Murdo having a set-to the other night?"

Duncan felt himself flush red and he tried not to meet her eye, instead pretending to be focussing on the road even though this stretch was as straight as a die and he had a clear view of the empty road ahead of them. "Murdo Grant?" he asked casually.

"Yes, Murdo Grant," she said, clearly amused. "Unless you picked a fight with another Murdo after I left."

"Ah… you heard about that then?"

"Yes, I did. What was it about? I would have thought the two of you should be old enough to have grown past that sort of behaviour."

Duncan cocked his head, clenching his jaw, irritated with Archie for opening his mouth, assuming it was he who had told Becky. "Aye, you'd think so. Besides… he started it." As soon as the comment left his mouth he realised he did indeed sound childish. Becky laughed, a sound that only worked to deepen his embarrassment.

"So?"

"So what?" he asked innocently, slowing the car to pass over a cattle grid.

"What were you two scrapping about?"

He looked across, seeing her smiling at him. He returned her smile and shook his head. "Which one of these is yours?" he asked, distracting her and avoiding the question as they approached the settlement. "I can't remember where Davey lived."

"Second right, with the old black house to the side."

Duncan turned off the road and through an open gate onto a basalt chip-lined driveway, drawing the car up before the front door. Adjacent to the house was a narrow strip of land within which was an old stone building. It was a traditional black house but had fallen into disrepair. The original thatch had been replaced with a corrugated metal roof lining, as had many on the island, and it was evidently used as a storage barn of sorts now, a wooden door midway along one side was rotten and partially hanging off its hinges.

"Come on," Becky said, "let's get this stuff inside and I'll make you a cup of tea."

"Can't argue with that offer."

Ten minutes later, the bags were stacked in a line on the kitchen worktop and Becky had excused herself. Duncan loitered in the kitchen, looking out of the window behind the sink over the range of nearby properties. This house was much as any other on the island. The older houses were built to withstand the elements; solid, thick walls and small windows. There were a lot of modern buildings springing up in every settlement he'd seen since he'd been back now though, many based on the Hebridean longhouses of old with state-of-the-art technology to both insulate and heat them. He could see one or two from Becky's kitchen. One of them looked to be a guest house or bed and breakfast, he could see a sign hanging beside the gate to the driveway and the surrounding gardens were well tended and landscaped. No easy feat in this climate.

The flow of land shifting to developers seemed steady, much as it had always been, and people moving to the island to live a simpler life was seemingly a real draw for incomers, keeping the likes of Dougal Mackenzie occupied. For most islanders though, life really hadn't changed all that much over the years. The roads were better, that was undeniable, and the infrastructure had come on since he'd left, catching up with and then keeping pace with the mainland. Skye was certainly changing, but he hoped it would be for the better rather than to become the seasonal playground of the wealthy. If that happened, the heart of this place would die.

"Sorry about that," Becky said, reappearing from the next room.

"No problem," Duncan said, smiling at her as she set about unpacking the cold goods and putting them in the fridge. Had she put some make-up on? He wasn't sure. She'd certainly put a brush through her hair though.

"Can you put the kettle on?" she asked over her shoulder.

A few minutes later they were sitting at the small table in the corner of the kitchen, Becky with her hands cupping a mug of tea. Duncan met her eye.

"Have you been to see your mum yet?" she asked.

"Aye." He lifted his cup, sipping at the drink but it was far too hot, so he set it down again.

"I see you still avoid awkward conversational topics with as few words as possible," Becky said, smiling.

"Aye," he repeated and they both laughed. Duncan sat back, drawing a deep breath. "Sometimes it's nice to listen."

"I see you're not wearing a wedding ring."

He glanced at his left hand, holding it up and extending the fingers.

"You never married?" she asked.

He shook his head. "Nope. Marriage and me don't really go." She smiled. It was artificial, forced. "You can't be surprised by that?"

Now it was Becky who shook her head, blowing the steam from the top of her tea, peering over the mug at Duncan. "I thought you might settle down at some point," she said, coyly.

"Maybe I have." She met his eye and he grinned. "I just—"

"Didn't get married," she said, finishing his comment. Silence. Becky was stewing on something. He could still read her. Not much about her appeared to have changed, and he found the prospect of her company to be compelling despite the years that had passed since they'd been together. "Are you in a relationship?"

He frowned, genuinely unsure of how to answer that. "I... don't think so."

She was amused. "You don't *think so*. How can you not know?"

"Well, I have a toaster... along with everything I currently own, in the back of my car outside... so..." He shrugged. "I don't know... but I don't think so. Maybe when I get back to Glasgow." The words sounded hollow. He and Natalie were over. He could be confident about that regardless of what he'd just said. The finality of it was something he didn't want to accept, at least not out loud. He considered that momentarily. Was it the fear of yet another failed relationship that made him defer acceptance of its demise or was it pure ego?

The silence grew and Duncan felt awkward. He found Becky watching him. Maybe she'd ask that question that was on her mind, whatever it was, any time now. He hoped not.

"Have you ever... wondered what things would be like if you'd made different decisions?"

He looked at her, trying to read the hidden meaning behind the question but unsure if there was one. "That depends..."

"On what?"

He cocked his head. "Which decisions you're talking about?"

She averted her eyes from his, staring at the cup in her hands, pensive. "I don't know... leaving for Glasgow... us... the baby. That type of thing."

"Oh... the big decisions," he said quietly. She looked up at him, nodded and smiled. He drew a deep breath. "It was all such a long time ago."

"Sorry," she said, hurriedly. "I shouldn't have brought it up."

"No, no… it's fine—"

His mobile rang and apologetically he took it out of his pocket, relieved by the timing of the interruption, but he did his best to hide that.

"Alistair. What's up?"

"I was just about to head down to Elgol to speak with Roddy Mcintyre. Do you feel like joining me or… do you still have errands to run?"

Something in the way Alistair said the word *errands* made Duncan feel like he'd been caught skipping school.

"Sounds good," Duncan said, checking his watch. "It'll take me a half hour or so before I can be back in town."

"Where are you?"

Duncan smiled. "I'm running an errand," he said, "but I'll be back soon."

"Aye, grand."

He hung up, glancing at Becky. "Sorry. Duty calls. I'll have to head back into Portree in a minute."

"No problem," she said. He watched her fingers absently toying with the sides of the mug before her on the table. "So… how long are you back for?"

The previous questions now seemed far from her mind. Her entire demeanour had shifted. Perhaps the moment had passed.

"A week or so. Maybe more, but it depends."

"Are you here working on what happened to Isla Matheson?"

He nodded and Becky shook her head.

"That's awful what happened to her. People are saying she was murdered. Is that true?"

He didn't want to obfuscate. "Well, we don't know for

sure, not yet, but someone buried her out near Trumpan, that's for certain. Why they did that? That's the question and it will probably answer all the others."

"Just awful," Becky repeated, looking down at her mug again.

"I have to go," he said, standing up and reaching for his coat hanging on the back of the chair. Her eyes followed him to the door but she didn't get up. "Thank you for the tea."

"Duncan," she called as he was leaving. He stopped and looked back. She seemed nervous, lowering her voice. "Do you ever think about me? About us?"

He held her gaze, biting his bottom lip... and nodded. She looked away from him without saying another word and he stepped back, gently closing the door behind him. Walking to the car, feeling a mixture of emotions, he forced himself to focus on the case.

CHAPTER NINETEEN

THEY MADE good time heading south from Portree to Broadford and then on to Elgol where Roddy Mcintyre's family business was based. The drive took a little over an hour and most of it was made in silence. Duncan found that odd. Alistair was hardly the quiet type, usually garrulous, but this brooding silence unnerved Duncan. Something must have got under his skin.

They were parked up alongside the jetty, waiting for the boat to return. A small wooden cabin was off to their right, a ticket office, with several posters mounted on the exterior walls providing information regarding available tours and pricing. Duncan cast an eye over them. Aside from the tourist-guided boat trips there were opportunities for hikers to be dropped off in remote places where they could then explore the wilds of Skye at their own pace, returning to be collected an hour or two later. In the lighter months these trips were offered daily, running through to later in the evening making use of the extended daylight hours, whereas in the winter the options were far fewer.

Sunset was mid-afternoon in the winter months and

tourists couldn't be caught out in the dark hiking the banks of somewhere like Loch Coruisk. People could die and had done, in such remote locations accessible only by boat or helicopter.

"A penny for them."

Alistair glanced sideways at him, meeting his eye. "Eh?"

"What's on your mind, Alistair? I don't doubt you're a cantankerous old sod when it suits but get it off your chest or else I'll walk back to Portree."

A trace of a smile crossed Alistair's face then, but it vanished a moment later. "I'm just thinking about you, Mr McAdam."

That piqued Duncan's interest. Alistair had been addressing him by his first name since they'd met but had now slipped into formality. It was like his mum using his full name when he'd been caught in his bedroom with the red and silver foil that'd once wrapped several Tunnock's Teacakes when he was barely eight years old.

"What's that then?" Duncan asked.

"I can't quite figure you out."

Duncan shrugged, turning his gaze back across the water and spying an ominous weather front crossing over the Cuillins to the north-west of them. "What's there to figure?"

Alistair took a deep breath, sighing as he exhaled, staring straight ahead and across the water. There was still no sign of the *Skye Explorer* returning from its last trip of the day.

"DCI Jameson doesn't like you."

Duncan smiled, leaning back against the head rest. "You got that too, huh?"

Alistair laughed. "I mean... he *really* doesn't like you."

"Yeah, he asked for someone else to come up here and he got me instead. I'm like the unexpected child who's then born the wrong gender."

"Yes, I can see that," Alistair said. "That's why you got saddled with us."

"And why did you get saddled with me, Alistair?"

He shrugged. "We island folk aren't important. Not in the big scheme of things." There was bitterness in his tone. "When all this is done, Jameson and his crew will disappear over the bridge to Kyle and it'll be me and the rest of the island who'll have to pick up the pieces."

"Is it ever anything different, Alistair?" Duncan said, rolling his head to face him. "It's always the victims, those in their circle and the community who have to find a way to move on. If Jameson is right… then it won't make too many ripples."

"If he's right? About the killer being someone from off the island?"

"Don't forget the pathologist is leaning towards natural causes, not murder," Duncan said.

Alistair cocked his head. "Aye… and pathologists can be wrong. Natural causes, my backside."

A boat appeared from around the southern tip of Soay, one of the many islands making up the Inner Hebrides. The boat was a small wooden vessel with a wheelhouse cabin towards the bow and open seating in the stern.

"Does anyone still live on Soay?" Duncan asked.

"Last I heard there were three residents," Alistair said, then glanced over at him. "If you don't include the sheep obviously."

They waited for another ten minutes for the boat to make its way across the sea loch before docking at the jetty. Half a dozen passengers clambered onto the wooden walkway, exchanging words of thanks with the crew before heading to their cars. It was getting dark now and the crew set about tying the boat up for the night. Once the passengers had filtered past, it left only Duncan and Alistair waiting patiently for the two crew members to come ashore.

Duncan watched the younger of the two men tying the boat up, presuming that was Roddy. The other was likely to be his father as the business was publicised as a family enterprise. Both men glanced over, aware of their presence but didn't speak until they were off the boat. Duncan made ready to present his warrant card, as did Alistair.

"Roddy Mcintyre?" Duncan asked. "We'd like to speak to you about Isla Matheson."

The elder of the two men stopped, his eyes flickering between them and Roddy. "Who's asking?"

Roddy smiled weakly, placing a gentle restraining hand on his father's forearm as both detectives displayed their identification. "It's all right, Dad. I'll be grand."

Roddy Mcintyre was in his late thirties, slim and with sandy hair hanging down across his forehead in curls. These ringlets couldn't be natural, and his hair was also highlighted with blond flecks. His father, likely in his sixties, in contrast was stocky and balding, standing before them clutching a woollen beanie in his hands, appearing pensive, and reluctant to leave them to it.

"I'll be fine," Roddy assured him. His father eyed both detectives warily before nodding. Duncan moved aside to allow him to pass them on the jetty.

"I'll wait in the ticket booth," he said, walking away.

"Sorry about my dad," Roddy said. "He doesn't care much for the police."

"I'm sorry to hear that," Alistair said, his tone implying he really wasn't. "Has a record, does he?"

Roddy smiled, shaking his head. "No, nothing like that. He just... takes issue with authority figures. It's nothing personal."

"We were surprised not to see you at the vigil the other night, Roddy," Duncan said, thrusting his hands into his pockets, protecting them from the breeze coming in off the loch. "People were kind of expecting you."

"Is that right?" Roddy said, his lip curling in a sneer. "I must have missed the invite."

Duncan sniffed. "I thought the two of you were close, you and Isla?"

"Yeah…" Roddy's demeanour softened. "We were. Very close."

"So why didn't you go?"

"The vigil?" Roddy shrugged. "I don't have to prove how much Isla meant to me by standing with a load of hypocrites holding candles just to look good on their Instagram."

Duncan was taken aback. To his mind, the event appeared to be quite touching for those in attendance.

"No love lost between you and some of them, then?"

Roddy grinned but it was malevolent. "A bunch of tossers, if you ask me."

"Can I quote you on that?" Alistair asked. "Just for the record."

"Aye, do that," Roddy said. He inclined his head. "Look, I suppose it was a nice thing to do… but I don't need to be up there to show people what Isla meant to me and… some of those people… I've no' seen many of them for years and if I go years more before I see them again then that'll be just fine with me."

"You think the motivations of some in attendance were less than honourable then?" Duncan asked.

Roddy snorted. "Too right. I stay away from most of that group these days, not that I was ever one of the gang, so to speak, anyway. Even back then."

"Care to name any one person or persons in particular you're referring to?"

Roddy smiled, this time it was one of genuine amusement. He shook his head. "I really don't want to get involved."

"In what?"

He shrugged. "All of it… none of it."

"We're trying to find out what happened to your friend," Duncan said.

"Tell me, what did happen to her?"

"We're still working hard to figure that out."

Roddy looked at him. "So, you're saying you don't know."

"Not yet, no."

"Twenty years of rumour, conjecture and gossip. Now you've found her… and you still don't know what happened."

"Don't you care?"

"Of course I care," Roddy said, shooting a dark look at Duncan. "But nothing good will come from dredging all that up again?"

"How about justice for Isla?"

Roddy half-smiled. "Do you think Isla gives a shit now?"

Alistair glanced at Duncan who raised an eyebrow. Roddy shook his head.

"Look, you have your job to do, I get it. But do you think whatever you uncover is going to change anything? Isla's still going to be dead, isn't she?"

"What about if someone killed her? The person who dumped her body out in the bog. Don't you think they should be held accountable?"

"Oh yeah, absolutely," Roddy said. Looking around, he outstretched both his arms. "And do you see him around here any place?" He raised his eyebrows, his eyes flickering between them. "No… I didn't think so."

Alistair scowled at him. "You don't seem particularly surprised by any of this, Roddy," he growled.

Roddy turned on him, frowning. "Surprised? About what?"

"About us finding Isla's body."

"I'm not." He shrugged. "I knew she was dead. I've known it for years."

"How could you?"

Roddy sighed, dejected. "Because I knew Isla. She wouldn't up and leave like that without a word to anyone. Not by choice."

"Then help us find out what happened to her," Duncan said.

"Like anything I have to say is going to be helpful." Roddy took a deep breath, a mask of resignation crossing his face.

"It might," Duncan said.

Roddy's expression deepened as he held Duncan's gaze, and Duncan thought he was about to relent but he shook his head. "I told you, I don't want to get involved."

"You gave us a statement at the time," Duncan said.

Roddy met his gaze with a steely eye. "Then read that. It should tell you everything you need to know."

Duncan assessed Roddy. He hadn't made a decent first impression, that was certain. Glancing towards the ticket booth, he could see Roddy's dad watching them; his stance hadn't softened at all. Like father, like son, perhaps. Roddy seemed just as spiky. A guilty conscience, perhaps or was it simpler than that, and he was shutting himself off from the pain? Duncan struggled with the man's attitude. It struck him as decidedly odd.

"If you're not bothered about wanting justice, what about closure for her family... and for the others who really cared for her?"

Roddy glared at Duncan, his lip curling into a snarl but he stopped himself from saying whatever threatened to spill from his mouth. He sniffed, breaking eye contact and drawing breath.

"Yeah... you're right, of course." He rubbed at his eyes, drawing his hands down across his face, marking a noticeable shift in his demeanour. "What would you like to know?"

"The night of the party, Isla was flirtatious amongst the group, yes?"

Roddy nodded. "She was, yes. Trying to make a point, I think."

"To whom?"

He shrugged. "Her ex mainly..."

"Alex Macrae?"

"Along with some of the catty lasses too. Catriona, Kirsty... Ashlee. All of that group."

"Why? I get the boyfriend seeing as he was moving on—"

"Moving on?" Roddy said, snorting with derisory laughter. "He still had eyes on Isla. He wanted to play the field, but he still wanted her at his beck and call should his need arise."

"How did Isla feel about that?"

Roddy exhaled through clenched teeth. "Isla... for everything else she was, was very loyal."

Duncan sought the context behind that comment. "So, she still had time for him, for Alex?"

"Yeah... the daft mare. He was a piece of work, Alex Macrae, I can tell you. She was far too good for him but she had a blind spot around the guy. She saw him as her saviour."

"Alex?" Duncan asked.

Roddy grinned. "I see you've met him then?" Duncan nodded. "Then you'll know. Not that I want to bad mouth the guy— "

"But you're going to," Alistair said.

"I'll say this, if I was in the hospital on a life support machine, Alex is the type of guy who'd unplug it to charge his phone. You know what I mean?"

"By accident or on purpose?" Alistair asked.

Roddy inclined his head. "Do the two need to be mutually exclusive?"

"And how might Alex have reacted to Isla's behaviour that night?"

Roddy shrugged. "He noticed. I'll say that."

"Would you say he was a violent young man?" Duncan asked.

"Alex? No more than any other teenager with too much time on his hands and way too much testosterone to throw around. He'd be up for a scrap as much as the next guy."

"What about you?"

"Me?" Roddy asked.

"Yeah, you and Isla were close. You spent a lot of time together according to others in your peer group."

"You're asking if I was upset that Isla wasn't making a play for me?" Roddy asked, smiling.

"Yes, I am." Duncan found his reaction curious. "It's a fair question. It could be galling for most young men if the object of their desire looked past them—"

"Or straight through them," Alistair added. Roddy looked between them, shaking his head.

"That's what my dad said would happen as soon as her body was found."

"What's that?" Duncan asked.

"You lot would start looking around for someone to blame."

"We're trying to find out why she died."

"And also, to find someone to blame," Roddy said. "It doesn't matter whether that person did it or not, you just need a bogeyman to hold up as the fall guy to reassure the public that you're doing your job, so they can all sleep soundly in their beds at night."

"That's cynical," Alistair said. Duncan thought that was a case of the pot calling the kettle black but didn't say so.

"Do you think Alex would have harmed Isla that night?"

Roddy let out an exasperated sigh. He shook his head. "I really have no idea."

"Take a wild guess."

He looked at Duncan, pursing his lips. "No... if you put a gun to my head, I'd say no. I don't think Alex is the type, but I don't think any of that lot are the type." He shrugged. "I don't like them, but would they hurt Isla? I doubt it." He looked at both detectives in turn. "Now, is there anything else or can I go? It's been a long day and I'm cold, tired and could do with a beer."

"No, you can go," Duncan said. Roddy nodded, turned back to the boat and stepped down onto the deck, retrieving a small backpack from near the cabin. He climbed back onto the jetty where Duncan and Alistair were still standing, passing by them and offering a polite smile. Duncan called after him. "Seeing as you were so close to Isla, I'll bet you knew she was pregnant."

Roddy stopped with his back to them only a few paces away. He turned back, biting his bottom lip, his eyes narrowing.

"Isla was pregnant?"

It was a question rather than a statement.

Duncan nodded. "You didn't know?"

He shook his head, taking a half step in their direction. "Isla never said anything to me about it."

"You were her closest confidant, weren't you? That's what everyone says."

Roddy arched his eyebrows. "Well, if everyone else says it then it must be true, eh?"

Duncan found the man's attitude somewhat baffling if not annoying.

"If she didn't come to you, then who would she go to?"

Roddy was thoughtful. "I don't know. Genuinely, I don't. With something like that, I'd have thought she would come to me in a heartbeat. I'm a bit disappointed to think that she felt like she couldn't if I'm being honest."

"I'd like it if you were honest," Duncan said. "How was she in the run-up to that night on Coral Beach?"

Roddy looked away; his forehead creased in thought. "Pre-occupied, I'd say. But with what, I couldn't say. Maybe that explains it, her being pregnant and all."

"How would it have gone down if she had told people?" Duncan asked. "About the baby."

Roddy snorted. "Alex would have folded, that's for sure. He's one of the most irresponsible people I know. Can you believe some folk let a guy like that look after their elderly relatives? They'd be better off leaving them in their rooms with an open tin of cat food rather than trusting that guy to care for them."

That comment cut Duncan deeply, bearing in mind where his mum was. He didn't react but he felt Alistair's eyes upon him.

"And her father?"

Blowing out his cheeks, Roddy arched his eyebrows. "That wouldn't have gone down well with Reverend Matheson, not at all. I remember Isla telling me once that Donnie, her brother, got a girl in trouble down in Glasgow. He was in his first year at Uni at the time." He shook his head. "Old man Matheson lost it, big time."

Roddy inclined his head, a gesture to see if it was okay for him to leave and Duncan nodded. As an afterthought, he called after him. "What happened to that baby? Donnie's, I mean?"

Roddy turned, looking at them whilst walking backwards. He shrugged, pushing out his jaw. "No idea, sorry." He spun away from them and continued walking. His dad, seeing him approaching, came out of the ticket office, shooting his son an inquisitive look as he locked up. Roddy nudged his dad's arm with his elbow as he joined him and the older man put an arm around Roddy's shoulder and the two of them walked away, side by side.

"What do you make of that then?" Duncan asked.

Alistair stood beside him, both of them watching the father and son climb into a four by four. The Mcintyres seemed to be paying the police no attention but Roddy and his father did glance in their direction when they felt they were not being observed only to quickly look away again.

Alistair sniffed hard, the nylon of his coat rustling on the breeze. "Something's not right there." He glanced sideways at Duncan. "Wouldn't you say?"

Duncan nodded. "Aye, something's not right at all."

CHAPTER TWENTY

THE OPERATIONS ROOM was abuzz when Duncan and Alistair returned to the station, so much so that the two of them felt in the way. The two men exchanged glances and while Duncan went in search of DCI Jameson to give him an update, Alistair went to find the local team. Jameson was in his office, situated just off the incident room, briefing several CID officers, none of whom Duncan knew. He knocked on the door, interrupting the DCI who was in mid flow. Begrudgingly, it seemed to Duncan, he beckoned him inside.

"What is it, Duncan?"

Two of the three detectives glanced up at the new arrival, but no one acknowledged him.

"I've just come back from speaking with Roddy Mcintyre, and I think—"

"Who?"

"Mcintyre, Roddy Mcintyre," Duncan said. "He was Isla's closest friend—"

"Oh yes, yes of course," Jameson said. His eyes lowered to his mobile on his desk, absently swiping a notification off the screen. He lifted his head, expectantly looking at him. "We're a little busy here, Duncan. What is it?"

"Roddy... there's something about his reaction to our visit that seems off."

"And?"

Duncan met Jameson's eye. The DCI seemed irritated rather than interested.

"He's named by most people who knew Isla as her closest confidant and the guy couldn't have been less interested in finding out what happened to her if he tried." He shrugged. "It doesn't add up."

Jameson sat back in his chair, glancing at the two men standing across the desk from him, a third leaning against a filing cabinet off to his right. The cramped room felt stuffy and oppressive with them all squeezed into it. The DCI frowned, clicked his tongue against the roof of his mouth and exhaled.

"You have this guy... what was his name?"

"Roddy Mcintyre."

"Yes, Mcintyre... in the frame?"

"Well, I wouldn't say that as such, it's just—"

"A hunch?" Jameson asked. The officer standing looked across at Duncan and he thought there was a trace of a smile on his lips.

"Not a hunch as such, but reading through the case notes, Roddy was always referred to as a happy-go-lucky character, quick with a smile and Isla's—"

"Closest friend. Yes, you said that." Jameson made a tent with his fingers before him. "Things have moved on a little, Duncan. Information you're not party to. I think it supersedes your... intuition."

The last was said with an inflection on intuition and a murmur of amusement passed among the men in the office. Duncan felt his hackles rising.

"May I ask what it is?"

"It's come to light that a German national by the name of…" Jameson glanced down at his desk, "Dieter Pohl was in the area around the time Isla went missing. He has several arrests for violent assault against women, here in the UK and back in his homeland." Jameson seemed triumphant. "Data analysis puts him on the island in mid-summer of that year and he doesn't pop up on anyone's radar for another six months, resurfacing in the borders in January of the following year."

"Forgive me… I might be slow on the uptake but—"

"Don't worry, Duncan. We know how it is here on the island. It must be good to be back among your own kind."

Duncan felt his neck and face flushing, particularly when a ripple of laughter went through the room. Jameson raised a hand, apologising for the joke.

"Pohl was travelling around the country in an old VW camper, picking up odd jobs here and there, working cash in hand, thereby making him hard to track. While he was here he got a gig doing odd jobs for a holiday-let business up near Dunvegan which puts him in the target area. We think it likely that after leaving Skye he chose to keep a very low profile, thereby not drawing attention to himself, giving him time to put distance between himself and Isla's disappearance. Obviously, with her body remaining concealed no one came looking for him and then he moved on again." Jameson flicked his hand towards one of the officers sitting opposite him. "Gerry, carry on for me, would you?"

The officer turned around in his seat, looking at Duncan.

"Pohl's currently serving a seven-year sentence for the rape and unlawful imprisonment of a teenager down in Kilmarnock, three years ago. We're fast tracking a DNA analysis and we're sending a team across to interview him."

"Where is he?" Duncan asked, deflated that his lead now looked to be quite ridiculous bearing in mind the direction the investigation was now taking.

"He's in HMP Grampian, over in Peterhead," Jameson said. Duncan must have worn his disappointment on his sleeve, and Jameson noticed. "It's okay, Duncan. You've done some solid work with the locals. This is obviously no reflection on you."

The words were positive but he felt the DCI was patronising him.

"What about the pathology update?" Duncan asked.

Jameson nodded. "The pregnancy?"

"I was thinking more the termination."

"Pohl has an MO where he tries to destroy the DNA evidence that might convict him. In one case, after assaulting a woman, he threw her in a swimming pool. The chlorine destroyed any trace evidence on her body that could have been used. On the charge that saw him sent down, he forced a victim to shower before agreeing to release her. It was only pure luck he was apprehended before being able to clean the vehicle he transported her in that proved she was in the car. He's a cold, calculating bastard, Duncan, but we think we can get him."

Duncan nodded. "You think Isla's injuries are a result of him trying to conceal his attack?"

"That's what we're working with." Jameson met his gaze, his eyes narrowing. "You disagree?"

Duncan couldn't say either way and merely shrugged. "I didn't know there were any DNA samples retrieved for comparison?"

"We're hopeful that new analysis methods will provide a link," Jameson said, "and the threat of that analysis might tilt Pohl in our favour, perhaps trip him up."

Duncan wasn't convinced but he nodded. "Right, what can I do?"

Jameson took a moment to consider it. "You know the area, Duncan. One of the lads will sort you out with the address. Head out to Dunvegan and speak to the owners of the holiday company who employed him. See if you can gather any information we can use in the interview with Pohl. You never know, they might have something useful to say."

"Today?" Duncan asked, checking his watch. It was pushing seven o'clock and the drive out to Dunvegan, where the Waternish peninsula met the Duirinish, would take a good hour or so.

"Yes, the team will be interviewing Pohl tomorrow morning and any extra ammunition we can arm them with before they go in would be beneficial. I know you're unlikely to get anything useful, but it's worth a check."

Duncan agreed, feeling like a fifth wheel, he glanced through the internal window into the incident room, seeing Alistair chatting with Ronnie and Fraser. Jameson dismissed him and Duncan left the office, making his way over to join Alistair. They all nodded a greeting as he approached, the three of them watching their fellow officers at work with the enthusiasm that a breakthrough in a case always generated. They seemed downhearted though.

"They've found their patsy," Alistair said to Duncan as soon as he joined them.

"You're sceptical of the Pohl link?"

"Oh aye. Aren't you?"

Duncan considered it. "Jameson's confident they can put this guy in the area at the time of Isla's disappearance."

"Pah!"

Duncan found himself smiling. "Is that your professional response based on the currently available evidence or…"

"They're reaching," Alistair said. Both Ronnie and Fraser nodded in agreement. "They think they have him on the island at the time. That's it. It's hardly a smoking gun."

"Yes, they're still to speak to his employer and try to officially place him in Dunvegan."

"After twenty years?" Alistair said. Angus appeared at Duncan's shoulder. "I pity the poor sod who has to get that information."

"Well, pity us, Alistair," Duncan said.

"Oh bloody hell! Do we have to go out to Dunvegan?"

Duncan nodded. Alistair sucked air through his teeth in dismay.

"I can't remember what I was doing twenty years ago," Angus said.

"You were still in short trousers," Alistair replied. "Your mum was still dressing you around then."

"She still does," Fraser added.

"Hardly," Angus replied.

Russell joined them, loudly chewing a mouthful of crisps. Alistair stared at him and Russell offered him the bag, but Alistair declined with a dismissive shake of the head. Russell shrugged. Duncan looked at him. He had a rugged face for a man in his early thirties, perhaps he'd been a boxer.

"You've done some boxing... or what do they like these days, cage fighting?"

Russell momentarily paused his chewing, frowning deeply and glancing around at the others' faces. "I like a bit of boxing, it's true. Why do you ask?"

"Boxers are gladiators... and the actor Russell Crowe— "

"Nah..." Russell said, grinning momentarily before putting another crisp in his mouth. "Nice try though," he said, spraying crumbs out of his mouth as he spoke. Angus snorted derisively while the others laughed and Duncan frowned.

He'd figure out the nickname sooner or later. Someone reached through the small group, handing Duncan a slip of paper with an address and a postcode. He held it up to Alistair.

"This is us," he said.

"Aye… us chasing a fart on the wind."

CHAPTER TWENTY-ONE

"This is pish."

Duncan glanced sideways at Alistair who was staring straight ahead of them into the darkness. Rain was falling steadily, much as it had been since they left the station and headed out towards Dunvegan. From the island's capital, Portree, they took the A87 as if they were heading to Uig and the ferry terminal. This was the best maintained road on Skye, necessary due to the heavy vehicles using it to cross the island linking the mainland with the main terminal serving the outer islands. Once they'd turned off and headed west however, the drop off in quality of the roads was noticeable and the going much slower.

"This is pish," Alistair repeated, his fingers tightening on the steering wheel of his pick-up.

"I heard you the first time," Duncan said absently, trying to read the file on Dieter Pohl and specifically his suspected movements during the period they believed he was on Skye. The team had already done a good job of building up a picture of his stay. A financial trail had been established, largely through payments made into his bank account while he worked in the area, confirming his presence on Skye along with places he visited provided he paid by card and not with cash. That was more of an issue in the past with fewer businesses using card machines which were now commonplace with the provision of technology to remote locations.

The town of Dunvegan was less than five miles south of Coral Beach, the last place Isla was known to have been seen alive. It was certainly coincidental to find a man with Pohl's record in the vicinity at the time. Even so, Duncan was wary about getting carried away with the investigation team's excitement. Judging by Alistair's sentiment, he wasn't on board with it either.

"This is—"

"I know!" Duncan said, feeling exasperated. It was like debating with a toddler.

"Well... we're out here chasing ghosts in the dark. You know why they sent us?"

Duncan nodded, giving up on trying to read from the minuscule amount of light beaming down from above him and reaching for his mobile and the brighter torch function. "Aha, yes, I do."

"Because it's pish. That's why."

Duncan chuckled which only seemed to further antagonise Alistair.

"They don't want any of their guys coming all the way out here at this time of night on a stab in the dark, and so they send us."

Duncan looked over at him. "Are you missing your favourite quiz show on the telly or something?"

"No... but the wife will be giving me earache if I don't get home at a reasonable time." He sighed. "And trust me, no man wants that."

"Certainly not me," Duncan said quietly, returning to his

file.

"You're not married, are you?"

Duncan shook his head, still reading. "Nope."

"Ever considered it?"

"Nope."

"Wise beyond your years."

"Thank you," Duncan said, glancing up and bracing himself as Alistair took a steep bend at a speed greater than he should have. The pick-up lurched around the corner which, unhelpfully, had an adverse camber to it. "That's the nicest thing you've said to me since I arrived."

"Aye. You'll likely die alone and unloved in a damp bedsit in Pollokshields, but… whatever," Alistair said with a wink and a smile that Duncan almost missed in the darkness. That wasn't a cheery thought, but he decided not to comment. They were heading out to meet Karen Graham, the owner of multiple holiday homes, chalets and a bunk house, all based in and around Dunvegan. Having owned the business since it started and developed it over a thirty-year period, Duncan was optimistic she'd be up on the detail of whom she employed and when.

Approaching Dunvegan, Alistair turned off the highway when they came to the first couple of buildings; a guest house and a restaurant. Many of the buildings in the town were traditional stone villas, a few of which had been converted into shops or restaurants to serve the booming tourist trade that passed through annually to visit the castle, museum or for camping on the headland. Most of the buildings faced the sea loch given its name by the village, although the waters of Loch Dunvegan lapped against the settlements of Galtrigill, Borreraig, and Colbost on its western shore as well as Claigan, where Isla and her fellow party goers had travelled past that fateful night, on the eastern shore.

Dunvegan was the ancestral home, as well as the seat of power, for the chiefs of the Clan MacLeod for the past eight hundred years. The impressive castle that bore the name of the village, one of Skye's most popular tourist destinations, was still owned and occupied by the MacLeod family.

Duncan pointed to a property set back from the road and Alistair pulled the pick-up between two brick pillars and across a cattle grid, drawing up in front of the building on a gravelled parking area. Their arrival was noted and the owner had already stepped out to greet them before they'd even got out of the cabin.

"Mrs Graham?" Duncan asked, reaching for his warrant card to identify himself. "DI McAdam. We spoke on the phone."

She shook his hand and smiled at Alistair who returned it with one of his own. It was forced. He was still unhappy at having to make the trip.

"I understand you wanted to ask me about Dieter?"

"Correct. Do you happen to keep records from that time?"

"DI McAdam... I keep everything! You never know when HMRC will start asking questions, do you?"

Duncan had no idea, but he smiled politely. "Dieter Pohl worked for you then?"

"He did. He was a lovely young man," she said, smiling. "He'd get stuck into what ever you asked him to do, never one to complain and always cracked on no matter the weather or how tedious the job was."

"Sounds perfect," Duncan said. He saw Alistair nodding sarcastically, pouting, eyes wide, in the corner of his vision.

"Oh, he was," Karen continued. "It was such a shame when he moved on."

"Planned was it," Alistair asked, "his moving on when he did?"

She looked at him and shook her head, frowning. "No, he changed his plans all of a sudden. At least, that's how I remember it. He'd never said anything about leaving but," she shrugged, "I guess if someone's transient in their nature, then that's just how it is."

"How long was he with you?" Duncan asked.

"A good six months or so."

"And he stayed with you? Did he have a room or anything?"

"No, he stayed in his van. He had this old VW thing. Heaven knows how he managed to keep it going, driving all around Europe. He was always tinkering with it." She smiled. "But as I said, he could turn his hand to most things, so I shouldn't be surprised." She looked at Duncan quizzically. "You never said what this was all about on the phone."

"Didn't I?" he replied innocently. "Just carrying out some background checks. You know how it is."

The look on her face showed she wasn't convinced, but with no reason to question him further, she pointed back to the house. "I have the paperwork on my computer if you want to see?" Duncan nodded. "I've dug out some old photographs from that time as well, if you'd like to see those?"

"We would yes, thanks."

"And I'll make some tea. I've got a freshly-baked cake ready as well."

Alistair's eyes lit up. "Now you're talking, Mrs Graham."

Once Karen was walking away, Duncan whispered, "You don't get fresh cake at home, do you?"

"No, and she hides the biscuits... and counts my bloody calories too," Alistair said glumly, hurrying to catch up with their host, a new-found spring in his step.

Inside, Alistair was happily tucking into a large piece of coffee and walnut cake along with a mug of tea. Duncan absently leafed through an old photo album of snaps taken twenty years previously. It was a while since he'd seen such an album. With the onset of the digital age, photo albums like this were becoming a thing of the past. How many photos do people have on hard drives and tablets that they never look at? Only a relatively short time ago, people had to develop camera film and therefore took shots sparingly whereas now the capacity was there to photograph everything, but ironically no one ever looked at them.

"That's him," Karen said, standing on Duncan's shoulder, leaning past him and pointing at a photograph. "That's Dieter there."

Duncan looked at the image of a man a similar age to himself, early to mid-thirties. He had blond hair that hung past his collar and was dressed in jeans and a thick knitted sweater, but he would comfortably have fitted into a surfing community such was his apparent athleticism, broad smile and good looks. His arms were folded across his chest and he was leaning against an old campervan, presumably his and a handful of others stood to the right and left of him.

"Handsome guy," Duncan said, angling the picture so Alistair could see it.

"Devilishly so," Karen agreed, smiling. "He was quite a hit with the girls. And he knew it too."

"Too handsome for this island," Alistair said between mouthfuls. "Lovely cake, Mrs Graham."

She acknowledged the compliment by patting the back of his hand.

"Was he involved with anyone during his stay as far as you know?" Duncan asked.

The door opened and a man entered shaking water from his coat. He looked at the three of them with an inquisitive look. Karen smiled.

"My husband, Ian."

Both Duncan and Alistair greeted him and Ian Graham hung up his coat on a hook beside the door before crossing to where they were sitting.

"They're with the police," Karen said. Her husband was a stern-faced, heavy-set man in his sixties, with a lined face reflecting his time spent grafting on a trawler.

"Oh aye. What's all this about then?" he asked looking at the photo album on the table.

"They're asking after Dieter. You remember him? He used to do odd jobs for us one summer a way back."

Ian thought hard. "I do?"

Karen moved a photograph lying on the table towards him and he peered over Duncan to see it.

"The German lad?" he asked. Karen nodded. "Aye. Flash lad... quick with a smile. Can't say I liked him much. What's he done?"

"We're just building up a background at the moment, Mr Graham," Duncan said.

"Ah... well I can't help you there. I barely knew him." He glanced at his wife. "I'm starving. Did you save me supper?"

Karen nodded, gesturing towards the kitchen, and with that Ian left them to it, heading off to find something to eat. Duncan watched him go and then turned his attention back to his wife.

"You were saying, about Dieter? Was he involved with anyone on the island as far as you know, romantically speaking?"

Karen thought about it. "Nothing regular that I know of. I mean, he could have been. There would have been no shortage of takers, I assure you. He was very popular. Intelligent, charming... fun to be around. I wonder where he is now?"

Duncan arched his eyebrows but didn't tell her he was in prison. "And how did he come to leave again? You said it was sudden?"

"Oh... yes, it was very abrupt," Karen said, frowning. "I did wonder if all of that nasty business around that poor girl who went missing tainted things." She was absently fingering a bead necklace as she recalled Dieter's departure. "He seemed to love being out here. We're really in the back of beyond in most people's eyes and it takes a certain type of person to enjoy living here, particularly if they're not born to the island."

"He left around the time Isla Matheson went missing?"

Karen nodded. "Nasty business. We were all scared for a time, even started locking our doors during the day and night." She shuddered. "There was a wave of fear that seemed to get washed up on the shore around then. I felt it. We all did. I was saddened to see Dieter go from a personal level and not just a business one. He made me feel safe out here." Duncan glanced at her. She smiled weakly. "Oh, my husband was never around, being out on the trawlers... a few days home and then away again for twelve at a time. None of the shallow water fishing either." She laughed, glancing towards the kitchen where her husband was pottering about in the background. She lowered her voice. "I swear he was just trying to get as far away from me as possible."

"And Dieter was reassuring to have around?"

She nodded. "He was a very capable young man. After he left I did feel vulnerable, but as time passed and the police seemed to think it was a case of a runaway teenager rather than anything sinister... things slowly got back to normal."

"And what do you think now?"

"Now that she's been found?"

Duncan nodded.

"It's awful. To think she's been so close to us all for all these years... Do you know what happened to her yet?"

"We're still investigating, Mrs Graham. How soon after the search for Isla began did Dieter leave? Do you remember?"

"Oh yes, I remember that summer very well." She thought about it. "Within a month I would say, perhaps less. He just upped and left one day. I found him packing up his camper-van. At least he said goodbye, I suppose." She smiled wryly. "I had the impression he might not have... but perhaps that's unfair to say."

"A bit odd, wouldn't you say, to just up and leave like that?"

She took a moment to consider the question. "To be fair to Dieter, he'd done all the work I'd commissioned him for, so he was twiddling his thumbs by that point."

"What had he been doing for you?"

"We had three chalets built along the way," she said, gesturing through the wall, "up on the east coast of the loch. They're not big or anything, just one bedroom, a seating area and a kitchenette. He helped us fit out the interiors. Nothing fancy, but he was quite a skilled handyman."

"Did he say why he was leaving, and why so soon?"

She shrugged. "Only that it was time to continue his exploring and that he had never planned to stay as long as he did." Karen's expression changed and she looked at Duncan suspiciously. "You're asking a lot about Dieter. You don't think he had a hand in this, in what happened to that wee girl, surely?"

"As I said, we're still investigating. Previously it was a simple – if you pardon the phrase – missing person inquiry but things have now changed, obviously. We're building background on people present in the area, those Isla may have come across or spent her time with. Do you know if Dieter had any interaction with Isla?"

Karen frowned. "I never knew Isla Matheson, and after she went missing her face was on display all over the island, so I think I would have known if she'd been around the place." She shook her head. "If he did, then it was done away from any of my properties."

Twenty-minutes later, Duncan and Alistair were walking out to the pick-up. Karen agreed to email the financial records displaying the dates Dieter Pohl was working for her and she'd offered to let him take the photo album. He'd declined for the time being, taking some pictures of the photographs with his mobile phone instead. Isla Matheson didn't appear in any of the shots as far as he could tell, which was disappointing.

They got into the pick-up and Alistair looked across at him. "Those chalets up the coast are pretty close to Claigan you know."

"I know."

"I mean… it's only five minutes down the road…"

Duncan stared at him. "I know."

"Pretty easy for him to slip out that night—"

"I bloody know, Alistair. All right!"

"I'm just saying, that's all."

Duncan didn't want to admit it, but perhaps Jameson and his team were on to something. At first, he'd thought the incident team's hypothesis would hinder the investigation rather than progress it. Personally, he'd always insisted on keeping an open mind in his approach to a case. The problem with a working hypothesis is that the team runs the risk of seeking evidence to fit it rather than following the path of where the evidence naturally leads. In this case though, he really felt they were on to something.

CHAPTER TWENTY-TWO

ALISTAIR PULLED up outside the police station back in Portree and Duncan got out, pleased it was no longer raining but there was still a nip in the air and away from the warmth of the pick-up he shivered as he waved off his DS. Drawing his coat around him, he crossed the square to where he'd left his car only to find a woman leaning against it. She turned as he approached. It was Becky.

"Hi Duncan."

He was surprised to see her. She looked frozen to her core, her skin paler than usual and her hair was damp suggesting she'd been caught outside in the rain.

"Hey. What… what are you doing here?"

"Waiting for you, on the off chance you'd be back soon."

"Working late?" he asked, glancing down the street towards the craft shop where Becky worked some hours. She shook her head, stamping her feet to generate warmth. How long had she been waiting for him?

"Just had a few bits to do in town." She indicated to the Portree Hotel on the far side of the square. "Do you fancy a quick drink?"

He looked round. The hotel, one of the largest and oldest in the town, didn't look to be busy and he agreed. "Sure."

"Shall we sit outside?" Becky asked him once they had their drinks, hers a lemonade while he got a pint of beer. The lounge bar was half full of patrons and it looked like a fiddle player had been lined up to provide an evening of entertainment. He was setting up his kit in one corner of the lounge. Once he got under way the bar would likely fill and they'd stand no chance of hearing each other. He nodded.

Outside, where Duncan recalled there was a line of short-stay parking bays, these had now been closed off and replaced with a decked seating area for use by the hotel and the one next door. There was a mix of outdoor tables interspersed by covered seating inside glass pods that were remarkably similar to domestic garden greenhouses. To incomers they'd probably wonder how on earth anyone could sit in them during the heat of summer, but those familiar with Skye would know the heat would barely last a week or two. Much of the year, these pods would be invaluable extra space offering shelter to patrons.

The rain held off and they chose a table in between the pods, coats done up to the collar, and sat down. A string of low light bulbs hung overhead offering a warm yellow glow. The shops were all closed now, so there was barely any traffic and the last of the buses had run for the day, so the nearby bus station was silent.

"Did you get the car fixed?" Duncan asked, puncturing what had become an awkward silence.

Becky shook her head. "I think it's had it, to be honest. I'm using Davey's van just now."

Something was on her mind, Duncan could tell. Perhaps not that first night when Archie had drawn them together, but certainly the next time they met when he'd given her a lift home he'd had the impression she'd seemed preoccupied, and that feeling persisted tonight.

"You said you'd seen your mum. What about Roslyn?" Becky asked. "I can't remember if you said you had or were going to."

"I was going to," he said. "And I have…"

"How is she?"

"Mum is… Mum." He frowned. "It's difficult. Ros is grand though. I think I upset her, mind."

"Doesn't sound like you at all," she said, sipping at her drink to mask the trace of a smile.

"No, not like me to do that, is it? I bring nothing but joy everywhere I go."

"A ray of sunshine," she said, smiling widely now. Duncan tilted his head, lifting his pint in salutation.

"Are you okay?" he asked, setting his glass down on the table but keeping his fingers curled around it.

"Of course. Why do you ask?" She sounded defensive. Typical, he thought. He was always guilty of pushing people to reveal whatever it was they had on their minds, often prior to their readiness to do so. Maybe it was a by-product of holding a warrant card.

He shrugged. "You just seem… preoccupied."

"Do I?"

Her tone was innocent, surprised even. But he knew her better. She was still Becky, and he'd grown up alongside her for nigh on twenty years since they'd first met at primary school, and a fifteen-year gap wasn't going to alter how he was able to read her.

"Tell me to mind my own business if you like."

She made to speak but hesitated, her eye drawn to something behind him.

"Oh dear God," she mumbled. Duncan turned to follow

her gaze. Stumbling down the street, lurching from one side of the pavement to the other was Archie Mackinnon. Seeing them, he almost lost his footing but managed to brace himself against the hotel wall which was all that saved him from keeling over. Pushing off the wall, he lurched in their direction, coming to stand before them on unsteady feet.

"My two-favourite people in the whole world!" he said, grinning. It was clear he'd had a few but he wasn't totally hammered.

"The whole world?" Duncan asked and Archie's grin changed to thoughtful and he shook his head.

"Maybe not the whole world. Maybe just the island."

"Or just Portree?" Becky said.

"Aye… but Portree is a big town," Archie said, smiling and sinking into the chair next to Becky. He met Duncan's eye. "Your round is it?"

Duncan frowned. "Maybe you've had enough for one day. What do you reckon?"

"Nonsense! You sound like my Fiona," Archie said, disapprovingly. "Mine's a pint, no hurry… but I'm parched."

Duncan laughed awkwardly.

"Pickled more like," Becky said. Archie thrust out his jaw before grinning.

"Then put me in a jar and roll me home." He looked at Duncan accusingly. "You still here?"

Duncan reluctantly got up, pointing at Becky's partially touched drink. She shook her head and he set off for the bar. He felt guilty for not having checked in on Archie. He'd planned to but had been side tracked with work. Archie and Fiona had been together since school and Duncan's thoughts turned to their daughter, at least if his memory served it was a girl, but he couldn't be sure. They'd kind of lost touch after school with Duncan going on to further education and Archie going to work on his father's croft. He wondered if his old pal got to see much of his child since the split.

The fiddler was under way and as expected the number of people in the bar had grown significantly, many of whom were now gathered around the table where he played. A woman had joined him and she was singing a song, accompanied by the strings, that Duncan thought he recognised but couldn't put a name to. Bypassing the bulk of the assembled audience, he squeezed his way through but found it still two deep at the bar waiting for service.

Absently scanning the room, his eye was drawn to the open fireplace, orange and red flames licking at a massive log, dancing in the hearth. Two men were sitting in a booth to the right on the far side of the room having an animated conversation. The one facing him was aggressively making a point, leaning forward and almost snarling, gesticulating with his hands. The body language of his companion sitting opposite him, although having his back to Duncan, was expressive, almost defensive. It didn't look like they were arguing as such, but it was clearly an animated conversation.

The song ended with a flourish and the audience clapped and cheered much to the delight of the performers and conversations sparked among people with the advent of the brief break in the entertainment. The queue for the bar parted and Duncan stepped up, catching the eye of the barmaid. He ordered two pints, one for himself and the other for Archie. While he waited, he found his eyes drift back to the men whose conversation appeared to have calmed. Perhaps it was the end of the music that had until now masked their discussion.

The visible one was in his mid to late forties, Duncan guessed, with an impressive hairline. Duncan hoped his would look as good in ten to fifteen years' time, swept up and away from his forehead with the aid of some styling product no doubt. It was jet black without a hint of grey. He was also tanned, which was no mean feat in this part of the world, with no hint of orange so not the result of a bottle or a salon spray as was customary down in Glasgow these days. Duncan assumed he was not local to the island, at least not a hereditary resident if he had a natural tanned skin tone.

If he had to guess, he'd have placed him as coming from southern European descent, maybe Spain or Italy. He also had the style of those guys, the ones Duncan found strutting about on the piazzas and plazas of the Mediterranean when he'd been down that way on holiday. He sported close-cut designer stubble, a tailored leather jacket and a roll neck straight off the fashion pages. These continental Europeans carried themselves with an air of confidence, or arrogance some might say, but were broadly considered cool. Scottish guys, in the main, just didn't possess that as a general rule.

Duncan watched as he leaned forward, jabbing a finger in the air at his companion who reacted, batting the hand away. Coolio, as Duncan decided to christen him, leapt up and for a moment Duncan figured he'd called it wrong, thinking it was about to kick off. Instead, Coolio stood there glaring at his friend before the flash of anger in his expression passed and he shook his head, holding his hands up by way of apology.

"Oh, to be a fly on the wall," Duncan whispered.

"What's that?" the barmaid asked him, setting two pints down on the bar in front of him.

"Nothing, just talking to myself," he said, reaching for his wallet.

"The first sign of madness," she said, winking. "That's seven-twenty, please."

"What… pounds or lira?" he asked, frowning. "I wanted a couple of pints not a new mortgage. I was going to offer you one but I figure I'll be collecting glasses to pay for it." She shot him a sarcastic smile which made him laugh. "You know, the second sign of madness is going to the pub for a pint."

"Or talking to blokes when you're in one," she said, gratefully accepting the ten-pound note from his hand before disappearing to the till and ringing it up.

"Seven quid," Duncan said to himself, sipping at his pint whilst waiting for his change. "I thought it was getting bad in Glasgow."

The musicians were getting ready for their next set and Duncan hurriedly walked around them before the throng came nearer. A quick glance towards the booth saw the two men had left. The blast of cold air as he stepped outside hit him and he shivered involuntarily.

"About time, Duncan. I was going to call the mountain rescue!" Archie called. Several heads turned to look at him and Duncan flushed. Two of those looking his way were the men from the booth, Coolio and his friend. Duncan recognised him as Roddy Mcintyre. The latter turned away from Duncan, bearing a nervous expression, and with a hand on his friend's back steered him away up to the corner, encouraging him to pick up the pace as they walked despite his friend's reluctance. Coincidence? Duncan didn't believe in them. His curiosity piqued, he put the pints down and looked over his shoulder at the departing men just as they rounded the corner and disappeared from view.

"What took you so—"

"I'll be right back," Duncan said, still looking in the direction of where Roddy had been. His eyes flickered between Becky and Archie. "I'll be right back," he repeated and hurried off up the street before either could speak.

At the corner he chanced a quick glance around it. A line of cars was parked on the right of the one-way street, a few people milling about on either side of the road but of Roddy or his companion there was no sign. A car pulled out from the parking bays and gently accelerated towards him, the headlights momentarily blinding him as the front of the car lifted. As it passed by, he glanced into the cabin seeing Coolio at the wheel but the passenger seat was empty. The driver seemed to look at Duncan and their eyes met for a fraction of a second as he passed. It was a silver Mercedes, a coupe, and only a couple of years old according to the year of the plate. Duncan made a mental note of the registration. However, of Roddy Mcintyre there was no sign.

Returning to his friends he found Becky looking irritated. Archie had always had that effect on people. You had to know him to appreciate him and even then, he could be trying. How he managed to get Fiona to marry him, heaven only knew. As for Archie, he was leaning back in his seat, arms folded across his chest with his head slumped forward, snoring.

"Strewth, Archie," Duncan said.

Becky shook her head. "What are we going to do with him?"

"I'll get him home... again," Duncan said, staring longingly at the two pints of beer that he was not going to get to finish, not if he wanted to keep his licence anyway. Archie's glass was empty though. He must have sunk it in one. Becky saw him looking.

"Don't be alarmed. He's been doing this for years."

Duncan cocked his head. "He could always put them away, but I thought we'd have all grown out of that by now."

Becky laughed. "You've been away far too long, Duncan McAdam." She checked the time. "Listen, I know this was my idea, but I should be getting away now."

Duncan felt disappointment. They'd barely managed a word. Nothing significant anyway. "Another time?"

She looked at him, glumly he thought, and then nodded.

"Yes, another time."

She got up, patted the sleeping Archie's forearm and then passed Duncan, hesitating as she came close to him. He caught her eye and for a moment he was eighteen again, looking into those big blue eyes and longing to touch her. He went to kiss her cheek but she moved away, consciously avoiding him or not he couldn't be sure. Maybe it was bad timing.

"See you soon, Dunc," she said quietly, turning and walking away.

"Aye," he said exhaling. "See you soon." He watched her go. Although she was somewhat fuller in the figure now, as were they all, she still had that wiggle of her hips in the way she walked, accentuating her curves, that he found so enrapturing.

"Davey will knock you spark out, you know?"

He turned to see Archie watching him with one eye open.

"Ah… what are you talking about, man?"

"You… and her," Archie said, pointing towards Becky. She couldn't hear the exchange but Duncan flapped his hands to quieten him down. "Mark my words," Archie said. "It'll all end in tears."

"Nothing is going to end in tears," Duncan protested. "There's nothing… to end."

"Aye, right."

It dawned on Duncan and he gazed upon his pal, his eyes narrowing. "Did you… pretend to be asleep?"

Archie smiled.

"You bloody did, didn't you?"

"Saving you from yourself, Wee Duncan."

"I don't need saving—"

"Impulsive," Archie said accusingly. "That was always your problem, controlling your impulses. And I saw it the other night when you floored Murdo – he's still pissed off with you about that, just for the record – that nothing has changed."

"Really?" Duncan said, indignant. "And what about you? Drowning in a sea of booze rather than facing up to real life."

"And what is real life?" Archie countered.

"Paying your electricity bills for a start."

Archie waved the comment away. "I've got my wind turbine... it just needs a fix. I'm on it. Windiest place in Europe, my old croft. Who needs the bloody Hydro anyway?"

"Well, when your turbine needs a new part for starters."

Archie frowned, his lips rattling as he exhaled. "Aye. True that."

CHAPTER TWENTY-THREE

DUNCAN WALKED through the incident room looking for one of the local officers, he didn't mind which. Fraser MacDonald was the first one he saw and he made a beeline for him.

"Morning Fraser. Are you busy?"

Fraser glanced up from his copy of *The Herald*, frowning. "Rushed off my feet, Boss," he said, folding the paper in half and putting it down on his desk, rearranging the location of his steaming cup of coffee to make room for it. "Sorry, I was just having a wee minute—"

"Never mind that, Fraser. It's fine." Duncan slipped him a piece of paper. Fraser opened it and read the registration number. "Can you take a look at that and see who owns it for me?"

"Aye, nae bother," Fraser said, sitting forward and focussing on his screen. Duncan crossed the room to where a young DC was sitting. They'd had a brief conversation in the canteen a couple of days previously and she seemed nice enough. She clearly hadn't got the memo that they weren't supposed to interact with the locals like most of the team. Maybe his being up from Glasgow confused things.

He sidled up to her desk. She glanced up at him and smiled. "Morning DI McAdam. What can I do for you?"

Maybe she'd since received the memo after all.

"Good morning, Lesley." He smiled. "Who says I'm after anything?"

She returned his smile and arched her eyebrows. Duncan relented, perching himself on the edge of her desk.

"All right, how are the interview team getting on with Dieter Pohl?"

She sucked air through her teeth, glancing around the room to make sure they couldn't be overheard. A couple of people were on the edge of being within earshot so she beckoned him closer. He leaned in, keen.

"More than my job's worth to say," she whispered.

He lifted his head, grinning. "That's so cold!"

She smiled. "Seriously though, Pohl's refusing to speak without his solicitor present, so they haven't got under way."

"Do we think he'll cough to it?" Duncan asked, believing it unlikely. Rapists and killers in general had a warped moral compass, if they had one at all, and confessing to crimes that would see their time in prison extended pretty much never happens. Unless of course there was so much evidence to the contrary that they could no longer deny it, and even then, the killers seldom own up, often preferring to maintain an element of power and control over the situation by staying silent. He knew that whether they spoke or not made little difference in those cases as the scientific proof alone was usually enough, but in this case all they had was his proximity to Isla's disappearance alongside his criminal record.

They were going to struggle to connect him to this particular crime and Duncan knew it.

"Jameson is upbeat, but he usually is."

"He holds himself in high regard, doesn't he?" Duncan

said. She nodded. "Any chance you can let me know when you hear something?"

She looked up at him, smiled and nodded before dropping the smile. "No chance in hell, DI McAdam."

"Ah come on. What can he do to you?"

"Besides destroying my career by putting a black mark against me and transferring me back into uniform, you mean?"

"Yes, besides that."

"Absolutely nothing," she said, smiling warmly.

"Thanks, Lesley," he said, getting up from her desk after seeing Fraser waving to get his attention.

"No problem at all."

Duncan walked over to Fraser's desk, resting a hand on the back of his chair he looked over Fraser's shoulder at the screen.

"Who do we have, Fraser?"

"The car belongs to Carlos Moreno," Fraser said, glancing up at Duncan. "Spanish national, resident in the UK for the last twenty-two years."

"Ah... Carlito..." Duncan said quietly, attempting a terrible Mediterranean accent. "Good work, Fraser."

"Easy really. He's applied for leave to remain post Brexit and it was granted in the summer of last year, so it didn't require a lot of digging."

"And what does Mr Moreno do in Portree?"

"He's a doctor. The car is registered to an address here in the town, so I'm guessing he works at the hospital."

"Bloody foreigners, coming over here and caring for our sick and injured," Duncan said, patting Fraser on the shoulder. "Good work. We'll make a detective out of you yet."

"Do you want me to find out anything else on this guy? Who is he anyway?"

"I'm not sure, to be honest. Is he known to us at all?"

Fraser shook his head. "Not so much as a parking ticket as far as I can see."

Duncan stood up, glancing across at the information boards currently dominated by information relating to Dieter Pohl and that branch of the investigation.

"Sir?"

Duncan turned back to Fraser. "What?"

"Do you want me to follow up on him? If so, what angle am I coming at him from?"

"Do you know what he does at the hospital?"

Fraser shook his head. "I can find out."

"Okay, but be discreet, yes."

"Float like a butterfly and sting like a bee," Fraser said, winking.

"Walk like an elephant and empty the vending machines, more like," Alistair said, coming to stand beside them. Fraser grinned at him. "What's the craic?"

Duncan frowned. "I'm not buying this Dieter Pohl link. There's something about it that's bugging me."

"Why not? He fits."

"He fits very well. Yes, that's true," Duncan said.

"So, what's not to like?"

Duncan shook his head. "It's the pregnancy... and more specifically, the termination. It's not right."

"What's Pohl got to do with that?" Alistair asked.

"That's my point, Alistair. Pohl has nothing to gain from it... and where would he keep Isla in the days it took her to develop septicaemia?"

"Maybe she went off with him for a few days?" Fraser said. "In his camper, like."

Duncan shook his head. "Unannounced? I don't see it. It

doesn't make any sense, and we've no established link between him and Isla."

Alistair opened a paper bag, producing a bacon roll. He held it up to Duncan and then took a bite, continuing the conversation whilst chewing his food. "Nothing about this makes any sense. It hasn't right from the start."

"That's another thing I've struggled with," Duncan said, "right from the start; Isla attends this hedonistic party on Coral Beach, there's alcohol and drugs available to anyone who wants it and yet her plan to get home is to call her father, whose reputation is well known on the island. It's plain weird."

"That's true," Fraser said. "But his lad, Donnie, went off the rails in spite of Ruaridh's position in the church." He shrugged. "Maybe Isla was going down the same path?"

Duncan conceded the point. "By Ruaridh's own admission he figured his daughter was staying with friends when she didn't call him that night, so at the very least he must have been expecting it as a possibility."

Alistair struggled to swallow a particularly large piece of bacon, then wiped the ketchup from his lips with the back of his hand. "I do hope you're not considering smearing the reputation of such a fine upstanding man on this island as Ruaridh Matheson?"

Duncan darted a questioning look at him, sensing sarcasm. He shook his head.

Alistair smiled. "Good, because if you were to do so then the community would be constructing the wicker man before sundown, and you'd wake up tomorrow morning with your toes feeling a wee bit warm!"

Duncan smiled. "While we're waiting on news coming through from Peterhead—"

"The hotly anticipated confession of a guilty man?" Alistair asked, his sarcasm seemingly unbridled now.

"Exactly. At this end we're going to continue focussing on where Isla was for those missing days between when she was last seen and where she ended up. If we can shed some light on her medical condition leading up to her disappearance then we may get some answers."

"Which one of you idiots is responsible for this then?"

All eyes turned to see DCI Jameson striding through the incident room holding a newspaper aloft. Concerned looks were exchanged by everyone present as Jameson came to stand at the front of the room. He threw the paper down in disgust.

"I swear I was clear that word of us speaking to Dieter Pohl was to remain within this room," he said, glaring at anyone who dared make eye contact. "Now, I know I was clear what I said because I was standing right here when I said it!"

Alistair cocked his head. "He seems upset."

"You're damn right I'm upset!" Jameson said, turning his ire on the DS. Alistair closed his eyes, pursing his lips, regretting having spoken as loudly as he did. "Now it's in the papers and will likely be all over the television and radio within the hour."

Duncan frowned. How could he reasonably expect to keep their focus on Pohl quiet? From what he understood, Dieter Pohl was something of an attention seeker at the best of times and therefore it wasn't beyond the realms of possibility that he would have leaked the news himself. Besides that, expecting a secret to be kept within an investigation involving dozens of officers was pie in the sky levels of expectation. People talked, sometimes they did it in exchange for money and at other times just to bolster their own ego. At least that was his experience in Glasgow.

"It beggars belief!" Jameson bellowed, storming off into his office. "I'm disgusted with every single one of you," he added before slamming the door.

"He got out the wrong side of the bed this morning," Fraser said, sniffing and returning his attention to his screen remarkably unfazed by the senior officer's outburst. In fairness to him, this inquiry would pass and with it, Jameson's presence in Portree. Then things would go back to normal; as normal as they ever were in this job anyway.

"Right, back to work everyone," Duncan said and heads turned back to their desks.

"Here we go," Fraser said, pointing at his screen. Duncan turned to him, Alistair coming alongside, finishing up his bacon roll. "I give you Dr Carlos Moreno... paediatric consultant, here at Portree Hospital."

"Paediatrics," Duncan said.

"Feet?" Fraser asked.

Alistair chuckled. "No, children."

"Ah right, of course," Fraser replied, flushing.

"That was quick, Fraser," Duncan said, looking over his shoulder.

"Social media makes things so much quicker than using the phone these days," Fraser said. "So much stuff online." He began scrolling through the doctor's timeline. "It all seems quite normal. I'm always surprised when people don't secure their feed." He shook his head, seemingly disappointed. "I can see he's been furry boots quite a lot this year."

"Furry boots?" Duncan asked.

Fraser glanced up at him. "Aye, he's got his furry boots on... away on his travels, out and about, you know?"

"Where's he been then?"

"Let's see… Spain – visiting home, I guess – and he's been away to Italy… Paris in February. Nice restaurant too, looking at the pictures. Attractive dinner partner… relationship status… in a relationship," Fraser said, "with Jojo Moreno. I guess that's his wife."

Duncan looked at him. "Unless it's his sister, you'd think so, wouldn't you?"

Fraser inclined his head. "Ah well, you know what these Mediterranean sorts are like. Big on family aren't they."

Alistair clipped him on the back of the head. "Not like that they're not."

"Anything else?" Duncan asked. "Who is Carlos spending time with?"

"Ah… hang on and I'll check," Fraser said, hesitating. "Well… at least he's securing his friends. Nothing to show unless I am friends with him, so he is conscious of security to a degree. I could always send him a friend request."

"Kind of bypassing the covert investigation side of things though, Fraser," Alistair said. "I can't see a guy like that wanting to get pally with a middle-aged polisman with a large paunch, can you?"

Fraser waved the comment away. "No, of course not. But I could create a fake profile… be another doctor from… Buenos Aires or something?"

Duncan patted him on the shoulder. "Steady on 007… let's not get carried away."

"Who is this guy anyway?" Alistair asked.

"I saw him arguing with Roddy Mcintyre last night."

"Arguing about what?"

Duncan shook his head. "No idea, but it was getting a little heated. I'm pretty sure Roddy saw me and then couldn't get away fast enough." He shrugged. "It got me thinking; Roddy is keeping something back."

"He's keeping a lot back," Alistair said quietly.

"Fraser," Duncan said, "can you bring up Roddy Mcintyre's social media feed?"

"Aye, I can that." Fraser tapped away, bringing up a list of Roddy Mcintyres on the social media site from all around the world. Duncan was surprised by how many there were. A casual scan of the list showed many of them seemed to be living in North America. "Here he is, our Roddy."

Fraser opened up Roddy's timeline. There was no digital security applied to his account. It was open to be viewed by anyone. There were a lot of posts relating to the boat tours, photos of smiling passengers posing with whales and dolphins or with scenic backdrops.

"What are we looking for specifically?" Fraser asked.

"Any ties to Dr Moreno?"

Fraser's fingers tapped away but he was unable to find Carlos Moreno tagged in any photograph on Roddy's account nor was he listed as a friend. Despite beavering away for a few minutes, he drew a blank, shaking his head apologetically. "Sorry, nothing doing."

Duncan found it interesting nonetheless. "Curiouser and curiouser said Alice."

"So, this guy is a friend of Roddy's and he's a doctor?" Alistair asked. "And he was around when Isla went missing?"

Duncan nodded. "Probably nothing in it though."

"Coincidence," Alistair said.

"Almost certainly."

"I know it's a long shot... but shall we ask him if he knows Isla anyway?"

Duncan frowned. "It couldn't hurt, could it?"

CHAPTER TWENTY-FOUR

PORTREE COMMUNITY HOSPITAL was situated on the south side of The Lump, a headland jutting out into Loch Portree, the harbour with the quayside and its famous brightly-coloured terraced houses could be found on the north side. Alistair parked his pick-up in one of the last available bays, squeezing the massive vehicle in between two smaller hatchbacks. Duncan had difficulty getting out.

"Aren't you worried they'll dent your truck when they get in?" Duncan asked, indicating the cars to either side of his.

"Nah. Look at the step plates." Duncan did so, seeing wide stainless-steel steps running the length of the cabin. "I've been sitting in it while people huff and puff about the size of my pick-up, one lass even smacked her door against my pick-up to teach me a lesson. She only managed to dent her own door."

"Teach you a lesson how?"

Alistair shrugged. "On not to have such a big vehicle, I guess. Worked out well for her."

They walked across the car park to the hospital entrance. Having already failed to find Dr Moreno at home, a neighbour telling them that he was home alone, his family away visiting relatives, and they'd seen Moreno heading off to work, they drove straight to the hospital.

The community hospital had a lovely view over Loch Portree and Duncan, having spent two weeks on a hospital ward in Glasgow one time looking out of a window at a solid brick wall, would have loved this landscape to accompany his convalescence.

"What do we know about the good doctor besides his consultant specialisation?" Duncan asked.

"Married for nineteen years... one child, a daughter... and he's never been in trouble with the police or any other governmental body," Alistair said. "The General Medical Council confirmed they've never had his name raised with them. He's squeaky clean. A model citizen."

"No one's squeaky clean, Alistair. You should know that."

"Pure as the driven snow, me," he said, grinning as they walked up to the entrance doors.

The sliding doors parted with a laboured swish and Duncan headed for the information desk to their right. People were milling about the foyer, heading in or out of the hospital or queuing at the small convenience shop offering basic refreshments, magazines and newspapers. Duncan asked for directions to where they could find Dr Moreno and were soon on their way through the building.

"I'm surprised this place is still going," Alistair said as they negotiated the patients, staff and visitors.

"How many patients can they take?"

"Last I heard it was fewer than twenty. It's been under threat of closure for years, but it's still here."

It only took a few minutes for them to reach their destination. The doors onto the ward were secured with a pass code lock, an intercom panel set into the wall alongside it. Duncan pressed the buzzer, hearing it sound at the nurses' station beyond. The intercom crackled and they identified themselves, Alistair looking up at the camera mounted above the door and grinning. They heard the door click and they entered.

The nurses' station was a few paces ahead and they found a stern woman waiting for them. "How can I help you?" she asked.

Duncan produced his identification, showing her his warrant card. She gave it a casual glance but nothing more. "We're here to speak with Dr Moreno. Is he about?"

"I'm Dr Moreno."

They both turned to see a doctor approaching them with an inquiring expression on his face. Duncan was surprised to hear him speaking English with a Scottish accent, expecting he'd still sound Spanish much like the footballers he'd hear speaking on the television in post-match interviews. It stood to reason though, seeing as he'd lived and worked in Scotland for decades now.

"Dr Moreno," he said, "DI McAdam and DS MacEachran from Portree CID."

He came to stand with them, smiling at the nurse who excused herself. "What can I do for you gentlemen?"

If he recognised Duncan from the previous night, he didn't let on.

"We would like to speak to you about Isla Matheson," Duncan said.

Moreno's eyes narrowed and he seemed puzzled. "Who?"

"Isla Matheson," Alistair repeated. "You must have heard of her, her name's been all over the news these past few days."

"Oh right, yes of course. That girl who went missing…"

"And has been found," Duncan said.

"Yes, yes… what's this have to do with me?" he asked, looking around. A couple of staff members passed by paying them no attention, but Moreno gestured for them to follow him into another room. It was an office, used by whichever staff were on shift by the looks of it with a lack of personalisation but an awful lot of paperwork lying around. Moreno closed the door. It was a little claustrophobic with the three of them in there. Alistair wasn't a muscular man, but very tall. Both Duncan and Carlos Moreno were heavier built, now standing almost shoulder to shoulder.

"How can I help? I'm afraid my forensic pathology knowledge peaked in the third semester of my second year at medical school," Moreno said, smiling.

"You're a paediatric consultant, aren't you?" Duncan asked.

"Yes... well, I was. My last post in that role was down in Broadford but here, we're more of a GP-led inpatient care facility as well as offering some outpatient services... audiology and the like. We've recently restarted the urgent care centre though, hence why we're much busier. And also why I'm here."

"Restarted?" Duncan asked.

"Yes, we've had a bit of a staffing issue for some time."

"Hasn't everywhere?" Alistair asked rhetorically.

"Indeed," Moreno said. "I'm only here on a secondment."

"I know the feeling," Duncan said, waving away his comment as the doctor looked at him. "Then back to Broadford?"

"That's the plan."

"So, how well did you know Isla Matheson?"

Moreno was puzzled, his eyes darting between him and Alistair.

"Know her?" He shook his head, his forehead creasing. "I don't... didn't."

"You were on the island when she went missing though," Duncan said.

Moreno exhaled. "Maybe... probably... so what? There are a lot of people on the island, then and now."

"True," Duncan said. "I just thought you might know her through your friendship with Roddy."

Moreno's eyes drifted to Duncan, his lips parting. Duncan didn't speak, allowing the silence to hang in the air.

"Roddy?" Moreno said at last. He nodded. "Yes, I know Roddy."

"How long have the two of you been friends?"

Moreno's expression darkened. "A while, as it happens."

"He was a good friend of Isla's. I guess he's mentioned her recently, since her body was recovered."

"No... I can't say he has."

"Really?"

He inclined his head. "Not that I recall, but... I haven't seen much of Roddy recently."

"When did you last see him?" Duncan asked. Moreno stared at Duncan, struggling to swallow. His mouth must have run dry.

"I... saw him last night. Why do you ask?"

"Oh right... a quick catch-up, a few drinks... that sort of thing?"

Moreno's patience was at breaking point. "What are you getting at Detective Inspector...?"

Duncan chose his next words carefully.

"McAdam. Duncan McAdam. Isla Matheson died following a medical procedure... which may well have been a factor in her subsequent death. We're trying to determine who carried out that procedure."

Alistair sniffed hard; his eyes fixed on the doctor. "You see, she wasn't admitted to any facility on the island and no hospital within a day's travel has her registered as a patient, so... anyone within her circle with medical training is... of interest to us. Isn't that right, DI McAdam?"

"Of great interest," Duncan agreed.

Moreno spluttered. "And you think it was me? Ridiculous."

"Is it?"

"Damn right it is!"

"Your friendship with Roddy Mcintyre, is it a close one?"

Moreno, still reeling from the previous question looked at him, wide eyed. "Sorry... what?"

"Can you describe the nature of your relationship with Roddy Mcintyre?"

"We... we're friends. Good friends."

"He's quite an avid poster on social media," Duncan said, remembering the feed Fraser showed him.

"Is he? I wouldn't know."

"No?"

Moreno frowned, looking at Duncan. "No, I wouldn't."

"It's true, the two of you aren't even friends on social media."

"Well... there you are. How would I?" Moreno challenged him.

"Curious though," Duncan said, "seeing as you have three hundred friends on your account and Roddy has even more, and yet the two of you are strangers... digitally speaking."

Moreno shrugged. "I was a med student for nigh on eight years... moving around to take up different residencies. So what? I know a lot of people. Is that a crime now?"

Duncan shook his head. "Strange though, isn't it? The two of you pretending not to know one another."

"I'm not pretending about anything."

Someone knocked on the door and it opened. Dr Moreno

looked across, irritated. A nurse put her head around the door, smiling awkwardly.

"Sorry to disturb you, Dr Moreno, but the others are waiting to start the rounds."

"I'll be right there!" he snapped and she retreated from view, closing the door behind her. Taking a deep breath, he closed his eyes and regained his composure. When he opened them again, he'd taken on a steely resolve. "Is there anything else you'd like to ask me or have you just come here today to talk about my social media habits? Maybe you'd like to know what I had for my breakfast? A sausage bap if you're interested in that?"

Alistair nodded. "Square or link?"

"What?" Moreno asked.

"The sausage… was it square sausage or a link sausage?"

Moreno let out an exasperated gasp. Alistair met Duncan's look and shrugged. "It matters. Lorne sausage is a must."

Duncan turned his attention back to Moreno. Their eyes locked for a moment. "Can I ask if one of those residencies you mentioned was ever on a maternity ward?"

Moreno baulked at the question, frowning dismissively. "No, it wasn't. What the hell are you asking me that for?"

Duncan smiled. "Thank you for your time, Dr Moreno."

The doctor moved towards the door, hesitating before opening it. He looked back at Duncan as if he was going to say something. His expression implied anger and frustration. Apparently thinking better of it, he stepped aside, holding the door open for them. They passed by and he closed the door before striding away without another word. Duncan looked at Alistair who arched his eyebrows.

"Tetchy, isn't he?"

"Aye," Alistair said, nodding. "I see what you mean though. There's something off with him."

"Come on, let's head back to the station."

"Sorry about the sausage thing," Alistair said as Duncan pressed the button to release the doors so they could leave the ward. "But I felt it was important to know. Square sausage is what the nation's reputation is built on."

Duncan glanced sideways at him, shaking his head.

Alistair spread his hands wide, sidestepping a slow-moving elderly man walking with a frame in the middle of the corridor. "Mark my words, if it ever disappears there will be *blood on the streets*."

Duncan laughed.

CHAPTER TWENTY-FIVE

THE DRIVE back to the station only took a couple of minutes and Duncan was surprised to find Karen Graham sitting in reception. The desk officer caught their attention as they crossed the lobby.

"She's been waiting to see you, sir," he said, peering over the rim of his glasses and indicating her with the end of his pen. "Wouldn't speak to anyone else but you."

Duncan looked across at her. She was sitting in the corner, her hands cupped in her lap staring over at him. She looked pale and somewhat lost. Duncan gestured for Alistair to continue whereas he crossed the room towards her. Nervously, Karen got to her feet, wringing her hands now as he greeted her.

"Hello, Mrs Graham. What can I do for you?"

She looked past him, anxiously scanning the lobby. The desk officer glanced over at them and his attention only seemed to make her agitation grow.

"Would you like to take a walk with me?" he asked. She nodded and they left the station together.

Duncan drew his coat about him. There was a stiff breeze

coming in across the water and although this day started with some heavy cloud cover, that had now been replaced by a clear sky, beautiful but cold. Leaving Somerled Square behind, they crossed the main road and descended the steep line of steps to where the many tourist buses and coaches would park up at the water's edge while their respective parties made the short walk into the town.

The tide was out and many small sailing and shallow water fishing boats were lying at anchor. Some had been drawn up out of the water for routine maintenance. There was barely a soul about today though. All they had for company were the gulls circling overhead.

"It's really beautiful here, isn't it?" Karen said as they walked. Her hands were deep in the pockets of her heavy woollen black overcoat with a contrasting red scarf.

"Yes, it is. Sometimes I miss it," Duncan said.

She looked over at him quizzically. "Where do you stay?"

"Glasgow."

"Urgh... big cities," she said, "I can't stand them. All those people, the traffic... and the noise."

Duncan smiled. "It has its good points too."

"I suppose so... but not for me."

They walked on in silence, rounding the bay and coming to the rocks revealed by the receding tide.

"You didn't come all the way over to Portree to tell me how much you hate Glasgow," Duncan said, stopping.

Karen stopped too, staring out across the water towards Ben Tianavaig in the distance.

"No... no I didn't, DI McAdam."

He waited but she remained staring straight ahead. He thought about forcing it out of her but sensed it had taken a lot to bring her to see him, and so he remained patient. After a minute, she looked at him glumly.

"Is it true?" she asked. "What they're saying on the news this morning about Dieter?"

Duncan inclined his head. "He's a person of interest, that's true."

"And he's in prison at the moment?"

Duncan nodded.

"For… attacking those women?"

Again, Duncan nodded. "Aye, not that he ever admitted to doing any of it."

Karen looked down at her boots, pursing her lips. "But he did, didn't he?"

"The DNA doesn't lie."

She smiled but it was a wry smile and one without humour. "I can't believe it. Dieter was so…" she looked at Duncan "… not like that when I knew him."

"You never felt threatened by him then? You never had any instinctive reaction to him?"

She shook her head. "Like I told you last night, it was quite the opposite. He was a reassuring presence to me back then."

Duncan nodded. "While your husband was away."

Her eyes darted to him and he held her gaze, waiting. She looked away. "You know, you didn't tell me Dieter was in prison."

"You didn't need to know."

She looked at him again, sighing.

"And if I had told you, would you be standing here talking to me this morning?"

She shook her head, and chuckled. "No, I don't suppose I would be."

Duncan felt the chill in the air. He shuddered, tensing his body to try and sink deeper into the warmth of his coat. "But here you are."

A trace of a smile crossed her face. "Here I am," she said quietly.

Duncan moved to her shoulder and they both looked out over Loch Portree, Duncan squinting as the low sun reflected off the distant water.

"So, how long were you sleeping with Dieter Pohl?" he asked.

If Karen was shocked by the question, she didn't react, her eyes still trained on the distant headland. There was no denial.

"Two to three months... on and off," she whispered, her eyes flickering between Duncan and the landscape.

He took a deep breath. "While your husband was out at sea?"

She nodded. "He works hard... like all fishermen. It's a tough life, but not just for them. It's difficult to be the one left behind to manage everything else; the house, the business... and then they just slot back in for a few days every couple of weeks and before they're away again."

"Lonely."

Karen nodded, smiling weakly. "Living out that way is remote enough... and living there alone you certainly feel it." She glanced at him. "Not that I'm looking for sympathy. It's not like I was the only one." She took a deep breath, shaking her head thoughtfully. "Most people who work the water these days, even back then, fish the inner sea but not my Ian. He had to go on the deep-sea trawlers. The money was worth the inconvenience, the greater risk, or so he said."

"And then there was Dieter."

She smiled but it soon faded. "Yes, then there was Dieter. He was so different to Ian; younger, charming... quite the dashing character and so, so funny. He could make you laugh like no other." She stared at her boots again, absently kicking a pebble towards the water. "I don't really know how it happened, but it did." She looked at Duncan. If she had remorse for the affair she didn't show it in her expression. "When Ian came off the boat, Dieter and I would cool it… there was no way he would ever have known what was going on between us. Not that I expected it to last. I mean, what would a man like Dieter see in me? I was nearly twenty years his senior."

Duncan wondered if the self-deprecation was artificial or if she suffered from low self-esteem, but it wasn't his place to judge. Whatever people got up to in their own homes had little to do with him, and he'd be a fine one to stand in moral judgement of another in any event.

"What about the night Isla Matheson went missing," Duncan said, "were you with Dieter that night?"

She snorted a laugh. "Possibly… maybe, who knows?"

"Is it possible?"

"I was with him most nights when Ian was away, days too sometimes, and he was certainly away when all that business on Coral Beach happened, that's for sure."

"But you don't recall that particular night?" Duncan asked sternly. "It's important, Karen."

She sighed, shaking her head. "I don't know. I really don't."

Duncan was thoughtful, allowing a moment of silence to pass by.

"When Pohl spent the night with you, did he stay the whole night?"

She nodded. "Only if I was expecting the cleaners or someone else to call round would we make sure he was gone first thing in the morning, otherwise, yes, he would stay through the night." She shrugged. "It wasn't as if Ian and I had children or anyone else who might walk in on us." Her expression took on a faraway look, remembering past times.

"It was so... hedonistic," she said, looking glum. "And now..."

"There's no pleasure without pain," Duncan said.

"My husband... Ian, can't know about any of this, Detective Inspector."

Duncan frowned. "He's going to find out." She looked at him, pleading with her eyes. He shrugged. "I'm not going to sing it from the rooftops, but what do you think Dieter will do when he's being accused of murder?" She was horrified. "He'll likely say he was with you, even if he wasn't."

Karen walked to a bench on the bank overlooking the loch, sinking down onto the seat, her hands still in her pockets. She slowly rocked backwards and forwards, her face bearing an impassive expression. Duncan sat down next to her.

"I've really made a mess of things, haven't I?" she said quietly.

"Easily done," he said and she looked at him. He cocked his head. "We've all made mistakes. Show me someone who hasn't and I'll show you a liar."

She smiled affectionately, nodding. "Thank you."

It was true and no one knew more so than Duncan himself. Although, he'd never been in a position to provide an alibi to a convicted rapist and suspect in a potential kidnapping and murder investigation.

"Will he use me as his defence, do you think?"

"I would," Duncan said, spotting what he thought was a dolphin out in the loch although it could have been a ripple on the surface and a trick of the light. "But I don't know if he's saying anything yet. You should brace yourself though."

She shot him a worried look. "For what?"

"The press will have a field day on every aspect of this case. It has all the elements that sell papers."

Her head lowered. "Oh... God."

He felt for her. "Do you have anyone you can go and stay with should the need arise; get yourself out of sight for a while?"

She frowned. "I have a sister in Edinburgh."

"It might be worth giving her a call and priming her."

"I'll do that."

"But don't go anywhere without giving us your contact details first," he said, meeting her eye.

"I won't," she mumbled. Conversation lapsed again, Karen troubled by her inner monologue, Duncan guessed.

"Tell me, do you think he could have done it?" Duncan asked.

"Could he have hurt that girl?"

"Yes."

She thought about it for a few moments, clearly wrestling with her thoughts.

"If you'd asked me that at any time in the last twenty years I would have said no, I don't think he could be responsible."

"And what about now?"

She was pensive. "Dieter was… aggressive. Not physically violent you understand…"

"Sexually aggressive?" Duncan asked.

She nodded. "But always in a consensual way."

"It's speculative, I know, but looking back do you think there were signs there that he could act without consent?"

She pursed her lips, meeting his gaze for a moment before looking away again. This was difficult for her in so many ways. "I don't know. I really don't. But is that because my view has been skewed by knowing he's now in prison?"

Duncan acknowledged the point with a curt nod.

"The relationship I had with Dieter, if you can call it a relationship, was… not one borne out of love or any real romance," she said, looking at Duncan. "We were not exactly

Rom Com material. It was two people coming together through… convenience, for want of a better word." Her face flushed. "I don't regret it. Does that make me a bad person?"

Duncan exhaled heavily, arching his eyebrows. "No, it doesn't." He couldn't help but think it did make her a terrible wife and partner though.

His mobile rang and he excused himself, leaving Karen on her own staring out across the water. It was Alistair.

"Go ahead, Alistair."

"You'll never guess what the rapist has had to say for himself."

Duncan glanced at the dejected figure of Karen, sitting alone on the bench. "Oh, I'm pretty sure I can."

Finishing the call, he walked back to stand on Karen's shoulder.

"I have to return to the station, Mrs Graham," he said. "We will need to take down an official statement detailing everything you've just told me. I know from your point of view that will cause problems, but a word of advice… and it's up to you whether you take it or not." She looked up at him expectantly. "However difficult it is, I would speak to your husband about all of this before he reads about it in the newspaper."

She held his eye for a moment before turning away and returning her gaze back over the water.

She didn't say a word.

CHAPTER TWENTY-SIX

DUNCAN PUT the statement down on his desk and sat back in his seat, flexing his shoulders to release the tension in the muscles. It didn't work. Drumming his fingers on the desk he sought to figure out what was preoccupying him. Reading through the original statements taken from Isla's friends and family following her disappearance, he'd cross referenced them with the follow-up interviews carried out in the last couple of days.

In the main, there were few differences; perhaps a few details forgotten or remembered slightly differently, but nothing earth shattering that might impact the case. He sighed. Maybe Jameson and his A Team were right and the answers to Isla's fate lay with an outsider. Statistically, that was so unlikely. Nine out of ten times the victim would know their assailant, either a spouse, an ex, friend or family member. Even a colleague was a long shot when viewed through the lens of the numbers.

So why was Duncan hung up on these people?

"Something on your mind?" Alistair said, sidling up to his desk and perching himself on the next desk along.

Duncan sighed, rubbing at his face. "Plenty, Alistair."

"Anything further on the interview with Dieter Pohl?"

Duncan shook his head. "We'll be the last to know. Jameson didn't take it well that he could have an alibi provided by Karen Graham. Not well at all."

"Well, look on the bright side, if Jameson is proved right, you'll be away home before you know it."

"There is that," Duncan said, smiling, but if the truth be known he didn't really know where home was anymore. The prospect of returning to Glasgow filled him with a touch of dread when he thought about his DCI's reaction let alone when he thought about where he might stay when he got there. The one-bedroomed apartment he rented in the West End was just a base, not a home. He'd made his home with Natalie over the last couple of years, although he'd blown that now. "You know what's really bugging me?"

Alistair cocked his head. "What?"

"The termination."

"Isla's pregnancy?"

"Aye," Duncan said, frowning. "We've not been able to find any record of where she had the procedure."

"Travelled further than we think... used a fake name, or a friend's name... there are a number of ways around it."

"Nah," Duncan said, sitting forward and resting his chin on a balled fist. "They have a duty of care, not to mention they're used to doing these procedures. Mistakes that could lead to septicaemia are possible... but statistically—"

"There you are with your numbers again," Alistair said. "Are you sure you didn't miss your calling? Maybe you should have been an accountant or something."

"I'll show you my bank balance to prove that's a terrible idea," Duncan said with a sideways smile. "No, this termination... if we can't find evidence it was done at a hospital through the proper channels then I can't help thinking it was carried out elsewhere."

Alistair frowned. "You mean like in the old days... a back-street amateur? That's hardly necessary here, is it? I know we can be seen as a bit backward in coming forward here on the islands, but we're only talking twenty years ago. It's not like it's back in the fifties or anything. Things weren't all that different to the way they are now."

"I know... and I agree but humour me for a minute. Who could have done it?"

Alistair exhaled, folding his arms across his chest. "Okay... Roddy Mcintyre's pal, for one."

"Dr Moreno," Duncan said, nodding. "Yes, I can see that. Not his speciality, but he's a surgeon... was on the island and would have the knowledge."

"No record of him knowing Isla at the time though, and he is older than her by what... a decade or more?"

"True, and why he would run the risk to his medical career to perform a back-street abortion escapes me," Duncan said. He had a thought. "When did he get married, do we know if he was single back then?"

Alistair shook his head. "No idea. Easy enough to check though if he married in the UK obviously. If not, how good's your Spanish?"

Duncan smiled. "About as good as your Gaelic."

"That bad?"

"Let's put him on the list anyway."

"This *hypothetical list*," Alistair said, glancing towards Jameson's office. "The DCI's already crabbit as it is without you fucking things up further. Who else have you got on it?"

"The vet," Duncan said.

"Oooh... James Turnbull," Alistair said. "Good shout, I hadn't thought of him."

Duncan splayed his hands wide. "He's used to medical procedures. Many of the drugs used to treat animals are also used to treat people, albeit in different forms and strengths. He's bright enough to do a bit of research and he has a sterile medical environment, equipment…"

"Motive?"

"To avoid his wife uncovering an affair with a teenage girl… the damage to his business and reputation. I've met him, and I thought he was an arrogant man."

"He had an alibi though, didn't he?"

"For when Isla went missing that weekend, yes," Duncan said, "but septicaemia is an infection that grows, weakening the body over a period. And even if that passage of time was short, Isla could have contacted him… travelled across to Uist…"

"And he tried to treat the infection himself," Alistair said, thinking aloud, "and failed. Interesting theory. Very speculative though. What about the wife?"

"By her own admission, Andrea Turnbull was away nursing her sick mother in Fife. He could have had Isla with him for days without her knowing. Maybe he underestimated how ill she was. I've read up on septicaemia and the person can go from feeling mildly ill with a slight temperature to a severe fever and slipping into a coma within the space of twelve hours."

"So, the good veterinarian gets it wrong… Isla slips into a coma—"

"Or dies," Duncan said.

"Or dies…" Alistair tilted his head towards him, "…unexpectedly. So what does he do? He *could* fess up and take his chances."

"And ruin his marriage, career… his entire life? Or…"

"Bring her back to the island," Alistair said, "and bury her not too far away from where she was last seen alive." He arched his eyebrows. "It's a cracking theory."

"Aye, but one without a shred of actual evidence to support it," Duncan said. "Isla couldn't have told anyone otherwise it would most likely have come up."

"And if Turnbull knew that she hadn't told anyone, he'd reckon on a decent chance he'd get away with it. Okay," Alistair said, his expression thoughtful, "let's think it through as if it is an accurate representation of what happened. Where did Turnbull say he was when she went missing that night after the party?"

"The annual BVA conference," Duncan said. Alistair looked at him quizzically. "The British Veterinary Association. That year their conference was held in Glasgow. Turnbull stayed for the duration, three to four days and then travelled back after it closed."

"So, he wouldn't have been around on the Saturday night?"

Duncan shook his head. "Presumably not."

"Perhaps he left early?"

Duncan angled his head. "Worth a check, but who's likely to remember that long ago if he did?"

"I'll have Russell look into it. He's good at that sort of thing."

Duncan nodded. "That's the list… two men, and only one of them has a motive as far as I can see."

"If he was having an affair with Isla," Alistair said, "which we also can't prove."

Duncan looked around, then lowered his voice. "It might be good for us not to speak about this too much around the office. I can't see it doing either of us any good if it comes up in conversation in front of certain people."

"Discretion is my middle name."

Duncan was sceptical. Of all the adjectives he would choose for Alistair, discreet was not one of them.

Alistair noticed and smiled. "All right, my middle name is *Falcon*, but if you tell anyone I'll knock you out."

"Really?"

"Aye," Alistair said, looking around to make sure no one was within earshot. "My mother had a thing about explorers... Columbus, Marco Polo and all those types."

"Robert Falcon Scott," Duncan said quietly, smiling. "Suits you."

"Aye, does it hell!" Alistair rose off the desk, jabbing a finger in the air at him. "I mean it, tell anyone and I'll haunt you until your dying day... and beyond."

"Lips are sealed, Alistair."

Alistair went to find Russell and Duncan was alone with his thoughts once again. Roddy Mcintyre came to mind, something he'd said was also troubling him. Leafing through the file on his desk, Duncan sought out the references to Isla's best pal. The descriptions of the teenage Roddy offered up to the original investigating officer were in stark contrast to the man he'd met the previous day. Without anything more pressing to do, Duncan figured he'd address the inconsistencies.

Tossing the file down, he picked up his phone and looked up the telephone number of the Mcintyre's tour business and dialled it.

"Good morning," a gruff voice answered. It was hardly the warm reception he'd anticipated.

"Mr Mcintyre?"

"Speaking."

"It's DI McAdam, we met briefly yesterday when I came out to speak with your son, Roddy—"

"I remember. What can I do for you?"

Duncan didn't need to be particularly empathic to sense the man disliked him.

"I was hoping to follow up on a couple of points raised in the conversation I had with your son. Is he about?"

"No, he's called in sick today."

"Nothing serious, I hope?"

"No… I don't think so, just feeling a bit off, so he's taken to his bed. It's not good business to infect your customers on their holidays."

"No, I can see that. Busy today?" Duncan asked, making small talk while contemplating his next move.

"It's always busy these days, even when it's quiet it's still busy."

"Do you think he'd be well enough for a phone call? I really could do with speaking to him."

"I guess so. I can give you his mobile number, if you want it? Is there a problem?"

"Nothing to worry about, Mr Mcintyre. It's just procedural stuff, you know?"

Duncan took down the mobile number, grateful for the assistance. Roddy's father mumbled something incomprehensible before hanging up. Somehow, Duncan didn't think it likely to have been anything complimentary. He called Roddy straightaway. The call cut to voicemail within three rings. He tried again, only this time the call ended immediately.

Perhaps he didn't answer unrecognised numbers, plenty of people didn't, himself included. Standing, Duncan picked up his coat and signalled to Alistair that he was ducking out for a bit.

CHAPTER TWENTY-SEVEN

THE DRIVE SOUTH TO BROADFORD, where Roddy lived, took just shy of three quarters of an hour and Duncan found his house easily, a white house on the outer edge of the town over-looking the Inner Sound towards Scalpay. Duncan parked his car in the street behind a silver Mercedes and was gently buffeted by the wind as he walked up the drive to the front door.

He rang the doorbell and waited, turning to admire the view, the gentle hum of distant traffic carried to him on the breeze. With no sign of activity from within, he stepped back and looked up at the first-floor windows wondering if Roddy was asleep. The curtains were open however. He rang the bell again.

"I'll be right there!"

Duncan waited, hands in his pockets. Moments later, a key turned in the lock and the door opened. Roddy's smile dropped as soon as he recognised Duncan.

"Hello, Roddy," Duncan said, casting an eye over him. Roddy was dressed in jeans and a knitted jumper; his hair neatly styled and possibly still damp from showering. His colour was good. Overall, he seemed refreshed. "How's your health?"

Roddy averted his eyes from Duncan's gaze. "Oh... all right, you know?"

Duncan smiled. He'd pulled the odd sickie in his time too.

"I'm sorry to drop by unannounced, but I did call earlier."

Roddy looked over his shoulder, then back at Duncan, shooting him a nervous smile.

"That's okay, honestly. I... must have my phone off or on charge or something."

"I felt like getting out of the office anyway," Duncan lied. "May I come in? I have a couple of follow-up questions to ask you. Nothing to be concerned about. It will only take a minute."

Roddy seemed anxious. "Um... yeah, sure." He stepped back and opened the door wider. "Come in, Detective Inspector," he said, unnecessarily loudly.

Duncan entered, politely wiping his feet on the mat in the hall, allowing Roddy to close the door behind him.

"Nice place you have here," Duncan said. "A lovely spot."

"Thanks. Yeah, it's not exactly close to where we dock the boat. My dad's always on at me to move closer but I'm not ready to live further out. I don't want my life to become all about the business."

"Like your father's?"

Roddy arched his eyebrows but didn't comment as he led Duncan deeper into the house and through to an open-plan kitchen dining room at the rear.

"Was it your first choice to join the family business?" Duncan asked as Roddy offered him a seat. He declined, preferring to stand. Roddy did likewise, folding his arms across his chest.

"I'd be lying if I said it was, but I can't say it was a choice. Besides, my dad wouldn't manage well without me."

"He could hire crew couldn't he?"

Roddy laughed. "Oh yeah, he could. They wouldn't stay very long if he did though. They just don't last."

"The job or the boss?"

"Definitely the boss," Roddy said, smiling awkwardly and taking a deep breath. "Dad's not an easy guy to work for."

"You manage."

Roddy smiled wryly. "But he's my dad."

"I would have thought that'd make things harder," Duncan said, shuddering at the thought of working shoulder to shoulder with his own.

"We do right by our family though, don't we?" He shrugged. "Business is good, but it's competitive and always has been. If there's a period where things aren't going well, your family can always take a pass on their wages right? You don't get that much loyalty from others." Roddy shrugged. "I never had the option to do anything different, and you can't miss what you never had, can you?"

"I guess not."

"So, what brings you down this way?" Roddy asked, his eyes flitting beyond Duncan towards the hall. Duncan glanced back, curious, but nothing was there. "I mean, it must be important for you to make the trip."

"I was reading through the old witness statements taken at the time Isla was reported missing. The way people described you caught my attention."

"Really?" Roddy was surprised, smiling nervously. "In what way?"

"Everyone described you as happy-go-lucky, quick with a smile and never taking anything too seriously."

Roddy shrugged. "Aye... so what?"

"Forgive me for asking, but what changed?"

Roddy's lips parted and he frowned. "I don't understand."

"Admittedly, I have only just met you but... you strike me as jaded, a little cynical perhaps." Duncan watched him closely. "Their description of you doesn't chime with my experience. Can you explain that?"

Roddy, stone faced, held Duncan's gaze. "Well, maybe things were different back then."

"So, what happened?"

He shrugged. "I grew up. What of it?"

"I was just curious."

Roddy snorted derisively. "Whatever. You came all the way down here to ask me why I'm not the same guy I was twenty years ago? Forgive me, but is that what you get paid for?"

"No, of course not. It was something you said when I met you the other day."

"Oh aye, what's that then?"

"You said nothing good would come from dredging all this up again," Duncan said. Roddy leaned back against the breakfast bar, frowning. "What did you mean by that?"

He held Duncan's gaze for a moment with an impassive expression, and then he shrugged. "Nothing, I guess. Just that... it won't existentially change anything."

"Existentially?"

"Yeah... that's right, it won't."

"At the time that's what I thought you meant," Duncan said. Roddy nodded. "However, I got to thinking... and the more I think about it the more it sounded to me as if you're aware of the consequences."

Roddy's eyes narrowed. "Yeah, what the hell are you talking about?"

"I think you knew," Duncan said. "You knew about the pregnancy."

Roddy scoffed. "Now I *know* you've lost the plot—"

"I don't think so, Roddy. The way you reacted when I mentioned it. I put it down to you being bothered about your friend choosing not to confide in you, but it was more than that wasn't it? You were *surprised* that I knew, not that you didn't."

Roddy looked away, shaking his head, but it was a gesture without conviction.

"So, I thought about it some more," Duncan continued, "and I figured that out of all the people Isla knew, family, friends... who would she turn to for advice or a shoulder to cry on? And the one name that keeps coming back to me is her best pal." He pointed a finger at Roddy. "Which is you, Roddy Mcintyre."

Roddy remained silent; his jaw clenched.

"So, I asked myself the question; why would you be surprised that I knew?"

"And I suppose you have an answer for that as well then eh?" Roddy asked indignantly.

Duncan nodded. "Funnily enough, I do. That's my job. It's because you knew about the termination. It's the only reason you would be surprised."

Roddy drew a deep breath, clearly reticent to comment but his silence in and of itself all but confirmed Duncan's suspicion.

"Now," Duncan said, "put your game face on and call me a liar."

Roddy closed his eyes, his lips pursed. He slowly shook his head, looking down at the counter in front of him. "I cannae."

"You did know, didn't you?"

He lifted his head and met Duncan's eye, nodding. "I knew… afterwards."

"After she'd had the termination?"

Again, Roddy nodded. "Aye. She told me she'd been late and had taken a test, one of those ones you get over the counter." He chuckled but without genuine amusement. "She'd driven over the bridge to Kyle to get it, so paranoid was she that someone she knew would see her buying it on the island and tell her father."

"But she didn't come to you beforehand?"

Roddy shook his head glumly. "No."

"You're sure?"

"Of course I'm bloody sure, man!"

"Where did she go, to have the procedure?"

"I wouldn't know," Roddy said quietly. "She told me she'd taken care of it." He spread his hands wide. "She'd taken care of it and it was sorted."

"Did she say when?"

"No, but I thought it must have been recent. She seemed… off."

"In what way?"

Roddy was circumspect. "Unsettled by it all… worried, maybe? But I'm guessing. She didn't want to go into detail."

"Did it surprise you, that she hadn't confided in you in the first instance?"

"Oh aye… I was annoyed, I have to say," Roddy said frowning. "We were close, you know? I'd tell her everything and I thought she knew she could always come to me as well."

"But not this time."

Roddy appeared dejected. "Apparently not, no." He drew a hand across his face, pressing into both eyes with the thumb and forefinger of his right hand. "I guess she didn't feel safe."

"That's an interesting comment to make."

Roddy looked at him. "Is it?"

"Safe from who? The baby's father?"

Roddy exhaled heavily. "I wouldn't know about that."

"Wouldn't know or won't say?"

"What the hell do you want from me?"

"The bloody truth would be a good start!" Duncan bit back. "Now stop messing me around!"

"I thought I heard voices."

Duncan turned to see a man standing at the threshold, just as surprised to see him as the newcomer was to clap eyes on Duncan standing in the kitchen.

"DI McAdam," he said quietly. Roddy exchanged a glance with him and Duncan looked at both of them in turn. The newcomer had a damp towel in his hands, his hair still wet and awaiting a comb after showering.

"Dr Moreno," Duncan said, glancing at Roddy. "Are you doing house calls these days? I thought they were a thing of the past."

Carlos Moreno entered the kitchen and Roddy smiled at him apologetically. Now it made sense why Roddy had raised his voice earlier; to give Moreno the heads-up they had company.

"They do still happen in general practice, depending on the situation," Moreno said, folding the bath towel neatly and draping it over a chair in the dining area. He seemed hesitant, gripping the back of the same chair with both hands, looking over at Duncan. Moreno, dressed in a pair of tan chinos and a pale blue shirt, unbuttoned, with a white vest beneath, eyed Duncan suspiciously. "What brings you to Broadford, Detective Inspector?"

"I was about to ask you the same question," Duncan said, his eyes flickering between the two men. "But I don't think it's any of my business."

Roddy was silent, agitated. Moreno crossed the room and gently placed a supportive hand on his shoulder, squeezing it.

"It's not anyone's business but ours," Moreno said. Roddy lifted his head at hearing the comment.

"I take it your wife isn't away visiting friends then?" Duncan asked.

Moreno shook his head. "No. She's gone back to Spain with our daughter. She's staying with family." His tone implied he was sad about that. "Whether she returns… we'll have to see." He locked eyes with Duncan, assessing him perhaps. "It was a long time before I realised who I was, Detective Inspector. I married young, before I even finished medical school." He shook his head. "Life is too short to live a lie."

"As I say… your relationship is none of mine or the police's business, but I have to ask how long the two of you have known each other?"

Roddy exchanged a look with his partner and shrugged. "Eighteen months… maybe two years."

"Dr Moreno, you were working on Skye when Isla Matheson went missing," Duncan said.

"Yes, yes, I was… but I told you the truth, I don't know this girl. Not at all." He glanced briefly at Roddy before turning back to Duncan. "I have nothing to hide from you."

"And what about you, Roddy?" Duncan asked him. "What do you have to hide?"

Roddy shook his head, despairing. "You don't understand, Mr McAdam, but to be fair, how could you?"

"Try me?"

"My parents… my mum in particular is…"

"Bigoted," Moreno said, drawing a fierce glare from Roddy. "Sorry."

"She's old school about this sort of thing," Roddy said.

"She's not a hater, but... she finds it hard to break with the values she was brought up with. I'm not like Carlos," he said, smiling. "I know who I am, and I always have, but I couldn't show it."

"You won't, more like," Moreno said, bitterly.

Duncan sensed the tension between them on this issue. Carlos was seemingly prepared to go public with his feelings whereas Roddy, established and comfortable with his sexuality, wanted to keep their relationship from his family. He didn't envy either of them their positions.

"It's not that I won't. I just can't right now," Roddy protested. "I just need a little more time."

"There will never be a good time," Carlos countered. "Trust me, I know."

"I'm sorry, I don't want to get in the middle of anything," Duncan said, "but I need to know what you meant by dredging it all up again? I don't for a second think you meant the harm it might do to you personally, although knowing what the press are like they'll be more than happy to run a story as an aside to the main event just to titillate their audience."

"That's exactly what I'm afraid of," Roddy said, relieved that Duncan had seen his position. "They'll make it sound sordid... twist the truth. That's why..."

"Why what?"

"Why I don't want to get involved," Roddy said.

"But you are involved, Roddy." Duncan shrugged. "Like it or not."

"Well, I sure as hell don't like it, all right? I've got enough going on in my life that I'm struggling to deal with as it is," he said, shooting a pained look at Carlos. "And I don't want to add any more."

"If you knew about the pregnancy, why didn't you say something at the time?" Duncan asked.

"Because *at the time* I didn't think anything had happened to Isla. As far as I knew she'd taken off for a while to get her head straight." He ran a hand through his hair. "I didn't think... no one thought she'd... died or anything. I knew she was wrestling with something and I thought she'd be back."

His passion was convincing but Duncan still frowned at him for keeping silent. Roddy took it as him passing judgement.

"Look, the longer it went without Isla turning up the more doubts I had—"

"Then why not say something to someone?" Duncan asked.

"Because your lot said nothing was wrong," Roddy retorted. "So, I'm supposed to go against everyone, am I? Stand up and announce to the world that she was pregnant? You must be kidding."

Duncan had to admit he had a point.

"Who was the father?"

Roddy looked at him, biting his bottom lip as he shook his head. "She never said."

"Care to hazard a guess?"

"At the time... I assumed it was Alex's child. They'd only just broken up, so that made sense."

"And later, did that opinion change?"

"It did," Roddy said, glumly, "but before you ask, I don't know. I really don't. Then or now."

"So why did you move on from Alex Macrae?"

"I didn't. I mean, I didn't discount him. I'm just not so sure it was his."

"Why?"

Roddy shrugged. "The whole thing... the pregnancy, the

way Isla handled it and her reaction when she told me, so cold and matter of fact. None of it seemed like Isla, you know? It just wasn't straightforward."

Duncan's mobile rang and he fished it out of his pocket, excusing himself and walking into the hall. It was Alistair.

"Alistair, what is it?"

"Russell has come up trumps again, and you're going to love it."

"Turnbull wasn't at the conference?"

"Oh, he was at the conference all right. It was held in Glasgow that year, just as he said."

Duncan was disappointed. "Right. Please tell me there's more."

"Aye, it was in Glasgow but not in August. The BVA brought it forward to the May of that year due to an outbreak of Avian Flu on the continent over the winter. They wanted to try and get ahead of the curve as they expected it to leap the Channel."

"So Turnbull's alibi is blown?"

"Aye, we've got him, don't you think?"

Duncan sought to quell the rising excitement. From being crestfallen at the discovery of what Roddy was keeping secret to a prime suspect landing in their lap within the space of ten minutes.

"Yes, Alistair," Duncan said, feeling his stomach flutter. "I think we have him."

"Shall we bring him in?"

Duncan couldn't do that without first running it past DCI Jameson and that was the last thing he wanted to do at this point.

"No, but we're going to speak to him. He doesn't know that we're about to torpedo his story and I don't want him to see it coming. We'll go over there."

"We?" Alistair asked. "As in, you and me... on the ferry?"

"Unless you have a friend who can fly us out there, yes. Is that okay?"

"I suppose."

Duncan heard the reluctance in his voice.

"What's up?"

"Nothing... I'm just not all that keen on boats," Alistair said. "I was army not navy."

"You live on an island, Alistair, surrounded by water. There's a fair chance you're going to need a boat from time to time."

"Doesn't mean I have to be too keen on drowning though, does it?"

"Book us on the first available sailing, would you?"

"I'll do that."

"And Alistair... keep this between us, okay?"

"Will do."

CHAPTER TWENTY-EIGHT

DUNCAN RETURNED TO THE KITCHEN. Carlos was making coffee and he raised a cup towards Duncan who declined. Roddy was sitting at the dining table.

"I have to head back to Portree," he said to Roddy. "If there's anything else you think I need to know then now is the time to tell me."

Roddy sniffed and shook his head.

"Are you sure because I'll be annoyed if I have to traipse all the way down here again having found out something else you should have told me already?"

"No," he said, shaking his head. "There's nothing, I swear."

"Right, seeing as we're finally starting to trust one another, I want to ask you about Isla's life. I understand why you don't want scrutiny coming on you," he glanced at Carlos, "and your life, but not wanting to *dredge up* the past... there's stuff in her life that is being kept from me. I think you know what I'm talking about, so let's have it."

Roddy sighed. "For Christ's sake," he said, putting his head in his hands.

"Whatever it is, I need to hear it."

"Off the record?" Roddy asked.

"If you like, aye."

Roddy looked over at Carlos who gave an almost imperceptible nod of approval. Roddy took a breath.

"Her father used to beat her."

Duncan arched his eyebrows. "Ruaridh Matheson… used to beat his daughter?"

Roddy nodded. "And his son. He beat Donnie, and Isla ever since they were wee bairns. Mainly Donnie… he got the brunt of it, right up until he left for university and then Ruaridh moved onto Isla." Roddy sat upright, drawing breath and casting his eyes to the ceiling. "And he used to knock their mum around too."

Duncan sucked air through gritted teeth. "That's a hell of an accusation."

"And Hell is exactly where that man is going, if there's any justice in this world or the next."

"Do you have any proof of that?" Duncan asked, pulling out a chair and sitting down opposite Roddy. He'd planned to leave momentarily, but suddenly that looked unlikely. Carlos came across and set a cup of black coffee down in front of Roddy. The aroma made Duncan wish he'd accepted the offer of a cup after all. Roddy wrapped his cup with both hands, appreciating the warmth.

"Only Isla's word…" Roddy said, glancing at Carlos, "… and seeing the bruises myself of course. He used to whip her, with a cane or a belt, on the backs of her upper legs and lower back. All places where people wouldn't see." He laughed nervously. "It's not like you get much of a chance to wear a bikini on Skye, is it? Sometimes it was because of her behaviour or so he said, or because she had the devil in her. Sadistic old sod. He'd lock her in the outhouse, sometimes for an entire day or night, if it suited him. She'd nae make a sound or he'd give her what for as penance."

Images flashed unbidden through Duncan's mind, distracting him, and he fought to push them aside. Feeling suddenly warm, Duncan felt his face flushing and his breathing pattern accelerating.

"She was terrified of the man," Roddy said quietly, "and he ruled that household with an iron will…"

The mental churn came from nowhere, threatening to overwhelm Duncan and he closed his eyes, disoriented and feeling nauseous, trying to stabilise his thoughts. The worst of it seemed to pass.

"Are you all right?"

Duncan finally shook himself free of his thoughts, opening his eyes to find both Carlos and Roddy looking at him with concerned expressions. Carlos had a hand on Duncan's shoulder, was staring into his eyes and apparently examining him closely. He had a pocket torch in his hand, the beam moving between Duncan's eyes. He blinked against the glare. Carlos had been making coffee only seconds previously.

"How are you feeling, DI McAdam?" Carlos asked. "Take it easy just now."

Momentarily dizzy, Duncan gulped two massive inhales and the sensation passed soon enough. Reaching up, his neck and cheeks were warm to the touch. Duncan was worried he was about to vomit and he suppressed the urge. This had happened before, but not for a long time. Embarrassed, he fought to move past the feeling and find his focus.

"I'm sorry… I must have zoned out there for a second," he said, pressing a hand against his forehead and feeling a clammy sheen of perspiration on his skin. "Do you have a glass of water?"

Roddy returned to the table with a glass of water almost

immediately. Duncan hadn't noticed he'd already got up. Accepting the water gratefully, he managed to drain the contents in one go.

"How are you feeling?" Carlos asked him again. He had a hold of Duncan's wrist now, having turned the hand over and was gently pressing his fingers into the skin. Duncan hadn't noticed him do that either.

"I… I'm okay. I think."

"Your pulse is erratic," Carlos said. Duncan withdrew his hand, suddenly self-conscious. "Has this happened before?"

"From time to time, I guess."

"Have you been under any significant strain or stress of late?"

Duncan almost laughed, but instead he shook his head. He was feeling better, although the moment was unsettling to say the least. If it'd been the first time he'd experienced it then he would've been more concerned, but it wasn't. For a brief period it had become a regular event, accompanied by insomnia lasting for days until he'd wrestled a prescription from his GP to help him sleep at night, but he thought he'd put all of this behind him and moved on.

Perhaps he'd been deluding himself.

"I'm fine, it was just a dodgy turn. Probably the square sausage at breakfast."

Carlos looked unconvinced, but retired to a few feet away, cupping his chin with thumb and forefinger, keeping a watchful eye on him. "You should get yourself a proper check-up, Detective Inspector."

Duncan nodded. "I'll do that, first chance I get."

"I'm serious," Carlos said, forcing their eyes to meet. "Whatever that was, it isn't—"

"Normal?" Duncan asked, smiling. Carlos nodded. "Not the first time I've been told that. I get it, don't worry." He looked at Roddy who had taken his seat again. "What were we talking about?"

"Ruaridh Matheson," Roddy said, looking at Duncan with a mixed expression, "and the fact he's a total bastard."

Duncan rubbed the side of his head. "Yeah, that was it." Learning of Reverend Matheson using violence against his family, particularly his children, wasn't a surprise to Duncan. Maybe it should have been, but parents of a certain age or generation saw corporal punishment as character building and indeed necessary. You only had to look at the outcry from many in the population when legislation was introduced to limit the levels of force a parent could use on an unruly child to see that. To a person who didn't hold similar beliefs in disciplinary action, the violence could easily be construed as over the top or even sadistic in nature.

"Isla wanted to get away from home, away from *him*, but she had no idea how to do it."

"Which is why you thought…"

"She might have taken off for a bit?" Roddy said, nodding. "Aye, that's right. I always expected her to come back at some point though. I thought she had no idea how to make a new life for herself without help from someone and I wasn't in a place to help her. I wish I had been. The longer it went on – the longer she was away – the more I figured everything was okay. Especially seeing as your lot hadn't found anything untoward about it."

Duncan raised an eyebrow, feeling himself returning to normal. As normal as he ever got anyway. "You thought she'd managed to do it, to leave and get on with her life elsewhere?"

"That's right." Roddy looked glum. "I figured maybe she'd gone to stay with Donnie down in Glasgow. I thought about asking him when he came home to help out after his father's accident, but I thought better of it. Ruaridh was in a coma for days and the word was that he might not pull through. If Isla had gone to Donnie's I figured the family situation would bring her back. When she didn't, I thought better of speaking to Donnie. When he moved back, having found his father's faith in God, I thought again about asking him... but Donnie... he'd changed."

"Changed? In what way?"

"From rock star wannabe to a man of the cloth. It was a surprise, I can tell you. It was like he wanted to put his old life behind him. The old Donnie... the party guy, had died," he said, the hint of a smile crossing his lips which faded rapidly. "He wasn't approachable anymore. Not like he had been before. And now... Isla turns up out there in the peats." His expression took on a thousand-yard stare. "I was shocked."

"Why didn't you tell us this as soon as Isla was identified?"

Roddy snorted. "Yeah right. And who's going to believe me over him? The respected clergyman or the closet gay from Elgol?"

"It's not the fifties," Duncan said. "The choices people make in how they live their life don't have the same stigma as they used to."

Roddy scoffed. "You reckon? A few years ago, I'd have agreed with you, but have you seen what's going on these days? Are you on social media at all?"

"I try to keep away from it to be honest, melts your brain."

"Well, things haven't moved on as much as you thought, DI McAdam."

Not for the first time, Duncan realised that Roddy had a point.

CHAPTER TWENTY-NINE

ALISTAIR WAS WAITING for Duncan when he walked into the incident room back at Portree. He was grumbling about something and everyone else was giving him a wide berth.

"Are we good to go?" Duncan asked.

"Aye," Alistair muttered. "I have us booked on the seven-thirty sailing. No shortage of places, seeing as no one else in their right mind wants to catch the last crossing."

"It's a night out, Alistair," Duncan said, smiling. "Most men would be pleased to get a free evening in the pub."

Alistair shot him an incredulous look. "A free evening, aye! One on Uist… not so bloody much. Unless you want to hit the sunset strip and the casinos with me?"

Duncan smiled at the sarcasm. Russell, up until now sitting at his desk with a phone clamped to his ear, hung up and turned to face them.

"Good work getting into Turnbull's back story," Duncan said.

"Thanks very much, but it wasn't hard." He indicated his phone with a nod. "That was the station chief from out at Dunvegan. They've just attended a house fire up Geary way."

Geary was a small hamlet on the east coast of the Waternish peninsula. "He thinks we should go and check it out. He's calling in a specialist from the mainland to take a look, but he thinks it's likely arson."

"Arson?" Duncan asked, surprised. "What was burning?"

"An old croft. Uninhabited he reckons, but he's confident someone's torched it."

Duncan and Alistair exchanged a glance, Alistair frowning.

"Who'd want to set alight to something all the way out there?"

Duncan's eyes flitted to the clock on the wall. "We can take a look," he said, much to Alistair's chagrin. "Come on, we've got hours to kill between now and the sailing this evening. There won't be much we can do other than take a look."

Alistair reluctantly agreed. Russell picked up his phone.

"Shall I call ahead and tell him you're on your way?"

Duncan nodded, signalling to Alistair to get his coat. He did so, muttering under his breath as he fell into step beside Duncan.

"How DID it go with Roddy Mcintyre anyway?" Alistair asked. He'd barely said a word to him since they'd left Portree.

Duncan wondered how much he should say, bearing in mind he didn't want to cause upset in the lives of either Roddy or Carlos.

"He was keeping something back but not about what we thought."

"Oh aye," Alistair said, looking over at him. Duncan maintained his focus on the road ahead, hoping Alistair would do the same seeing as the weather was closing in around them now. A bank of sea fog was rolling in off Loch Snizort and visibility was reducing along with it.

"Roddy told me that Ruaridh Matheson used to abuse his family. He'd beat the kids… and his wife too."

"What?" Alistair asked, astonished. "Reverend Matheson? I don't believe it."

"I know," Duncan said, with a wry smile. "That's what Roddy figured most people would say… and the reason he kept quiet. Looks like he was right."

Alistair grumbled something inaudible, feeling slighted.

"Roddy says Isla used to show him the bruises."

"Well, I'll be damned."

"If it's true, hopefully Ruaridh will be."

"Do you believe him?" Alistair asked. "Roddy, I mean?"

Duncan thought about it for a moment, although he'd been doing that for much of the drive back from Broadford. He nodded. "In my eyes, he's credible."

"That's what we say to journalists."

Duncan laughed. "I do believe him, yes." He cocked his head at Alistair. "Proving it this many years down the road would be a stretch though. Somehow, I doubt Donnie's going to confirm it, do you?"

"Nah… and with Isla and their mother gone, why would he ruin what's left of his family. You think it's relevant?"

"To Isla's death?" Duncan asked and Alistair nodded. Again, Duncan paused for a moment of reflection. "On the one hand, yes, you can't say it isn't. If Isla was going to expose her father then he'd have a motive to silence her, but there's no evidence that Isla was going to do anything of the sort. At least, not that she told anyone. Roddy thought she wanted to get away but didn't have any actual plans to do so, or none that she confided in him about anyway. Watch the road, Alistair for crying out loud!"

Alistair swerved to avoid a sheep wandering aimlessly across the carriageway as they were wont to do in this part of the world, waving away Duncan's exclamation with a casual flick of his hand.

"Relax, would you? I was driving while you were still itching in your father's underwear," Alistair said, shaking his head, although he did keep his focus on the road from then on. "But on the other hand?"

Duncan had momentarily lost his thread. "Right... on the other hand, no it's not relevant. We're assuming she'd already had the termination procedure before she went missing, and so there was no reason why the pregnancy would be related to her abduction, if you follow?"

"Maybe the father of the child didn't like the idea of her terminating the pregnancy and got angry about it," Alistair said.

"Maybe. Although we still don't know who the father was. Roddy assumed it was Alex Macrae, seeing as he'd been dating Isla up until recently."

"You sound like you might disagree with that?"

Duncan sighed. "I'm not sure about any of it, to be honest with you. Every time we pull on a thread it only leads to more questions and even fewer answers. If we are looking for someone who attended the party that night then it's more likely to be someone who made a pass at her and she rejected them... one thing leading to another..."

"But the pathology doesn't reflect that nor do the witness statements."

"Which is why none of this makes any sense," Duncan said mournfully.

Their route took them across the base of the Waternish peninsula from Edinbane and then up the west side through Waternish itself, Lusta and then Hallin before they arrived at

Lower Halistra. From here they cut across to the east coast passing through desolate peat bog which lay to either side of the single-track road.

When they arrived at the high point overlooking Aros Bay, the road split. To their left was the hamlet of Geary whereas taking the right turn would lead them down to Gillen. Alistair headed up the coast towards Geary, the northernmost inhabited part of the peninsula. Beyond here, only hikers and crofters with their all-terrain vehicles could pass on the land. The road was a dead end and neither man knew exactly which croft had been burning, however all the houses were located on the left with the bulk of their narrow crofting land gently sloping away towards the water on the opposite side of the road, culminating at the cliffs some distance away.

They came across the scene soon enough. A liveried patrol car was parked across the road to stop traffic, what little traffic there was, from getting too close. The constable got out of his car, recognising Alistair immediately and pointing up the track to where the fire brigade's appliance was parked. Smoke was still billowing from the house, the flames long since extinguished but the crew were still damping down the charred remnants. Unusually, the croft was one set back from the road by some thirty metres, positioned behind the neighbouring properties which were all built in a straight line, more or less. The access track was grassy and overgrown and didn't appear to have seen much traffic pass over it for quite some time.

Alistair parked his pick-up alongside a stone boundary wall separating the croft from its neighbour's land and the two of them got out. Fortunately, the prevailing wind was carrying the smoke away from them and across the moorland at the rear. Duncan drew his coat about him and came alongside Alistair, whose long nylon coat rustled on the breeze as they walked. The station officer came across to greet them, shaking Alistair's hand.

"Long time no see, Al," the man said, nodding a greeting at Duncan.

"Tommy, this is Duncan McAdam," Alistair said, dispensing with the formalities of title as usual. He turned to Duncan. "This is Tommy Muir. Retired draughtsman by day, all action firefighter by night... or when needed."

Tommy shook Duncan's hand. "Nice to meet you, Duncan."

"What do you have for us, Tommy?" Duncan asked.

"A proper bùrach is what we have," he said, gesturing behind him towards the smoking stone house. "Come and see."

He led them the short distance towards the building, three members of his part-time fire crew were busy ensuring the fire wouldn't spring back into existence, hosing down the smouldering roof trusses and ceiling beams that had collapsed in on the building due to the ferocity of the flames.

"I'm afraid we haven't left you much," Tommy said, indicating a path for them to follow that would safely get them closer to the scene. "The fire burned so hot that all we could do when we got here was to ensure it didn't pass to the neighbouring properties on the wind. It's a good job the wind switched to a westerly or we would have struggled to contain it."

Duncan looked to their left, seeing the next house had a thatched roof in the traditional style, a rarity these days. Most of the thatched long houses had been replaced by imported slate or metal panels, steel, aluminium or zinc. The old stone croft house had been gutted by the fire. Aside from the gable end walls and the stone surrounds to the upper dormers, everything else was now smoking on the ground floor amongst a pile of charred timbers.

At the rear of the building, butting up against the wall of the house was the remains of an old caravan. It was burnt out with only the metal chassis and wheels identifiable. The thin plastic walls and metal frame had melted and buckled under pressure from the extreme heat. Judging by the size of the frame, it was likely a two berth.

"Any idea what started it?" Duncan asked, scanning the ruins of the house and the wreckage of the caravan.

"The concentration of flame was over there, at the rear here," Tommy said, pointing to a section of wall that stood out between the caravan and the house. "You can tell by where it's more blackened than elsewhere. The soot deposits are far stronger in that area. It's obviously where the fire began, either inside the caravan or it was started against it. Then everything properly went off when the old gas canisters stacked outside the caravan caught."

"Explosion?"

"Heard down in Gillen," Tommy said. "Luckily, I don't think there was a lot of propane left in them otherwise it could have been even nastier. The explosion ripped the guts out of the caravan, tearing through it like it was made of paper, before carrying the flames over to the house."

"Who called you?" Alistair asked.

"Willy Robertson. Do you know him?"

Alistair shook his head. Duncan looked around. "The neighbours didn't see or hear anything?"

Tommy grimaced. "They're mostly self-catering holiday lets along here these days. A couple of the lads still work the land, but no one was home when this got going. They've all been for a nose around since we got to work though."

Alistair and Duncan exchanged a glance. "No witnesses then?" Alistair asked.

"Your job no' mine," Tommy replied with a wink.

Duncan glanced around. "How do you think it got started?"

Tommy fixed him with a stern look. "An investigator will be coming onto the island tomorrow, but I'd hazard a guess that it started with the caravan and then the flames caught on the roof of the house. This old croft house... the timbers would have been the perfect path to feed the flames right enough."

Duncan looked at the rear of the house where the stones were indeed badly charred.

"And you say it started there?"

"I reckon so, aye. Someone's used an accelerant to get things going too, in my opinion."

"Any idea what?"

Tommy shrugged. "Nothing exotic. My money's on good old petrol or perhaps paint thinners, if they had enough of it."

The wind changed, gusting a cloud of acrid wood smoke across them. The stench caught in his nostrils and Duncan covered his face, happy when the next gust blew it away from them. He looked out over the water, not that he could see the land across the other side of the loch anymore, so thick had the fog become now.

"Anyone living here?" he asked, confident the house and caravan were unoccupied due to the poor state of repair of the croft in general.

"No, Willy said no one's lived here as far back as he can remember," Tommy told them. "The land is tenanted out, but as far as he knows the croft itself is pretty much abandoned these days. Has been for years."

"Kids?" Duncan asked drawing a chuckle of derision from Alistair.

"You've been in Glasgow too long!" Alistair shook his head. "The weans start beach fires around here, they don't go about burning people's homes to the ground," he said, pointing at the house and caravan for emphasis. "They'll no' be giving it laldy all the way out here, and especially not on a night like this."

Duncan smiled. "I suppose not." No one had been hurt which was the main thing, although he found the prospect of an arsonist running about remote communities to be disturbing. The island had three fire stations with another just over the bridge at Kyle, but the island was big and the roads were difficult to pass at times. This house was unoccupied, but the next one, if there were to be a next one, might not be. Duncan couldn't ever remember an arson on the island, at least not in a case like this. "Could be an insurance job. Who is the landowner, do you know?"

Tommy shook his head. "No idea, sorry."

"We'd better head off if we're going to make the crossing," Alistair said.

Duncan checked his watch. Alistair was right. They'd be pushing it as it is, and he was keen to speak to James Turnbull and didn't want to leave it another day.

"Can you make sure your investigator gets in touch with me tomorrow?" Duncan asked, handing him one of his contact cards with his mobile number on it. The station officer nodded, glancing at the card. Duncan thanked Tommy and the two of them walked back to the pick-up.

"Look at you," Alistair said, opening his door. Duncan looked at him quizzically. "Make sure the investigator calls you tomorrow."

Duncan shrugged. "And?"

"It's almost like you're settling in to stay for a while."

Duncan shook his head. "Nonsense," he said quietly. Alistair got in and Duncan stayed where he was for a moment, looking over the scene of the burnt out house. He beckoned the constable over from where he was leaning against his patrol car.

"While you're here, I want you to go door to door, see if anyone saw someone they didn't recognise coming or going this evening. Anything out of the ordinary at all, however small."

The constable nodded. "I will, but there's no' many folk about tonight."

"Do what you can."

He got into the pick-up, catching Alistair smiling at him. Duncan chose not to acknowledge the look. He pointed down the road, back the way they'd come and Alistair started the engine.

CHAPTER THIRTY

THE CROSSING from Uig to Lochmaddy was delayed for an unexplained reason and therefore they arrived in the Western Isles shortly before ten o'clock at night, an hour later than scheduled. Once they'd left the terminal and passed through the town they were out into the wilds of North Uist. The night was overcast and beyond the beams of the headlights the only light pollution emanated from the properties dotted around the open landscape, pin holes of light punctuating the darkness.

Alistair slowed the pick-up as they entered Carinish, Duncan directing him through the gloom. The mist hung thick over the machair, reflecting the light back at them, making passage across the island slow going. Even Alistair with his heavy right foot had to concede the journey was perilous if you didn't know the roads.

Arriving at the entrance to the track that took them up to the Turnbulls' home, Alistair stopped after crossing the cattle grid. Duncan looked over at him quizzically.

"What are you expecting to happen?" Alistair asked. "We

don't have anything substantial on him and without some form of a confession none of this is likely to stick."

It wasn't anything Duncan hadn't already thought himself.

"If he has any sense about him at all, he'll refuse to answer any questions without a solicitor present."

"That'll take all the fun out of it," Alistair said dryly. "It'll make him look guilty as hell though. I've not met the bloke, but do you think he might try to style it out?"

"Let's see."

Alistair drove the pick-up forward, drawing up in front of the main door to the house. Lights were on inside and Duncan rapped his knuckles on the door, Alistair coming to stand just behind him. A dog barked from inside and soon after the exterior light overhanging the door came on, Duncan blinking against the glare. James Turnbull opened the door, visibly surprised to see the two policemen standing outside his home.

"Mr Turnbull," Duncan said. "This is DS MacEachran. We're sorry to call so late, but we have a few more questions for you."

James Turnbull's eyes flickered between them and he nodded, beckoning them to enter. A spaniel appeared from somewhere in the house, tail wagging furiously as it inspected them, although it quickly chose to give Alistair a wide berth which was telling. Somehow dogs seem to know whom to safely approach and whom to avoid.

Their host led them along the hall and into the kitchen, an open-plan dining and family room were beyond that with a large wall of sliding glass doors offering a panoramic view across the machair to Baile Sear, a low-lying tidal island just off the coast slowly being reclaimed by the sea. Tonight however, the view was just an expanse of inky gloom. Even the wind was barely audible within the house, such was the quality of their renovations, keeping the wild Atlantic winds at bay.

Andrea entered the kitchen behind them. "I thought I heard voices," she said, looking between Duncan and her husband, glancing at Alistair.

"The police have a few questions, love," James said.

"At this time?" she asked surprised, but she didn't seem bothered by the hour of their arrival.

"Apologies for the timing," Duncan said, "but the ferry was delayed."

"No problem," James said. "Would you like a cup of tea or something?"

Duncan declined. Neither of them took a seat when offered either.

"So... what can we do for you?" James asked.

Alistair moved to stand to James' left, Andrea's eyes following him warily. Duncan had the impression their arrival may not have been wholly unexpected.

"When we spoke previously, we still didn't have the full set of results from pathology. It would appear that Isla had been pregnant," Duncan said.

James' lips parted but he said nothing, however he did shoot a furtive glance at his wife who remained steadfast and impassive, sitting on a stool at the breakfast bar.

"I... I had no idea Isla was carrying a child."

"You're sure about that?" Duncan asked. Now Andrea's expression made an almost imperceptible involuntary twitch which Duncan noticed.

"No... I mean, yes," James said. "I had no idea. Why would I?"

Alistair cleared his throat. "So, Isla didn't call you for help about it in the week she went missing?"

James looked at him, his brow furrowing in disbelief. "No,

I didn't hear from her at all that week, and why would she call me? What a preposterous notion."

"She could have called you while you were down in Glasgow the night she went missing to talk about it?" Duncan asked.

"No. Why would she?"

"To get some medical advice perhaps?"

James' head whipped around to Duncan; shock evident in his expression.

"No!" James barked. "Of course not."

"No contact with her at all while you were in Glasgow?" Duncan asked for clarification. He saw Andrea's head lower in the corner of his eye.

"No," James said fiercely. "That weekend I was working amongst my peers. A conference isn't necessarily a jolly, DI McAdam. I worked very hard."

"Oh... did yer, aye?" Alistair said.

James glared at him detecting the sarcasm so often missed by others.

"Yes," he growled. Shifting his gaze to Duncan. James then glanced at his wife who had her head in her hands.

Duncan pointed casually to Andrea. "I think she knows, James."

"Knows what?" James asked, confused.

"She knows your story is falling apart around you," Duncan said. "Don't you, Mrs Turnbull?"

She lifted her head and met Duncan's gaze. Lips pursed, she exhaled deeply through her nose and nodded.

"How about we start again, and the two of you drop this pretence?" Duncan asked.

"The game's up, James," Alistair said jovially. James Turnbull's face drained of colour and he looked to his wife, possibly for guidance. "Time to correct the record. Whenever you're ready, take your time... but it's late, so please do crack on."

James looked lost. Duncan took the initiative.

"We know you weren't at a conference in Glasgow, James. We checked."

Turnbull covered his mouth and nose with one hand, steadying himself on the kitchen island with the other. He shook his head, dejected. Was it because he'd been caught out in a lie or relieved at not having to continue repeating it.

"No... you're right, I wasn't in Glasgow," he said quietly. "Not at the conference. It had been brought forward."

"Now we're getting somewhere," Duncan said. "So, you were here that week after all."

"No, he wasn't," Andrea said, interrupting Duncan before James could answer. "He was with me."

"You were visiting your mum weren't you?" Duncan asked. Andrea shook her head. "Please make certain you're clear on what you're about to tell us, Mrs Turnbull. Fashioning a fresh alibi off the cuff to mask the failure of the first rarely works out. Is this where we are now?"

"It's not like that," she said, looking down. James moved to stand beside her, placing a comforting hand on her shoulder. She shrugged it off and James' face dropped at the rejection.

"Right," Duncan said, irritated. "James, you'd better tell me what's going on or I'll have you on the next boat to Skye and you'll be spending a lot of time in a cell until you start making sense."

James Turnbull stepped away from his wife, folding his arms across his chest. Andrea was still staring down, refusing to meet her husband's silent, almost desperate pleas for eye contact.

"Let's start with your relationship with Isla, shall we?" Duncan asked.

James nodded, briefly closing his eyes. "Isla was such a... spirited girl," he said, a genuine smile forming on his lips. "She was captivating. Intelligent, fun... more mature than her years. It was so obvious when you met her."

Duncan saw Alistair roll his eyes at the description and he knew why. Claiming underage, or barely above age, girls were *older than their years* was the go to justification for older men, who should know better, as well as paedophiles who couldn't care less if the girl was old enough.

"Was the child yours?" Duncan asked bluntly.

"No!" James snapped. He looked at his wife, her head bowed. "It wasn't mine... I don't think it could have been."

Alistair snorted. "You don't think..."

James glared at him. "It wasn't mine," he growled.

"You had a relationship with her though, didn't you?" Duncan asked.

James looked at him. "Not like you're no doubt thinking, no." Andrea was still refusing to make eye contact with anyone. "It wasn't like that."

"Then tell us what it was like."

"It was... a... an infatuation."

"On whose part?"

"Hers!" Andrea said, lifting her head and glaring at Duncan for having the apparent impudence to ask the question. "She was obsessed with James. Flirting... dressing provocatively... appealing to the base desires of men."

Alistair raised an eyebrow, Duncan assumed he was thinking *not all men* but he didn't say it, thankfully. "Oh, aye..." Alistair did say, barely concealing an incredulous smile.

"It's true... to an extent," James said. When Isla came to work with me, she was like a breath of fresh air to have around the place." Duncan saw his wife wilt at hearing the comment. "You see, Andrea and me... we were having our problems." He looked across at her but she didn't reciprocate. "Like any marriage, I suppose. We... we'd recently found out that we couldn't have children and we so desperately wanted to have a family. More than anything."

"And you still blame me," Andrea whispered.

"I don't... and I never have," James said with feeling. She still wouldn't meet his eye.

"It must have been absolutely gutting for you to find out Isla was pregnant," Alistair said.

"I didn't know!" James said. "How many more times do I have to tell you that?"

Alistair shrugged. "Until one of us believes you, I guess."

James shook his head defiantly. "And you wonder why I didn't tell you the truth."

"I do still wonder that, James," Duncan said. "So, you were describing your relationship with Isla. Go on, please."

James took a breath. "Okay... as I said, Isla was in love with animals, nature... she could see herself trying to become a vet, or a veterinary nurse, working in the profession in some capacity. I think that was my appeal to her." He looked sheepishly between Duncan and Alistair. "She saw in me, and in my life, a lot of what she wanted."

"And what did you see in her?" Duncan asked. He pointed at him as he was about to respond. "And I suggest you tell the truth because it's been a bloody long day and I'm sick of people telling me lies."

"I saw... attention. Isla made me feel..." he glanced at Andrea, "... like I did when I met my wife; important, special... and loved." Andrea looked at him then, tearful. "Things between us had been so measured, so cold, with both of us tiptoeing around each other, walking on eggshells, frightened to say the wrong thing. It was awful... for both of us."

"And Isla?" Duncan asked.

"The flirtation was... intoxicating, I admit." James shook his head in resignation. "I used to love seeing her. Our time together wasn't restrained by the baggage of our lives. It was simple, pure and... passionate."

Alistair grimaced but said nothing.

"And how far did your relationship go?" Duncan asked.

"Like I said, it was an infatuation on her part and a flirtation on mine," James said. "And it went no further than that."

"Let me be clear," Duncan said. "You're denying there was any form of sexual relations between you and Isla Matheson?"

"I did not have *any* physical relationship with Isla at all that could have led her to become pregnant with my child," James said, meeting Duncan's eye. He then turned to face Alistair, cocking his head. "Is that clear enough?"

"I'm still thinking about you *thinking* it couldn't be yours," Alistair said flatly. "Now you're certain it wasn't. You're a learned man, so I reckon you'll know how weans come about."

"It was not mine," James snarled. "It couldn't be."

"Why did you lie to us?" Duncan asked. James's stance softened and he shook his head, sighing. "Why lie about where you were if you had nothing to hide?"

"Because... I couldn't say and I... panicked."

"You panicked?" Alistair asked. "Why would you panic?"

"Because I knew what it might look like. Isla... made a pass at me the last time she was here and..."

"You responded," Duncan said.

He nodded. "It was just a kiss... barely anything, for crying out loud."

"A kiss is physical," Alistair said dryly.

"Oh come on…" James said, exasperated. "Hardly."

"If it was just a kiss, why the lie?" Alistair asked. "You don't lie about a kiss. Come on, man, do you think we're stupid or something?"

"Because he had no choice," Andrea snapped, exhaling heavily and rubbing her face with her hands. "Because I told him to." Duncan exchanged a glance with Alistair before coming to stand opposite her across the island, encouraging her to continue. "Because I was in such a state. I needed… help, help that we couldn't get here on the island. We had to go to the mainland."

"Glasgow," James said, reluctant to elaborate. "I was in Glasgow, just not for the reason I told you."

"I was voluntarily sectioned, DI McAdam," Andrea said, meeting Duncan's eye. "You'll no doubt find it on record at Leverndale Hospital."

"Andrea was processed through the acute admissions unit and she spent four days on the assessment ward, with a further week in treatment before she was discharged," James said. "I visited her every day, even when they wouldn't let me see her I was there, hanging around like a bad smell." He looked at Duncan. "I'm sure my presence will have been recorded too. I was even given a consultation regarding the state of my own mental health, such as it was back then. The stress of it all… it nearly broke me." He looked at his wife. "It nearly broke the both of us." Andrea smiled weakly at him.

"We will check all of this out," Duncan said, "and if it turns out you're lying to me again, you can stand by, I tell you."

James spread his hands wide. "By all means do. We're telling you the truth." He shrugged. "We have nothing left to hide."

"And when was Andrea admitted?"

James was thoughtful. "I don't recall the specific date…

but I spoke with the hospital on the Monday and we trav- elled on the Tuesday... and were in Glasgow for the duration."

Duncan thought it through. Isla was last seen at the party on Coral Beach the following Saturday night. Could it still have been possible for James Turnbull to have performed the termination prior to their leaving? It was possible but seemed unlikely.

"We believe Isla visited Uist the week she went missing, and it would have been prior to your leaving for Glasgow."

"I know that," James said, "you told me the last time you were here, and I'll repeat what I told you then. If she was on the island that week, then it wasn't to come and see me. I hadn't seen her for a while, not since the... since she came on to me. Why would she come to me after I'd rejected her?"

"Because she was pregnant and had a back-street termina- tion in the week before we believe she died. That's why," Duncan said.

"And you think..." James stared at him, "you think I would do such a thing? Have you both completely lost your minds?"

"You have your clinic, surgical instruments and a sterile environment," Duncan said. "As well as a lot to lose if it came out she was carrying your child."

"You're mad," James said, shaking his head in disbelief. He looked at Andrea. "This is insane. I'm not the father... I didn't do any of this."

"You know, if that's the case, you could have saved your- self a lot of grief by telling us all of this when you were first asked," Duncan said accusingly.

"Hindsight is a wonderful thing, DI McAdam," James said, "and maybe if when I was asked Isla was considered a kidnapping or murder victim, then I would have, but your lot said she'd run away. So, am I supposed to wreck my life, my marriage for the sake of satisfying the gossips?"

Duncan tilted his head. "Aye... all things considered; I'd argue spinning a web of lies isn't the best course of action."

"On that... we can agree," James said, glumly. "However, we're entitled... my wife... is entitled to a private life, DI McAdam. You know what people are like; society has progressed in so many ways, but one thing you still don't want to be and that's tarred with the *mad brush*. You'll be forgiven most things, but mental fragility is still viewed as a weakness of character by many. And this is a small community... supportive, yes, but everyone knows your business."

Duncan bit his lip, nodding slowly. "I can appreciate that."

He looked at Alistair who appeared as disappointed as he felt himself. The trip hadn't garnered the result he'd half expected and certainly not the one he'd hoped for. Gesturing towards the door with a flick of his hand, Alistair nodded and readied to leave.

"Is... is that it then?" James asked, surprised.

Duncan inclined his head. "For now. We'll be checking with the hospital though... and if it's not right, rest assured we will be back."

"And we'll no' be so nice about it either," Alistair said.

James swallowed hard.

"We'll see ourselves out," Duncan said, glancing at Andrea Turnbull who looked devastated. "Thank you for your time."

With Alistair a step behind him, they walked out into the night. James Turnbull escorted them out anyway, closing the door after them before they'd even reached the pick-up. Alistair hadn't bothered to lock it and Duncan clambered in, deep in concentration. He realised Alistair had said something, but he'd been lost in thought and hadn't heard.

"Sorry, what was that you said?"

"I was saying it's plausible." He intimated towards the house with a nod. "What your man there was saying. It's plausible."

"Aye," Duncan said, "it is."

"I really thought we had him," Alistair said, turning the key in the ignition. "I thought we had the lying sod."

"Aye, me too," Duncan said.

"Forgive me for saying so," Alistair said, eyeing Duncan nervously, "but you don't seem too depressed about it."

"It's not that necessarily… but…" Duncan sighed, "there's something about all this that I'm not getting. It's all there or thereabouts, but I'm missing it. And it's annoying me now."

"Let's get back to the hotel before the bar closes," Alistair said, turning the pick-up around and accelerating down the track. "A few medicinal beers will help clear things up."

Duncan doubted that very much. The Lochmaddy Hotel was within sight of the ferry terminal and they were booked on the first sailing the following day. Duncan didn't like the idea of leaving the islands empty handed again. He'd been so sure they were on to something this trip, but now he had the feeling they were further away than ever in resolving this case.

CHAPTER THIRTY-ONE

Duncan awoke from troubled sleep, casting off the duvet and stumbling through the darkness into the bathroom. His head banging, a sheen of perspiration on his skin, he was reluctant to put the lights on for the brightness was sure to only make the pounding worse.

Running the tap over the basin, he cupped his hands and threw freezing Hebridean water over his face and neck. The shock of the sensation not only woke him up but it also offered a measure of relief. Blinking the water away from his eyes he stared at his reflection in the mirror before him. The thoughts running in circles through his mind were dissipating which was a relief. Images of situations coming at him through the darkest recesses of his memories only to pass by him and repeat over and over again. The fire inside his head burning so intensely that he thought his skull would crack under the pressure.

It had all seemed so real, so fresh, like it was happening now and not years ago when he was barely in his teens.

Pressing the sides of his head with both palms, he squeezed as hard as he could, feeling more sharp pain in doing so. This was a technique taught to him years before at a meditation class he'd attended. The class itself was a bust, Duncan had never been able to settle long enough to achieve the benefits, but a classmate had taught him this as a relief for a headache. Usually, it was done by another to you but seeing as he was alone, he'd do what he could. Just when he could bear the pressure no longer, he dropped his hands and the release lifted the throbbing pain from within his skull.

The pain soon came back, only less so than previously. It was a success of sorts.

Walking back into the bedroom, he glanced towards the window. The curtains were still open, Duncan always slept without drawing them as he liked to wake with the dawn. It was still dark outside. He could hear the howling of the wind whipping across the machair and buffeting the hotel. He stood in the centre of the room for a minute, staring out across the water of Lochmaddy. The fog had dissipated as the wind had increased overnight, and he could see the white caps of the waves as they moved against the scattered islands of the South Basin. It would be a rougher crossing back to Uig this morning.

Duncan found his watch and checked the time. It was nearing four o'clock. Holding the watch in his palm, he sank down on the end of the bed. The disturbing images of his dreams were ebbing away now, but he knew they'd return again once he sought sleep. It was the nature of these things. Returning to Skye only seemed to make them more vivid and intense. Perhaps he shouldn't have come.

Isla Matheson came to mind and he felt more comfortable thinking about the case than his own life, and he thought over the previous evening's conversation with James and Andrea Turnbull. They had been convincing, and if they were still lying then Leverndale Hospital would prove it. However,

Duncan doubted they were. He sensed James Turnbull was a dead end. He'd been wrong about why Isla had come to Uist that week. Or had he?

Crossing to the chair where he'd cast his clothes the night before, He got dressed. Alistair had indeed headed for the bar once they'd checked in, whereas Duncan had gone to his room for a bit of space to try and figure things out. Giving up around one in the morning, he'd got into bed and fallen into a fitful sleep of troubled dreams.

Slipping on his coat, Duncan stepped out into the corridor and walked the short distance along it to Alistair's room. He knocked on the door and waited. It took several attempts but eventually the door unlocked and a bleary-eyed face peered out at him, bags hanging beneath his eyes and dressed only in a pair of boxer shorts and a once white but now greying vest.

"What the feck do you want?" Alistair asked.

Duncan couldn't help but smile which only made the lines on Alistair's forehead deepen further.

"I need to borrow your pick-up."

"You need wha..?"

"The keys to your pick-up. I need to go for a drive."

"Do you know what time it is?"

"I do," Duncan said, "and I still need to borrow your pick-up."

Alistair muttered a curse, disappearing back into his room and returning with his keys. He thrust them into Duncan's hand and slammed the door shut. Duncan turned away and the door swung violently open, Alistair stepping out into the corridor behind him.

"You don't need me to come with you, do you?"

Duncan shook his head. "No, not unless—"

"No!" Alistair said, retreating into his room and shutting the door. Duncan smiled and set off down the corridor.

THERE WAS something curiously spiritual about being out on the islands at that time in the morning. Seeing the sky lightening to reveal the sweeping, almost desolate landscape of the machair to either side of him and the waves gently crashing against the causeway as Duncan drove across to Benbecula, was magical to the eye.

He'd been unable to get a thought out of his mind ever since he'd heard Isla had travelled to Uist. On learning she'd been pregnant, the exploration of her relationship to James Turnbull and the apparently undocumented termination of her pregnancy all pointed to the vet as the reason for her visiting the island. However, she hadn't confided in her closest friend, Roddy. This was something he'd been unable to understand and Roddy knew her better than most, in fact he knew her darkest secrets.

So Isla, when in a traumatic situation or suffering, would be willing to turn to Roddy, but on this occasion she hadn't. Was it as simple as this time she'd kept it to herself? Duncan couldn't see it. Something this big, with such a massive impact on her life, she would need to confide in someone. And that thought was what had put him in the pick-up driving across the Western Isles as dawn broke. Who did Isla trust more than Roddy? Who would she turn to if she was in real trouble?

The five-bar gate to the croft house was open and Duncan drew the pick-up onto the gravel drive and switched the engine off. A wisp of smoke was escaping the chimney, broken and dispersed on the wind. It was five o'clock in the morning now. He got out and walked up to the front door. He didn't have to wait long before it opened and Iona Sutherland looked up at him.

"Detective Inspector McAdam," she said, smiling. "What a lovely surprise."

"Good morning. I'm sorry it's so early— "

"No matter, come in, come in."

She opened the door and beckoned him in, then she ushered him through into the sitting room. The fire was banked up, crackling away with the television on in the corner. The sound was down and the subtitles were on the screen. Iona saw him looking at it.

"I can't be dealing with their shrill voices while I'm busy getting ready for the day, but I can see what they're saying if needs be. I have it on for the company more than anything else. I'll just pop the kettle on."

"Don't go to any trouble on my account," he said. She waved away his comment, shuffling into the kitchen. "Yes, you said when I was last here that you lost your husband. When was that?" Duncan asked, strolling over to the fireplace and scanning the collection of photographs arranged on the mantelpiece.

"What was that dear?" Iona popped her head out of the kitchen.

"Your husband. When did he pass?"

"Oooh… almost twenty-seven years ago now," she said, disappearing from view.

Duncan found a grainy picture of a young Iona standing next to a man in a grey tweed suit, his arm around her shoulder. She was grinning whereas his smile was measured. He carried himself quite upright. Iona entered the room and Duncan angled the picture so she could see it.

"Is this him?"

"Yes, that's my Ian. A fine figure of a man."

"How did the two of you meet?"

"At work," she said.

"I thought he was a crofter and that's what brought you across to Benbecula?" Duncan asked. "Because your family is originally from Stornoway, aren't you?"

"That's right," she said. "We moved from Stornoway when my father took on our uncle's croft after he died, but Ian was never a crofter. Our house here was one of the first on this part of Benbecula to be de-crofted. Ian was unwell, so we needed somewhere to retire to and there's no finer place. Tea or coffee? I only have instant."

"Yes, tea please," Duncan said, putting the picture back where he'd found it. Scanning the other pictures while the sound of Iona busying herself making tea in the kitchen carried to him, he found a family shot of Ruaridh and who he assumed was Ruaridh's wife, Èibhlin, standing with two children, presumably Donnie and his sister Isla. The children looked uncomfortable, Isla especially with her father's hands placed on her shoulders. Was that fair or was he projecting an emotional feeling upon them influenced by Roddy's accusations? He couldn't be sure.

He found a picture of Iona standing with roughly a dozen people outside of a nondescript building, a concrete slab facade likely constructed in the sixties. Most of them were wearing lanyards, so he assumed it was a picture taken with colleagues. There was a sign on the wall in the background and he picked up the picture, examining it closely but the detail wasn't great and he couldn't tell where it was taken.

"Where did you say Ian worked?"

"What was that, love?" Iona said, coming back into the room bearing a tray with a small teapot and two cups on it. Duncan put the picture frame aside and hurried to take it from her but she shooed him away, setting the tray down on a small table in the centre of the room.

"I was asking what Ian did for a living. You said you met at work?"

"Oh, he was a surgeon," Iona said, sitting down. Duncan's curiosity was piqued. He looked at her, trying not to appear overly interested. "A vascular surgeon, but he could have had his pick of specialisations. Ian was so talented."

Duncan nodded, choosing his next words carefully. "When did your husband pass away?"

"1994," Iona said, looking out of the window wistfully. Duncan bore his disappointment in silence. "And it doesn't feel like more than a month has passed. I miss him every day."

Iona set about pouring the tea and Duncan sat down opposite her. She passed him a cup and saucer and he immediately put it down on the side table next to him.

"So, you worked in the NHS as well?"

Iona glanced at him and something changed in her expression. She nodded curtly. "Yes, for a time."

Casually pointing up at the picture he'd been holding, he said, "I'm not a photographer, but that looks like a farewell shot."

"Aye… that was my last day, when I took early retirement so that Ian and I could come out here to Benbecula."

Duncan watched her closely. Iona didn't appear to notice his attention, but he sensed she was reticent whereas previously she'd needed no encouragement to revisit her past.

"And what did you do for the NHS?" Duncan asked.

"Oh… you didn't come all the way out here to listen to me talk about the ancient past—"

"Not at all, I love hearing people talking about their lives. It's a huge part of my job," Duncan said, forcing a smile to put her at ease. She seemed unconvinced. "Were you a nurse?"

Iona nodded, sipping at her tea. She wouldn't make eye contact with him.

"We found something out about Isla that we were previously unaware of," he said.

Iona looked at him and smiled. "What was that, dear?"

"Isla had been pregnant." Iona pursed her lips, averting her eyes from Duncan's gaze. "And we believe she had a termination shortly before she went missing."

Iona's lips parted, her eyes flickering up at him and away again. Still, she said nothing.

"Upsetting to hear, isn't it?"

She looked at him, cowed. "Yes," she said quietly.

"Isla was pregnant and she told almost no one, only confiding in her closest friend after she'd already had the procedure," he said. "She was in quite a state over it. A teenage girl... struggling emotionally..." Duncan shook his head, "...would turn to someone... someone she trusted. Wouldn't you agree?"

Iona remained impassive, making a show of sipping at her tea but Duncan could tell she was struggling to swallow.

"And who would Isla trust above all others, if not her closest friend?" Duncan sat forward, forcing Iona to meet his eye. "And you told me there was *nothing you wouldn't do for that wee girl.*"

CHAPTER THIRTY-TWO

IONA HELD his gaze with a steely expression. Slowly setting her cup and saucer down on the table, the kindly old lady facade dissipating with every passing second.

"We look after our kin in our family," she said in a measured tone. "It is the way of things... it always has and shall always be."

She wouldn't make eye contact with him.

"Does that include carrying out an unlicensed abortion?" Duncan asked coldly.

"Isla was in trouble, and she... trusted me enough to bring her problems to me."

"There are ways to—"

"With respect, young man, do not attempt to lecture me on the rights and wrongs of—"

"The procedure tore a hole in her uterine wall..." Duncan said and Iona gasped, raising a hand to her mouth, "... and it's likely that is what led to the infection that ultimately killed her."

"I... I... thought you said she was... murdered by someone."

Duncan shook his head. "We didn't know when I told you that, but we believe she died from septicaemia."

Iona shook her head, her guarded demeanour collapsing to be replaced by fear. "But I was so careful... I swear I was. I–It all w–went so well," she stammered. "There was some bleeding but that was to be expected."

Duncan felt his anger building towards her but quelled it. "Iona, who knew what you'd done?"

She shook her head forcefully. "No one knew. No one at all, only Isla and me."

"No one? What about the family?"

She shook her head, avoiding his gaze. "No one."

"I don't believe you, Iona."

She glared at him. "No one, I told you."

"And who was the father—"

"I don't know," she said, shaking her head again, wringing her hands in her lap. "Isla wouldn't say."

"Did you ask?"

"No... I don't know. None of my business."

Duncan took a breath, watching her. She glanced up at him, her eyes darting to the photographs on the mantelpiece and away again.

"I don't know," she repeated quickly.

"And when she went missing, what did you think?"

"I didn't know what to think... I don't know," she said, her eyes looking heavenward, out of the window, anywhere but meeting Duncan's intense stare.

"You must have thought something; that she's run away, perhaps? That something had happened to her? Maybe she'd spoken to the father and he'd reacted badly?"

"I don't know," she said, shaking her head. "I don't."

Duncan sat back, exasperated. They sat in silence for a few minutes with only the crackling fire to listen to. Duncan's mobile rang and he answered it. The line wasn't great, presumably he was some distance from the nearest cell tower. Rising from his chair, he moved towards the front of the house in search of a better signal, finding it improved next to a window.

"Sorry, say that again," he said. "You broke up."

"It's Russell Mclean, back in Portree. Sorry to call you so early, sir—"

"No, it's okay. Go ahead."

"I'm following up on this suspected arson last night. I called the Keck but his phone must be off or something."

"What did you find out?" Duncan asked, wondering if Alistair was nursing a hangover or if his waking him earlier had upset his sleep and he was still out for the count.

"It's one hell of a coincidence, but that croft that was set alight belongs to—"

"The Matheson's," Duncan said, looking over his shoulder to see Iona standing in front of the fireplace, her back to him, reaching for a picture frame.

"Aye... right. Weird huh?" Russell said. "How did you know?"

"That's why I'm the detective inspector," Duncan said, hanging up.

He put his phone away and walked over to Iona. She glanced up from staring at the photograph. It was the one of Ruaridh and his family. Isla couldn't have been more than ten or eleven in that picture. Duncan noticed the background for the first time. It must have been taken on a campsite some-where. There were tents off to the left behind the family and they were standing next to a caravan. It looked like new in this particular picture.

"Ruaridh had us all take a trip to Gairloch that particular

year," Iona said, angling the picture so Duncan could see. "Ian was so busy working that year… so I travelled up from Glasgow by myself and met Ruaridh and the family there."

"It's a cracking spot."

"Aye, isn't it?" Iona said, looking at Duncan and smiling. She traced the image of Isla slowly with her fingertips before gently putting the frame back on the mantelpiece. Quite emotional now, she put a balled fist to her mouth. It was shaking. "I didn't know…" she said quietly, "… what was going on. I saw them once, maybe twice a year with the occasional phone call in between. Everything seemed… fine."

"But it wasn't fine, was it?"

She shook her head. "No. Far from it."

"So, when did you know?" Duncan asked. Her eyes drifted up to meet his. "About your brother."

Iona stared at him; her expression unreadable. "Ruaridh?"

He nodded. "Yes, when did you realise your brother was abusing his family?"

She was pensive, perhaps gauging the depth of his knowledge or considering how much she should say.

"I can appreciate your desire to protect your family, Iona… but this isn't the way." He focussed a stern look on her. "It really isn't."

Taking a deep breath, Iona nodded reluctantly. "I always knew he was a stern father… but I figured that came from his beliefs. The strong, protestant work ethic and all of that. After all, that was how we were raised and believe me, our father was more than willing to use the belt or the back of his hand if he felt the need to."

"But this was more than Ruaridh's religious fervour?"

"Aye… much more. One time, I remember wee Donald – Isla's brother – was caught helping himself to some freshly-baked biscuits Èibhlin had made that morning and were cooling on a rack." She dismissed the misdemeanour with a flick of her hand. "It really wasn't a big deal, but Ruaridh... oh... he made it so much more than it was. More than it needed to be. That poor young man was given a proper thrashing. One of many, I expect."

"What did you do?"

"Me?" she said, surprised. He nodded. "What was I supposed to do? That was the way of things. Parental discipline is a personal choice and it's not for those outside of the family to intervene."

"The law says otherwise."

"Maybe these days, yes, but not back then, and even now who's to say what goes on behind closed doors."

Duncan could feel that familiar churn of anxiety and hatred in his stomach. Why would people choose to turn a blind eye when it was so obvious that they should step in? Was it fear of confrontation, of overstepping boundaries or simply that their own world view was so warped that they thought it acceptable?

For the life of him he couldn't understand the code of silence. He'd never understand those who knew and yet failed to act.

"You judge me, don't you?" Iona asked, bringing Duncan out of his preoccupation. "I can see it in your face."

He shrugged. "It's not my place to judge you."

"And yet you do."

"They were children."

"And Ruaridh is my brother."

"And that justifies your inaction?" Duncan asked, irritated by her reasoning.

"You think I should have brought him to task?"

"I do. I would have."

"Would you indeed?" Iona said, eyeing him scornfully. "Even if it meant destroying your entire family, ruining everyone's lives?"

"There are ways—"

"So you keep saying… and yet still these things go on… and have always gone on within families. Blood is thicker than water, Detective Inspector McAdam, and it always will be."

It was this attitude, a view held by so many, that allowed these patterns of behaviour to repeat time and time again. Why children, spouses… entire families could find their lives blighted by fear and suffering, for what; to appease the wrath of the abusers and to maintain a public facade. The stance disgusted him. Roslyn came to mind and he forced the image of his sister away, back into the recesses of his mind, focussing instead on Isla.

"Ruaridh fathered the child, didn't he?" Duncan asked. Iona looked away. "Didn't he?" Duncan's voice rose and Iona shrunk a little before his eyes. She nodded. "And he sent her to you?"

"No," she said quickly, shaking her head. "No, he knew nothing of it… not until afterwards. He would never have sanctioned the taking of a life."

"Spare me the religious morality," Duncan sneered. "The man was raping his daughter!"

Iona, blinking back tears, stood head bowed, hands clasped in front of her. "I'm so sorry."

"Sorry for what, for protecting an abuser or just sorry you've been found out?"

"I'm sorry," she whispered. Duncan took a step towards her and she backed away, clearly feeling threatened and vulnerable, terror visible in her face. Duncan stopped, realising his fists were clenched by his side. Embarrassed, he backed away, confused by his reaction. Iona was frightened, if not terrified, of him.

It dawned on him that Ruaridh's shadow cast further than over his wife and children, reaching as far as Benbecula too. Iona's reaction was a pattern of behaviour instilled in her by her own upbringing. It wasn't a conscious choice she'd made to enable Ruaridh, but more a result of a lifetime of grooming. A pattern as easy to undo in adulthood without help as it would be to disconnect a finger. The entire family were victims, depending on your perception.

"After your father passed away, your family held onto the croft out in Geary, didn't it?"

Iona nodded, calmer now Duncan had both retreated and adopted a measured tone. "We tenanted out the land, renewing it every five years with the Commission."

"And is that where Ruaridh took Isla," Duncan asked, "when it became clear she was unwell?"

Iona bit her bottom lip, nodding. "I didn't know, I swear. He didn't tell me until much, much later."

"What did he tell you about Isla?"

"He called me on the phone that night... saying that Isla had fallen ill... that he'd picked her up from the party as agreed – although I don't think she wanted him to – and that she'd been unwell. Isla told him what I had done and she asked him to take her to the hospital. He wouldn't do that nor did he want to take her home, you see. Èibhlin would have insisted on taking her to the doctor and... we couldn't have that."

"Because you knew what would happen."

"Yes. Doctors ask questions... a lot of questions. Ruaridh said he would take care of her... and that it would all be okay," she said, peering up at Duncan, wary of his reaction. "He was so angry with me... because of what I'd done. I dared not challenge him," she said, shaking her head furiously. "I couldn't. He… stayed away. I phoned several times the next day and I always spoke to Èibhlin who was so, so worried about where Isla was. The longer it went on the more distraught she became, the poor wee thing."

Duncan suppressed the sarcastic comment that came to mind.

"Èibhlin thought Isla was genuinely missing?"

"Aye, Ruaridh never told her about any of it. Eventually, he called me… it must have been the second or maybe the third day, and he said Isla was fine and that they had to figure out a way to bring her home and deal with all of the hulla-baloo of her disappearing. The police had already been in touch with me by then… and of course I had to tell them I hadn't seen her. What else could I say? And then Ruaridh had his accident."

"The car crash?"

"Yes, he'd lain unconscious in that car for at least twelve hours through the night. The Lord must have been watching over him."

"Aye, it seems the Lord was not too keen for Ruaridh to join him obviously."

Iona looked away.

"Go on, please."

"Well, we didn't know if Ruaridh would make it. He slipped into a coma… Èibhlin called Donnie home, what with Isla missing and then Ruaridh… she needed her family around her."

"Did you go across?"

She nodded; her lips pursed. "It was dreadful. I couldn't say anything at all. I didn't know where Isla was. I expected her to walk in at any time, especially once she heard about the accident. The fuss around where she'd been, would die down soon enough, what with her father being in a coma. I figured it was only a matter of time."

"But she didn't, did she?" Duncan said. "Come back, I mean."

Iona frowned. "No. I was... perplexed. I assumed Isla had been sent away somewhere, perhaps to a retreat to recover until she felt strong enough to return. It was only once Ruaridh regained consciousness that he confided in me where she really had been."

"Out at the family croft," Duncan said.

Iona nodded, sitting down. "I wanted to go out there right away, but Ruaridh made me promise to leave it to Donnie."

"Donnie?"

"Aye." She shook her head. "Well, Ruaridh was still in hospital and paralysed by that point, and so he had to send Donnie. He couldn't very well send Èibhlin, could he?"

"And?"

"Donnie couldn't find her. Isla had gone, taken her opportunity with Ruaridh in the hospital and set off before he came around. He'd never have given her leave to move off the island. He'd lost that battle with Donnie," she said, shaking her head, "and there's no way he would have let her go." Her expression took on a distant look. "I'm ashamed to say it aloud, but I've been thinking it for years..."

"What's that?" Duncan asked.

"Isla... I've been so angry with her for running away like that. I couldn't believe she didn't get in touch with someone in the family to say how she was. I mean, not to tell us where she was if she didn't want to, but to not even let her poor mother know she was safe... I was so, so angry with her."

"She wasn't safe though, was she?" Duncan said.

Iona looked downward, wringing her hands in her lap. They sat in silence while Duncan considered his next move.

"I'll need you to come back with me," he said. "To Portree."

"Today?"

"Yes," Duncan said, reaching for his mobile to call Alistair. "Today."

CHAPTER THIRTY-THREE

DUNCAN OPENED the door and walked out into the incident room. He could feel the tension in the room as well as see all eyes were surreptitiously following him. Glancing over his shoulder, Duncan noted the stern gaze of DCI Jameson watching him leave. Alistair came over to meet him.

"Are you sure this is how you want to play it?" he asked.

"I am. Jameson has signed off on it."

Alistair lowered his voice. "He can't have liked that much?"

"He didn't but gave us leave to do it."

"Good," Alistair said, "they're waiting for us in the lobby and Russell has everything arranged."

Duncan and Alistair made their way downstairs. Duncan paused at the security door and took a deep breath before reaching for the door release button.

"It's no' too late to change your mind," Alistair said.

"It is," Duncan said with a wry smile. "Treading softly just won't cut it now."

He pressed the button and opened the door to the public lobby. Both Ruaridh Matheson and his son, Donnie, turned to see them. Donnie smiled a warm greeting whereas Ruaridh had his ever-present nasal cannula in hand ready to ease his breathing if required.

Donnie bounded across to greet them, offering his hand to Duncan. His hand and wrist were bandaged and Duncan hesitated, viewing the dressing.

"Good morning, Reverend Matheson," Duncan said. Donnie withdrew his hand, nodding towards it sheepishly.

"I had a wee accident, fixing up the chapel."

Duncan cocked his head at the injury. "Nothing too serious I hope?"

"It's a little tender, but I'll be fine."

Duncan looked past Donnie, acknowledging his father seated behind him in his wheelchair.

"Thank you both for making the trip in to see us on such short notice."

"You're welcome, DI McAdam," Donnie said. "You have some news for us, I take it?"

Duncan looked past him, seeing a woman crossing the road outside and approaching the station entrance.

"Perhaps we could go somewhere more private," Duncan said, offering an open-hand gesture towards the security door leading into the station.

Donnie nodded and Alistair tapped the code to unlock the door before stepping through and holding it open for them all to follow. Donnie went first and his father steered his motorised chair after him. With Duncan bringing up the rear, they made their way through the corridors towards the interview rooms. Rounding a corner, Duncan saw Russell standing at one door and, as they approached, he nodded to Alistair in the lead before stepping inside the room to his left and keeping the door open.

As the small group came upon the entrance, Alistair

slowed and Donnie, as was human instinct, found his curiosity piqued and his eyes flickered into the room. Iona Sutherland, his aunt, was sitting there alone, her hands clasped together in her lap. At the sight of her, Donnie paused, open mouthed. His eyes darted to Ruaridh, whose expression didn't change, and then back at Iona. Duncan came alongside them, intimating towards Iona with a curt nod.

"Your aunt has been very informative," Duncan said. "She's managed to fill in a lot of the gaps around what happened to Isla."

"Gaps?" Donnie asked, his eyes narrowing, tension evident in his tone.

"I'm so sorry, Donnie," Iona said, wringing her hands and looking between her brother and her nephew. "It's just... Ruaridh... what was I supposed to say?"

Donnie's lips parted and he glanced at Duncan and then his father. Ruaridh was breathing faster now, forced to insert his cannula to ease his breathing difficulty. He took a steep intake of breath and glared at his sister.

"You say nothing, Iona!" he said, angrily. "Do you hear me?"

"It's a bit late for that, Ruaridh," Duncan said, shaking his head. "We have everything we need."

Ruaridh's eyes widened, sucking air through gritted teeth, fumbling with his oxygen canister, his chest heaving as he broke out into a fit of coughing. Donnie, belatedly, sought to assist him, reaching for the controls only for Ruaridh to bat his hand away with a fierce swipe.

"You... say... nothing!" he barked at Iona who lowered her gaze to the floor.

"I'm so sorry..." she all but whispered.

"Nothing!" Ruaridh repeated in between hacking coughs,

reluctantly accepting Donnie's help who, by now, looked horrified, his eyes searching Iona for an explanation.

"It was the termination, Donnie," Duncan said. "The need to get rid of the child threw it for me. Why couldn't Isla go through the proper channels and who could have performed the procedure, let alone been willing to do so? Once I'd figured that out, everything else fell into place."

"What on earth are you talking about?" Donnie asked without conviction. Ruaridh's breathing was ragged, his chest heaving with every exaggerated breath, and even if he wanted to contribute to the conversation, Duncan figured he'd be unable to do so.

"Your father wasn't out searching for his missing daughter that night when his car came off the road. He was heading home after leaving her at your family croft—"

"Now… you look here—" Donnie said, turning on Duncan, but he was having none of it.

"But only Ruaridh knew where Isla was… perhaps your mother too, but we'll never know, will we?"

At the mention of his mother, Èibhlin, Donnie lost his air of righteous indignation, stammering a rebuttal, "I… I… don't see where you're going with this…"

"Really? Do you want to maintain the charade for a bit longer, do you?" Duncan said. Donnie glanced at Alistair, whether expecting support, Duncan couldn't tell, but Alistair stood firm, arms folded across his chest, staring back at him. "Perhaps your mum was also kept in the dark… at least for a while. Did she know about the child? Did she know her husband was not only beating his children but raping his daughter too?"

"How dare you…" Donnie said. Inside the room, Iona was crying now whereas Ruaridh was glaring at Duncan, eyes wide with barely controlled rage.

"Your father couldn't have known about the uterine tear resulting from your aunt performing the abortion. And without medical training, he probably didn't notice the onset of the septicaemia from the ensuing infection brought on by that tear."

Donnie looked at his father and then back at Duncan.

"He left her in that croft... perhaps locked inside the caravan to the rear," Duncan said, "only he didn't foresee his accident, the coma... or the reality that no one knew she was there until after he came round. Which is when he told you, Donnie."

Donnie Matheson met his eye and Duncan could almost see the fight dissipating from them as the seconds passed.

"And you found her, didn't you, Donnie?" Duncan asked. "When your father told you, you went out there and you found her... locked inside the caravan," he looked at Ruaridh who refused to meet his gaze, "the very same caravan you set fire to last night."

Donnie's head snapped up, staring at Duncan open mouthed. Duncan reached out and gripped Donnie's bandaged hand and the reverend gasped.

"Did you get overly enthusiastic with the petrol," Duncan said, "trying to make sure that we would never be able to prove Isla was ever there? Your paranoia must have been absolutely raging for you to go and do that."

Donnie shook his head, disconsolate, tentatively withdrawing his hand from Duncan's reach.

"A hell of a risk," Alistair added. "If anyone had seen you," he shook his head, "then it'd have drawn out all kinds of questions."

Donnie, breathing heavily, raised his chin as he looked squarely at Duncan.

"My whole adult life," he said defiantly, "has been spent in the service of the Lord; serving the community and steering my flock on the righteous path."

"Whitewashing your guilt," Duncan said accusingly. "And I'll tell you now, it won't be enough."

Swallowing hard and breaking eye contact, Donnie's defiant stance broke and his intake of breath stuttered. Ruaridh lurched forward in his chair, scrabbling to grasp his son's arm. Donnie snatched his arm away, eyes gleaming.

"What should I have done?" he asked Duncan. "What could I do? I'd already lost my sister… was I supposed to lose the rest of my family too? Leave my mother with the knowledge of… of what my father—"

"Donald!" Ruaridh shouted, but it was all he could say before collapsing into another fit of coughing. Donnie looked down at his father, almost apologetically. He turned back to Duncan, despairingly.

"Your mother," Duncan said, "did she take her life because she couldn't live with the weight of the secret?"

"My mother didn't know… she couldn't know," Donnie said, fiercely shaking his head. "It would have…"

"Killed her?" Duncan asked. Donnie met his eye and nodded. "And yet, not knowing led to her taking her own life anyway, didn't it?"

Again, Donnie nodded. Ruaridh had hold of Donnie's sleeve now, tugging on it with as much strength as he could muster which had very little impact. Donnie ignored his father.

"Had I known she would do something like that… that she was struggling so. I'd have done something," Donnie said. "I swear I would have done something. I loved my mother."

"Funny way of showing it," Duncan said, bitterly.

"I cared deeply for her," Donnie protested.

"Oh… did yer, aye?" Alistair said.

"I did, aye," Donnie retorted angrily, triggered by the sarcasm.

"Did you care for her while you were burying your sister out the ways at Trumpan?" Duncan asked pointedly. Donnie lowered his gaze. "Dress it up however you like, but that was a horrific thing to do, Donnie. Isla deserved so much better than that."

"I think of her... Isla," Donnie whispered, "a lot, you know? How must she have felt out there... all alone... waiting for someone to come. It is torture for my soul... to know that one day, despite the penance I've performed every day since... that it will never be enough when I face my judgement." He looked at Duncan. "It won't, will it?"

Duncan took a deep breath, shaking his head as he exhaled. "I know nothing about spiritual things... to me that's such a cop out, so I've no idea if you'll ever face such a trial. Perhaps when you die that'll be it, and the sins of this life will pass away with you, but know this," he said, fixing Donnie with a stern look, "you will face a reckoning, in this world before the next," he said, looking down at Ruaridh, still refusing to make eye contact with him. "And I'll use every available means at my disposal to ensure that happens."

RUSSELL SET down two cups of coffee on the desk, moving one closer to Duncan who was lost in thought. Alistair picked up the other, thanking Russell with a wink. The door to the office opened and DCI Jameson entered, closing the door behind him. Russell made to leave whereas Alistair leaned back in his chair, making himself comfortable.

"No need for either of you to leave on my account," Jameson said. The look of surprise on Alistair's face made it clear he'd had no intention of moving anyway. "Duncan..." Jameson said, getting his attention.

"Sir?"

Jameson nodded approvingly. "Good result... well done."

"Thank you, sir," Duncan said graciously.

"I've no idea what the procurator fiscal is going to make of it, mind," Jameson said, frowning. Duncan had to agree. It was a mess, and what the family would be charged with depended on what they could prove although Iona's confession and Donnie's apparent willingness to cease the charade should make it easier. "Anyway," Jameson said, looking at all three of them in turn, "solid effort. Well done."

"Thank you, sir," Alistair and Russell said in unison. Jameson turned to leave and then looked back at Duncan. "I suppose you'll be heading back to Glasgow soon enough?"

Duncan arched his eyebrows and exhaled. "I... guess so. I hadn't really thought about it. I didn't expect everything to come to a head so quickly."

"Well..." he looked at Alistair and Russell, "I don't think it's something for broadcast to the masses, but... I've had word from above regarding DI Johnston. You all know he's been off for a spell—"

"I know, sir. He's unwell."

"Yes, and he's not coming back any time soon. Central are looking for someone to cover for him... a secondment of sorts. Interested?"

"Me?" Duncan asked.

Jameson shrugged. "I cannot think of anyone more suited. You've proved yourself adept at reading the community here. They... and you, could do a lot worse."

"I'll... give it some thought, sir."

"Happy to put a word in for you if you want me to," Jameson said, making to leave. Duncan acknowledged the offer with an appreciative smile. "Anyway, great job. Well done."

Jameson left and no one said a word for a few moments. Alistair leaned back, craning his neck to ensure the DCI had indeed left before he spoke.

"That must have hurt," he said, chuckling.

"What's that?"

"Him… being nice to you!"

Duncan laughed. Russell returned to munching on his crisps, rummaging around at the bottom of the bag to gather the last of the crumbs.

"That's it…" Duncan said, looking at him.

"What's it?" Alistair asked, his eyes narrowing.

"Why you call him *Russell*. It's because he's always eating crisps."

Alistair and Russell exchanged a knowing look.

"Ah… I don't believe it," Alistair said. "He's only gone and done it." He sighed, putting his head in his hands. Russell grinned, enacting a celebratory jig from his seat. Alistair grimaced, shaking his head. "This is going to cost me a fortune…"

Duncan laughed and Russell rubbed his hands together gleefully before reaching for his mobile, likely to inform the others about the development. Alistair sat forward.

"The drinks are on you, Mr Keck!" Russell said with evident delight.

"What do you reckon?" Alistair asked Duncan.

"Reckon to what?"

"To staying here for a wee while?"

Duncan exhaled. "I don't know really. Back in Glasgow, I'm…"

"About as popular as a floating turd in a swimming pool,"

Alistair said, cocking his head knowingly. Duncan frowned. "I know it's true. I checked… it's common knowledge."

"Oh… is it now?" Duncan asked, mildly put out.

"Aye, it is… Come on," Alistair said, "you can't beat staying with your own ones… at least for a while. You never know, you might find you like it here after all. You don't need a skinny latte in an organic cup on your way to work every day. The big smoke is overrated, it smells… and it's busy, all folk rushing here and there."

Duncan grinned, meeting Alistair's gaze and appreciating the sentiment. "I promise… I'll think on it."

Alistair stared at him, lifting his coffee cup to his mouth. He tipped it towards him in a casual salute. "Aye, will you pish!"

CHAPTER THIRTY-FOUR

DUNCAN LINGERED in the corridor outside his mum's room, making minimal eye contact with any staff who passed by and avoiding small talk at all costs. *What was he even doing here?* The knot in his chest, ever present when he thought about his mum, felt as if it were tightening with every passing movement. He wanted to see her, almost needed to. His feelings were conflicted between the pull of seeking a mother's love and the push to run away from the expectation of almost certain disappointment.

"This is ridiculous," he muttered to himself.

Roslyn appeared from the room, startled by his presence. "Duncan?"

"Oh... hey, Ros. How are you doing?"

She walked up to him, a warm smile on her face. "This is unexpected."

"I had a bit of time, so I thought I should drop by, you know?"

Roslyn searched his expression with an appraising look. "I figured you'd be too busy working on your case."

"Aye, well we've found a resolution to that... so..."

"You've caught the man who did it?" she asked, narrowing her gaze, studying him and sensing his reticence.

He grimaced. "Aye... from a certain point of view." He shrugged. "It's complicated."

"Where you're concerned, Duncan, it usually is," she said, her smile broadening.

"Hey! That's a low blow."

"Fair comment though," she replied. He tilted his head in acknowledgment. "At least the family will have some closure."

Duncan nodded. "After a fashion, aye."

Roslyn cocked her head but didn't ask for anything further which he was grateful for because once it became public knowledge all hell was likely to break loose among the community.

"So, you'll be heading away back down the road then?"

He arched his eyebrows but didn't confirm anything. "I thought I'd pop in on Mum... see how she's doing, you know?"

Roslyn frowned. "She's no' having a good day today, Dunc."

"Ah right."

"But maybe you can cheer her up," Roslyn said, reading his disappointment. "Sometimes familiar faces can jog the memory and bring her back to us for a while."

Duncan snorted. "Or send her further away."

Roslyn shrugged. "Worth a try."

"I suppose."

He tentatively took a step towards the room, Roslyn shaking her head. "She'll no' bite you." He smiled weakly. "I'm just going to get a cup of tea. Do you want one?"

He nodded and Roslyn headed off down the corridor. Duncan entered the room, hesitating for a moment as he spied the old woman sitting in a chair in front of the window. She had a blanket draped over her knees; her hands cradled in her lap. Coming to stand alongside, he looked upon her face. His mother made no acknowledgment of his presence, maintaining her thousand-yard stare out of the window and over Loch Portree. Rain was falling over the mainland, drifting across the horizon, a cloud burst with hazy sunshine to either side of it.

His mum seemed so fragile, pale and expressionless. Duncan sat down in the chair opposite her, likely recently vacated by his sister.

"Hi, Mum," he said, smiling. "How are you today?"

She didn't look at him. It was as if he was invisible to her; a feeling he could relate to from his childhood. However, she was a very different person now. The woman of his memories, the one with her uncompromising hard edges and her razor-sharp tongue, had been worn away by the passage of time and the disease that had stripped her of her personality, memories and much of her dignity. She was a shell of the woman he knew.

The anxiety he'd been feeling on the way over, the same feeling that'd been manifesting since he'd set foot back on the island dissipated, replaced by sadness; a longing for what he'd once craved and had hoped for one day in the dark recesses of his mind, resolution. It wouldn't happen now. How could it? His father was long gone... not that there would ever have been any form of resolution there. With his mum though... there had always been hope but it was a longing for something he knew would never come about now.

Several times over the years he held the mirror up to her, but she hated so much of what she saw that she subsequently refused to look. And this was their impasse. Now, it would never change.

Sitting with his hands clasped together in his lap, Duncan looked towards the door as a nurse walked by the room. She paid him no attention. He felt little emotion, like an unused part in a nonspecific repair. *Perhaps he should just leave.*

"Are you here to see my boy?"

He looked over to see his mum eyeing him warily.

"Mum?" he asked, sitting forward. "It's me, Duncan."

Her lips parted slightly but there was still no emotional reaction to him, then a hint of a smile crossed her face and her expression lightened.

"Duncan," she said. "You'll need to get your tools back into the shed before that rain comes across," she said, lifting a bony finger towards the storm clouds ominously approaching Raasay to their east.

"I'll do that, Mum," he said quietly.

"I have to collect wee Duncan and Roslyn from the bus stop in a minute," she said. "That son of yours forgot his coat… again. He'll be wet through."

Duncan took a breath, feeling his eyes filling. "Aye… I was always forgetting my coat, wasn't I, Mum?"

"The lad's such a daftie. He looks a lot like you, Duncan," she said, reaching across to him. He slid off the chair and onto his knees in front of her, allowing her to touch his face with her hand, cupping his cheek in her palm. "Such a handsome man, Duncan McAdam. You had your pick of the lassies… but you still chose me."

Duncan was crying now, leaning into her touch. Her hands were cold, the skin rough.

"It's because you're beautiful, Mhari," he said. "Why would I choose anyone else."

She smiled at that, tilting her head and gazing upon him.

"You're just a boy, aren't you?"

"I am," he said, as she withdrew her hand. The movement

away, the loss of that one intimate moment was crushing. He wanted it back, but he was still smiling.

Her eyes narrowed and the smile slipped from her face, but she maintained the eye contact.

"You're my boy... aren't you?"

His smile broadened into a grin; his vision blurred. He nodded. "Aye, it's me, Mum. It's wee Duncan."

Her expression changed, almost as if a veil had been lowered over her eyes and her gaze drifted back to the window. She began to hum quietly, staring at a random point in the distance. For a moment, he was thrown but as the melody played out it sounded familiar. Taking her hand in his, he squeezed it gently, hoping to bring her out of it so they could talk some more. He had so much he wanted to tell her... so much for them to catch up on, but the tune ended and she was lost to him.

Standing, Duncan placed her hand back into her lap alongside the other and leaned over to kiss her forehead. She didn't react at all. Once again, he was invisible.

"I love you, Mum," he whispered before slowly withdrawing.

Unaware of her presence, Roslyn stood in the doorway, one arm across her chest, a hand to her mouth. She was crying too and Duncan didn't feel the need to hide his own emotions. She crossed to meet him and they hugged. Neither of them spoke. They just held one another for a few moments. Duncan couldn't recall them ever doing so before.

Stepping back from her, he sensed her reluctance to release her grip on him but she did so, letting go of his hands after a few seconds. He looked at their mum.

"Does that happen... that she drifts off like that?"

Roslyn nodded. "Yes, when she has her more lucid

moments… that's what happens. She stays with us less and less these days."

"She thought I was Dad again."

"I know… I heard," Roslyn said, wiping her eyes and sniffing gently. Duncan's gaze lingered on the woman in the chair overlooking the island she loved so much. "You should make your peace with her, Duncan."

He shot her a quizzical look. "What do you mean?"

"You need to move past it… all that stuff you've been carrying around with you for the last thirty years. Otherwise, it'll only hurt you more."

He shrugged. "What are you on about? I'm fine."

She laughed dryly, a sound without genuine humour. "Come on, Duncan. I know you, remember. You've been running from it for years… but it doesn't matter how far you run, or how long you stay away, it's all still there waiting for you when you stop." She shook her head. "I know you'll never forgive Dad—"

"No, I won't. He was a proper bastard—"

"I know," she said, reaching out and grasping his forearm supportively. "I know what he was, we all do, but you need to let it go."

"I hate him… for what he did to me… to you, to all of us," he said, glancing at their mum. "But I'm over it."

She laughed again. "No, Duncan, you're not. I can see it."

"Really? You have a spirit guide into my psyche or something?"

"No, of course not," she said, lowering her eyes, "but I can tell you what I do see."

"Oh, please do," he said, genuinely smiling. She took his hands in hers, squeezing them.

"I see a man who's alone… lost…"

Duncan made to pull his hands away and dismiss her, but she pressed on, refusing to let him back away.

"Do you ever wonder why you're alone, Duncan? Why you can't seem to hold onto a relationship beyond the early stages—"

"Nonsense," he said. "Back in Glasgow I was living with someone. We'd been together for a couple of years…"

"And what happened?" she asked. He averted his eyes.

"You can't do it, Duncan," she whispered, lifting his hands to her chest and pulling them to her. "You're still running… and it's time you stopped."

Lifting his eyes, he met hers and he could see them gleaming, her lips pursed. He knew then exactly what she meant. The same reasons he managed to sabotage every good thing that came his way, Becky, Natalie and a dozen in between, were the same reasons he couldn't find peace of mind in his life. It all stemmed from who he was when he was formed, growing up on the island.

"I should go," he said.

"If you feel you have to, yes," Roslyn said, smiling and letting go of his hands. He looked at her, feeling the outpouring of love in her expression. "But I mean it, you need to move past all of this otherwise it will eat away at you… and it will destroy your entire life." She tugged on his hands, imploring him. "Find a way through it, Duncan. Please."

Duncan nodded solemnly, accepting a hug from his sister. The embrace lasted longer than anything previously and when they stepped away from one another, they both had to wipe tears from their eyes. Duncan returned to their mother and kissed her on the top of the head. Again, she was unmoved.

"Ros," he said as he walked to the door, looking back at

her as she sat down in his seat, "I was thinking… about the old croft—"

Roslyn shook her head, holding up a flat palm to him. "I told you, I've no intention of selling it."

"No, no," he said, waving the comment away. "I was thinking… maybe I could fix it up? Make it habitable again, you know? What do you think?"

"You mean like a holiday let or something? I don't really need the hassle. I'm busy enough these days."

"No, I meant… for me…"

"For you? What, to live in?"

He cocked his head. "Aye… well, maybe. What do you reckon?"

She smiled warmly at him. "I think it would be a great idea."

"All right… leave it with me."

Duncan left without another word, feeling a sense of positivity for the first time in what felt like ages. Alistair's earlier words chased around his mind.

"Stay a while with your own ones, Duncan," he said, quietly to himself.

FREE BOOK GIVEAWAY

Visit the author's website at **www.jmdalgliesh.com** and sign up to the VIP Club and be the first to receive news and previews of forthcoming works.

Here you can download a FREE eBook novella exclusive to club members;

Life & Death - A Hidden Norfolk novella

Never miss a new release.

No spam, ever, guaranteed. You can unsubscribe at any time.

Enjoy this book? You could make a real difference.

Because reviews are critical to the success of an author's career, if you have enjoyed this novel, please do me a massive favour by entering one onto Amazon.

Type the following link into your internet search bar to go to the Amazon page and leave a review;

http://mybook.to/JMD-skye1

If you prefer not to follow the link please visit the sales page where you purchased the title in order to leave a review.

Reviews increase visibility. Your help in leaving one would make a massive difference to this author and I would be very grateful.

THE DEAD MAN OF STORR
PREVIEW

SIX HOURS. If she was able to fall asleep now, then she would get six hours of sleep before the alarm would wake her. Watching the hands of the clock pass around the face for what seemed like moments, but in reality had been almost an hour now… another hour since she'd made the same calculation.

How long has it been since I've had six hours of unbroken sleep?

The truth is, she had no idea. It hadn't happened any time recently and it certainly wasn't happening tonight. Her eyes strayed to the window where the warm orange glow of the streetlights filtered through the gently shifting curtains hanging to the side of the bay window, disturbed by a slight breeze that did little to cool her clammy skin on this strange summer night.

Throwing off the sheet, all that covered her bare skin, she made her way into the bathroom without flicking on the light. At this time of the year, even under a night sky shrouded by cloud cover, it seldom ever got properly dark and the resulting light permeated her bedroom stretching as far as the en suite.

Peering at her reflection in the mirror, hanging the full width of the bathroom wall behind the double basins, she stared at the dark circles beneath her eyes. Everything she'd been through in these past eighteen months registered in this expression, every facial line, every strained contour of her skin... and it would all culminate in that short walk she'd need to take tomorrow morning in the full glare of the waiting press, peers... and of course, the police. The thought of the coming day set butterflies away in her stomach and she shuddered. Until this time her anonymity had been secured... at least from the public. Others knew... and had done so for some time, although many never quite believing it was plausible, if at all even possible.

Aren't they in for a wake-up call.

Cupping her hands beneath the cold-water tap, she bent forward and gently splashed her face, running her cool hands down her cheeks and around to the nape of her neck where she pressed firmly. Her head was throbbing and she momentarily thought about the prescription she'd been afforded earlier; painkillers and a mild sedative to aid her sleep before the big day.

That's what the barrister had referred to it as: *her big day.* There were very few people she'd ever come across more arrogant than silk looking forward to their moment... all she is, is a prop in his performance, one no doubt practised in front of a mirror much like this one. Her imagination pictured him standing in his bathroom, butt naked, rehearsing his lines as would an experienced thespian preparing for their performance on stage at *The Royal Lyceum.* Is he likely to be nervous? She doubted it. He didn't seem the type. It had often been said that if they couldn't make it as musicians or stand-up comedians, they became the next best thing; barristers, the centre of attention, commanding all present to focus solely on them as they hammered away at the court.

Oh, how she hoped that would be true but tomorrow...

She doubted that too. A car alarm sounded in a nearby street, the shrill pitch of the sound breaking the silence over the city. Usually, such a sound wouldn't trouble her but tonight was different. Knowing she was on edge, she should just dismiss it as one of those things you find living in a city and normally she would, but tonight she made her way to the window, clinging to the relative sanctuary of the curtain as she peered down into the street below.

The setts were gleaming, a sheen of moisture left by the passing showers earlier in the night; a brief rain storm that everyone no doubt hoped would break the humidity but in the event was too ineffectual to make much of a difference. Nothing moved as she watched, and seldom did in this part of the city in the early hours this far from *Prince's Street*. A yelp behind startled her and she turned to see her dog sleeping on the chaise at the foot of the bed. She hadn't heard him come into the room, so she must have slept after all, at least for a time.

Moving away from the window, she gently sat beside her dog, reaching out and stroking his head. He was dreaming, his front paws and his nose twitching. The movement ceased as she touched him, his eyelids parting ever so slightly as he eyed her warily. She smiled.

"You go back to sleep, darling," she said, scratching behind his ear before standing up. The curtain wafted inwards as the breeze increased, accompanied by a creak from somewhere in the house. Her head snapped towards the open door and beyond that onto the landing. Perhaps that wasn't the breeze but a draught. Had she imagined it? The doors and windows of the ground floor were all closed. She'd checked, and then checked again several times. The dog slipped off the chaise coming to stand beside her, ears erect. It couldn't be her over-active imagination, not if he'd heard it too.

She listened intently, craning her neck to capture even the slightest sound from below but all she could hear were the night time sounds of the city beyond the window.

"What is it, boy? Did you hear it too?" she whispered.

The dog glanced up at her and then trotted out onto the landing, pausing at the top of the stairs and staring down into the hall below. Realising she was holding her breath, she released it and drew a sharp intake, holding that too as she watched the dog. It growled. A low murmuring sound suggesting he wasn't sure either. Then he barked, startling her, before he took off down the stairs at speed before disappearing from sight.

She waited... hearing nothing but her own breathing, the speed of which was steadily increasing alongside her fear. The dog would be barking if someone was there, surely? He didn't care for strangers and would always go for people in the street if they got too close or startled him. He'd certainly attack if he felt she was ever under threat.

Nothing. No sounds came to her from downstairs.

Pulling on her dressing gown, she edged out onto the landing, her skin tingling either from the heat or her fear, she didn't know which. Should she summon the dog? If no one was there then he'd come, but if she wasn't alone then they'd know where she was. Her mobile was by her bed... and they said to call if there was a problem, but... she was imagining it. She had to be. It was the lack of sleep, nothing more. To be so skittish was unlike her. It had been eighteen months. That was a long time and no one had said or done a thing. Why leave it until now? It's stupid.

Dismissing her fears, she took the first step down, gripping the banister as she slowly descended. Halfway down, a shadow moved beneath her and she shrieked before realising it was just the dog returning to the foot of the stairs.

"Oh... you bloody... thing!"

He clambered up to where she stood and she sat down allowing him to nuzzle his nose into her stomach, his tail wagging furiously.

"You scared the life out of me, do you know that?" she said, petting him.

The dog looked up at her, almost apologetically. She stood, relieved, and made her way down to the ground floor, intent on making herself a drink seeing as she was up anyway. A sneaky gin and tonic might help her sleep. Her four-legged shadow followed but as she entered the drawing room, he sloped off towards the kitchen, no doubt in search of a drink of his own or to find somewhere to get his head down.

Pouring herself a generous double, she dispensed with the need for ice or fresh lemon, instead choosing to fill the glass to the rim with tonic water, but the last of this bottle was barely enough to fill it halfway. Hunting through the pantry for a fresh bottle of tonic in the dead of night wasn't appealing, so she figured she'd make do. Who needs tonic anyway, she thought as she sipped at the liquid. It was strong, too strong and she baulked at the taste, putting the back of her hand to her mouth as her eyes watered.

Swallowing hard, her attention was drawn to the photograph, framed and mounted above the Victorian fireplace. Something was wrong... it didn't look right. It was offset to one side now, the slant visible even in the gloom. Clutching the tumbler, she slowly walked towards it. The sepia picture of the two of them standing together, her with her arms wrapped around his waist, both smiling into the camera... only... her eyes... were missing, both crudely cut out before rehanging the picture. She spun on her heel, looking across the room to the far wall where another picture of the two of them stood proudly on a table beside a lamp... the eyes were missing here too.

The dog barked from the kitchen and she dropped her glass, shattering it on the varnished oak floor. Backing out of the room and into the hall, ignoring the stinging pain from the soles of her feet as she trod on shards of broken crystal, she turned to see a figure in the shadows at the threshold of the kitchen. There was no sign of her canine guardian. The man was tall... powerful and he slowly raised a hand, placing his forefinger silently against his lips.

She screamed.

Publishing November 2023

ALSO BY THE AUTHOR

In the Misty Isle Series
A Long Time Dead
The Dead Man of Storr*
PRE-ORDER - RELEASE DATE NOV 2023

In the Hidden Norfolk Series
One Lost Soul
Bury Your Past
Kill Our Sins
Tell No Tales
Hear No Evil
The Dead Call
Kill Them Cold
A Dark Sin
To Die For
Fool Me Twice
The Raven Song
Angel of Death
Dead To Me
Blood Runs Cold
Life and Death**
****FREE EBOOK - VISIT jmdalgliesh.com*

In the Dark Yorkshire Series
Divided House
Blacklight
The Dogs in the Street
Blood Money
Fear the Past
The Sixth Precept

AUDIOBOOKS

In the Misty Isle Series
Read by Angus King

A Long Time Dead

In the Hidden Norfolk Series
Read by Greg Patmore

One Lost Soul
Bury Your Past
Kill Our Sins
Tell No Tales
Hear No Evil
The Dead Call
Kill Them Cold
A Dark Sin
To Die For
Fool Me Twice
The Raven Song
Angel of Death
Dead To Me
Blood Runs Cold

Hidden Norfolk Books 1-3

AUDIOBOOKS

In the Dark Yorkshire Series
Read by Greg Patmore

Divided House
Blacklight
The Dogs in the Street
Blood Money
Fear the Past
The Sixth Precept

Dark Yorkshire Books 1-3
Dark Yorkshire Books 4-6

Printed in Great Britain
by Amazon

32243171R00209